VEOS,

THE STORY OF A DUNGEON

VEOS,
THE STORY OF A DUNGEON

VICTOR STORM

Podium

Cover design by Jason Nathaniel Artuz

ISBN: 978-1-0394-6866-5

Published in 2025 by Podium Publishing
www.podiumentertainment.com

Podium

VEOS,

THE STORY OF A DUNGEON

CHAPTER ONE

Awakening Underground

The first sudden twinges of awareness seared through the void of non-existence in a way that can't really be explained. The presence of something where moments ago there had been nothing, and that something knew of the nothing, yet was not itself wholly the something. It was . . . No, *I* was . . .

I wasn't sure what I was. I was me—I was sure of that. I had a concept of what "me" meant. A separation from the self and the not-self. Yet I was sure that what I was should go deeper than that, although where that sense came from I had no idea. I struggled with my burgeoning thoughts for a moment until clarity struck like a . . . like a something . . . Like . . . lightning from a clear sky! Why had I thought of those words just now? But that wasn't important, because I now knew what I was.

Dungeon Core, I thought. That was what I was.

What was that, though? I wasn't entirely sure, actually. I hoped I'd figure it out eventually. I felt like I had things to do, things sitting just out of reach of my thoughts that would flee right as I reached out for them. What was the other stuff around me? I tried to stretch out with my thoughts, but they wouldn't go. Something else then . . . Something to make me aware . . .

Senses! The word appeared in my mind like I'd known it all along. I needed senses. With them I'd be able to know more things. Maybe even figure out what the hidden thing I was supposed to be doing was.

How would I get them?

I thought for a long while on that problem, which turned out to be quite a tricky one. I knew I was me, and there were other things that weren't me, but where the line was I couldn't quite tell. It was infuriating, this lack of knowledge. I *needed* to see. I *needed* to know . . .

Wait a moment . . . See! That was it. That was the word. That's what I needed to do!

As the thought went through me, a foreign one followed. Like a thought, but coming from not-me. It pulsed through me and showered me with a soft sound and buzzing sensation, and an image appeared within the void that was my inner world.

Hello and welcome, Dungeon Core! Congratulations on reaching the required level of cognizance to interface with the System. As a Core your connection will be a bit more special than most, and so I will guide you through the introduction.

The sound reverberated through my mind for a few moments as I reeled from the new flood of impressions. This was communication, between me and another. How exciting! Maybe they'd be able to help me get senses and expand them outward.

Greetings, I thought. No reason to be discourteous; at least I didn't think so.

If you are ready for the introduction, we can begin right away.

I sent a quick message of assent, and the voice continued.

Good. First things first: You need a name. Something that represents what you are.

That was a good thing to have. Nice idea, voice! I thought for a moment, trying to come up with a good name, and then like lightning from a clear sky, it struck me.

Veos, I sent. *I am Veos.*

Veos. All right, your choice is confirmed. I'll unlock the system for you now. Brace yourself.

What does that mea—

A torrent of intense heat and suffocating cold stormed through me. I gasped, which was strange given that I didn't have a mouth, nor had I really known what a gasp even was before I did it. Suddenly I realized I could *sense*. I knew what was me and what wasn't. I couldn't *see* exactly . . . or maybe this was what seeing was? I wasn't sure, but somehow it felt wrong to call this sight. I was aware of everything that was around me, and I could sense what it was and how it wasn't me. I realized that I was a sphere. A spherical crystal of some sort. Around me was a bunch of nothing, and beyond and below that a wall of rock. I felt the distinct difference between the rock and the sphere that was me. I was covered with pulsating lines that streaked across in different frequencies and patterns.

It was a dizzying experience, one not made any better by the sudden appearance of a . . . What was the word . . . I *knew* it, somewhere . . .

A status screen! A blue screen filled with patterns and shapes. Words, I realized. I examined the screen closely, reverent.

Name		Veos	
Race		Dungeon Core	
Floors		-	
Level	1	Experience	0/1000
Mana	10/10	Mana Regeneration	5/Minute
Edicts		None	
Skills		None	

Woah, I thought with excitement. *That's me!*

I see you've already accessed the status screen. Good. It is a good idea to keep a close eye on it, as it is a key part of your existence. Now, we still have some work to do. It will be easier if I show you. Here . . .

I felt a pull on my mind. A strange sensation drawing my attention to . . . something. A new screen! It was there, just minimized, waiting for me to shift my attention toward it and read its contents. I did so with glee.

Introduction: First Floor begun! Select a Guardian.

As a Dungeon Core, many people will want to learn your secrets and gain the rewards you offer. Most of them will act in accordance with the custom of Challenge, but you also have very limited personal abilities for self-defense against those who don't. Other than preventing their access completely, you will have to rely on tricks, traps, and the power of others to defend you. As a result, all Dungeon Cores can conjure a variety of creatures to act as their stalwart defenders. The last line are the Floor

Guardians, who will protect their Floor against any and all who seek to delve past it.

As a young Core, your options are limited by your level and your mana. Please select your first-Floor Guardian from the list below.

Rock-Claw Mantis: A large version of the mantis species that sports particularly sharp claws. Typically mantises are ambush predators who like to lie in forests or tall grass waiting for their prey to come close enough to strike. However, with claws that can grow strong enough to cut through stone, this species often take up other forms of hunting, as their size makes hiding less practical.

Young Wyrmling: A fledgling Wyrm is still quite a deadly foe, especially for those who underestimate it due to its small size. As it grows in strength and size, however, those who would underestimate it quickly disappear.

Green Jelly: A green slime that uses corrosive acid to absorb nutrients from whatever they can get their slime on. Mostly they eat plants, but those that grow enough can have acid strong enough to melt bone and steel just as easily as flesh and plants.

Leatherwing: A cousin of both the bat and the manta. An ambush hunter that is just as at home in the darkness of a cave as it is in deep water. Their sharp teeth, spiked tail, and swift yet sturdy wings make them adept grapplers, who bite down on their foes and bleed them dry, if they don't drag them down to the depths and drown them first.

I read through with what would have been a happy smile, if I'd had a mouth. This was *cool.* A creature of my very own. Something to keep me safe while I spent my time . . . doing something important, surely? I wasn't quite sure exactly what I was going to do yet, but I was getting there. My thoughts were becoming clearer by the second.

As for the choice of creature itself, there I paused. I felt instinctively that this was an important decision. One that might lead to my downfall just as easily as to my meteoric rise to power. I took my time, reading through the different options over and over, before finally making my decision. It had to be powerful enough to defend me, yes, but that wasn't enough. I wanted something more. I wanted something that fit with the . . . with the *narrative* of where I was. Something suitable for an underground environment.

I want the Leatherwing. I thought. I waited for a moment. There was no notification, no change in the screen, nothing. I frowned mentally but soon realized that there was a distinction between *thinking* that I wanted the Leatherwing and *choosing* it. It was a subtle difference, but an obvious one once I knew it was there. I rearranged my thoughts and *selected* the fourth option. The screen immediately blinked out of existence and I was filled with a surge of mana, which just as quickly rushed out of me and into the air of the cave.

Cave . . . nice word.

The mana pooled, then started to spin. With a final surge of light and color, I felt a *change* as the Leatherwing appeared in front of me. It stumbled slightly as it held itself up on awkward forelimbs. Its large wings, folded behind the forelimbs, were as black as the cave around it. I could see a mouth filled with teeth, as well as a pair of pincers on either side of the face, made for gripping hold and not letting go, and the head and spine extended back beyond the large wings and thinned out into a long tail covered in small spikes and ending in a hook. I instinctively knew it was made both for gripping and hanging, as well as grappling onto anything it caught, getting the hooked claws to catch and rip through flesh.

It seemed to sense my attention as it peered in my direction. It gave a small screech, then unfurled its wings and took up its post hanging from the cave's ceiling just above me. Its red eyes glowed faintly as it scanned the small cave for anything that could threaten me. I couldn't help but shiver. This was my first *Guardian*, and it was perfect.

Ah, the Leatherwing. An excellent choice for a cave-like Floor. The voice once more entered my mind. We're almost done with the introduction. All that's left is for you to finish your claim to your first Floor. Take your time and get it the way you want it, because it won't be easy to make drastic changes to the layout once a Floor is finished. Think over what you need in a Floor, and your instincts should tell you the rest. I shall leave you to it, and return once you are finished.

Introduction: Lay claim to your first Floor!
Now that you have contracted your first Guardian creature, it will need a place to guard. Create a space for your Guardian and its fellows, a place they can call home.
Requirements for first Floor: An entrance and a clear reward.

All right then, time to make a Floor . . .

CHAPTER TWO

The First Floor

How did I make a Floor again? The voice had said that my instincts should guide me, but how could that be true when I didn't even know how to start? I thought furiously for a while, I'm not sure how long, but once I snapped out of it—after not coming up with an answer, I might add—my mana was once again full.

Now that might be something. My thoughts became mana, the feeling of buzzing energy within me. That had to be part of it. It had been how I'd summoned the Leatherwing, after all.

Speaking of . . . I should probably come up with something to call my Guardian other than "the Leatherwing." A name that, like I had chosen for myself, seemed suitable. How could I go about naming something other than myself? Or maybe it already had a name and I just didn't know it? That was certainly a possibility . . .

No, I was getting distracted. First things first: I had to claim my Floor.

I had to *expand*.

That word struck a chord within me. It resonated with the very Core that was me. I was supposed to expand. And I knew how to. With a mental command, similar to how I'd selected the Leatherwing, I sent my mana out and away from myself. My senses went along for the ride, scanning across the far wall of the cave. I scanned across crevices, boulders, pools of water, and some other kind of rock hanging from the ceiling that looked different from the others. Maybe it was special somehow? I'd have to investigate later. I pressed onward, pushing my mana out farther and farther. The rock walls were much harder to pass through than the open air, but I managed with a bit of effort. And once I realized I could use the mana to move and shape the rock to suit my needs, I began doing that as well. Little by little the cavern began to grow. From a few meters in diameter to over a dozen, gaining equally in height. And, except just around where I lay, I dug away much of the cavern floor, leaving myself perched on a tall pillar. It felt much safer than being on the same level as everything else. Though not quite safe enough—after a moment I also dug a small hole right beneath myself, leading into a smaller separate cavern within the pillar. There I excavated my own little nest, leaving just enough room for the Leatherwing to enter easily and nothing else.

After I felt assured of my personal safety, I continued my work with the rest of the cave. I carved bewildering and seemingly arbitrary tunnels through the rock, making some lead to nowhere and some to sudden deep pits. There was just something about the trickery that felt right to me. Especially the pit with rock spikes at the bottom. That felt *exceptional.* So good, in fact, that I made several more and spread them out within the passageways I'd already finished. It was a simple trap, but in the dark and covered with a thin layer of mulch and gravel, who knew whom it could fool. Most people, I hoped, but I had no real way of knowing. I found myself wishing for some adventurers to find me so that I could pit my defenses against them. I paused. Yes, that felt right. That was another thing I was *supposed* to do. Lure adventurers in with the promise of treasure, then reward the strong and discourage the weak. Let those who proved themselves rise to the heights they deserved.

That was the *duty* of a Dungeon.

Expansion was the *reward.*

With my new insight fueling me, I got back to work with a redoubled effort. I sent my mana out as fast as I could, making the final adjustments to what would be my first, and for now only, Floor. The harder rock I left alone, instead continuing to make the same erratic pathways I'd started with, only now I made them with purpose. They were meant to confuse, to distract, and to slow down any intruders so as to let my Guardians catch them off guard.

I should probably have more of those. I felt safe with my Guardian, but having only the Leatherwing for the whole Floor felt wrong. Could I make more? No . . . I searched my mind and found that I was limited to only a single Guardian for each Floor I made, so until I could manage to grow, I'd only have the single Leatherwing as a Guardian. But that didn't mean I had to be completely bereft of other guards. As I scanned through my system interface, I learned that I already *knew* how to make other, smaller creatures. Two of them, in fact: the *Shadewing Bat* and the *Darkfin Manta.* It seemed my choice of Floor Guardian had given me these related creatures to populate the Floor with. That was nice. I wondered if I could mix and match once I got more Guardians, or if they'd be locked to this first Floor where the Leatherwing was. Whatever the case, I was happy I had them, and I started to populate my little cave as fast as my mana would let me. I made roosts for the Bats in the ceiling and along the hanging rocks, and filled the two pools of water in the cave with a few Mantas. Each was costly to my mana, but eventually I felt I'd made enough.

I inspected my Floor, its many nooks and secret little crevices for my Bats to roost in, the pools and channels for my mantas, all together with the confusing layout and some traps for good measure. A profound sense of satisfaction pulsed through me. It was finished. All I had to do now was come up with a suitable reward for those who managed to clear it, then I could connect it to the outside world.

For a moment I wondered exactly how I was going to do that, then instinct, or the system, kicked in and I knew what to do. I opened a different section of the system interface and selected the first and cheapest option, the only one available at this level.

Dungeon Chest
Cost: 15 mana per clear (taken from future mana regeneration)
Will be filled with a random assortment of rewards, depending on the selected category.

The system didn't really give me a lot of information on that one, but I found that instinctively I already knew a lot about how this was going to work. Dungeon Cores like myself had a certain dominion over creation, apparently. It was how we turned mana into creatures to defend ourselves, and how we could carve out and create our Floors. However this was mainly driven by the connection we had to the system, and many of its functions were either instinctual or beyond the conscious control of the Core itself. The rewards were one such function. The mana came from me, but I couldn't control what the reward was going to be. I frowned at that. I didn't really like the idea of not having control over my own Dungeon, but there wasn't anything I could do about it at the moment. Once I grew stronger and could create more things, I could certainly give out rewards by just leaving them around the place. But changing the rewards from the Floor Clear was beyond even the grandest of Dungeons. I sniffed—metaphysically, of course.

I'd just select something crappy then. That would show them.

Actually, never mind. If the reward were crappy nobody would want to brave my dangers to get it, and I'd have nothing to do. That would just get boring.

Let's see here, what were those categories again?

Mineral Chest
Armor Chest
Weapon Chest
Random Chest

That last option seemed unnecessarily vague, so that was out on pure principle. And why was one of the options "mineral"? Maybe because I was in a cave? Still, it didn't quite fit with the weapon and armor chests. After all, those who'd Challenge a Dungeon like me did so in order to get stronger and gain experience, and I had no idea how minerals would help with that. That one was out as well. I also didn't really like the idea of giving weapons so early, since they could very well be used against me. Armor it was.

Once I selected the chest, I programmed the command to release it upon the defeat of my Guardian, although it pained me to do so as I didn't want my Guardian to die. But such was its purpose.

At least its death wouldn't be permanent, and I'd just need to wait a while for it to respawn. Actually that was true for all of my creatures, I realized. As existences made from mana, they would not ever truly die but instead come back after a time at the cost of my mana—similar to the rewards being given from my future mana regeneration. The risk of death was mine alone, which was why my Guardians and creatures were the ones doing the actual fighting.

I chose the final location for the chest. Then I moved on to pushing outward, making a slope upward from a far wall, going even farther away from my cave. It was time to make the entrance and finish the Floor.

Sometime later, I'd managed to carve out a sloping passage through the stone and then through a section of softer soil before finally breaching the surface. I paused there for a moment, taking in the open sky and the sun. I wasn't exactly *seeing*, but something pretty close I thought, and even without eyes I could still appreciate a nice view and a cloudless sky. I was in a meadow, and I could faintly make out trees swaying in the wind surrounding me. A forest clearing then. A good spot for an entrance.

Before I could get to it, though, the voice sounded once more in my head.

Great job finishing your Floor! You've cleared the introductory tutorial and are now a proper Dungeon. My work here is done, but before I go, I want to mention a few final things.

Firstly, your purpose is to Challenge, reward, punish, and expand. How you do so is not that important, but cruelty and too many deaths of explorers you will likely lead to your destruction. Nobody wants an unfair Challenge, after all.

I'd already figured most of that out, not that I was planning on doing anything unfair anyway. The strong should be rewarded, but people should also be urged to grow. If I made things too hard, then those who'd need to test themselves the most would never have the courage to do so. And at that point I'd lose my purpose, wouldn't I?

The voice continued.

Secondly, as you've noticed, the system takes care of some of the things outside of your control. That can be temporary, if you become good enough at manipulating the different elements of mana to achieve a similar effect without its assistance. You will notice that your choice of Guardian strongly affects which of those elements you will come to favor, in addition to the pure mana used for expansion and construction. Therefore if this is a path you wish to go down, getting many different Guardians is something to look into. Such breadth comes with its own difficulties, of course.

Achieving independence gives you more freedom in how you may structure your Dungeon and your rewards. But it of course comes with more responsibility as well. Still it is a path you could go down, if you wish.

The voice paused before finishing with, *Good luck, young Veos.*

Thank you, voice. I sent it politely, but before I could begin thinking over the voice's words, a fresh prompt from the system appeared in my vision.

Tutorial completed!

You have now taken your first step as a young Core and are ready to emerge into the world. Requests from the Dungeon System Interface are complete for now, however more may appear on occasion depending on circumstance. As "requests," they are not mandatory, but they are strongly recommended; the system would not request something that would damage the Core.

Now go forth! Dig down and spread into the veins of the earth, and provide Challenge to those who seek power!

Tutorial completed perfectly! Tallying delayed rewards . . .
System Inventory opened!
Received [Random Creature Template (Mundane)]!
[Swift Descent] skill unlocked!
Leatherwing Guardian choice grants +10% proficiency with Darkness-element Mana!
Leatherwing Guardian choice grants +10% proficiency with Blood-element Mana!
Leatherwing Guardian choice grants +5% proficiency with Water-element Mana!
Experience gained . . .
Level up!
1 new Dungeon Perk available!

CHAPTER THREE

Rushing Down to Floor Two

The flood of information and sensation that came over me was overwhelming, and for a moment everything went black. I don't know how long, or even exactly what happened, but when I was conscious again my mana had recovered to full. I sent a panicked scan through my Floor but found everything as I'd left it, which let me relax a bit. At least I hadn't been found while I was unconscious. That would be a truly horrible way to end, without even a chance to defend myself.

Since everything in my dungeon seemed fine, I decided it was high time to really inspect my status. I had gotten several rewards from finishing the tutorial and I was curious what they were.

Name		Veos	
Race		Dungeon Core	
Floors		1	
Level	2	Experience	286/2000
Mana	20/20	Mana Regeneration	10/Minute
Edicts		None	
Skills		[Swift Descent]	

Perks	None
Rewards Inventory	Random Creature Template (Mundane)

I'd thought the mana I was holding felt a bit more . . . voluminous wasn't quite the right word but it almost described it. My capacity doubling would explain that feeling. And I can't help but smile at the new *1* next to *Floors*. I had a Floor. It made me giddy with excitement. I almost hoped someone would walk into it right then.

But no. There would be time for that later, ideally after I'd moved myself down into the ground to be farther away from any potential invaders. That was probably where the [Swift Descent] skill came in, I figured.

> **[Swift Descent]**
> Use all your available mana to quickly carve a shaft down toward the planet's core for your own Core. Makes more efficient use of mana than normal expansion, but limited to a tunnel no wider than half a meter. Distance traveled based on mana used. Can only be used once per finished Floor.

I activated it, and my senses became blurred and my mind unfocused. I felt a buzzing, a humming all around me, as a wave of new information and a staggering increase in awareness hit me like a rock to the . . . rock, I suppose. After an unknowable amount of time, it suddenly stopped. *I* suddenly stopped. I gradually came back to myself, my mind returning to normal. I examined my newly claimed area with gusto. There was twenty meters of shaft, and almost a meter of claimed rock and other materials beyond the shaft. Which explained where the massive influx of sensation came from. The shaft was just that: an empty hole in the rock going straight down. But it was surrounded by a variety of different rocks and a few natural openings intersecting the shaft. I realized there were even a few with water and some mushrooms I'd claimed as well. Which meant I could make mushrooms now. Neat.

The fact that the tunnel went straight down irked me. The second Floor wasn't supposed to be just a shaft with nothing in it. It was supposed to be expansive, and while it should be below the first Floor, that descent should be done through *stairs*. I had a lot of work to do. Plus I felt the area I'd claimed wasn't nearly enough to be considered a full Floor. I'd gone deep enough, but I knew there was more Floor to claim.

First things first though: a staircase. I pushed with my mana and claimed more and more stone surrounding the shaft I'd made until it was about three meters wide. After that I began claiming the rock behind me until I was able to carve out a more diagonal passageway down from my first Floor to this new level. I didn't mind the stairs being steep, but they did need to be stairs.

After several cycles of spending and recovering mana, I was finally finished. I now had a twenty-meter-deep staircase that also claimed twenty meters horizontally into the rock. I thought that was symmetrical and nice. After that I made my new stairs end in an archway leading into a larger room. It took a while, especially since I had to be more precise with how I carved out the stone to make it look more like something created. It was worth it, as I didn't want both floors to look like natural caves. No, the first floor should be the most natural, being the one closest to the surface, but after that the dungeon would begin in earnest. I experimented for a long while until I figured out how to not only dig through the stone, but shape it more deliberately into structures. I even learned how to transform it into a smooth, sleek stone, which I used, guided by a mysterious instinct, to make chambers a bit like you'd find in a mausoleum, complete with empty stone coffins and even a mysterious altar. Eventually I felt a resistance. Something invisible that stopped me from pushing outward. At the same time I felt something I'd experienced before while excavating the first Floor. But it was different this time, more suffocating. Earlier I'd felt a sense of completion—now there was something missing that made everything feel cramped. Suddenly I realized I'd lost myself in excavating and had ignored several messages from the system.

Second Floor begun. Would you like to select a Guardian?
Second Floor aesthetic intention detected. Modifying Guardian options. Would you like to select a Guardian?
Second Floor size at 50% capacity. Would you like to select a Guardian?
Second Floor size at 75% capacity. Would you like to select a Guardian?
Floor aesthetic solidified. Modifying Guardian options. Would you like to select a Guardian?
Second Floor size limit reached. Further expansion prohibited. Please select a Guardian.

Uhhh . . . oops. I'd missed a lot. I really needed to pay more attention. At least my inattention didn't prohibit my selection, I'd just delayed it.

Still, I'd need to pay much closer attention to the system in the future, since apparently now that the tutorial was done they wouldn't be shoved in my face whenever they appeared, but rather relegated to a slight pulsing at the corner of my awareness, obvious once I noticed it, but ignorable until I did. I resolved myself to be on the lookout for these messages in the future and steeled myself as I accepted the Guardian selection prompt.

Second Floor begun! Select a Guardian!

Floor Aesthetic: The Necromancer's Mausoleum. Due to the Core postponing the selection of a Guardian, the options will be altered to fit the Core's intended aesthetic. Note that Guardian creature selection is still affected by the current Floor and the Core's level.

Skeleton Golem: A large amalgam of bones from a variety of skeletons. This hulking brute of a monster lacks any form of subtlety, but more than makes up for it in durability and sheer power. It can absorb the bones of any non-dungeon creatures it finds in order to increase its health, defense, and size.

Skeletal Necromancer: The skeletal remains of a necromancer that has retained a spark of their former powers. It is not a Lich, not by a long shot, but it has taken the first step toward becoming one. Sporting a much higher intelligence than your average undead, this monster makes a natural commander, if slightly weaker in one-on-one combat.

Ravager Ghoul: Rabid madness and a craving for taking life given form. The Ravager Ghoul is relentless, thoughtless, and ravenous for anything living. The ghoul will single out the weakest member of a party and focus all its energy on consuming them to gain a boost in power and health.

Specter: A spirit of a restless dead, ethereal yet not always incorporeal. A specter does not have much in the way of offensive power compared to more powerful spiritual entities, but in return has a very high rate of survival. It has a hard time attacking the living, and the living has a hard time attacking it back.

Oh this was *cool!* Maybe delaying the selection hadn't been a bad idea after all if it got me these goodies. Well, the specter left something to be desired, and the ghoul seemed a bit too much of a relentless killing machine than I'd prefer, but the necromancer and the golem were both *very* interesting.

This would require some serious deliberation. The golem might seem a bit lackluster at first glance, but my instincts screamed that a monster that could grow innately was both rare and had the possibility to be extraordinarily powerful for its Floor. On the other hand a necromancer was *literally* what I'd pictured when I was designing the Floor, so not picking it just seemed wrong. And the line about having taken the first step toward becoming a Lich wasn't something my instincts told me I could just ignore either. I realized I knew monsters could evolve. More specifically *I* could evolve them, but seemingly only after they'd gained enough experience from defending the dungeon against intruders. So while I couldn't evolve anything now, neither my normal monsters nor my Guardians, it was definitely something I'd need to keep an eye on. I wouldn't want to miss an evolution, as I'd done just now with the Guardian selection, even if this time it had worked in my favor. The future evolution and how well it fit my theme were what made me make the choice in the end. The [Skeletal Necromancer] just fit my ideals for my second Floor too well. The Golem would have been nice, but I liked having a spellcaster as a Guardian a bit more. It would also serve as a more tactical 'commander' type Guardian, which was a nice way to differentiate this Floor from the more animalistic first one. With those thoughts reinforcing my decision I made my *selection.*

Like it had when I'd selected the Leatherwing all that time ago, mana began to rush from all directions, swirling together in front of me. It coalesced into a twister, then with a surge I felt the change, and the necromancer materialized in front of me. It was tall, almost twice as tall as a Leatherwing at a full two meters, and was clad in a hooded brown robe covering most of its wiry bones. The only exceptions were its hands, which stuck out of the robe and held a black staff with a suitably magical-seeming crystal orb at the top. Its face looked typical for a skeleton, apart from the blue glint of intelligence I could see in the glow deep in its eye sockets. I felt a surge of satisfaction run through my Core. This was my second Guardian, and it too was perfect.

Skeletal Necromancer Guardian choice grants +15% proficiency with Death-element Mana!
Skeletal Necromancer Guardian choice grants +10% proficiency with Darkness-element Mana!
Skeletal Necromancer Guardian choice grants +10% proficiency with Arcane-element Mana!
Experience gained!

The Necromancer stood still for a few seconds, as if growing accustomed to its new body, before taking a step toward me and bowing at the waist.

"Greetings, sire," he said. The voice was surprisingly crisp and clear for having come from a skeleton. "Thank you for your gift. It will be my honor to serve you in whatever way you wish."

I nodded mentally, then sent my thoughts to it the same way I had with the voice back when I first woke up. *Thank you. This Floor will be yours—it's called the Necromancer's Mausoleum. Its creatures will be yours to command in whatever way you see fit, provided I do not step in.*

"I will do my utmost." The Necromancer said, rising from his bow.

I *really* needed to give my Guardians names. I couldn't just call him "Necromancer" forever. But the Leatherwing should rightfully be named first, as it had been my first Guardian.

Go familiarize yourself with the layout. I shall give you subordinates momentarily.

Once I had my mana back up to full, I sent my awareness up the stairs and focused my attention on the Leatherwing hanging on its perch above the stairs. The pillar I'd made was gone, leaving nothing but a round chamber with a hole in its floor. But given that defeating a Guardian was a system-enforced prerequisite for descending, it didn't bother me that much, other than in an aesthetic sense. Still, since the first Floor was supposed to imitate a natural cave leading down deeper into the unknown, it wasn't that bad. I'd have to be more careful once I leveled up and could start my third though, as I didn't want tits entrance to be just anywhere on the other Floors. But that was a matter for later. Now it was naming time.

I focused on the Leatherwing, examining it closely. The dark red eyes, the sharp teeth and hooked claws. The way its hide seemed to almost shift its pigment to better blend in with its surroundings. Perfect for stalking unsuspecting prey, before grabbing them and dragging them into the darkness.

Stalker. I sent it. *Your name will be Stalker.*

I felt a surge of mana leave me, flowing into the Leatherwing, strengthening and enhancing it before my very eyes.

You have named your first creature!
Experience gained!
Your creature *Stalker* is being strengthened!
Stalker has become a [Leatherwing (Elite)].

CHAPTER FOUR

A Guardian's Status

I blinked mentally at the sudden influx of system notifications. Naming things had such power? Names were truly amazing. Though when I thought about it, naming *myself* was one of the first things the tutorial voice had instructed me to do. Maybe I got power from my name as well. Regardless, I was happy for Stalker, as I watched it . . . no, *her* . . . inspect her new form. It looked very similar to her old one, except she was slightly larger, and blended in with the cave around her in a more ethereal way. Her eyes also gleamed with more intelligence than before, similar to those of the Skeletal Necromancer. Maybe I could speak to her too? She didn't have a mouth shaped for words, but then again neither did skeletons, so it shouldn't be that bad.

The first Floor is yours to Guard, I sent. Stalker shifted her head toward my Core, immediately attentive to my words. *Go familiarize yourself with the layout and with the Floor's other inhabitants.*

I will do this, and do it well, Stalker sent back. Interesting. Instead of speaking aloud like the Necromancer, she'd used a kind of telepathy similar to mine. Her voice, such as it was, felt more like music and an assortment of tones than words, though the meaning was quite clear. I sent back affirmation, then returned my attention to the Necromancer. Might as well name him as well while I was at it. Let me think . . . A good name for a Necromancer . . .

Your name will be Krazad, I sent it. *Krazad the Necromancer.*

This time the surge of mana was much more intense. I'd recovered most of my mana in the time since the first naming, but I wasn't quite back to full. Plus, Krazad seemed to require much more mana for his naming than Stalker had. I half wondered why, but mostly I was occupied with feeling like I was being wrung inside out as I spent mana as quickly as it recovered. The edges of my awareness turned dull, almost black. Like the void before existence. Thankfully I was able to hold on, though only just, until eventually the process finally finished. I sank deep into myself, shutting down most of my external senses as I gathered myself after the ordeal. That had been *horrible.* Note to self: do not underestimate naming. I'd have to figure out what caused that sort of thing to keep it from happening in the future. For now though I was just glad to be in one piece.

> Your creature *Krazad the Necromancer* is being strengthened!
> Krazad the Necromancer *has become a* [Skeletal Necromancer (Elite)]!
> Experience gained!

I was vaguely aware of the new notification from the system, but I still spent a few moments within my Core, recentering myself. Afterward, I began to stretch my awareness back out to examine the new appearance of my second Floor boss, only to find that it hadn't changed. At least outwardly. I could feel that Krazad was different, stronger, than the Skeletal Necromancer had been. But outwardly he looked the same. That didn't matter to me though, as long as the naming did what it was supposed to. I only wished I could see exactly what was different.

I flinched mentally as a status screen suddenly appeared to my senses. One that was not mine.

Name	Krazad the Necromancer	Level	20
Race	Undead (Arcane, Darkness, Death)	Grade	Elite (Guardian)
Attributes			
Strength	40	Vitality	132
Dexterity	38	Perception	58

Spirit	90	Force	100
Health	1320	Mana	900
Skills			
[Mana Bolt], [Detect Magic], [Darkness], [Raise Skeleton], [Necrotic Aura], [Death Mark]			

My first thought was that this was incredibly unfair. My status wasn't anywhere near this extensive. And that wasn't even mentioning the skills and mana Krazad now had access too. But then I realized that if he had access to them, *I* had access to them as well, so I relaxed and began going through the page in earnest. The thing that stood out the most was that Krazad had many more attributes than me. In fact, the only one we shared was mana; the rest were foreign to me. Though I could sense something about their function and domain through my connection to the system, and the attributes were pretty much standard across the native creatures of this world. To check, I opened up Stalker's status as well.

Name	Stalker	Level	10
Race	Leatherwing (Blood, Darkness, Water)	Grade	Elite (Guardian)
Attributes			
Strength	35	Vitality	81
Dexterity	61	Perception	56
Spirit	32	Force	41
Health	810	Mana	320
Skills			
[Water Jet], [Blood Poison], [Darkness], [Meld]			

She was a lower level than Krazad, and her attributes were substantially lower as well. That made sense to me, considering that she was on the first Floor and Krazad was on the second, but I didn't really know where that feeling of supposed order came from. Because at the same time I also didn't particularly want Stalker to be weak just because she was *supposed* to be. That didn't feel right either. More stuff I needed to ponder about. Lovely. At this rate I'd never get anything else done *but* pondering. When I first awakened I'd been nothing but a bundle of excitement, but the more I learned, and the more I became aware that I didn't know anything about anything, the more frustrating it became to not know. Maybe I'd been too eager, too responsive to my impulses to grow and expand, when what I should have been doing was taking things more slowly and learning *why* things were happening.

Well, it probably wasn't that big of a deal. And I got this sweet new Floor aesthetic as a result, so everything worked out fine in the end apart from the naming issue. Still, I felt that I should take a break from growing for a bit, regardless of how counter that sentiment was to my sensibilities, and examine what I could actually *do*. Not just with mana, but with the system as well.

With that decided, I dismissed Stalker's status window and checked on the Bats and Mantas. They had statuses just like the Leatherwing, though their grade was Mundane instead of Elite, and of course they weren't Guardians. They were also all level 1, and had vastly lower attributes than Stalker, with only one skill each: [Meld] for the bats, and [Water Jet] for the mantas. Even though they were all the same level, there was some variety between their attributes, which let me work out how health and mana worked: health was ten times vitality, and mana was ten times spirit. Something I really should have noticed instantly, but oh well.

After that I summoned some Skeletons on the second Floor to check their stats; the new creature type was unlocked to me after selecting Krazad as Guardian. Their status looked pretty much the same as the other monsters, though they started at level 10, and cost a noticeably larger amount of mana to create. In fact just a single one cost 15 mana, almost my entire mana pool, so I had to wait a bit after each summon. It also seemed that instead of a different creature I'd gotten a subtype of my Guardian this time. At least that was how it was organized in my system window. There was the normal Skeleton, and below that was a subtype called Skeletal Archer. They cost 5 more mana to summon, but had higher stats on average and even came with their own equipment. Though they weren't Elite and still spawned at level 10. On a hunch I tried spawning a Skeleton on the first Floor instead, both to see what would happen and just to check if I could. I selected the base Skeleton from the system list and waited with baited breath. Then, just like normal, I felt the now familiar feeling of mana draining from me as the summoning began. I checked the new Skeleton status. Level 1 this time, and much lower stats than the others. Then I frowned when I noticed that it had still cost me 15 mana to make. That was three times as much as the Manta or the Bat for something at the same level. Still, it was an interesting discovery. It seemed there was some kind of level range on each Floor. Maybe you could only be below 10 on the first one, since that was the level of the Guardian . . . No, that didn't seem right. The Skeletons had been level 10 even on the second Floor . . . Whatever—I didn't have to learn everything right away. And I had plenty of other things I needed to investigate. Like my own status page. I hadn't checked it once since I leveled, and at that time I'd been too excited to think clearly about anything other than continued expansion. I remembered I'd received *rewards* from leveling up and I hadn't even checked out what they were yet, apart from the skill. I felt a profound sense of disappointment in myself. Bad Dungeon. Everyone should always check their rewards.

I decided to check out the thing called "Edicts" first . . . Only to find very little in terms of information. I had two Edict Slots, I could feel that instinctively. But exactly what they were *for* I had no idea. Something about defining Rules, with a capital R, that everything within the Dungeon had to follow. It seemed nice in theory, especially if I could make one that made people unable to kill me, but I didn't know how to use it. My mysterious instincts brought forth by the system weren't much help, either. With a mental sigh I moved on to the next thing on the list. Dungeon Perks.

This subject had much more information, and further cemented me as an utter *moron*. Perks were, as it turned out, passive abilities that would steer a Dungeon's growth. There were ones that made different creature types cheaper to make, ones that improved creatures based on their innate elements. There was even one that increased a Floor's maximum size and how much mana was generated through certain processes.

The last two were the most interesting to me. I *could* take one focusing on darkness-attuned mana, as that overlapped between my two Floors. But I didn't feel like restricting myself like that. Maybe I'd take the one that increased the power of a Floor's creatures for each element that Floor had that *wasn't* on any of the other Floors. That one could've been interesting. Though selecting it now that I already had an overlap . . . No, I couldn't do it.

After some more reading, I got bored and simply narrowed down the Perks I'd already read through to three contenders.

[Improved Mana Flows]	Dungeon Perk (Common)
Increases the Core's mana generation by 10% for each Floor in the Dungeon.	

[Spatial Expansion]	Dungeon Perk (Uncommon)
Increases the maximum size of a Floor by 1.5x the normal limit.	

[Elemental Darkness]	Dungeon Perk (Uncommon)
Grants the Core's minions attuned to the Darkness element +15% mana and health.	

I frowned internally. All of them were good, making it difficult to pick just one. But I also refused to wallow in indecision. That was *not* who I was. I was *Veos*. I *acted*.

I picked [Spatial Expansion]. It was the only choice really. Though the other ones might have given me an actual power increase but . . . I'd been forced to stop my mausoleum before I'd been happy with it. I hadn't thought it had bothered me that much until I'd seen this Perk, and realized just how much I *needed* to change it into the Floor I actually wanted.

Unfortunately the first Floor was already done, and so I couldn't expand it with this. But that was okay. I was happy with that Floor as it was anyway. The Mausoleum, however, needed more work. I dismissed my status window and was about to get started, then forced myself to stop.

Hold on. You're not done yet. There are still things left to go through.

The Random Creature Template specifically. I dejectedly opened up the status again and started going through my sudden influx of memories about the subject. I instantly became fully alert, and I felt excitement once more start to build in my soul. This was . . . I couldn't quite put it into words. But something about getting something at random was *incredibly* attractive to me. Was that what people felt when they got my Rewards Chests? I could only hope so, for their sake.

With rapt attention, I activated the template and felt a massive die started rolling around in my head. It spun and spun, each face representing a different creature. All my attention was focused on it as it began to slow down, gradually at first, before it finally landed.

You have unlocked the [Flame Wisp]! Experience gained!

A Flame Wisp . . . I tested the name on my tongue, mentally speaking. It was definitely different from the other creatures I had. Which was both good and bad. Good, because they might come as a surprise to future delvers. Bad, because they wouldn't fit with any of my Floor aesthetics. Bah, maybe that wasn't a big deal. Maybe one wandered in from outside. With my mind made up, I activated the system and summoned one to my first Floor. Then I quickly checked its status. What I saw caused my elation to deflate slightly. These Wisps had even lower attributes than my Bats!

But they did have [Flame Conjuration], and quite a lot of mana. So my instincts told me they could still be quite useful. Though I probably wouldn't use them on any of these first two Floors—they didn't match their themes.

With the chores left to me by my own foolish eagerness taken care of, I was *finally* able to get back to constructing my second Floor. I'd made the critical path, the boss room, and a pair of chambers that I felt fit into what a mausoleum should look like. My issue was the area around the staircase. My area of control wasn't broad enough to make anything before, while still wasting a lot of my precious Floorspace. Now, though, I could expand the area around and underneath the back parts of the staircase, and make a final, hidden, chamber. It wouldn't be vital to completing the Floor. But it *would* allow better rewards. I smiled internally as I worked, unaware of the passing of time. Around me my two Guardians, their minions, and a singular Wisp wandered or floated around, wordlessly protecting me while I hummed to myself and decorated the stonework along the corridors of the mausoleum. This Floor was going to be *so cool!*

CHAPTER FIVE

Aira's Awakening

Aira stood together with a dozen or so of her fellow villagers as the Awakener's carriage rolled down the main road into the village. Flanked by high-level guards on both sides, the mana-powered carriage rolled surprisingly silently, letting out nothing more than a soft hum despite how it towered over most of the buildings it passed. It was made of as much metal as wood, which, combined with its height, gave off an imperious and authoritative air that seemed to push the villagers into silence. Aira had of course seen this procession at last years' Awakening ceremony, but she hadn't felt like this then. Sure it had been impressive even then, but it was different watching from the sidelines, than watching it come straight toward her. The only way she could describe her feelings was awe mixed with healthy doses of anxiety and fear. She felt something squeeze her hand, and saw Athilana at her side.

The elven girl stood half a head taller than Aira, with the curly green hair common to her people tied up in ornate braids for the occasion. She gave Aira a reassuring smile, who returned it and squeezed her friend's hand in thanks before turning back to the procession.

It was stupid to worry, anyway. Everyone Awakened. Everyone got their Class and Glyph. Why did they always make such a big deal out of it?

Because there is always a chance someone gets a special Class, she reminded herself. That was what her mother had told her. It was the reason the Church and the Guilds cared to send their own members of the Awakeners, even to a small village like Coltmoon—just for the tiny, tiny, chance that one of them Awakened with a Tier 2 Class at Tier 1.

It would never *actually* happen here, of course. Things like that didn't happen in small villages. They didn't even happen in large metropolises more than once every few decades. But the ceremony was also an opportunity to recruit those with impressive Glyphs, regardless of their Class. Her eyes sought out Vireld, the symbol of the Kiyan Church embroidered on his chest. She hadn't known him very well, but his Glyph had caused quite a stir in the village when he'd Awakened three years ago. Aira understood the reason. An additional skill slot at each tier was already good, but an ever-increasing boost to vitality every tier up on top of that? That was a *good* Glyph. One any organization would want to recruit.

Her gaze turned back to her compatriots. More specifically Vireld's brother Daren, who's Awakening was the reason he was back in town today. She knew him better than she did Vireld, they were the same age after all, but she wouldn't call him a friend exactly. Still she hoped he'd get a good Glyph. She looked at the group of people crowding around Vireld and shivered. If anyone had reason to be nervous today, it would be Daren. Compared to him, what expectations could people have of her? None whatsoever. She felt a bit bad about it, but the thought did help relieve her anxiety somewhat.

The *thump* and *buzz* of the carriage's Magitech powering down jerked her mind back to the moment, and she returned her attention to the procession. It was almost time now.

"Next!" an Awakener in front called out. Aira squeezed her clammy hands together. This wasn't a big deal. She shouldn't be this nervous about it, especially after she'd managed to calm herself down a minute ago. Athilana had even been *excited* when her turn had come. Why couldn't she be more like her? She shook it off and forced herself to step forward. The Awakener took her name, checked it off his list, and guided her silently into the carriage. Once inside she was surprised by how light and airy it was. The outside was domineering, but the inside was downright comfy. She forced herself to pay attention and sat down at the Awakening table. Opposite her sat another Awakener, this one with a sigil for the Adventurers' Guild on her white robe. She gave Aira a friendly smile.

"Hello, young lady," she said.

"H-hello," Aira stammered.

"No need to be nervous," the woman said. "I will talk you through the whole process. You can have a second to take a deep breath if you need to." Aira nodded and did so, then the woman continued by gesturing to the items on the table between them.

"This is the Mana Crystal we'll be using." She said. "It came from a mine outside Ebereya, and it's certified at ninety-eight percent purity by their Miners' Guild."

"Oh", Aira said. She supposed that was impressive, though she didn't really have a frame of reference to understand why. She really didn't know much of the world beyond a few days' walk from Coltmoon. Even the nearest town, Aspenfield, was farther away than she'd ever been before, and all she really knew about it was that it was the place where the count who ruled this land lived. She also knew he answered to the Duke of Alash, who in turn served the King of Ebereya. It all seemed so far away, to the point where it lost its meaning. Seemingly noticing her confusion, the Awakener began explaining the process that had been used to mine the crystal. As well as how it was used to speed up the Awakening process.

She talked about the natural Awakening that would happen on the seventeenth day after a person's nineteenth birthday. Why that day specifically was so often the topic of research and discussion, much of which went way above Aira's head, and even the Awakener admitted to only understanding the basics of it. Still, she explained that finding everyone on their own specific day was simply not feasible, regardless of how large their organization was. And relying on people to travel to *them* was beyond what could be expected of the freshly Awakened. This was why Awakeners existed. As Aira listened to the woman talk about her role within the Order, and how life was on the road, she found herself calm. Her breathing slowed, and her heart rate steadied. Before she knew it she simply wasn't that nervous anymore. The Awakener, on the other hand, seemed keenly aware of her anxiety, because not even ten seconds after Aira herself realized it she stopped her story and transitioned to the actual Awakening procedure. Aira listened attentively, though her role was extremely simple. All she needed to do was hold her hand on the crystal and wait patiently.

She placed her hand atop it. It felt cool to the touch, yet alive with a kind of energy crackling just beneath the surface. She hadn't felt mana like this before. Sure her parents, and every other Awakened adult for that matter, had mana within them. But not like this. Not this concentrated. She shut her eyes and breathed.

In . . . and out . . . In . . . and out . . .

She briefly wondered how long it'd take.

> System connection established. Initiating Awakening process.
> . . .
> Awakening complete.

Aira's eyes snapped open as she felt an insane rush of mana flood into her and flow through her body. Everything from the base of her feet to her scalp tingled with energy. She gasped and threw herself backward into her chair. The edges of her vision grew blurry, and her mind struggled to adapt to the surge of new sensations and information.

She shut her eyes and breathed. She'd known this would happen. She could get through it. Eventually the rush faded, and though she still felt lightheaded she could at least think properly. She opened her eyes and couldn't help but smile. She'd Awakened.

It wasn't an accomplishment, really. Everyone did it, after all. But it still felt special. She felt . . . alive in a way she hadn't before in her life. Was this how Classers felt all the time?

She blinked. Right! Her Class and Glyph!

"Status open," she said aloud. She knew she'd eventually be able to open her status with a thought. But for now she felt it best to speak the commands, just to be safe. She couldn't help but grin as the slightly transparent blue window manifested in front of her eyes for the first time.

Name		Aira Carinon	
Biological Age	18	**Numerical Age**	18
Bonus Years		6	
Species		Human	
Glyph		Glyph of the Silent Hunter	
Tier		1	
Level		1	
Class		Ranger	

Strength	15	Vitality	16
Dexterity	17	Perception	15
Spirit	15	Force	16
Attribute Points	5		
Innate Class Skills	[Detect Entity] [Focused Shot]		
Skills:	[-]		
Talents	[-] (1)(1)		
Health	160/160		
Mana	150/150		

A Ranger . . . she thought. Not a Tier 2 Class, of course. Why was she a bit disappointed? She shook herself back to the present. Ranger was not what she'd guessed she'd get. Though it wasn't that big of a surprise. Glyphs and Tier 1 Classes tended to go hand in hand. She forced herself to check the description of the Glyph before the butterflies could sneak their way back into her stomach.

Glyph of the Silent Hunter	Human Glyph
This Glyph allows the holder to see clearly, both in the dark or through obscured terrain. They move silently without rousing the attention of those around. Skills that are *imbued* onto bows or arrows inflict increased damage per Tier (+10%). Gain an additional talent point on odd levels, only to be spent on *imbuing* talents.	

That was . . . good? She thought it was good. It wasn't remotely close to the type of Glyph she'd thought she'd get, or had hoped for, but it was definitely powerful. Most Glyphs only had an effect on the system and how you interfaced with it, whether it be making skills cheaper, or available earlier, or more powerful. This one did that too, though the increase wasn't nearly as high as she'd heard it was for other Glyphs. That was made up for by the additional talent points she'd receive, even if she'd be restricted in how she used them. You could say that the Glyph was half power increase, half talent increase, with some restrictions on both sides. What made it stand out, though, were the passive everyday life bonuses. Moving silently and seeing clearly weren't game changers and probably wouldn't work a hundred percent of the time, especially against magical detection or concealment. But it was active *all the time*, which made it all the more usable.

"Something good, I take it?" the Awakener said from across the table. Aira flinched and tore her eyes from her system window. She blushed awkwardly. She'd actually forgotten she was still in the carriage. She took a deep breath to center herself.

"I think so," she answered. "I'm not that familiar with all the effects, to be honest, so I'm not sure."

"Oh?" the woman said, raising an eyebrow. "Multiple effects, you say? Interesting. Most Glyphs only do the one thing. Would you describe the effects for me, please? This is of course private and won't be shared with anyone outside the Awakeners. Oh and if I could get your Class as well?" She turned to a blank page in her book.

Aira nodded. "I got Ranger as my Class, and my Glyph seems to be derived from that. Or the other way around—I'm not sure."

"It isn't fully known either way." The woman shrugged. "It's the subject of some debate whether our initial Classes determine our Glyphs or vice versa. Though the opinion held by most is that it is the Glyph that influences the Class."

Aira nodded. "Well, the Glyph is called 'Glyph of the Silent Hunter', and it helps me see clearly and move silently, regardless of terrain, I think."

"Passive benefits outside the system connection," the woman said as she wrote. "These kinds of bonuses aren't the most common, and they're often harder to rank. But with enough testing you should be able to get some idea of exactly how much it helps."

Aira nodded. "The Glyph also has a mild strengthening to skills that are imbued onto bows or arrows, and grants me additional talent points on odd levels that can only be spent on imbuing talents."

She looked at the Awakener woman curiously, trying to ascertain her reaction to what she said. The woman only looked focused, if a bit pensive, as she dutifully recorded Aira's words in her ledger. Once she was done she looked up and gave Aira a small smile.

"I can tell what you're thinking," she said, then tapped her pen on her lips in thought. "It's certainly a very *wide* Glyph in how it spreads out its benefits. Yet it's still united in purpose. In a way it's restrictive despite its variety of effects, since you'll have to utilize them all to gain the most you can out of it. If you go down that path, though, it seems like a good Glyph to me. Besides, what are Glyphs if not lanterns sent by the system to guide us along our individual paths?"

Aira smiled and nodded eagerly. That was true. The Glyph was just a guide. It would be up to her to take full advantage of it and walk the path to its conclusion. The Awakener closed her ledger and took out a piece of parchment, which she handed to Aira. She looked it over, then stared back up at the woman with wide eyes.

"Like I said, the Glyph could be powerful if you're able to take full advantage of it. And it'd be downright irresponsible of me *not* to invite you to take the Ranger course at the Adventurers' Guild. We are the Guild with the most members for a reason. We can help you, and in return you can eventually help us." She smiled at Aira. "What do you say? Do you want to become an Adventurer?"

CHAPTER SIX

The Third

I didn't know how long it took me to finally be satisfied with my second Floor, but it was definitely much longer than I'd spent on the first. But since my first Challenger hadn't arrived yet, and I had my first Floor as a buffer, I felt safe enough to take my time. Most of the work was tweaking the look and feel of the space, rather than changing the layout. I finished that almost right away. The staircase led down into a main chamber which split off to the other three directions. Each of the corridors had small room offshoots, which I imagined would have been for the people who'd served in this place before it had become a tomb. Each of the three hallways eventually ended in a larger room, in which I placed a number of sarcophagi to house the Skeletons and Skeletal Archers. I sculpted from stone furniture I thought would suit the place. A table here, some chairs there. Beds in each of the small rooms. I wasn't a hundred percent sure where this stuff was supposed to go, my instincts only helped so much, but I thought I was at least mostly right.

From there the three larger rooms had their own smaller hallways connecting each other. Then I created two last rooms. One for my Guardian, farthest away from the stairs, ensuring any Challenger would have to go through at least two of my large rooms to reach it. And one underneath the staircase. I filled that one to the brim with sarcophagi for more Skeletons, and even spawned in a bonus Rewards Chest. You'd get one for clearing the Floor, but you could get a bonus one by clearing this room as well. I still didn't feel comfortable enough to give out weapons just yet, but I also didn't want to keep using the same reward all the time, so I made the bonus a Minerals Chest. If it turned out that they weren't that valuable, my Challengers wouldn't have to tackle the room, since it wasn't on the critical path.

Other than that I worked on artwork, carvings in the walls depicting what I thought were epic scenes. Mostly featuring Skeletons, and many focusing on my Guardian as the hero. I spent some time carving runic messages as well, though they were mostly meant to confuse rather than communicate anything specific. This Floor wouldn't have many traps in it, so I wanted to add something to slow a Challenger.

Speaking of traps . . . I did make *a few*. Not many, and only ones that had to be triggered manually, either using mana or another more mundane mechanism. That way my Skeletons wouldn't accidentally activate them while nobody was here.

I had some problems getting the instructions to stick. As it turned out, Skeletons were *dumb*. Apart from my Guardian, who'd been blessed with intelligence and an ability to plan, the rest were dumb as bones. Still, eventually I managed to make them understand how to trigger an arrow trap, and when to do it so as to not shoot themselves. There was no chance I'd get them to figure out the mana-activated ones. They only barely used mana as it was, and most of that was passive benefits from the system. They simply didn't have the skill to manipulate mana on purpose. I had to leave those traps to my Guardian.

All in all it was a nice Floor. Six rooms all connected via hallways, three of which were trapped and three of which weren't. Around two dozen base Skeletons and a dozen Skeletal Archers made up my creatures for the Floor, since apparently that was limited as well, just like the Floor size. I admitted it made sense, since otherwise a Dungeon could just make creatures until the space was entirely filled with them. Maybe they'd even spill over to the outside. It still rankled a bit to be left with some unused sarcophagi in my bonus room, but eventually I gave a mental shrug and just left it as it was. It didn't matter that much, and maybe they'd serve as bait or accidental trickery for those trying for the bonus.

I made some final adjustments to the staircase, then declared the Floor finished. I felt a *shift* as the mechanics of the system locked my designs into place, strengthening the walls and borders beyond anything I could have made myself. This strengthening was how a Dungeon could avoid having people just break through the stone and go directly to the Core room, and was also the reason it was so difficult to change the layout of a Floor once it was complete. As tradeoffs go, it was well worth it.

> Floor finished!
> Experience gained . . .
> Level up!
> 1 new Dungeon Perk available!
> Skill [Swift Descent] unlocked!

All right, now we were talking.

I'd been keeping track of my experience after excavations and summonings, and neither did much at all for my progress. I had gotten some from summoning my Guardians, but the rest was chump change. It seemed most of my leveling would come from finishing a Floor. It made sense. After all, making more and more Floors was what I was *supposed* to do. Though something told me it wouldn't be as simple as just making one new Floor for every level. Pretty soon I'd need to do more to level, and maybe that was already true, considering my experience requirements. Unless something changed when I attracted Challengers. Oh I could hardly wait. I was *so* curious to see what people would think of my Floors.

No use sitting around. Might as well get started on my third Floor! *[Swift Descent] activate!*

I felt the same faint blurring of my surroundings, and a buzzing to my senses, as I rapidly began claiming the rock beneath my Core. It didn't feel as overwhelming as last time, and I was able to keep a loose mental awareness of the differences in material and environment as I descended, so that when I stopped it didn't come with the same confusion as the first time. This time I was also paying attention to my status, and noticed the prompt when it first appeared.

> Third Floor begun. Would you like to select a Guardian?

I hesitated. Did I want to select a Guardian right away? If I didn't, I'd be able to mold this new Floor to an aesthetic, like last time. The problem was that I had no inspiration for what the third Floor should *be*. With the second, I'd had a clear image in mind. Now, I had several ideas, but none of them stood out more than any other. Maybe picking a Guardian would give me the inspiration I needed? If nothing else I felt like I *should* know how creating a Floor based on a Guardian worked. That way I'd know which method I preferred in the future.

With that thought I accepted the prompt.

Third Floor begun! Select a Guardian.

Vampiric Gargoyle: A creature made from blood and stone, which is not alive yet feeds on the living. The Vampiric Gargoyle is a sturdy creature, often used for protection by Vampire Lords for their ability to survive prolonged engagements without permanent damage, even against the strongest of foes.

Sunfire Eye: An elemental of light and fire, who burns through lies and reveals truth. Sunfire Eyes are the justices of the Firelight Realm, employed for their reasoning, intellect, and magical prowess. Some even shift into the material plane when particularly difficult judgements need to be made.

Shadowborn Wraith: A being of anger and darkness, of revenge and anguish. The Shadowborn Wraith is the tragic spirit of a soul drenched in the blackness of betrayal. A creature feared and despised by most, and that revels in the torment of the living.

Greenscale Naga: A Greenscale Naga appears to be a solitary creature when observed. They make their home in underwater caverns, and only meet in person when absolutely necessary due to their ability to communicate telepathically. Being adept Arcane mages and fearsome fighters, they are not to be trifled with on land. Many never even try to engage with them beneath the waves.

I studied my options for several minutes, pondering what I might want for my third Floor, and searching for inspiration. The Shadowborn Wraith was out right away. It was much too vile for what I wanted my Dungeon to be. Sure I would have danger, and even death, but the Wraith was too hungry for it. Rather than Challenge, it sought to hurt and kill for its own sake. That wasn't me.

Narrowing from three was trickier. My first Floor emulated a natural cave, focusing on traps and unseen danger. The second evoked the feeling of uncovering something old and forgotten, with the danger being more organized and tactical. I wanted something different for the third. Also there was the Guardian itself. I wanted each Guardian to require a different type of strategy to defeat them. I had a stealthy ambusher and a tactical spellcaster. What I wanted for the third was more of a frontline fighter. A wall that stood between the Challengers and the rest of my dungeon. That felt right. On top of that, I also wanted the Floors to feel at least somewhat connected in theme if not in tactics. Which really left only one choice. The Vampiric Gargoyle it was. It was tough, undead, and also a bit similar to Stalker in that they both could feed on blood. I admit it wasn't the strongest connection ever, but it was good enough. It also helped me figure out what kind of Floor to make.

A gauntlet. A trial of endurance and perseverance.

The Challengers would have to contend with the Guardian, who would then leave to recover while my normal creatures attacked. Once the Gargoyle had recovered a bit, it would jump back into the fray. Rinse and repeat until the Challengers managed to defeat all my creatures.

For the design I started with a hexagonal cave, then I made the floor appear constructed, and raised walls around the edges. On the far end I made stairs leading directly up the cavern wall, where I placed a door and made a small room. The wall itself I carved to look like it was part of a castle, with tall towers and parapets for my Guardian to sit on. I then connected the castle walls to create a sort of courtyard and placed gates in each wall that lead to smaller rooms. These sub-chambers would hold my creatures, and the Guardian could utilize its ability to fly to escape to the parapets.

The Floor would be rather small, but that wasn't bad. I could exchange the leftover Floorspace for additional creatures to really hone in on the theme of constant battle.

I frowned mentally. When had I realized I could exchange Floorspace for more creatures? And how did it make sense that a *smaller* Floor could have *more* creatures placed in it? The seeming lack of logic bothered me, so I searched my mind until I found an answer. It turned out that not only was there a maximum Floor size, but a *minimum* one as well. Only once that had been reached could a Dungeon decide between adding more creatures or having a larger Floor.

I sighed. It made some sense—if there wasn't a minimum size I could make the Floor so tiny nothing could fit inside it and therefore nothing could beat it, but it annoyed me to no end that I hadn't realized this earlier. If I had known I could have tweaked the mausoleum to fit all the creatures I wanted . . . I needed to pay more careful attention to these instincts. It was knowledge I didn't know I had until I thought about it, so unless I really thought about a problem or question, an answer would never reveal itself.

I made a note to really think through whether there was anything else I wanted, or something I was curious about that might change, before finalizing this third Floor.

The size minimum was a bit annoying, as it was about twice what I'd planned for the Floor. In the end I just made the castle larger by making the roof higher and adding more fake towers and spires. Now the cavern was almost thirty meters high, more than halfway back up to the second Floor. But with the system enhancements to structural integrity, I wasn't worried. With the layout done, it was time to populate it.

I checked what new creatures the Gargoyle had given me.

Oh, there were three of them! The Stone Gargoyle, the Stone Thrall, and Blooddrinker Lichen.

The Gargoyle seemed to be a smaller version of my Guardian, though without many of the abilities that came from its Vampiric prefix. Nevertheless they were solid fighters with high defenses and surprising mobility due to their ability to fly.

The Thralls were . . . slow. Lumbering humanoids of rock with very little skill for thinking or planning. Even less so than my Skeletons. But they were difficult to kill and didn't tend to run low on stamina, so they weren't quite as disappointing as their attributes first made them appear. In addition, they took up much less of my creature budget per Thrall than the Gargoyles did. Exactly how much was difficult to tell, as the cost of each creature was affected by all the current creatures already on the Floor, but a ballpark would put them at three Thralls to one Gargoyle. Which made the comparison much more favorable, though the Gargoyle might still win in a direct confrontation. That didn't matter so much though, since their main purpose would be to delay and drain the resources of the Challengers, not outright defeat them.

The Lichen was something entirely new. For one it was a plant, which I'd never been given before. Even so, it had a form of intelligence—in fact about the same level as the Thrall. Still, without an ability to move around it was lacking in proactive strategy. What it could do, however, was release spores that drained the stamina of those who breathed them in, while encouraging the act of lying down atop the Lichen. Once the creature was asleep, the Lichen could then enter its bloodstream and feed off its life force.

That last part was a bit disconcerting, as I didn't particularly like the vibe that would give my dungeon, but the stamina drain was exactly what I wanted. I would have to place the Lichen so that it would be difficult to lie on top of, but where its spores could still reach the battlefield. The courtyard walls and the parapets were the obvious candidates. And since my Gargoyles and my Thralls were all immune to the stuff, the gated sub-rooms could also be filled with it, provided the spores could reach from there. I'd have to test it to be sure.

First and foremost, though, was summoning my Guardian itself. I waited until my mana reserves were full, then activated the summoning. The creature was much larger than my other two bosses; standing almost three meters tall and powerfully built, the stone construct gave off an imposing air. It flexed its wings and arms, which moved surprisingly smoothly for being made of stone, before growling a greeting toward me.

I greet the Lord. It sent, and though it used telepathy like Stalker had, the feeling, or sound, of their message was completely different. Where Stalker's had been a chorus of musical tones, this was words. Gruff words that felt like grating stone, but still words. It was neat that even telepathically a kind of personality differentiated my Guardians. I sent it an approving greeting and told it to familiarize itself with its domain. It bowed and flew off, and I waited for my mana to recover before naming it. I did *not* want a repeat of what happened last time. Luckily my regeneration was fast, so I didn't have to wait long.

But before I could name my newest Guardian, a faint tingling sensation gave me pause. What was going on? It felt like I was being watched, yet at the same time . . . more.

A message from Stalker immediately clarified the situation, and I instantly focused all my attention on my first Floor.

I had been discovered.

CHAPTER SEVEN

The First Challenge, Part I

I *told* you I felt a change in the mana flow!" Alerio said excitedly. "There really is a Dungeon here!" He was nearly jumping up and down where he stood he was so giddy.

"It would seem so, yeah," Noracin said. He turned to the rest of his party. "All right, we listened to Alerio and confirmed that there indeed is a new Dungeon nearby. The question now is what do we do about it? Challenge or report?"

"Challenge," Alerio said immediately. Emmalia and Ceria, however, were more reserved, both with thoughtful frowns on their faces.

"It's risky Challenging a Dungeon you don't know anything about," Emmalia said. "My father taught me that many young people Challenge too eagerly and end up paying a price for it."

"Adventuring as a lifestyle is risky," Alerio countered. "But how are we supposed to improve if we don't take any risks? The Gods grant favor to the bold, as they say."

"We are all level ten. Beating any Tier-one Floor would give us the right to Tier up," Ceria added.

"That's the point exactly." Alerio nodded eagerly. "Come on guys? Aren't you tired of being stuck at level ten? I know I am. And we'd have to travel all the way to Alash to even have the chance of Challenging another Dungeon."

"Challenging isn't the only way to Tier up. There are other ways—ways that are safer and don't involve delving blindly into a Dungeon you know nothing about," Emmalia said.

"'Adventurers shouldn't be afraid of taking risks,'" Alerio quoted his former instructor. "Besides, those 'other ways' aren't exactly something we can realistically expect."

Noracin couldn't help but sympathize with Emmalia's worries, but Alerio was also not wrong. Being adventurers at the peak of their Tier, this was when they were *supposed* to Challenge a Dungeon. To prove themselves worthy of advancing to higher levels. He frowned, his head agreeing with Emmalia, but his heart with Alerio. He turned to their Fighter for a hopeful deciding vote.

"What do you think, Ceria? Do we Challenge or go back home?"

She thought for a moment. "I—"

Her words stopped abruptly when a sudden system alert appeared in front of each of their eyes.

Quest received! Welcome to a new Dungeon!
The Dungeon Veos wishes you welcome into his halls, and he is eager to meet your Challenge. As the first people to enter the Dungeon, Veos will grant you all a bonus reward for Challenging this Floor in the form of two Talent Points each, as well as 1 Armor Chest, if you begin the Challenge Floor within 1 hour!
Time remaining: 59:51

"Well now, this is definitely something," Noracin said, surprise clear in his voice.

"We *have* to try it now," Alerio said.

"Okay, this *can't* be normal," Emmalia said. "I've never heard of people getting those kinds of rewards for simply Challenging the Floor."

"You're probably right that this doesn't happen that often. But strange doesn't mean it's insidious." Alerio turned a wide grin toward the other members of the party. "We can't not try this now. We'll get more than the normal clear reward even if we don't finish the whole Floor!"

"It's clear to me," Noracin said, "that this Veos is extremely eager for us to Challenge it right away. But why?"

"Maybe he's young and impatient?" Alerio said. Ceira scoffed, but he pressed on. "I'm serious. I don't know much of the more advanced stuff about Dungeons, but I do know that young Dungeons are *very* eager, both to be Challenged and to expand."

"I get it, the Dungeon's just like you," Emmalia said.

"Yeah, but you're missing part of the point. He gave us a Quest. I think he might be insulted if we don't Challenge after this kind of gesture. I don't know about you, but I don't want to end up on the blacklist of one of the few Dungeons in the whole southern region."

"Surely that's not likely to happen just because we don't take the Challenge?" Ceria said, then paused and furrowed her brow as she thought about the Quest again. "Three Hells, it might not be that far off. Gods above . . ."

"We have an opportunity here," Alerio said. "Or maybe eternal regret if we end up missing out."

"I hate to say it, since he's going to be smug about it for *weeks*, but Alerio's winning me over here," Ceria said, and even Emmalia seemed to waver at the possibility of being blacklisted.

Noracin inspected the faces of his party thoroughly and saw a gradual change from worry to determination across two faces. And the third was just grinning the entire time. He sighed. "He's convinced me as well," he said. "Emmalia, you too?"

She glared at Alerio. "Damnation. Yes, he has."

"A Challenge it is, then," Noracin said. "Let's hold a strategy meeting, make sure everyone knows their roles, and see what this new Dungeon is so eager to show us."

Five minutes later Noracin had taken up the rear as the party took their first steps into the Dungeon. Emmalia led the way, using her enhanced perception to scout for any traps or other dangers. Right behind her, Ceria held her shield high, ready to leap forward at the first sign of trouble to take the hit for the Rogue. Alerio walked a bit farther behind, almost right in front of Noracin, and was focused on feeling the direction of the mana flows.

The slope gradually leveled out into a roundish cavern. The ground was rough and seemed unworked, with stalagmites and stalactites creating a maze throughout. Noracin could hear the faint sound of water droplets falling from the stalagmites down onto a pool of water below, in the center of the small cavern. There was a narrow path around the pool leading to three different paths branching out of the chamber. He called for Emmalia to halt and turned to face Alerio. "Which way?" he asked.

The Mage shut his eyes and focused, his arm gradually raising, seemingly of its own free will, and pointing straight ahead. "That one is faster, but they all lead to the next Floor. No dead ends."

"That you can sense," Emmalia said, to which Noracin grunted agreement. "So which way, boss?"

"I told you not to call me that," Noracin said. He thought for a moment. "Anyone have a problem with the straight-on approach?"

"Not me," Ceria said. The others gave their assent as well, and the party started down the center path. The gray and brown of the cave became darker and darker as the group moved farther and farther from the entrance. Noracin tsked at the Dungeon not providing any light.

"Wait a moment." Noracin held out a hand and activated a skill. "[Orb of Light]," he called out, letting his party members know what was happening. "I'll walk alongside you, Emmalia. Ceria, you take the lead."

"Got it, *boss*," Ceria said. Emmalia laughed as Noracin walked up beside her.

The two of them exited the cave into a passage that gradually narrowed before widening back out again.

"Hold!" Emmalia hissed. "Listen . . ."

A soft sound like shifting leaves rustling overhead drew Noracin's attention up, and with the aid of his [Orb of Light] he could see the roost of Bats hanging down from the ceiling.

"Great . . ." Ceria muttered. "Bats."

"It is a cave. Bats make sense," Alerio said.

"I know. I just wish there weren't so many of them."

"Why aren't they attacking?" Emmalia asked, looking up. "We're standing right under them."

"The light, maybe? They don't have the element of surprise anymore," Noracin suggested.

"That doesn't seem—"

Emmalia was interrupted by a shout from Alerio. Noracin whirled around to face the Mage, a [Healing Touch] ready in his hands. He found Alerio staring back the way they had come, toward the first cave. As he took a step toward him, suddenly the Bats overhead flapped their wings and dove down toward the party as one. Ceria immediately yelled out, activating her [Taunt] and drawing the majority of the Bats toward her. Emmalia spun and the steel of her daggers flashed as they slashed, each swipe hitting a Bat and taking its life. Noracin swung his mace over his head, but was mostly focused on getting to Alerio, who had pressed himself to a cavern wall and out of range of whatever was attacking them from behind. His eyes were on the Bats flying overhead, and his [Flame Bolt] made short work of those that dared stray too close. But there were *so many* Bats; some were bound to get a hit in. And when they did, Noracin let himself relax a bit—they barely did any damage. That meant Ceria and Emmalia could handle themselves for a while.

"Are you good on health? What hit you?" he called as he finally got to Alerio.

The Mage paused in his barrage to meet his eyes with a smile. "Water, I think. And yeah, it didn't even do twenty damage."

Noracin nodded, canceling his skill and raising his mace to fight in earnest.

Once the surprise had worn off, the party made short work of the flock of Bats. Whether by fire, mace, sword, or dagger, a single hit would lead to a kill more often than not. And what few attacks the Bats managed through their armor barely moved their health bars.

Noracin slammed down on the final Bat with a heavy crunch that ended as swiftly as it began, the summoned creature dissipating into motes of mana. He stood back and took a deep breath. "Everyone good?" he asked. When everyone nodded he added, "Let's move away from the water, then."

Emmalia led the party farther along the passage that curved away from the entrance. Once they were out of sight from the water, Noracin had them stop to go over the battle. Everyone's status was good, almost full, but the encounter still led to a lively discussion.

"Considering the damage we took I'd say neither the Bats nor whatever the things in the water were could have been much higher than level one. Three at the most," Alerio said.

"Agreed," Ceria said. "My [Taunt] is normally way less useful on a large number of enemies, but these flocked to me like flies to a corpse."

Noracin frowned. "Why keep them all at level one?" he asked.

Ceria said, "Maybe the Dungeon doesn't know how to increase their level directly? If he's young and we're his first Challengers like the Quest said . . . "

Alerio scoffed. "That'd be a sight. A Dungeon that can create Quests but can't do level management." He shook his head.

"It might be true," Ceria insisted.

"I think it's more likely that since Veos hasn't had any Challengers before, he has deliberately kept levels low as he doesn't know exactly how dangerous the encounters are yet. Keeping everything at a low level gives more room to tweak the difficulty later until he gets it right," Alerio said.

Noracin nodded at that. That made sense and was in line with what they had already found out about the Dungeon: that it was well above average in intelligence and awareness for its age.

"That could be it," he said. "Though we should still keep our guard up. Maybe the later enemies will be a higher level."

Everyone nodded at that, and the party resumed their advance. Emmalia in front with Noracin, Alerio in the center trying to sense the right way to go, and Ceria at the rear, ready to defend the Mage in case of an ambush. They crossed two more chambers similar to the one where they had entered without issue. No Bats in the ceiling, and no attacks from the water. The only danger was a smattering of pitfalls throughout the various passages, though with Emmalia at the head they weren't a real issue. Noracin still made sure to make a mental note of their locations. Most parties wouldn't have a Rogue with a perception-enhancing Glyph at the front, and to them these traps could be deadly. This party, though, needed only make their advance a bit slower. Especially now that they had determined that the Bats weren't a real threat to them, Emmalia could focus almost solely on the ground in front of them as they walked.

After five minutes of honestly rather boring delving, Alerio signaled for a halt as the passage began to widen out into a full cavern again.

"This one feels different," he said. "I think the way to the next Floor is somewhere in there."

"Then the Guardian is there too," Noracin said. "Stay sharp. With the cave aesthetic and the Bats, the Guardian is probably bat-like itself. Keep your eyes on the roof. And remember, Guardians are always at the max level for their Floor. No more level ones."

Everyone nodded, their faces becoming more serious and their grips on their weapons tighter. After a nod from each of them, Noracin signaled for Ceria to advance into the room. He followed right behind, his [Orb of Light] held high, and his gaze scanning the roof and walls of this final chamber. Appearance-wise it wasn't much different from any of the other spaces, except that it was larger—even with his light he couldn't make out the details of the far wall. And there was something about the *aura* that made the hair on the back of his neck stand up.

"Movement," Emmalia called out. "Up there, near the ceiling. There seem to be small tunnels in it."

"Everyone get—" Noracin began, but was interrupted by a screeching cry from above. A second later, half a dozen jets of water sailed out of the darkness of the cave, heading straight for them. Ceria instantly stepped forward, raising her shield.

"COMBAT!" Noracin yelled, raising his mace and readying a [Healing Touch].

The real Challenge was about to begin.

CHAPTER EIGHT

The First Challenge, Part II

As half a dozen different jets of water soaked the Challengers from all sides, the swarm of Bats descended on Noracin from above. He swung his mace wildly, desperately trying to keep both himself and Alerio clear of attackers. The wave of relief he'd felt when these Bats had also turned out to be level 1 quickly drained away when he realized just how *many* of them there were.

All the packs that would've been spread out across the Floor were probably moved here after our first encounter. He guessed as he swung. Each swing scored a hit, and each hit scored a kill. Yet the swarm didn't seem to be diminishing at all.

"Guardian!" Emmalia called out. Noracin's gaze flew toward where she was pointing up into the cloud of black wings.

"I see it!" he called back. "Ceria! Left and up, near the ceiling."

"Yeah, I see it too," the Fighter said. She backed away from the barrage of water, positioning herself closer to the other members of the party as the creature dove down toward him and Alerio. No, toward *Alerio* specifically.

"Three Hells. It's smart," Noracin yelled and swung his mace, but the creature weaved out of the way, moving with much more grace than the Bats despite being more than thrice their size. It spun around and rose back into the air, whipping its spiked tail at Alerio. He tried to dodge, but the attack had taken less than a second, and he had no hope of actually getting out of

the way in time. Noracin winced at the squelch as the tail pierced Alerio's shoulder, causing the Mage to scream in agony. A second later Noracin used his [Healing Touch] on Alerio, but he felt a resistance to his magic he instantly recognized.

"It's got poison of some kind," he called out, reaching into his satchel. He pulled out an [Antidote] and poured it into Alerio's mouth.

"That wasn't one of the elements we knew about," Emmalia shouted, dodging a diving attack from the Guardian. With Ceria now standing protectively over Alerio, the Rogue became the only clear target, only she was much nimbler than the Mage, and could twist out of the way of its attacks. In the meantime the Bats seemed happy to keep the rest of them occupied, swarming back and forth and attacking relentlessly, seemingly heedless of their own losses.

"It's . . ." Alerio started from the ground, then coughed. "It's [Blood Poison]."

"Alerio? Are you good?" Noracin called down to him without looking. He swung his mace, hitting and killing another Bat.

"Yeah, think so," Alerio said. "Bastard did over a hundred damage though. Can't take many of those hits."

The cave was plunged in [Darkness], causing them all to freeze in place for a second.

"I lost it!" Emmalia called out.

Noracin cursed, trying to conjure a second [Orb of Light], only to find that it didn't illuminate anything. He guessed the Guardian's [Darkness] was stronger. Not wasting any time, he dismissed the skill and reached into his satchel to retrieve a warm yellow stone.

"Using a [Sunstone]! Shield your eyes!" he called out and hurled the stone into the ground. Light exploded from it in a silent pressure wave, forcefully pushing the [Darkness] away. Though it didn't dissipate completely. It continued swirling around the edges of the stone's affected area, creeping closer to them with every second. The screech from the Guardian told Noracin that the stone had been effective enough, and Alerio didn't waste the opportunity.

"Ceria!" the Mage yelled. The Fighter could hear Alerio's unspoken message, hastily placing herself behind the Mage.

"[Flame Nova]!"

A wave of fire burst from Alerio's outstretched hand, quickly spreading up toward the Guardian and the roof of the cave, through the swarm of Bats. Two dozen shrieks echoed through the cave as Bat after Bat died, followed by a stronger, more musical one when he struck the Guardian itself. The flames continued harmlessly past Emmalia, Alerio's Glyph of the Dancing Flame hard at work, and stopped just above the jets of water. There they remained, dancing in the air as Alerio maintained the conjured fire. The Mage stood on unsteady legs, reached into his coat. and pulled out a blue vial, then chugged the party's [Mana Potion] in a single gulp. Noracin winced but didn't speak. He knew it needed to be done.

At the same time Ceria, now freed from her duty of blocking the constant jets of water, was able to switch her attention to the Guardian and activate her [Taunt], focusing on it and it alone. Noracin knew that a Guardian would be resistant to [Taunt]-like effects. But resistance wasn't immunity, and there was a huge difference between a [Taunt] spread across three dozen Bats and one focused onto a single creature. The Guardian spun in the air, glaring and screeching at Ceria before diving down in attack, sending a stream of its own [Water Jets] at the group. Ceria held up her shield to block, while swiping at the giant bat-thing with her sword, but it evaded her attack easily and dove for her now relatively unguarded legs. Noracin swung his mace down to cover, and Emmalia hurled her dagger while sprinting back toward them. All three attacks hit at once, causing both the Guardian and Ceria to cry out in pain. The Fighter reflexively swiveled her leg to try to shake the creature loose, but it held on, twirling its long tail around her leg and biting down to keep itself locked in place. Noracin abandoned attacking with his mace; he knew he wasn't good enough to hit the thing while it was attached to Ceria's leg without hurting her as well. Instead he activated several [Healing Touches] one after the other, applying them to the wounded Fighter.

Alerio, still focusing on maintaining his dancing flames, backed up a bit to give Ceria some room to maneuver, which she utilized to stomp her leg hard, then slam her shield down onto the creature, trying to pry it loose while gritting her teeth against the pain. Despite her best effort, however, the thing didn't budge, and Noracin was forced to use [Healing Touch] after [Healing Touch] to maintain the Fighter's continuously draining health. Ceria shook from excess damage, but managed to keep her [Taunt] active until Emmalia arrived and stabbed the creature where its tail held it in place. It screeched a musical crescendo and twisted itself free from Ceria's leg.

A second [Darkness] dimmed the light of the [Sunstone] temporarily, distracting the Fighter for just long enough that the creature could free itself from the [Taunt] and launch itself into the air, the remaining Bats descending to give the creature cover. Noracin gave Ceria two more [Healing

Touches] to drain the [Blood Poison] and let her recover enough health to reduce her shaking, though she was still having difficulty putting weight on the damaged leg. Meanwhile Emmalia slashed at the Bats with her daggers. There were only a few left, most having been burned by Alerio's spell, but the ones that remained were able to stall Emmalia long enough to allow their Guardian to fly to the cavern's ceiling.

The Guardian spun in the air, then started raining down a series of rapid-fire [Water Jets] toward Alerio, who seemed to be its priority target now that it was no longer under the effect of a [Taunt]. Noracin did his best to shield the Mage—he knew that too much damage could break the man's concentration—letting the flames keep the creatures in the water from firing dissipate. The [Water Jets] stung where they struck. Noracin grunted and moved to use a [Healing Touch] on himself, but stopped before activating it. He was almost out of mana. Even with his Glyph, he had two, *maybe* three uses left before he'd be completely drained. He couldn't afford to waste them on himself. Letting out a frustrated screech at its failed attack, the Guardian flew up and vanished into the tunnels in the ceiling. The few remaining Bats followed suit, hiding themselves in the rock. Noracin looked around suspiciously for where those tunnels might lead, until a glance at the dancing flames told him everything he needed to know.

"It's waiting for Alerio to run out of mana," he growled. "Then it'll rejoin the battle with additional fire support."

"What the hell is this thing?" Ceria gasped, limping toward him. "It's way too tough for a Floor one Guardian, surely?"

"My instinct says yes, but I haven't done any more Dungeons than you, so I only know what others have told me." He turned to Alerio. "How much longer can you maintain the flames?"

The Mage stood with an intense focus in his reddening eyes that had continuously stared right into the flames. Now they flickered to the side as he checked his status.

"One minute," he said. "I have a hundred and twenty-seven mana left. The potion's worn off too."

Noracin swore as Emmalia also rejoined him and Ceria after collecting her thrown daggers.

"I say dissipate them now," she said, looking up at the ceiling. "It could just wait up there forever. We, however, have a time limit."

Alerio grunted, but he lowered his outstretched hand and shut his eyes. He slumped a bit as the flames faded, feeling the effect of spending so much mana at once now that the skill wasn't active. Noracin took a step toward him just as *something* struck the Mage in the back. Alerio let out a soft whimper at the sudden and surprising burst of pain, and all but collapsed onto the ground. The Guardian faded into existence on top of him, its spike sticking into his back.

Ceria screamed in frustration and desperately activated her [Taunt].

Emmalia raised her daggers, yelling as she prepared to hurl them at the monster.

Noracin screamed and started running. He felt his feet slide across the ground, slick from the Guardian's [Water Jets]. Time slowed down as he lost his balance, and he thought he could see the health draining from Alerio faster and faster as his body approached the ground. He was only two steps away. It would take him less than a second to get there. If he hadn't slipped he'd have made it. Yet now it seemed so far.

He landed with a grunt and instantly tried to push himself back up and forward, but his feet once more slipped on the wet stone and sent him flailing. He stared at Alerio, and a wave of helplessness washed over him. He wasn't going to make it. His friend was going to die, and he wasn't going to be able to help him.

Time slowed further, almost to a standstill, as a faint rumbling began. It didn't come from the ground or the ceiling. Or anywhere specific for that matter. This rumbling was from the very *world,* as it itself seemed angry at what was happening in front of Noracin's eyes. A *ripple* spread through the Dungeon, originating from everywhere and going in every direction. It passed through him in an instant, and he thought he could feel *frustration* in its wake. Then it vanished as quickly as it had come, leaving everyone and everything in the cave too stunned to move.

To Noracin's horror, the Guardian was the first to react. But then something unexplainable happened.

It let Alerio go.

Not only that, it picked him up and dragged him over to where Noracin lay, dropping the man next to him. He stared blankly at the beast as it turned to look straight at him. It opened its mouth and sang in dissonant tones.

Heal him. This one's story is not supposed to end by mere misfortune.

Then it beat its wings and flew up into the darkness of the tunnels above. Noracin reached out, more from instinct than any actual thought, and activated his [Healing Touch].

CHAPTER NINE

Resolution and Resolve

Two minutes earlier.

The Challenge had been an excellent source of information so far. I'd already learned so much about how to improve the Floor—for instance, I was an utter and complete fool for never even considering the possibility of manually increasing my creatures' levels. I also learned the annoying fact that Mages could somehow *feel* the correct path by sensing how the mana flowed through my Dungeon. And those learnings came in just the first few minutes.

The battle with Stalker was proving to be even more enlightening, not to mention exhilarating. My first Guardian was *strong*. Much stronger than the Challengers had been prepared for, though with my other creatures lacking in level, the outcome of the battle was still uncertain.

I watched as Stalker dove down toward the Fighter, who seemed to be caught by surprise at my Guardian's ability to avoid rushing straight at her even while under the effect of her [Taunt]. Both the Cleric and the Rogue reacted, but not in time to stop Stalker from latching on with her tail and her claws and activating her most damaging skills. Both she and the Fighter sang in pain, though Stalker did more damage and had much more health to work with than her opponent.

Now let me see how you're going to deal with this situation . . .

I watched, all my attention laser-focused on the different characters in the scene.

The Fighter stomped her leg and slammed down with her shield, trying to pry Stalker off, while the Cleric pumped heal after heal into her to slow down her rapidly draining health, but it wasn't until the Rogue managed a stab that did an exceptional amount of damage that Stalker was forced to disengage her [Darkness]. The Fighter was still standing for now, though she looked haggard and wobbly. I felt like laughing, exuberant at the Challenge offered by both sides. Two combating narratives, trying to determine which will be written out as truth. The concept resonated within me as nothing had ever done before, as if rewarding me for doing what I was supposed to be doing.

Stalker flew above the party, raining down a series of [Water Jets] against the Mage, but her effort was rebuffed by the Cleric, who stepped forward to shield the man with his own body. Stalker screeched in annoyance, though I felt a swell of pride at the man's willingness to sacrifice himself for the greater good. Truly rising up to the Challenge.

Stalker disengaged, flying and calling the Bats up into the tunnels above. I frowned at that before I noticed her activating [Meld] and sneaking along the stones toward the Mage. A true stalker in action.

"It's waiting for Alerio to run out of mana," the Cleric growled. "Then it'll rejoin the battle with additional fire support."

I laughed inwardly. A reasonable deduction to make, but oh so wrong.

"What the hell is this thing? It's way too tough for a Floor one Guardian, surely?"

Yes, praise her more. I swelled with pride.

Stalker herself, however, didn't pay any attention to the words, fully focused on creeping ever closer to her target. She was almost upon him now. Just a few more seconds . . .

As the Mage staggered slightly from deactivating his skill, she pounced, landing on his back and stabbing forward with her tail. It squelched as it pierced flesh, and the Mage tumbled forward with a whimper, his health falling below 50, and draining quickly from Stalker's poison.

I focused with all my senses. This was the climax of the fight. I felt like I could see everything play out in slow motion, even before it happened. The Fighter screamed, but couldn't run on her still-wounded leg, so was left to activate a [Taunt], which, unfortunately for them, Stalker was able to resist this time.

The Rogue raised her daggers to throw, but I could see that she knew they wouldn't be much help.

But the protagonists of this final sequence were neither of those two. The heroes were the Cleric and Stalker. He was the closest, and could not only try to pry Stalker loose, but keep the Mage alive long enough for the others to be able to help. I could see it in my mind's eye: the Mage lying on the ground, downed but alive, as the others desperately tried to shield him from Stalker's attacks while low on mana and with their own health dwindling. A fight that seemed almost hopeless, yet one from which heroes could rise.

Then the man slipped on the wet stone. My perfect story shattered into a million pieces as he fell onto the ground with a grunt. Time felt like it stopped as I struggled to comprehend the sudden twist to the story.

No, it wasn't supposed to go like that.

This wasn't the ending I wanted. It wasn't even satisfying.

I could accept bad luck as a cause for a death in the case of ineptitude, overconfidence, or if the person was just incredibly annoying. But this party was none of those things. Sure they might have braved danger where they didn't have to, but that was what they were *supposed to do.* That wasn't over-confidence. That was a fulfillment of purpose.

Here, now, bad luck just felt like a slap in the face. I felt like the fates were laughing at *me* just as much as at the Mage. Even if the Cleric had made it over to the Mage, the fight would have been heavily in my favor, and the Mage still wouldn't likely survive. But he might have. The result was still undetermined. My story still unresolved.

No. I wouldn't stand for this. The fates might toy around and decide the endings outside. But not here. Not in my domain. In here, [I Decide How the Story Ends].

I felt a faint rumbling from the world, coming from everywhere and nowhere all at once, like an ominous thunder that had somehow come *before* the lightning. Then my mana vanished. It didn't rush out like it had with the naming, nor did it flow out as it did when I normally used it. It simply disappeared. Then something *else* rushed out. Something more . . . ethereal. Something that was a part of me on a deeper level.

It *hurt.*

I felt like my soul was being peeled alive, flayed from the inside out. The something twisted itself into thin threads that pulled on the world, causing a ripple that spread throughout my Dungeon in an instant. Then it vanished, leaving me feeling tattered and drained, but filled with determination. I ignored the relentless flood of system messages, fighting against the black void of unconsciousness that threatened to overwhelm me if I didn't focus.

There was still work to be done. I *stopped* the Mage's health from reaching zero, temporarily diverting the damage elsewhere. I couldn't do everything, even with the Edict, but I could do enough. Once I was done I sent a message to Stalker of my intentions, and only then did I let myself see the notifications as the blackness overcame me.

Action restricted due to low Tier . . . Overruled.
Action restricted due . . . *Overruled.*
MANA LEVEL INSUFFICIENT! High risk of consciousness degradation!
Alternate method reached . . . Draining Core experience.
You proclaimed an Edict!
Substantial experience gained!
Core status critical.
Entering repair mode . . .

"It did *what?!*" The Hallmaster of the Aspenfield Adventurer's Guild yelled, rising so quickly from her chair that she sent it flying backward. It hit the wall of her office with a crash. Katherine Verantz took a deep breath to recenter herself, then turned her sharp gaze on Noracin. He flinched back in his chair at her outburst and stared up at her with startled eyes.

"Apologies," she said after a moment. She took a deep breath and schooled her features. "Would you please repeat what you just said?"

"Ah," Noracin started, then swallowed. "I said that there was this ripple, then the Guardian told us to heal Alerio. Said he wasn't supposed to die 'due to mere misfortune.'"

Katherine closed her eyes and breathed, slowly in and out, as she seemingly tried to process this information. He could see part of her didn't believe it. Three Hells, part of *him didn't* believe it, and he'd been there. It would without question be the biggest thing to happen to the Aspenfield Hall since she'd taken over, if not ever in the history of the whole Hall.

"You're dismissed," Katherine said a moment later. "Go see your friend. I suddenly have a lot of work to do." Noracin nodded and stood to leave.

"Wait!" The Hallmaster called out as Noracin approached the door. He turned to face her.

"Don't tell *anybody* else about this. Don't even talk about it with your party except outside the city walls. You understand?"

"Yes, Hallmaster," Noracin said. Katherine nodded, then waved for him to exit.

Once outside, Noracin took a deep breath and leaned against the wall. That had been *heavy*. Even though he'd been an active Adventurer in Aspenfield and Coltmoon for more than five years now, he hadn't ever really interacted much with the high tiers. After leaving the Order, he'd had enough of people telling him what to do; he decided he could do it all on his own.

And look where that got me. He let his head fall back against the wall and sighed. Five years later and still Tier 1. Not only that but now you almost got a friend killed.

He shook himself. Alerio wasn't dead. He'd screwed up, but the worst hadn't happened. Noracin pushed off the wall and headed to the infirmary.

The Guild Hall had its own healing area, as Adventurers often suffered the effects of toxins or semi-permanent debuffs that simpler healing spells couldn't treat. It had its own entrance from the outside of course, so as not to make the main building too busy, but Noracin could also access it from inside by walking through the basement.

As he walked up the stairs to the infirmary's reception area, he noticed Emmalia sitting outside one of the doors, waiting. She looked up as he approached.

"How'd it go?" Emmalia said.

"Honestly I don't know," Noracin said. "She basically kicked me out as soon as I was done speaking. But from her reaction I'd say something big is going to happen."

"That's underselling it, I think," she said.

"Maybe." Noracin turned toward the door. "How is he?"

"Fine, mostly," Emmalia said. "The healer's in there right now doing some 'sealed knowledge' mumbo-jumbo, but I was in there earlier, and he seemed fine. Says he lost some Vitality but that there wouldn't be any other permanent issues. He's mostly upset about not knowing what happened while he was unconscious."

"He almost died, and he's just fine now?" Noracin said.

"Why wouldn't he be?" Emmalia asked, cocking her head.

Noracin blinked, then just stared at her. He couldn't find what to say to that, as he hadn't expected the question. Why in the Lady's name *would* someone just be fine after they almost died?

"Sometimes I forget just how different a life you've had," Emmalia said, seeing the look on Noracin's face. He frowned at her. She shrugged.

"It's true," she said. "You grew up in the safe and stable environment of the Order. Then once you left you still leveled slowly by only doing safe

Quests where you could plan and prepare well in advance. To you, and to some extent maybe Ceria as well, death is scary and foreign. To me and Alerio, it's just something that happens to people. Sometimes to people you know, sometimes to strangers. Eventually it'll get you as well, so no use going around worrying about it." She paused and frowned.

"Though that is no reason to take life for granted or rush into danger. If you ask me I think Alerio can be a bit *too* easygoing on that front, but it works for him. The point I'm making is that death shouldn't scare you into stagnating by being too safe. Once you stop trying to improve, you might as well be dead anyway."

"You really believe that?" Noracin said after a moment.

Emmalia shrugged. "Sort of? Maybe partially? I like life, and I'm not one of those danger-seeking hooligans you sometimes see in the guild. But what I'm *not* is afraid of dying. And neither is Alerio."

She turned to look up at him, seemingly studying his expression as she tried to decide what to say next.

"You're a pretty good leader, Noracin. People like Alerio need people like you to keep them reined in. Though you might want to ease up on the guilt, and maybe be more aware of the fact that the dangers you're always warning us about are not things to run away from. They're things to be overcome." She stood and stretched.

"Anyway, now that you're here I can go stretch my legs, maybe see if I can pry Ceria loose from her overbearing instructors. I'll be back in a few."

Noracin stared after her as she left, unsure what to say. She was at least partially right, maybe, though there were several aspects of what she'd said that didn't sit right with him. First and foremost was the fact that he hadn't had any idea that this was how she and Alerio felt in the first place. They had been members of the same party for over a year now and completed several missions together, though none had been especially dangerous. Maybe that was the reason? Or had they tried to tell him, and he'd just been too set in his ways, too sure that as the eldest he knew better, that he hadn't actually heard what they'd been saying?

Had he been hamstringing himself, along with the rest of his party, by being too cautious? And had that left them all unprepared when danger came?

He realized he might have.

Maybe it's high time I took a hard look at myself, he thought. *Started acting more like an Adventurer, and less like a protector from the Order.*

CHAPTER TEN

Waking Up

Gradually the blackness faded to a disjointed awareness, which was accompanied by intense confusion.

Where was I? Who was I? What was going on? Why was it so dark in here?

I descended into full-blown panic as dozens of thoughts sped through my mind at once, joined together with several notifications from the system that I didn't recognize. Instinctively, I retreated my awareness back into my Core in an attempt to hide from everything and everyone. Something had caused the emptiness—I knew that. And I didn't want to meet whatever it was ever again.

Slowly I remembered who and what I was.

I was Veos.

I was a Dungeon Core.

I was in my Dungeon.

I blinked bleary metaphysical eyes, then paused. How had I forgotten *that?*

What in all of creation had happened? I had . . . I had proclaimed . . .

The memories of what had happened returned to me in a rush. Of the Challenge, of all I'd learned. Of the end of the story. Of the ripple in the world and the tearing of my soul that had caused it.

Ah, right. I checked the system for any notifications I had missed and found several, mostly detailing my status throughout my stay in the blackness.

A few caught my attention more than the others, and as I read them I felt not a small amount of trepidation bubble up within my Core.

> Core integrity 76% . . . 62% . . . 51% . . .
> Risk of permanent damage imminent. Searching for solution. Solution found.
> Unused [Dungeon Perk] used by [REDACTED].
> Core integrity restored.
> Experience drain ceased.

I stared at these messages even after I was finished reading them, while the reality of what had almost happened smashed down on top of me like a crushing weight.

I had almost *killed myself.* It wasn't a particularly nice realization, especially since it had been entirely by accident. Even now I had no idea whatsoever how I had proclaimed that Edict. I could remember a desperate desire, a *need* for the story to play out the way I wanted. But not how that desire had been turned into . . . whatever the hell happened. A simple thought had turned into something more that had turned into something larger still, and that in turn had almost resulted in my own death. And *had* resulted in me losing my hard-earned experience as well as my unspent perk! Though that last one didn't hurt as much, since I'd actually forgotten I even had it.

No, it was the almost dying that drew my attention. I didn't want to die. In fact, I *very much* wanted to stay alive as long as I possibly could.

And yet, despite that, I found that I didn't regret what I'd done. Which was surprising to me in and of itself. Did I really care about the story of some Challenger more than my own life?

No, that wasn't what it was. What I cared about was telling the story, not so much the outcome itself or who the story was about. Some stories would end in ways I didn't want, or ways I couldn't even see coming, but they should at least still end in a way that made narrative sense. They shouldn't end weirdly just because some annoying outside force like luck interfered in their resolution.

I felt better once I'd come to that conclusion. Good, even. I felt certain of myself, and what I would do in the future, in a way I hadn't before. Up until now I'd mostly just been following my instincts, testing stuff out and not really thinking that much about why I was doing this thing over that one, making plans and promises then just ignoring them and pushing forward regardless. That would change now. From this point onward, I would think before I acted. I would plan ahead, and my Dungeon would tell a story.

With my thoughts on that settled, I steeled myself and opened my main status screen. There was something I needed to know.

Name		Veos	
Race		Dungeon Core	
Floors		2	
Level	3	Experience	3/4000
Mana	40/40	Mana Regeneration	20/minute
Edicts		[I Decide How the Story Ends]	
Skills		[Swift Descent]	
Perks		[Spatial Expansion]	
Rewards Inventory		-	

I sighed inwardly. Of course my experience was all the way down to freaking *3*. Though I suppose I should be thankful it hadn't dropped down to 0 and beyond, reducing my level to 2. I wasn't sure if I'd even have survived if that had happened. Regardless, with my experience from making the third Floor and the Challenge all gone, I'd probably have to wait a while before starting on my fourth Floor. I supposed I *could* start it without going up a level, but I had a specific plan for what the fourth would be, and I didn't want to give that up by making a new Floor with the same maximum level as the preceding one. After all, what kind of Vampire Castle wasn't stronger than its gargoyle guards? That was still a bit in the future though. I was eager to get back to expanding.

First of all, I had to improve my first Floor. I had learned a lot from observing the Challengers. For starters, my traps weren't that good, or at least had the potential not to be if the Challengers had someone at the front focused on Perception. The same could be said for my Mantas, who were a great support in the final fight, but when they were by themselves it was possible for the Challengers to just walk right past them. To fix that I'd have to station my Bats and Mantas together so that they could help make up for each other's weaknesses.

It seemed like a good idea on paper, but with the first Floor being finalized, I couldn't make any changes to the layout itself. All I could do was move the creatures around or unsummon them completely. That meant there were really only two places the Mantas could be while also allowing the Bats to remain hidden for their ambush: just beyond the entrance of the first cave, and in Stalker's chamber. In a few levels I felt I'd be strong enough to carve through system-enhanced materials. Then I'd be able to make the actual final version of this first Floor properly. But for now this would have to do.

After unsummoning the remaining Mantas and repopulating the Floor with more Bats to make up the missing creature count, I also spent a long time pumping Mana into them to push their level higher. The Bats had been a great distraction in the Guardian fight, but that was down to sheer numbers more than anything. A smaller number of Bats had proven almost entirely useless. And I didn't want to simply put all my Bats at the end, because that would leave the rest of the Floor completely barren, and would also pull focus from Stalker as the final fight.

I decided on a three-layered approach. The first chamber with both Bats and Mantas would have the second-lowest level, ranging from 5 to 7, to make the initial breach a proper first Challenge. The roosts with Bats alone would be higher, at level 10, to make them pack more of a punch without the support of the Mantas.

The smallest group, the ones supporting Stalker, would remain at level 4 or below. That way they would be an obstacle, but the focus of the fight would still be on my Guardian.

Once I was happy with the plan, I got to work pumping mana into my creatures.

It took a *long time.* Over twenty minutes of constant spending and regenerating mana to max out a *single* bat. And I had *dozens* of them. Luckily I didn't need to max out all of them, but this would still be an ordeal. I was helped by my new *determination* to make my Floors *right.* To make their internal story consistent and to keep their aesthetic natural to that story and the environment. I could stand boredom in the quest for excellence. I hoped.

It was well into the next day by the time I was done with the creatures on the first Floor. I wasted no time and moved on to those on my second. This was work that needed to be done, and I preferred getting it over with as soon as possible so I could get back to the fun stuff. I decided on a pattern of gradually increasing levels between the squads of Skeletons and Archers from 13 at the start to 20 by the end of the Floor. For the bonus room I decided to only increase them to level 15, as it was a room with a large gathering of creatures and I didn't want to accidentally make it too difficult. I'd check on it again after someone had Challenged it. Plus the Skeletons took a lot more time to level up than the Bats. And while my patience had grown since I'd affirmed my commitment to crafting my Floors properly, there was still *a* limit to what I could handle.

While I was diligently working on the bonus room, a tingling sensation informed me of another human near the entrance of my Dungeon. I froze, then focused all my attention on the new potential Challenger. Making improvements to my creatures was all well and good, but this was a new person. Someone whose story I could watch. Someone who made things change.

I frowned as I watched the person. They were just standing there outside my entrance. Why didn't they walk inside? Were they afraid because they were alone? The first group had been wary, and there had been *four* of them. Though this one felt stronger than that lot. Could I grant a new Quest to get them to . . .

My thoughts were interrupted by a notification from the system.

Request for passage!

Human "Katherine Verantz" is automatically on your [Blacklist] due to being above the highest level of your lowest Floor. She has made a system oath of nonviolence and is requesting passage to your first Floor for the stated purpose of "inspection and investigation." Do you want to grant her passage?

Yes! I would have screamed my acceptance of the prompt, but I didn't have a mouth. I watched excitedly as the person walked inside, then a shiver went down my spine as the full weight of her presence descended on me. It didn't feel threatening, but it did showcase just how large the difference in power could be between different people. I felt excited that I could maybe learn something new, but it was mixed with a touch of anxiety and wariness, even with the protection of the oath.

CHAPTER ELEVEN

Questions of Names and Power

The woman walked slowly through the various paths and dead ends that made up my first Floor, stopping occasionally to poke and prod at some rocks or plants seemingly at random. She stopped to check out the pools of water and the Bat nests, which did make sense to me, as did her detailed examination of my various traps. Those were actually made to be a part of the Floor experience, after all.

While the woman investigated, I couldn't resist doing a little of my own into the woman's status, comparing it to my previous Challengers' and to my own creatures'.

Ah crap. She wasn't just stronger than the Challengers. She was *much* stronger. The others had been level 10. This woman was level *57* and had more in her *weakest* attribute than any of my creatures had in their *strongest*. I was suddenly *very* grateful to the system for imposing a limitation on who could enter the Dungeon without my permission. If that wasn't there, this woman or anyone even close to as strong as her could kill me and there would be nothing I could do about it. As it was now, I felt an albeit somewhat tenuous sense of safety, which encouraged my curiosity. Someone as strong as her surely must be able to tell me something new and interesting, right? There was so much I didn't know. So much I wanted to learn. About how Dungeons usually worked, since apparently I was unusual in some way according to the previous Challengers. And about what had happened with the Edict—most importantly how I could avoid that happening again.

I just wished I could speak, so I could ask. My telepathy didn't work with anyone not created by me, so that was out of the question.

Wasn't it? I remembered that Stalker had spoken to the Challengers. Well, more accurately she'd sang and clicked. But they had understood what she meant.

I sent Stalker a message to prepare her. The woman was still one cave away from her chamber, but I wanted her out in the open and ready to ask my questions as soon as the woman stepped into view. The Leatherwing dropped from where she'd been hanging from the ceiling and landed on the ground just in front of the entrance to her cave.

A minute later, the woman stepped around the corner. She paused as she saw Stalker standing there, then looked past her to examine the rest of the cave. She didn't step inside, though. Perhaps she didn't think I'd appreciate her approaching my second-Floor entrance, oath or no oath. I didn't care either way, since I was busy crafting the perfect opening for Stalker to sing.

"You seek new information. Veos does the same. I will ask his questions."

The woman froze and looked around, her eyes widening slightly as they turned to Stalker. For a few seconds there was total silence, before the woman closed her eyes and took a slow breath.

"Right. It could speak," she said, though I didn't think that was meant to be a response to my previous statement.

"Very well," the woman said. "In exchange for allowing me to investigate, it is only fair that I do the same for you. Ask away. Though there are some things I won't be able, or want, to answer."

All right! Question time. What did I want to know, again . . . I had thought this out a moment ago . . . Ah, right.

"What is the best way for me to learn the things I don't know about Dungeons and the system?" Stalker sang. The woman seemed taken aback for a moment as the more complicated words seemed to not translate perfectly from notes to words, but it looked like she got my meaning.

She contemplated for a moment before she answered. "That is a very complicated question, as it depends heavily on what you want to learn. Most Dungeons learn over time, though whether they do so by experimentation or by getting information from the system, I don't know. What you could do is ask someone who is more studied regarding Dungeons, as they might know more. There are some things I might know, but I'm afraid I don't know if there is a how-to guide for how Dungeons learn."

Drat. Well it was worth a shot, at least. I supposed I would have to wait to learn more about the general system-related stuff. For now, though, there were some more specific things I was curious about.

"What is the cost of an Edict, and how can you learn that ahead of time?"

This time the silence was longer, though I suspected it wasn't because she was taking time to understand Stalker's words, rather it seemed to be *because* she understood exactly what was said that she was careful in how she answered.

"An Edict is a powerful thing," the woman said eventually. "I don't know how they work, or how they are made. All I know is that the strongest Dungeons hold them sacred and rarely share knowledge about their details to outsiders. I'm afraid if you want to know more you'll have to ask another Dungeon or one of its emissaries."

I could talk to other Dungeons? How? And what were emissaries? I shook myself mentally. Why was I asking *myself* when for once there was someone right here that could actually answer?

"Dungeons can talk if their territories overlap, or almost overlap." The woman answered after Stalker sang the question. "I don't know exactly the process, but those kinds of meetings mostly happen far below ground, when Floor sizes become sufficiently large. Emissaries are contracted outsiders. They function a bit like unofficial Guardians and spokespeople, helping a Dungeon interact with the outside world." The woman paused. "Though before you ask I don't know how it works. Emissaries are rare, as most Dungeons don't bother much with the outside. And the ones that do have them are all at around my tier or higher. At least those that I know about."

Yikes, not something I could do anytime soon, then. Which was becoming a trend, I was noticing. How infuriating. Why must all these cool things I wanted to do be locked behind some ethereal level requirement? I felt a sudden and intense urge to finalize my third Floor and continue my expansion but forced myself to remain present in the conversation. I had so many more questions and I wanted to ask as many as the woman was willing to answer.

Which turned out to be four more questions, most of the answers to which could be boiled down to "this is a cool feature that you can't access right now," or "I don't know, ask someone else." Were all investigations this annoying?

There was one question that got a proper answer, however: "How does naming work?"

"A Dungeon can grant a name to its creatures at the cost of mana, though sometimes experience can be required as well. The mana can come from either the Dungeon or an external source, most often a Mana Crystal, that the Dungeon possesses. But the experience has to come from the Dungeon itself. The exact cost depends on a variety of factors, many of which are unique to each naming and can't be accounted for ahead of time. Some general rules though are that the higher the creature's level, the more expensive it will be. Other factors are how well the name suits the creature, and the intent the Dungeon has while giving it."

When she was done speaking, I had Stalker thank her, then answer some of the woman's questions in return. I felt pretty good about that, since unlike her I was actually able to answer the questions I was given. How old was I? Easy. What is this Guardian's name if it has one? Even easier. How many names have you given? How many Quests?

All questions I was able to easily give complete and correct answers to, without stumbling even once.

After we were both through with our questions, the woman said she had to go, which by that time I found an exciting prospect. I was beyond eager to get back to working on my third Floor, especially since the woman had been kind enough to leave behind *two* Mana Crystals. Additional thanks for my excellent ability to answer questions, no doubt.

I had been a bit hesitant about naming my third-Floor Guardian, considering the Edict and how naming Krazad had gone. But with the crystals in my possession, I was full of confidence and roaring to go.

After a cursory examination of the Floor to remind myself of what I was doing, I got to work. Now that I had a proper story in mind, there was a lot of editing to do on the Floor layout, but I was driven to see it through. Instead of simple empty rooms set into the wall for my normal creatures, I carved out small but proper dwellings, and placed them inside the courtyard. I then populated the buildings with different numbers of creatures depending on their size, and made proper parapets for my normal Gargoyles around each. I then found I could add timed automatic locks to the doors through the system, making each building open one at a time without me having to do it myself. I could even randomize the order, making the gauntlet something Challengers had to drudge through without being able to prepare for anything ahead of time. Plus the locked doors also made it difficult for more than one set of enemies to attack at once, as I was worried that would make the Floor a bit too difficult. Not to mention how it would be off the gauntlet theme if more than one group were in the fight at the same time.

I ended up with four buildings, one in each quadrant of the courtyard, with one large fountain in the center. My Guardian would be at the end farthest from where the Challenger entered the Floor, atop the main castle parapet, looming in the distance the instant they entered the Floor.

Once I was done I took a moment to take in the Floor in its entirety. It felt good. Right. The different creatures and layout came together both in function and aesthetic to not only tell a self-contained story, but to also connect to the overall narrative of my Dungeon as I continued to expand. This I felt was the true start of my Dungeon; the first two Floors were experiments in trying to figure out what was best.

I checked my mana, and once I saw it was full I moved the Mana Crystals to where my third Guardian sat. It was time to give him a proper name. I thought for a moment.

Your name will be Obelisk. I sent. *Guardian of the deeper Dungeon. Gatekeeper of the castle. Your task is to test the strength and perseverance of all who'd Challenge this place, and remind them of the price to do so.*

I felt mana drain out of me. Much faster and with greater intensity than when I'd named the Necromancer, but being still conscious, I was not even close to the rate of proclaiming an Edict. Still, my mana pool was drained in seconds, and I felt a slight shift as mana was pulled through the Mana Crystals. It was an *incredibly* strange sensation, like I was a straw and something was drinking through me, yet I was also the water, and the glass. It wasn't painful, and I didn't feel the enclosing blackness, so it was much better than the second naming. After it drained the first crystal and started to work on the second, I began to feel a bit worried, and that worry only increased as the second stone gradually became emptier and emptier as the seconds passed. The second crystal cracked; it was empty. The drain once more started coming from me, and I felt the now annoyingly familiar sensation of being sucked out of myself and drawing ever closer to the infinite void. I steeled my resolve. My mind was stronger now, and my thoughts more solid and focused. Thankfully most of the mana cost had been paid already, and it ended soon after my drain started up again. I sat back and watched as the strengthening took hold of my Guardian.

Your creature *Obelisk* is being strengthened!
Your creature *Obelisk* has become a [Vampiric Gargoyle (Lord)].
Experience gained!
You have successfully made a *Lord*-grade creature for the first time!
Experience gained!

This would turn into yet another big deal once people outside found out, I was sure of it. Though as I watched my new Guardian try out his new body and examined his new status, there were only two words that came to my head: *Worth it.*

Name	Obelisk	Level	30
Race	Undead Construct (Stone, Death, Blood)	Grade	Lord (Guardian)
Attributes			
Strength	150	Vitality	280
Dexterity	120	Perception	100
Spirit	100	Force	100
Health	2800	Mana	1000
Skills			
[Drink Stone], [Blood Curse], [Raise Thrall], [Stoneskin], [Drain Life], [Darkness], [Shadowstep], [Stonespear], [Stone Barricade]			

CHAPTER TWELVE

Plans and Interruptions

A while later, once I'd managed to stop admiring my newest and strongest Guardian, I moved on to checking my own status. I wanted to see how much experience I'd gained from the woman's visit, making the finishing touches to the Floor layout, and naming Obelisk.

I wished I'd remembered to check it *as soon as my guest left*, but I'd been too eager to get started. A lesson for the future. At least I remembered before *finalizing* the Floor, which was the thing that actually prompted the experience boost. I hoped that meant finalizing was more important than the actual building process.

I had 1189 of 4000 experience. That was pretty good. Better than I'd been expecting, certainly. I'd gained over 1000 points since the visit, as manually increasing the level of my creatures naturally didn't give *me* any experience. I wasn't sure how much I was going to get from finalizing the Floor, but I wasn't going to waste time trying to work it out with calculations. I would just finalize it and see.

Floor finished!
Experience gained.
Level up!
1 new dungeon perk available!
Skill [Swift Descent] available!

I almost let out an excited yelp as I felt the system enhancements settle into the designs across the courtyard, strengthening them and locking them into place. I actually leveled up! A part of me had hoped, but mostly I hadn't expected to get enough experience. I really had to thank that Katherine Verantz when she came back. Thanks to her I could proceed with my fourth Floor as planned. I already knew what I wanted to do, and I was eager to see if I could do an even better job than I'd done on the third.

I forced my mind back to the present. I wasn't going to rush ahead again. I was going to think things through properly. I checked my status again, and confirmed that finalizing the third Floor had given me 3000 experience. Maybe that was the pattern? Finalizing a Floor gains 1000 times its number? Or maybe it's 100 times the maximum level of my creatures?

I noticed that the requirements for reaching the next level had once again doubled, from 4000 to 8000. If the Floor number determined the gain, it would give me much more experience on later Floors than if it were determined by the level of the creatures, assuming the doubling of the requirements continued and I'd be forced to make more and more Floors per level. Which I had no reason to doubt it would. I supposed I'd have to wait to find out after I finalized the fifth Floor, because I didn't think creating the fourth would be enough to level up again unless there was a sudden influx of new experience from somewhere.

Moving on from there, I managed to resist the urge to activate [Swift Descent] and instead moved onto selecting my new perk. No more forgetting and accidentally having the perk be deleted, thank you. I took my time reading through the options, stubbornly fighting the everlasting battle against boredom to try to get the perfect perk that would help me create my stories.

It took an hour, but eventually I managed to narrow it down to a list of three candidates.

[The Power in a Name]	Dungeon Perk (Uncommon)
Increases the strengthening from a Core's naming by 15%. Naming costs 25% more mana.	

[Spatial Contraction]	Dungeon Perk (Uncommon)
Reduces the minimum size of a Floor by 50%.	

[Vampiric Blessing]	Dungeon Perk (Rare)
Core minions attuned to both the Death and Blood elements gain 15% mana and health, and recover health based on damage dealt to living creatures outside the Dungeon's control.	

Unfortunately I wasn't able to find any perks regarding Edicts or emissaries, but considering how rare the woman had said those things were, that wasn't that surprising. I even tried to find ones that would increase my own experience gain, or reduce the requirements needed for a new level, but again had no luck. Still though the ones I did find were pretty interesting in their own right. I was especially drawn to the first one, though I was also a bit hesitant since I wasn't sure what it would do to the Guardians I'd already named. It might be overly sentimental of me, but it didn't feel quite right to leave them out of it. And I wasn't a hundred percent sure that it wouldn't apply to them, either. It was a risk, and a downside that slightly dulled my interest in the perk. The main downside was the increased cost. I wasn't sure I'd be able to get enough Mana Crystals to be able to name my higher-level Guardians quickly enough. And even with my increased resistance to boredom, I still didn't especially *like* waiting around, hoping for enough Challengers who might have spare Mana Crystals lying about.

Maybe I could send out a Quest? "Mana Crystals wanted. Paying in talent points."

It might work, though I had no idea how valuable either of those things actually were. Argh dammit, I definitely should have asked the woman about that while she was here. As it was, taking that perk was a risk; it might not actively improve my current power level, and I might also find it difficult to use the perk at all. *But* it was the most open-ended perk that both strengthened and would help tell a variety of stories if it *did* work out.

On almost the opposite end of the spectrum stood the [Vampiric Blessing]. It was the most straightforward power-increasing perk of the three, but it was severely limited in whom it would actually benefit. Right now the only creature that would gain any strength was Obelisk. None of my other Guardians had that combination of elements, nor did any of my ordinary creatures. Not even the ones from the third Floor. But what it would do, and why I was interested in the perk in the first place, was boost what I was planning to build on my next Floors. And that was the story I was most invested in at the moment. The [Spatial Contraction] perk was just an all-around solid benefit that worked well with the perk I already had and would greatly increase the variety of Floors I could develop in the future.

I pondered for a moment, but discarded the second option first. The effect would be nice, but I wouldn't need it right away. My fourth Floor wouldn't be small, after all.

As I was deep in contemplation, a fourth perk caught my attention. It would give me the ability to split a Floor in the middle, with each half getting one slightly less powerful Guardian, which could definitely be interesting for the future. But the reason it brought me out of my contemplation was that the idea of splitting a Floor in two was one I'd already begun accidentally with the courtyard and the castle. Instead of *literally* splitting the Floor, I could split it narratively, making the exit of one Floor the entrance to the next, and allowing the story to flow seamlessly between them. That way I could integrate the higher experience requirements of several Floors per level into the narrative, and I wouldn't have to wait around for Challengers after finishing each one.

That possibility, combined with the risks of the first perk being at least temporarily useless, pushed me to select the [Vampiric Blessing] as my level four perk. With two Floors of the castle ahead of me as well as the courtyard receiving benefits, I would definitely get enough value out of it for the perk to be worth the slot.

With that decided, it was time to get started on the fourth Floor. This one would be the upper castle, and would end in a grand meeting hall, which would then allow the Challenger to descend into the lower castle.

I worried the order didn't make the most sense, as castle leaders were typically found near the top, not at the bottom. Then again, castles weren't normally made underground like this. I should be able to make it work. I'd have to make some adjustments to the design and plot, but I could only work within my own abilities. Maybe if I made the lower section a prison of some sort . . . Yeah, that could be a good strategy. I could work with that.

I activated [Swift Descent], and my surroundings blurred as I moved rapidly downward from the courtyard. I went much farther this time, reaching almost a full hundred meters below the third Floor before I stopped, but that was good. I'd need the space to get the Floor I wanted.

> Fourth Floor begun. Would you like to select a Guardian?

Nope. This time I was going to design the Floor first to make sure I was able to select the Guardian I really wanted. I dismissed the notification and felt a gleeful surge of enthusiasm as I went to work claiming what would be the dimensions of the Upper Castle, starting from the initial staircase down and continuing on with the different rooms and hallways.

And the final hall with the Guardian will be there . . . and then the staircase can go over there . . . Oh right, I need proper tables for this room . . .

A faint buzzing of my senses and a call from Stalker pulled me out of my focus. There was once again someone outside my Dungeon. Several some-ones, in fact. Two men and one woman. A quick check of their statuses told me they were all at the cap of my second Floor at level 20. For once I wasn't that thrilled at the prospect of a Challenge, but I still forced myself to pull away from my creation and pay attention to the group of three as they stepped onto my first Floor. I quickly signaled to my Mantas and Bats to stay away. No good would come from attacking this group with the level difference. The trio walked down the slope, then stopped and looked around when they entered the first cavern.

"I told you Katherine was acting weird," one of the men said. "But to think she was hiding something like a new Dungeon from us . . ."

"What else can be expected from the Adventurers' Guild?" the other man scoffed. He turned to the woman. "You ought to know better than anyone, having been one of that lot, right Lenore?"

The woman just shook her head, her attention instead focused on the cave around her. "There is something strange about this Dungeon," she said. "It doesn't feel like a normal first Floor should."

The first man frowned. "Now that you mention it, there is something different about the air here compared to in Lash. You think that's why they're keeping it secret?"

"If they think they can exploit it for profit, I wouldn't put it past them," the second man said. "Or maybe they just don't know how to handle this stuff properly. You know, one time there was this adventurer who found a . . ."

"Would you focus, Trald," the first man said, annoyed. "We have a report to make for the Bishop."

"Yeah, yeah," the man called Trald said. "Speaking of that, now that we found what Katherine was hiding, shouldn't we, you know . . . go make that report? Why did you guys even want to go in here?" He shivered and rubbed his hands against his arms. "This place gives me the creeps. And it's just a standard freaking cave Floor anyway. There's nothing interesting to even find in here."

I let out an offended scoff. What did that man know about Dungeon design? Or design in general for that matter, considering his outfit. If his level were lower, I'd have sicced my Bats on him, taught him a lesson. For now though all I could do was wait, and hope they went farther down.

"Don't be a baby, Trald," the woman, Lenore, said. Then she frowned, and continued with a sigh. "But you're right; we do have a report to make. And as much as I'd like to stay and Challenge for Tier 3, Katherine and the Guilders already have several days' head start on us. Come on, let's get going. We need to be a bit closer for our lower-tiered Message Stone to reach."

The woman spun on her heel, leading the men back up the slope and out of my Dungeon. I was left a bit stunned as I watched them go, a strange mix of frustrations boiling up within me. At first I'd been annoyed when they arrived and interrupted my work. But now I was irritated that they just left without actually *doing* anything. I especially wanted that Trald guy to Challenge my second Floor. He didn't have the look of someone who could handle it well, and he was annoying enough that I was eager to see him brought down a peg or three.

Anyway, whatever was going on up above didn't matter to me that much—it was time to get back to doing something actually worth my time. I had a castle to make.

CHAPTER THIRTEEN

Excavations and Annoyances

Once the annoyances were gone, I returned to plans for my fourth Floor. I marked out the different rooms and hallways in my mind and soon felt ready enough to start claiming and carving the structure itself from the surrounding rock. Though as I began work, some system restrictions forced me to change my design a bit, since apparently system Floorspace and actual, physical space did not have a one-to-one correlation.

A cubic meter of solid rock used up more Floorspace than one filled with nothing but air, which made sense. What I hadn't realized was that if the cube was filled with both rock and air, it could take up *more* Floorspace than solid rock if the free space allowed for passage by walking or climbing. Basically the system determined how much Floorspace something took up based on the volume that was *usable* by Challengers. Squeezing more rooms into a smaller space wouldn't cheat the system at all.

I grumbled for a while about how few loopholes there seemed to be in this system, but there wasn't anything I could do to change it, so eventually I got over it and got back to work. Overall my layout wouldn't need to change much to meet the Floorspace limit thanks to my [Spatial Contraction] perk. All I had to do was remove two rooms and the hallway connecting them and make some of my tunnels a bit narrower, and everything fit.

Once the full layout was claimed, I took a moment to check over everything. The Challengers would enter the castle from what would be the ground floor if it had been on the surface, and would have to delve deeper through the castle's various basements and catacombs to find the secrets hidden below. That was the narrative of the castle Floors. I further subdivided what made up the fourth Floor into three sections. The first section would be the ground level of the castle, followed by a series of increasingly narrow hallways and staircases leading down through the basement into a secret area beneath the castle, where the Fourth's Guardian would be fought. Beyond that there'd be the entrance that would lead farther down and into the castle's prison, but I'd leave the details of that area until I was actually making Floor five.

Once I was satisfied with the layout, I got to actually building it. The first section would be the largest, with an entry hall from which three paths would diverge. One to the servants' quarters, one to the kitchens, and one to the main feast hall. I carved out the various rooms in each section, then began connecting each of the different sections through a series of winding corridors, some of which would lead to nowhere, though narratively I decided they'd lead to other areas of the castle. From the feast hall I carved the staircase that would lead down to the second section. This middle section would be the smallest and would mainly consist of a series of narrow tunnels and passageways that would lead the Challengers deeper and deeper underground, uncovering darker and darker secrets as they went. Eventually these pathways would lead them to the third and final area of the Floor, which I dubbed the Warden's Office. It would be a basic, functional room in which the Guardian would stand watch, both keeping the Challengers out and the fifth-Floor prisoners in. Of course the creatures couldn't actually leave their Floor, but it worked as an element of the story.

Once the main layout of the fourth Floor was complete, I started working on sculpting details into the stone to make pillars, walls, and a floor made from stone bricks. I even made statues depicting the castle's former and current residents. I lined the walls of the feast hall in enormous windows, which was a bit tricky and took some trial and error since I'd never made glass before. This castle being underground and all, the windows weren't functional, so I covered them in painted artwork depicting the history of the castle. Each window displayed a chapter of the events leading to the Warden tossing the previous rulers deep into the earth in an attempt to protect the world from their heinous acts. I even figured out that I could spawn some of my [Flame Wisps] on the other side of the glass to create a sort of artificial glow that would shine through and highlight the colors of the artwork. It didn't look realistic at all, but it did look extremely *cool.*

With the first third done, the Floor was almost complete, as the latter two sections would represent areas underground meant to be hidden from view, they didn't need much ornamentation. I made some adjustments to the Warden's Office, carving out giant gashes in the stone to make it appear as if a difficult battle had been fought there in the past. Finally I moved my Core to the prison entrance and sat back to admire the Floor. It was a masterwork, if I did say so myself. The Floor where I'd cemented who I was. If the first two Floors had been me discovering the world, the third was where I'd started to discover myself. And this fourth Floor put into steel what it meant to be Veos. The Floor was made to Challenge, yes, but that wasn't all it was for. I also wanted it to intrigue, invest, and ask questions of those who attempted it. It was a representation of me. Of who Veos was at this moment in time.

I let out a metaphorical breath and allowed the notifications of the system to wash over me. Then I opened the Guardian selection window.

Fourth Floor begun! Select a Guardian.

Floor aesthetic: Castle of the Vampire Warden
Due to the Core undertaking the risk of postponing the selection of a Guardian, the options will be altered to fit the Core's intended aesthetic. Note that Guardian creature selection is still affected by the current Floor and the Core's level.

Blood Clan Vampire: A vampire of other vampires. A creature of the night, yet the night is its enemy as much as the day is. The Blood Clan is seen as a plight by the other vampire clans due to their intense obsession with feeding not only on mortals but also on other vampires. Their bloodlust and intense hunger make them fearsome combatants akin to berserkers, and their special blood magic make them all but unkillable when they're well fed.

Shadow Clan Vampire: The Shadow Clan likes to stand apart from the other vampiric clans, interacting only when necessary. Being mercenaries and assassins by convention, they are not trusted by those who don't know them well. Those who do know them know how strongly a Shadow holds to a contract, and the dangers of agreeing to one.

Nosferatu: A failed experiment by a Lich who grew too ambitious for his own good. However they do not see themselves as failures. What they might lack in beauty and stealth they make up for in tactics and mentalism. Where the Shadows can strike so fast as to be invisible, the Nosferatu can strike without being there in the first place.

[Special!] Pureblood Vampire: A vampire who can trace its origin all the way back to the true primogenitor, and who has kept its traits. The nobility of vampires, the Purebloods can be found in most clans, though they share more traits with each other rather than their closer kin. They are the overseers of Vampire kind, watching and judging their lesser cousins from the frontlines of a battlefield just as easily as from atop a throne. Masters of both blood and shadow, brains and brawn, with a control over the creatures of the night rivaling even the strongest druid, the Purebloods are rare, yet never weak.

I cheered to myself. This had worked *wonderfully.* And considering the special offer, the system seemed to have understood *exactly* what I was going for. At that moment I took back everything bad I'd said about the system and my instincts. They weren't stupid after all.

Just as I was about to select the Pureblood Vampire as my Guardian, a buzz from above let me know that there were once again people at the entrance. I let out an annoyed growl, but I couldn't resist looking to see who it was.

The trio with the annoying Trald had returned. And they had brought with them a tiny illusory man made of glowing yellow light, standing atop the woman's outstretched palm.

That seemed weird. Especially since I couldn't access the status of this man made of light. In fact, if the other three hadn't been speaking with him and I hadn't been able to see the statuses of the others, I would have guessed him to be a skill made by the woman in whose palm he stood.

This time the party didn't stop at my first cavern but moved directly to Stalker's chamber. I sent her a message, but she was already well aware of what was happening. Unfortunately for both of us, there would be very little she could actually do to stop people twice her level, Guardian strengthening or no.

She still gave it her best effort, and I praised her for focusing on that Trald fellow. While her attacks hadn't hurt him much, it did seem like she disturbed him quite a bit just by being nearby, and her flight made it at least a bit tricky for the three to defeat her quickly. It was a nice surprise at the end of a very unfulfilling first Floor Challenge. I knew they were twice its level, but was this how it normally went? Surely I wouldn't have to suffer through higher-level Challengers demolishing my carefully planned stories every time they wanted to reach a Floor that would actually test them. Right . . . ? I thought there must be something I could do.

Eventually Stalker's hit-and-run tactics proved insufficient, as the tiny glowing man caught her in chains of light. There was little she could offer in terms of resistance. I sent feelings of encouragement and reassurance as her health dropped to zero.

"Damned insect," Trald spat as Stalker dissipated into motes of mana. "Why do they always have to go for me every time?"

"It's your charming personality," the other man said.

"Very funny, Victar." Trald said. He shivered. "Can we get a move on? I want to get this over with as soon as possible."

Victar began, "Why did you even volunteer for the reconnaissance troupe if you can't handle doing the—"

"Children," the man made of light interrupted. Both men instantly closed their mouths. "My time is limited. Keep moving if you wish for my protection."

"You heard the Bishop," Lenore said. "Let's move."

As the party descended the stairs toward the mausoleum, I paid closer attention. If nothing else, they would at least provide me with information about how well I'd designed the Floor.

At least that was what I thought. But even that was too much to hope for. Apparently now that the group was in for an actual Challenge, the man of light decided to take a more active role in the fighting. A shield of yellow light encompassed the party, fully stopping any and all attacks my creatures attempted, while seemingly empowering the Challengers' own attacks with some kind of burning property that chewed through my Skeletons like they were made of paper.

This wasn't a Challenge at all. As the party continued onward through the hallways of the mausoleum, as if on a casual stroll, I felt anger and frustration continue to boil up within me. They were making a mockery of my Floor. Of the very concept of a Challenge.

And it was all the man of light's fault. If he hadn't been there, these three wouldn't have stood a chance. I could tell. My first Challengers had been of a lower level, sure, but they had been much more skilled and organized. This party . . . They were undeserving of their success. The only one with anything resembling talent and a proper attitude was the woman, but she was completely unable to contribute to the Challenge herself because she was too busy being coddled by the man of light.

If the Challenge was corrupted by the presence of the man of light, all I had to do was *remove him from this place, and the story would be told properly.*

I felt a surge of power as my Edict activated, then everything went black around the Challengers, plunging them into [Darkness].

CHAPTER FOURTEEN

The Second Challenge

Far away from the Dungeon, within the Chapel of the Order of Our Lady of Light and Wisdom, Bishop Nicomedes El-Ecien winced slightly as the link to his [Messenger of Light] was forcefully broken. He recollected himself less than a second later and tried to reestablish the connection, only to find himself rebuffed and with a notification from the system hovering in front of his face.

> This action is not permitted.

He tried again.

> This action is not permitted.

Then there was an additional message.

> Cheating will not be allowed.

Nicomedes took a deep breath and wiped the blood that had begun to drip from his eyes. A quick glance at his status told him that his health hadn't dropped much, but it was a testament to the restriction that it was able to affect him at all. There were only two things in the world that would make the system do that. Either a Covenant made by someone who had reached his own tier, or an Edict made by a Dungeon. Ordinarily the former would be much more likely, even considering the location. But with this Dungeon being so recently 'discovered', Nicomedes thought it unlikely the Adventurers' Guild had set up that kind of security already. Because though the light of the sun could hide the less bright light of a candle beneath its shine, it wouldn't exactly be subtle about it.

So unless they had come up with some new combinations of skills to hide the existence, let alone the specifics, of a Dungeon, the second option was much more likely. And was also the one Nicomedes's instincts said was the probable culprit in this case. A Dungeon that was strong enough to create an Edict was rare, but rarer still were Dungeons that actually made one. Just because they could didn't mean they would, after all. The fact that the Order only had *two* such Dungeons in their roster across all ten nations of the continent spoke volumes of just how rare they were. And here one had managed to conceal itself, probably with the help of the Adventurers' Guild, until it grew too strong for their control. He wished he could have used his [Mana Sense] while in his [Messenger of Light] to be able to sense how many Floors the Dungeon had, but his guess would be somewhere in the low to mid-teens. If it had spread much deeper than that, it definitely would have gotten in contact with one of the other Dungeons in the area. Then again the closest Dungeons, Lash and Part, both had close connections to the Guild as well, though they weren't tied to the Guild as closely as the Order's Dungeons were. Still it wouldn't be a surprise to Nicomedes if the pair had come to some kind of agreement with the Guild to keep quiet about this new Dungeon's growth. The only questions were why had they hidden it, and why were they coming forward now? Why send Katherine there and risk exposing themselves? Did they really think the Order wouldn't figure out what they had been doing?

Nicomedes scoffed and looked down at the report from one of his men within the Guild.

> Tier 1 party finds a new Dungeon in the Lashwood.

He shook his head. Just how naive did they think he was?

The Bishop stood from his desk and walked out into the chapel proper. Lower clergy and servants all bowed and scurried out of the way as he passed, but he paid them no mind as he strode with swift steps toward the inner sanctum. This called for a gathering of Bishops. It rankled, but this was much too big a situation to keep secret, and there would be too many questions if he tried. His own work would need to be put on hold for the moment.

"What's happening?!" Trald yelled out into the darkness. One minute they were walking along, completing an important yet *boring* mission for the Bishop. And the next, the Messenger vanished and they were all plunged into chaotic darkness.

"The connection broke!" Lenore yelled back from somewhere to his left. "[Orb of Light]," she added a second later. Trald reflexively shut his eyes just in time to keep himself from being blinded when the light from Lenore's skill pierced the darkness around them.

Only that's not how the skill performed. It barely did anything. Although at least now he could see well enough to make out his own hand in front of his face. He looked around in a daze, trying to figure out what was going on, when a gurgling sound to his right made him jump. He reached out, catching Victar by the arm as he collapsed down onto his knees, an arrow sticking out of his throat.

"It isn't just dark. It's [Darkness]!" Lenore yelled.

"Victar's been hit!" Trald called out at the same time. Seeing the blood pour down his friend's chest slowed his spinning mind and forced him back to the present.

"[Healing Light]!" He quickly pulled out the arrow and activated his skill to sew the wound shut and stop Victar's health from draining further. Victar let out a relieved breath and activated his own healing skills to restore his health back to full.

A second arrow whirred past through the [Darkness], clanking against the stone less than a meter away from Trald's leg. He flinched backward away from the sound.

"It's Skeleton Archers," Lenore said. "There were still one or two of them when the Messenger was cut. I can't see them in this. Someone else use [Orb of Light]."

Right. Trald shook himself and activated the skill. With two lights active at once, they were able to pierce the [Darkness]. Now, cut off from the safety of the Bishop, Trald was forced to really pay attention to their surroundings for the first time. They were standing just beyond the doorway in a rectangular room, which only had one other exit, directly opposite where they were standing. The hallway behind them was straight and would lead back to the rest of the Floor. To their right was a single closed sarcophagus against the wall. But it was what was in front of him that drew his attention. Four Skeletons and two Skeleton Archers stood in formation in the middle of the room. The ordinary Skeletons remained where they were, seemingly guarding the Archers as they raised their bows and pointed them right at him.

He reflexively took a step backward right as Lenore burst into action, sprinting toward the undead monsters and drawing her sword. Trald's training took hold, and without thinking he cast [Blessing of Light] on the charging woman. A yellow smoke began to wisp off her body, the glow of it extra visible in the [Darkness]. She fell onto the undead with righteous fervor, cleaving through them with ease despite being without the Bishop's much stronger [Blessing]. Victar rose to standing with a groan and started to pull out his own sword.

"Don't," Trald said. "You were hit. Focus on restoring your health. You'll only be in the way besides."

Victar grunted but put his sword back in its sheath and instead activated his own [Blessing] on Lenore. Trald stood as if bewitched as their leader seemed to dance through the Skeletons' attacks with ease, avoiding their strikes with minimal effort, while keeping close enough to land attacks of her own. Within fifteen seconds she'd felled one of the Archers, and after twenty more passed the other was dead, and two of the ordinary Skeletons were nothing more than piles of bones on the stone floor.

"Was she always this good?" Victar said, sounding equally as stunned as Trald felt. Trald could only shake his head in disbelief. He was having a hard time believing she was the same level as him.

"It looks like we won't even have to do anything," he said.

A blast of arcane energy slammed into Lenore from their right, as if making a mockery of his words. The impact knocked the woman off balance, allowing the two remaining Skeletons to get their own attacks in. Lenore cried out in pain and quickly retreated back toward Trald and Victar.

Trald spun to the side, finding himself staring at a single Skeleton standing by the now-open sarcophagus. Its eyes glowed with an intelligent malice, and it seemed to be looking straight through them. He shivered, knowing instantly what manner of monster this was.

"Guardian!" he yelled, activating [Burning Ray] at the monster, which only seemed to make the thing slightly more annoyed, if it did anything at all. It turned its empty yet glowing eyes toward him, and *spoke*.

"You should not have come here." The voice had a clear and crisp tone, not at all in congruence with the creature's appearance, the disconnect making the effect even creepier. Trald felt like his entire skin wanted to crawl up and down his spine over and over again.

"Your sire interfered where he should not have, and allowed for you to perform beyond your own capabilities. This has been stopped, and you should be grateful that my sire is more virtuous than yours. Your Challenge will be fair from here on."

The creature raised its staff. "Come. I, Krazad, shall test your mettle."

The Guardian's staff began to glow an ominous red, which then turned to black smoke. It pillowed down onto the stony ground by the hallway that lead back the way they had come, and Trald could hear the crackling of bone within the swirling mists.

"May the Lady light our way, and shelter us from the darkness beyond," Victar said, gripping his sword tighter. Trald echoed the words in his heart, though his mouth wouldn't move to speak them aloud. Lenore had backed away enough to stand just ahead of the two of them, her head held high and her sword raised, pointing a Challenge toward the Guardian. Their leader's attitude made some of Trald's fear dim slightly, and he raised his wand as well, readying another [Burning Ray]. The mist dissipated, revealing a pair of Skeletons akin to the ones Lenore had just cut down.

"I'll take the Guardian," Lenore said. "Victar, keep the ordinary Skeletons off my back. Trald, you focus on supporting us both from range."

"Understood," Victar said.

"I will," Trald said.

Lenore took a step forward, then a second one turned into a sprint. The Guardian raised its staff, arcane energy surging toward the gem nestled at its tip. Victar's charge waived off to the side, targeting the pair of Skeletons blocking the doorway. Trald fired his [Burning Ray] at the sole surviving member of the original group of Skeletons to keep it off of Lenore. The Guardian fired its spell at her. She seemed to blur for a moment, glitching in and out of the world, causing the magical energy to pass straight through her without hitting anything. Trald blinked, momentarily losing his focus but managing to regain it before he lost control over his skill. Lenore covered the remaining distance in a second flat, her sword screaming through the air as she cleaved toward the Guardian's neck. It seemed just as taken aback by her actions as Trald had been, because it didn't block the attack. Instead a black filament emerged from within the bones of its chest, stretching to cover the point of impact. The sword hit with a reverberating *clang* that spread throughout the room.

"More cheating," the Guardian said with a sigh. Trald would have sworn it sounded *disappointed.*

Lenore suddenly let out a scream of pure agony, which stopped just as abruptly as a ball, that made him nauseous to look at, was forcefully pulled out from her chest and hovered in front of the Guardian. She collapsed onto the ground in a heap.

Trald didn't need to be a trained healer to know she was dead. The Guardian turned its burning glare toward him as one of the Skeletons got a hit in on Victar's hand, making him cry out in pain and drop his sword. A second hit made him fall to one knee.

The Guardian raised his staff once more.

Trald turned and ran.

CHAPTER FIFTEEN

The Unidentifiable

Trald died quickly once his will to fight gave out and he started to flee, as was appropriate. Victar lasted a bit longer, but it was clear that while his level was the same as Krazad's Skeletons' he wasn't actually that practiced in fighting, especially against multiple enemies simultaneously. He fell without defeating a single Skeleton. I let out an annoyed huff, but I withheld my personal feelings when I sent an acknowledgement of effort to Krazad. That hadn't been a very satisfying Challenge either, but that didn't mean Krazad hadn't been doing *his* own work properly. Again it was the Challengers who upended the story, though this time was worse. This time it was done intentionally, an attempt to mess with the natural order of things. And to make matters worse, defeating them didn't even feel satisfying. Sure it would have ended the same way if their Challenge had been fair, but the trio had attempted to cheat and go farther than they should. If they had Challenged properly from the beginning, they would have realized their own inadequacies and given up well before they'd reached Krazad's chamber. They died because someone was trying to carry the weight for them, making them unable to hold themselves afloat once the aid was removed. So that ending should be proper, no? Try to cheat, get knocked down by your own hubris. Then why didn't it feel satisfying . . . ?

Because they weren't the main offenders, I realized. The man made of light had been most responsible. The trio had just been doing as they'd been told. And the man of light had gotten away freely because he'd never actually been here in the first place. The would-be main players had been turned into minor participants in the story of their own demise. That was why the story felt incomplete. I would have to rectify that eventually. Bring this story to a proper conclusion.

For now though there was the minor issue of the floating sphere of impossibility in my second Guardian's chamber that I had to tackle. I'd first sensed the bead-sized sphere within the woman Lenore during her initial charge against my Skeletons, but it wasn't until Krazad's skills had been nullified that I understood it had been responsible.

Exactly how and what it had done I still didn't know—I couldn't see any information about it through the system. In fact the only reason I could tell it existed in the first place, and why I was calling it a sphere, was because other things occasionally stopped behaving normally in a sphere surrounding it. Sometimes mana and my senses would pass through the space as if nothing was there; sometimes it would feel like they hit something more solid than rock. And when I tried to peer deeper into the thing using the system, I only got spotty results, and even then it didn't tell me anything useful.

I couldn't make myself look at that message for very long. Just having it in my system window gave me a feeling of wrongness stronger than I'd ever felt before. Stronger even when I'd made my Edict. It felt universally wrong, like it came from something that couldn't, and more importantly *shouldn't*, exist in the world. Yet there it was, noticeable if only by the absence of ordinary interactions between things that normally would have an effect on each other. Like the light from Trald's orb—before it dissipated as he died, it sometimes simply skipped over the area around the sphere. Though that hadn't made that area dark, and neither had Krazad's [Darkness]. It had simply stayed as dark as if no skill or mana had been used in the first place.

I dismissed the message and pulled my focus away from the sphere. I would have to investigate this in more detail, but for now I just wanted it away from my second Floor and my immediate attention. Despite its glitchy nature I found I could move the thing easily enough, though doing so felt extremely strange. Like I was moving something heavy that at the same time didn't even exist. I pushed past the strangeness and moved the sphere down to the fourth Floor, where I still had the ability to carve through rock and claim more space. I didn't want it to be a part of my Dungeon, but I also didn't think it was proper to try and destroy the thing without knowing what it was and how it worked. I couldn't carve out a completely separate area as everything had to be reachable from my Core, but that didn't mean I had to make it easily accessible. I carved out a small tunnel in the ceiling of the upper castle, even smaller than the ones my Bats used. Once I had tunneled a bit away from the main path, I carved out a small chamber in which to place the sphere. To make everything fit within the Floorspace limits, I had to make the main room slightly smaller, but it was the best idea I could come up with on short notice. Once the Floor was finalized, I'd probably move it again, though I wanted to do some tests on it first, maybe delve deeper into my system-powered instincts, before I made any permanent decisions.

Once the sphere was safely tucked away, I moved my attention back to the three corpses on my second Floor. I stared at them for a moment, unsure exactly what I should be doing with them, until my instincts showed up and provided some actual answers.

Just claim them and absorb them, they said.

I wished they didn't make it sound like it was so obvious—like they were speaking to an idiot.

Once I did so, I got several notifications and bonuses from the system, rewarding me for my first defeated Challengers. I guessed only dead things counted as "defeated." I would dispute that, but all right.

Everything that had been on their persons was also added to my Rewards Inventory, which went from being completely empty to suddenly being filled with random crap. I also learned I could exchange the stuff I didn't want for additional experience, so I quickly sorted through the mess of random knick-knacks, from clothes to coins to swords, in search of something useful.

And to my surprise, there actually was something I wanted to keep. Lenore had a pouch of four full Mana Crystals, as well as one cracked and drained one. I quickly separated the pouch from the rest of the junk, which then got turned into experience. Once I was done I looked at my status again, checking to see how much experience defeating an actual Challenge could give me.

Name		Veos	
Race		Dungeon Core	
Floors		3	
Level	4	**Experience**	3867/8000
Mana	80/80	**Mana Regeneration**	40/minute
Edicts		[I Decide How the Story Ends]	
Skills		[Swift Descent]	
Perks		[Spatial Expansion], [Vampiric Blessing]	
Rewards Inventory		Mana Crystal x4, Empty Mana Crystal x1	

Apparently it gave a lot.

I hadn't checked since I began carving out the Fourth, but I knew from experience that carving out a Floor didn't give nearly as much experience as finalizing it did. Given the 189 experience I'd had before starting, I'd gotten over *3000* experience from this Challenge. That seemed like a lot compared to the previous ones. Was the reward really that much higher if the Challengers died? Or maybe it had something to do with the man made of light, or the strange sphere?

So many questions, so few answers.

But at least this was exciting, even if it was something unknown. If the trend held, I would be getting 4000 points for finalizing the fourth Floor, which would put me just under the requirements for reaching level 5. I probably wouldn't need to be at the same level range as the fourth after all, considering I hadn't even selected, and more importantly named, the fourth Guardian yet.

Speaking of, now that the interrupting Challenge was over with, and the necessary post-Challenge cleanup as well, it was high time for me to get that done. I opened the Guardian Selection window again and selected the [Pureblood Vampire] before anything else could interrupt me.

Mana flowed out of me in a rush, before coalescing into a humanoid form. The Vampire's skin was a pale gray, contrasted with flowing jet-black hair and glowing red eyes. She wore a dark blood-red suit over a black shirt, and her cufflinks were ornamented coffins in gold. At her waist was a sword with a hilt that ended in a crescent moon made from a dark ruby that glowed in the darkness of the warden's office. As she manifested she seemed momentarily confused, before her head snapped in the direction of my Core and understanding bloomed in her eyes. She performed an exquisite bow in my direction, then twirled around where she was standing to survey the room. Her eyes landed on one of the gashes in the wall, ostensibly performed by her in a moment of triumph over her enemies.

"Well now . . . " she said. "*This* definitely seems interesting." She ran a finger across the gash in the wall. "I remember making this cut," she said. "Yet at the same time I know the memory to be a false one." She turned her attention to me. "I also know what you would have me do. Act as the warden, serve as a player in your story." She trailed off, turning to look at the sealed door that ostensibly would lead to the fifth Floor. "I know there is nothing down there yet. But I still feel an intense *need* to shield the world from the evil that lay within. An evil I don't even know yet."

I didn't know what to say to that. This entire conversation had shocked me to my Core, if I was being honest. I hadn't expected the Guardian to be quite so self-aware. Or aware in general. And I *certainly* hadn't expected her to come with memories of a life I'd just made up around a week ago. I didn't know how to feel about that.

The Vampire shook her head and gave my Core a small smile. "Do not feel guilty. I don't feel particularly bad about it. It's just a strange feeling, is all."

I shook myself out of my contemplation, forcing myself back to the present. My work still wasn't done. Though I felt I should tackle this next thing a bit differently than I had my previous Guardians.

I will be granting you a name, I sent her. *Do you have any wishes or thoughts on what you'd like it to be?*

The Vampire looked away from her inspection of the door and furrowed her brows in thought.

"A name, you say?" she said. "I suppose I ought to have one. I feel I must have had one before now, yet it's one I've forgotten. Something regal, I think, yet also menacing. I am a Guardian, after all."

Something regal yet menacing . . . I thought hard about it, considering and discarding names as they came to me. I wanted to get this one *right.* It took a while, but eventually one came to me.

Your name will be Morrigan. I sent. *Countess of the Purebloods. Warden and Ruler of the Castle above the Prison. Enemy of the Aberrant.*

I added that last sentence without having a single thought about it, or even fully understanding what I meant when I said it. But it felt right all the same.

Mana flowed out of me as the power of the naming took effect.

CHAPTER SIXTEEN

Level Five

It took a few moments and drained three of my newly acquired Mana Crystals, but the naming was finished without any significant issues for once. I left Morrígan alone to familiarize herself with her newfound power and to organize her memories. She'd felt that something was a bit different about them after the naming, though she couldn't say exactly what had changed. Except that her memories now somehow went beyond, or at least were more detailed and nuanced, than what I'd come up with initially.

I'd deal with the implications of *that* some other time.

Right now I had a Floor to populate and finalize, and a new Guardian's status to examine.

Name	Morrígan	Level	40
Race	Pureblood Vampire	Grade	Lord (Guardian)
Attributes			
Strength	210	Vitality	300
Dexterity	231	Perception	148
Spirit	200	Force	256
Health	3000	Mana	2000

Skills
[Blood Curse], [Raise Spawn], [Drain Life], [Darkness], [Shadowstep], [Arcane Barrier], [Animal Transformation], [Partial Monster Transformation], [Aphotic Nova], [Invisibility]

Like Obelisk, Morrígan was a Lord, and her attributes and skills showed how exceptional that was. Though without any other creatures of similar levels to compare to, it was hard to know exactly how big a difference grade made for a creature.

I was being stupid, wasn't I? Selecting Morrígan as my Guardian hadn't summoned just her. She had also come with three different creature types. Looking at my system I saw that they were the Vampire Spawn, the Vampiric Wolf, and the Leatherwing.

I confirmed that Morrígan's Leatherwings were indeed the same type of creature as Stalker. A quick summoning also proved they had similar attribute preferences, if not specific numbers. Stalker had a Guardian and name boost and was an Elite, but Morrígan's Leatherwings were three times Stalker's level, which evened their attributes. I felt a bit miffed about that. Like Stalker was being somehow cheated by the presence of Leatherwings that were more powerful than she was. I pushed that irrational feeling away. It was a stupid reason to be upset. And these new Leatherwings could actually be a good thing for the first Floor's story. Before now the cave and the mausoleum felt pretty disconnected from the rest of the Dungeon, but the addition of these creatures could help tie the early Floors together with the later ones. I'd have to think a bit about how to structure it narratively.

For now, though, I forced myself to return to the task at hand, which was a proper investigation of the difference a creature's grade made on their attributes. Now I even had a much better way of checking than what I'd first planned, since I could now simply summon a normal Leatherwing to my second Floor, and it would be the same level as Stalker. Then I could compare the two stat blocks together . . .

The difference was *substantial.* Stalker's attributes were more than *twice* as high as a mundane Leatherwing's. Unfortunately I couldn't get a complete picture, since the grade wasn't the only thing that separated the two, Stalker being a Guardian as well as named, but it put the difference in power a bit more in perspective for me, and made me reaffirm a pair of conclusions I'd already come to long ago.

One, names were amazing. Two, Guardians were also amazing.

It took me a few minutes, but eventually I had a populated and developed fourth Floor. In my opinion, Wolves didn't really fit into the castle aesthetic in my opinion, but both the Leatherwings and the Vampire Spawn were perfect for the place. I even threw in a few Stone Thralls and some Skeleton Archers to round out my creature composition a bit. Once the creatures were all summoned I did a quick check to confirm the Floor was good to go, then finalized it. I felt the now familiar sensations of the system strengthening the layout and formalizing the connection between this Floor and the ones above it. Next came the surge of experience, and just as I'd suspected, the finalization combined with the naming pushed me over the edge to level 5. A barrage of system messages hit my view.

Level up!
Skill [Swift Descent] available!
Skill [Spatial Connection] acquired!
Skill [Dungeon Management] acquired!
Perk [Mana Mastery] acquired!

Quest received: Advanced Dungeoneering!

You have almost succeeded at something at which many of your fellow Dungeons have failed, and you have the chance to officially enter the latter half of your development. As a stronger Dungeon, you are given more freedom but also many new responsibilities and expectations. Prove yourself capable enough to continue on this path. Future levels will be locked until the requirements listed below have all been accomplished.

Name a Guardian (1/1)
Defeat 10 Challengers (3/10)
Provide completion or Quest rewards (4/10)
Finalize five Floors (4/5)
Create a custom Floor clear condition (1/1)
Create a custom creature (0/1)

Time limit: none

That was a lot of new information to get at once, especially given what it implied about me, and Dungeons in general. For starters the fact that naming a single Guardian was a partial condition for this "advanced" Quest told me just how unusual it had been for me to name them almost as soon as I'd made them, and served to explain at least part of why the outsiders had seemed to think I was so strange. And why Stalker had been so unexpectedly difficult for that first party.

The next few requirements were more self-explanatory and understandable, even if they were a bit of a letdown in terms of leveling prospects for the immediate future. It meant that regardless of the additional experience I'd gotten from my naming and Challenges, I'd still be forced to make the fifth Floor the same level range as the fourth. I'd made my peace with that once already, so the frustration was short-lived, helped along by the last two conditions.

When had I ever made a custom clearing condition? I hadn't even known it was *possible.* I distinctly remembered instinctually knowing that the defeat of the Guardian was a system-enforced requirement to descend through my Floors. And yet now I was learning I could have made a different requirement all along? Were my instincts just stupid?

No. I felt quite sure that before this Quest, I couldn't have made a Floor that didn't require the Challengers to defeat a Guardian. It was only now that I'd been given more manual control with the [Dungeon Management] skill that I'd unlocked that capability. But that left the question of how I'd already completed the requirement, if the requirement was something that I hadn't had the ability to complete until now.

Did the bonus room I'd made on the second Floor count? I'd made it give out an additional clearing reward, and it was technically a custom clearing condition, even if it wasn't strictly required to clear the Floor. I wasn't sure, but it was the best guess I could make with the information I had, and it was an answer I found plausible enough that I could accept it, at least until I could ask someone who knew more.

My new [Spatial Connection] skill allowed me to set up a portal between the entrance and any Floor I wanted, provided the ones entering it were at the proper level for that Floor. The portals wouldn't take up any actual space in my Dungeon—they were a service powered entirely through the system, and one I was very grateful for. It was an answer to the problem of high-leveled Challengers needing to massacre their way through my early Floors to reach the one they were after. Just a single Challenge by those overleveled for my first Floor was enough for me. I didn't want to have to sit through any more excursions like that in the future.

Acquiring the [Dungeon Management] skill was like having a light turned on in my mind. Things that I hadn't understood or that had been hidden from me before were suddenly clear as day. For starters, I could man-ually remove and replace the system's reinforcements on my Floors. *Finally!* That would let me actually complete, maybe even redesign, the first couple of Floors now that I had a proper story in mind.

Secondly, it also let me create and manage custom effects and clearing conditions on a Floor-by-Floor basis. And I could even give the Floors offi-cial names! I'd named them for myself already, of course. But now I could *do it through the system.* A Floor didn't have a level or attributes to strengthen, of course, but I could strengthen the custom effects I could now add. In addi-tion, named Floors seemed to alert Challengers to their presence in a way that unnamed ones simply didn't. Each time a Challenger entered the Floor, they would be given a notification from the System regarding its name and effects.

It was all a bit overwhelming if I was honest, but it was still extremely exciting stuff. But none of that even held a candle to the excitement I felt when I thought of combining the skill with my new perk. That combination was the key to experimentation and self-expression—to telling stories that were completely and wholly my own, instead of ones partially authored by the system.

It would allow for custom creature and, more importantly, Guardian creation.

The process was extremely complicated and involved, and even though I now had a faint idea of how it was done, I had no confidence I would be able to pull it off yet. The mana requirements were high, but mana costs could be overcome with time and effort. No, the main barrier I faced was still a lack of understanding of how different kinds of creatures and elements worked. Before I could start making any creatures of my own, I had to understand what made different types of creatures tick, and how their elemental attune-ments worked. Otherwise I'd just be fumbling around in the dark, hoping against hope to stumble on the one-in-a-billion chance that the complex series of magical and non-magical interconnected systems worked together properly.

It wasn't going to happen by brute force. I had to go beyond simply absorbing the various animals that occasionally wandered into my domain. I had to study them and the creatures that had been provided by the system. Then I *might* be able to attempt to create something of my own. Provided I had a clear enough idea of what to make, of course. Which at the moment I didn't. Maybe once Morrigan got her memories in order she'd be able to provide some inspiration. In the meantime I could always start by studying the creatures I'd already unlocked, as even if I didn't end up making something similar right away they'd still provide me with valuable information and experience about this new and exciting world of advanced dungeoneering I'd found myself in.

A hissing screech from Morrígan drew me out of my reverie. In an instant my full attention was on the Vampire. I'd expected to find her in her chambers, but instead she stood in the entrance hall of the castle. She was staring up at the ceiling with a look of murder and violence on her face that even made *me* uncomfortable, and I was partially connected to her mind.

What is it? I sent.

"The enemy," Morrígan said. "The experiments my predecessors did, if they actually existed. The things they became. What the world did to us as a result. *That* is at fault for all of it. *WHY IS IT HERE?!*" She screamed out that last sentence in a voice of fury and anguish, not a small amount of it directed at me. I followed her gaze to the ceiling. No, she was looking up *through* the ceiling, toward the impossible sphere I'd found on the woman Lenore. I frowned.

Explain in detail everything you remember, I sent. Morrígan growled, but did as I asked and started talking.

CHAPTER SEVENTEEN

A History of Blood Gone Aberrant

According to what my memories tell me, these experiments were begun during a particularly difficult inter-clan war. Once one clan started it, the rest followed soon after," Morrígan said. "Nobody ever told me exactly when, since even after being captured and tortured at length by other members of the clan, the perpetrators of these experiments either wouldn't say or actually didn't know which of them started it. Regardless, *I* first learned about it what feels like twenty years ago, though how that could be true is of course a mystery to me, as I also know I didn't exist even twenty *days* ago. Yet my memories are crystal clear of not only those twenty years, but of *centuries* spent in the Blood Court..."

What is the Blood Court? I sent. Morrígan paused and blinked at my interruption, but answered after a moment.

"The Blood Court can mean either the main castle where the high nobility of the clan would meet to discuss and oversee the ruling of the whole clan. Or it could refer to the members themselves. Those that participate in those meetings and serve as representatives of the clan in issues affecting Lariet, or the whole Elorian Empire." She paused. "Though, as a concept, it isn't that relevant to the story."

Apologies, go on. I sent. Morrígan shook her head slowly, then thought for a moment as she tried to remember where she'd been.

"Anyway, what I wanted to say was that I have a lifetime worth of memories of serving within the Court, as well as on the battlefield. A lifetime as clear to me as if they just happened."

She paused. "We will have to talk about that someday. About whether you stole my soul for your Dungeon."

That is not how Dungeons work. At least, I don't think so. But I promise we can talk about it later. For now I think we ought to focus on the sphere.

"Yeah, the *sphere*," Morrígan growled, then took a deep breath to calm herself down a bit before continuing. "When I said *it* was the cause, that might have been a bit of an exaggeration. That *specific* sphere isn't actually the same object the perpetrators used, it just has the same aura. Though this one is lesser in strength, the stench it gives off is unmistakable. It is the stench that nearly drove the Vampire species to extinction, and turned all of the planet Nerian-Silex against us."

How do you know this is true, and not simply a part of my Story? I sent.

"I feel it in my *soul*," Morrígan said, then sighed dejectedly. "But I also know that might not be the most reliable source, considering my situation."

I took several moments to think about what was best to say in response.

I think that what you know is different and more evolved from what I created, but I can't be sure that wasn't the system stepping in and making things up. It has been frustratingly vague about giving me answers, and even now I feel there is much I don't know or understand.

"That's not frustrating at all," Morrígan grumbled sarcastically.

Wherever the memories come from, I would still definitely like to hear them. Tell me your memories about the sphere, and how it is relevant to you and your story. Start at the beginning.

"All right, from the beginning then." She took a deep breath. "I was one of twelve Purebloods within the Blood Clan when all of this began. Back then I still lived in my uncle Rovian's castle, and I was a general of the Blood Clan's army. The Clan wars were in full conflagration, and we were losing to the alliance of the Shadow and Beast Clans." She shook her head. "It must have made my uncle desperate, because while we were at our lowest, the strangeness began right here in the castle. Keeping secrets. Staying within the castle walls for weeks at a time. And an overall eerie aura that even put other Vampires off. The same kind of aura that is coming from the sphere right now. Only back then I didn't know that. Back then I only felt it was *wrong*, but didn't have the context to know why. I didn't know it was the sign of the Aberrant."

What exactly were, are, the Aberrant? I sent.

"An enemy of the world. Of the system itself. A race of monstrosities without levels and beyond the system that still somehow can hold sway over some parts of it even we don't have access to. I don't know where they came from, but I do know they weren't always here. But now they have a three-layered occupation of this dimension, what we came to call the Three Hells, and they are fighting a constant battle to enter into this world and destroy it. We Vampires were members of an alliance of the five races fighting a secret war against them for *decades,* and it was thanks to us we were able to push the Aberrant back."

She paused, then continued in a pained voice, "But without an outside enemy to defeat, we turned our attention to each other. Years spent in near-constant battle had changed many of us, my uncle among them. It didn't take long for infighting to begin. As I mentioned, nobody knows who started it, but it was someone from *my* clan *who first* experimented with combining themselves with the Aberrant. Simple experiments in the beginning. Trying to figure out how to use their system manipulation to gain an edge over our enemies. But experiments beget experiments, and soon the corruption took root in the hearts of all of the clans. Many were changed forever, their personality partially or completely overtaken by some monstrous desire for consumption of others. Some even got tagged as Aberrant by the system and were designated as the enemy."

Morrígan sighed. "And though it shames me to say it, it was only then that I noticed what had been happening all around me. Even within my own family's castle. My uncle wasn't among the ones labeled Aberrant, but he was changed."

And so your uncle is the one you remember placing in the prison? I sent.

Morrígan nodded. "Him and some of his coconspirators. They hadn't undergone the full transformation, so I'd hoped to be able to find some way to save them eventually while keeping them from harming the rest of the world in the meantime."

She shook her head. "I don't know if I succeeded in the end. Or if any of what I just said actually happened, for that matter. That is where my memories end, with me tossing my family in prison. The next thing I knew, I was being summoned by you into this Dungeon."

I stayed silent for several moments as I tried to figure out how to respond. My link with my Guardians wasn't a link to their thoughts or even fully their emotions, but there was some kind of connection that made me able to understand how saddened and vulnerable Morrígan was feeling. Completely different from how she'd been when I first summoned her, now that she knew who she was. Or who she thought she was, anyway.

I promise you we will figure out what really happened. It might take a long time, as I have only ever spoken to anyone from outside once. But since I did it one time, I can do it again. And someone out there should be able to confirm your story.

"Or confirm that it never happened and that it is all in my head," Morrígan said.

Or that, I agreed. *But wouldn't you rather know the truth?*

After a few seconds Morrígan shook herself and I sensed a feeling of determination bubble up through the link. "Yes, I would rather know the truth," she said. "And thank you for helping."

Of course. I sent. *Now, what are we to do with the sphere?*

"Destroy it," Morrígan said immediately. "It will do no good to have that thing anywhere in the world."

I thought about that for a moment. Could I even destroy it? I could absorb it like I'd done the Challengers and the rocks around them, but I hadn't wanted to because of the feeling of wrongness the sphere gave off. And now that I knew more, I was even less eager to do so. Unfortunately I didn't have another way of destroying it other than through absorption. Just tossing it outside was *definitely* a terrible idea. I explained as much to Morrígan, who got a look on her face like she was talking to an idiot.

"I can just smash it to pieces," she said. "Move it down here and I'll do the rest."

Are you absolutely sure that destroying it is the best plan? We might need it in the future. I'm almost certain the man of light is the one responsible for it being here, and he wasn't among those who died.

"A man of light?" Morrígan asked. I quickly explained the Challengers who'd attacked my second Floor just before I'd summoned her, as well as how I'd sent away the man of light who'd been protecting them.

"The woman definitely sounds like she had a basic application of Aberrant enhancement," Morrígan said. "But I haven't ever seen someone with an Aberrant implant within their body *not* start to go insane." Morrígan shivered as a particularly strong memory caused an emotional fluctuation through our connection.

"If this man of light has figured out a way to make an Aberrant enhancement stable and remove the side effects, that definitely makes him someone we can't look down on. Added to that, he's at least Tier eight, possibly even

Tier nine, considering the skill he used." She looked forlornly at the ceiling, then shook her head. "I suppose holding off on destroying the thing is the smarter choice," she admitted grudgingly. "For two reasons. Firstly to avoid insulting someone so far above you in power. The [Blacklist] keeps him from being able to kill you, but there are other ways that he can harm you, or hinder your growth."

Great, I thought, then sent to Morrígan, *And the second reason?*

Morrígan smiled grimly. "Just as there are multiple ways for him to hurt you, there are also ways for you to hurt him. While I don't know exactly how the world out there works anymore, if I ever did, there is simply no way that these kinds of things are an accepted practice you can just do out in the open."

He's doing it secretly, just like your uncle did, I realized.

Morrígan nodded. "Exactly. Which means that you can threaten to expose him if he starts acting aggressively."

I pondered that concept for a moment. Morrígan's words were all true, but there was something about them that didn't feel right—didn't feel like me. Was I the blackmailing type? Not really. I hadn't even thought about the concept before now, and now that I did, it felt icky to my sensibilities. Not wrong in the same way the Aberrant felt wrong, but still like something that didn't suit who Veos was supposed to be.

Then was I someone who would use the Aberrant to serve my own purposes and to gain an advantage?

No.

I was surprised at how vehement that response was. It came from the very Core of me. Or maybe from beyond my conscious self, originating in my instincts themselves. I *would not* accept the Aberrant, nor those who utilized their power. I'd die first.

All right, then. That helped me come to a decision.

We will hold onto the sphere for now, but only as a precaution, and only until we can come up with another way to destroy it. Once we do, we will also try to hold the man of light accountable. Someone outside has to be capable of doing that, surely.

Morrígan nodded. "Sounds like an acceptable solution. But could you remove the thing from my Floor? The aura it gives off is *vile.* I can't stand being near it."

I'm afraid the fourth is the only Floor I can . . . I trailed off. That wasn't true. I could just start the fifth and put the sphere in there. With what the

Quest had said about locking my later levels, I wasn't sure exactly how that would work, but it did renew my [Swift Descent] skill, so I should be able to do something.

I checked my status.

Name		Veos	
Race		Dungeon Core	
Floors		4	
Level	5 (4)	**Experience**	LOCKED
Mana	80/80	**Mana Regeneration**	40/minute
Edicts		[I Decide How the Story Ends]	
Skills		[Swift Descent], [Spatial Connection], [Dungeon Management]	
Perks		[Spatial Expansion], [Vampiric Blessing], [Mana Mastery]	
Rewards Inventory		Mana Crystal x1, Empty Mana Crystal x4	

That wasn't what I'd been expecting, but it sort of made sense considering what the Quest said. I sighed. It seemed I was level 5 in nothing but name, as both my mana and mana regeneration were the same as they were when I was level 4. I even showed as level 4 in parentheses, which would explain why I felt that my creatures would still be locked out of the higher level cap until the Quest was completed. Fair enough, though why the system worked this way instead of just not allowing me to level up at all made very little sense to me. Maybe it had no other way of giving out the management and connection skills or the mastery perk.

I dismissed the status, the specific reasons why it worked this way didn't matter right then. The important thing was that while I was still functionally level 4, I could use [Swift Descent] and begin work on the fifth Floor right away. I returned my attention to Morrígan, who was still staring up at the ceiling with a disgusted frown on her face.

I will move it to the fifth Floor in a moment, I sent.

"Thank you." She breathed out a sigh of relief.

I activated [Swift Descent] and felt a rush as the surroundings blurred past and through me as I burrowed through the stone, before stopping with an abrupt lurch. I took a moment to examine this newly claimed area. It was again almost a hundred meters back up to the fourth, the distance dictated by my similar mana count. Still, it would be more than enough for my purposes. It was time to get started carving out a prison.

CHAPTER EIGHTEEN

Setting Things Up

I wasn't exactly the most focused while carving the prison layout. In my defense, my mind was still reeling from the story Morrígan had told. A part of me still didn't believe it could have happened. Surely Dungeons didn't steal souls from beyond the grave to make their creatures? My instincts hadn't indicated *anything* about that being the case, and I thought if that was how Dungeons worked it should have at least been mentioned. But Morrígan's story was much too divorced from what I'd envisioned to have come purely from my own narrative, so the only other explanation would be if the system itself had *made it up from nothing*. Though for what reason I had no idea.

There was also a third option, which was a mix of the first two. Perhaps the events Morrígan had described had actually happened in the past, but she wasn't the creature or soul who had experienced them. She was something wholly new, yet implanted with memories of a false past that was similar to the story I was creating, to make a sort of duplicate or copy of the person who had once existed.

None of the options were comfortable, if I was honest. That last one especially I hoped wasn't true, since it would mean Morrígan didn't even have a story of her own. It would be someone else's, and she'd just be forced to play it out because I wanted a specific kind of performer.

I shook myself. No use getting drawn down by could-bes and what-ifs.

I'd definitely need to ask someone about this as soon as possible, but for now the best thing would be to drop it and focus on what I was actually doing.

The prison would be a chasm, I decided. A deep hole going from the entrance at the top of the claimed fifth Floor all the way down to the bottom. A spiral staircase would run along the walls, with occasional rooms, or cells carved into the rock. These cells would hold the creatures of the Floor. Initially I had thought to only have a few very strong creatures, but unfortunately even with my newly found freedom thanks to [Dungeon Management] I was limited to a single Guardian per Floor. And judging by the Vampire Spawn, there was an enormous gulf between even the strongest of my normal creatures and the strength of a Guardian. The creatures would have to come in groups, like normal.

I could, however, make changes to the victory condition. Rather than having Challengers beat the Guardian, I could make them seal it back into its cell. That fit much better with the narrative, and would also give the Guardian a stronger buff since the party didn't have to fully defeat it to clear the Floor. I would scatter clues to how to perform this sealing throughout the various cells to make the Challengers be on constant lookout if they wanted to learn the ritual. That would also make them pay more attention to the Floor's story, as the Floor's ritual would be found within the narrative. The sealing itself would be triggered by a variant of mana-powered traps that I changed to allow Challengers to activate. If done improperly, however, the trap would blow up in their face, making the job of Guardian-sealer a risky one.

As I was working on the cells, a faint buzzing to my senses told me there were people walking around outside my entrance, but after giving them a glance it didn't look like they were planning to go inside any time soon, so I ignored them and went back to work. After telling Stalker to send a message if their attitude seemed to change, of course.

I finished up carving and claiming the cells. There would be seven in total, each one containing the solution to one step of the Guardian-sealing process, except the final one, which would contain the order in which to perform the steps. Once I was done, I looked everything over.

I decided to add a secondary clear condition of killing the Guardian outright. That way if a party missed the proper way to handle the Floor but were still able to rise to this much harder Challenge, they wouldn't be barred from completing the Floor.

After that came the rewards. I had *much* more freedom with my new skill. I could still give out the Rewards Chest for a random item relative to the level of the Floor. But now I could also be more specific, granting unique items I'd designed myself, or even grant more esoteric rewards such as experience or even talent points. Though my instincts were against those last two—they were too valuable for a level 4 reward.

I wondered briefly why they were against *this* reward and not the Quest I'd created earlier. Then it dawned on me that this Rewards Chest was *repeatable,* while a Quest only happened once. I still wasn't quite clear on exactly how valuable talent points were, but a large and repeatable chunk of extra experience . . . Even I could tell what kind of allure that thing would have.

All right, no experience or talent points for now. But I still wanted to be a bit more personal with my reward, and I also wanted to differentiate the rewards for clearing the Floor using the ritual from those for clearing it by killing the Guardian. Maybe clearing the Floor "normally," by defeating the Guardian, would give the normal Rewards Chest, but performing the ritual would grant a more special item. Yeah, I liked the sound of that.

But what would the item be? I wanted it to be tied to the narrative of the Floor of course and to the Guardian itself. Which meant I needed to leave it until after I'd selected the Guardian and populated the Floor with the rest of its creatures.

But before I did that I wanted to experiment a bit with the [Spatial Connection] skill. Something about the skill nagged at me. I thought there must be some way for me to use it better than to just ferry people from the entrance to the proper Floor for their level. According to the skill description, it made a connection between two Floors of the Dungeon, either temporary or permanent, and could be between any two Floors even if they weren't next to each other. That way I could send high-leveled people directly from my first Floor to the fourth, for example, and wouldn't have to endure them slaughtering their way past defenses that had no chance of stopping them. It seemed pretty straightforward, but my instincts were telling me there was something I was missing. Some way I could use it to enhance the story of the Dungeon . . .

Oh I'm an idiot! I thought. I could make the connection *permanent.* Meaning I could use the portal as the main way of travel between Floors, and I wouldn't have to use a literal staircase leading downward every time. The realization lit a fire of enthusiasm within me. That was the *perfect* solution to the narrative dissonance I was feeling about the connections between my

Floors. Because what kind of cave had a staircase that led to a mausoleum, which in turn had a staircase that led down to a castle courtyard?

It just wasn't realistic, but I had accepted it as a necessary cost to connect everything within the Dungeon.

But with this the connection didn't have to be so literal. With this I could *really* turn my first two Floors into proper parts of the story. Putting down hints that would connect the narrative thread between the cave and the castle, yet keeping the locations ostensibly separated.

I turned my attention away from the fifth Floor onto my second. With shaking metaphysical hands I activated the skill, making a permanent portal between the second and third Floors. Then I used [Dungeon Management] to remove the system protection on the stairs leading down from Krazad's chamber . . . and filled the space with conjured stone.

Yes! I pumped a mental fist. It worked!

Instantly ideas started rushing through my head of how I could alter these first two Floors and really make this story flow. I got to work.

Aira walked near the back of the group as they trudged across the leaf-covered ground. As a level 6, she wasn't really in a position to help out against most monsters of the Lashwood, but she was still a member of the Guild as well as a native of Coltmoon, so she was asked to help set up the new outpost. Or rather, Athilana was asked to help—Aira was just someone who tagged along out of inertia. But it was still a great opportunity. A new Dungeon was rare, and one so close to home even rarer still. As natives to the area, she and Athilana would be given priority access to this new Dungeon once the outpost was set up. Though considering there were a lot of people from the area who also had priority access, many of whom were at the peaks of their tier and ahead of her in line, it was a minor boost at most.

No, Aira corrected herself. *It is still a world's difference from the waiting list I'd be on if I were from somewhere else. That could be* years.

"Whatcha thinkin' about?" Athilana's voice came from behind, causing Aira to jump. She coughed awkwardly and tried to play it off as if nothing had happened.

"Just the future, and the Dungeon," she said. "We're lucky it's so close, since it means we won't have to go on the list in Lashwood."

"That's true," Athilana said, coming into step beside Aira.

"I thought you were with the others up front," Aira said.

The elf shook her head. "Nah, they're boring," she said. "Most of the ones from the Guild are organizers and paper pushers. And the Adventurers themselves keep pretty close to their party, and aren't quick to open up to strangers."

She pointed to a red-haired woman in leather armor with twin daggers at her waist. "That one was the only good conversation up there, but since she's a scout she has to leave and come back all the time." Athilana shrugged. "So here I am, talking to the only person here who'll speak to me who's actually interesting."

"So I'm not the second or even third option? I'm . . ." Aira counted on her fingers in mock outrage. "Your *last* option?"

Athilana laughed a bright laugh and opened her mouth to speak, but she was interrupted by the sound of a whistle coming from ahead of them in the forest.

"A monster's been spotted nearby," she said gleefully. She grabbed Aira by the hand and started off toward the sound. "Come on. Its level might be low enough for the other parties to leave the job to us."

"Not likely this deep in the woods," Aira said as they ran.

"A chance is a chance," Athilana said. Aira shook her head with a smile and kept on running alongside her friend.

Nicomedes surveyed the array of specimens in front of him. Each wiggled slightly in their tubes, as if in response to some wind that they all could feel and he couldn't. On the table in front of them the [Infernal Blaze] was roaring and in full conflagration, but thanks to the barrier he didn't feel even slightly hot. He reached down for the first specimen. He grimaced thinking of the thousands of hours of work that would go to waste with what he was about to do. But it couldn't be helped. Lenore hadn't returned, which had come as a surprise and likely meant the Dungeon, or possibly even the Guild, had learned of her enhancements. Thankfully their workings had been kept secret, apart from what could be expected between a Bishop and his priests, but the risk of keeping these things here was still too high. Just shutting down the experiments wouldn't be enough anymore. Especially with Bishop Harean coming to the Chapel.

He tossed the tube into the fire, and the thing inside screeched as it burned.

CHAPTER NINETEEN

Outside Happenings

Noracin looked out across his hastily set-up desk at the area around the entrance to the new Dungeon. In just a few days, the rather small forest clearing had grown substantially as everyone worked to remove the surrounding trees. The clearing was filled to the brim with people carrying supplies back and forth as the new outpost was being set up, and even now a group of people were hard at work expanding the perimeter. The Hallmaster herself scurried between the various stations, as it was her team in charge of leading the operation. Under normal circumstances—and even in the case of a new Dungeon—he would have found this extremely unusual, as a Hallmaster was usually a more political position. And they were often too busy with different dealings between the Guild and other organizations to handle day-to-day operations.

But these weren't normal circumstances. As one of the few who had entered the Dungeon and lived, Noracin should know that better than anyone.

He'd overheard the leadership talking one night during the journey out here. A scouting team from the Order had sneaked into the Dungeon, and they never walked back out.

He'd spent the night praying for them when he'd heard, asking the Lady to light their path to the afterlife and for them to reach the safe harbor of Astrala. Though he *was* disappointed in their actions, as he felt that sneaking about wasn't proper behavior for members of the Order, their souls still deserved well wishes for the Great Journey. Though he wasn't naive enough to think that the Order didn't partake in the same politicking that other organizations did. Not anymore, at least. More to the point, he didn't believe for a second that the scouting team had decided to sneak on their own accord, so they deserved his well wishes even more.

It had been a few days since he'd learned of the lost scouts, and the workload he'd been given as the leader of the only official Challenger party had done wonders to distract him from the morose parts of Dungeon Challenges. He looked back at the stack of papers in front of him, only for a second pile to be dropped unceremoniously on top of the lot.

"The Guild says the outpost should be made ready for Challenges to begin in three days," one of Katherine's senior clerks, Redar, said. As a high Tier-3 Scribe, ordinarily he would have outranked Noracin by *leagues*, but as discoverers of the Dungeon he and his party had been granted a few privileges. Such as priority access to Challenges and a seat at the table when any decisions were made regarding the Dungeon. But just because the Scribe had to follow his directions during this excursion didn't mean he had to like it.

"This is a new list of applications for entry from weeks two to four. When you have a free moment, the Hallmaster has requested you go through these and work out a good schedule for the Challenges," Redar said.

With privilege came increased responsibilities, and so Noracin was now sat with over a dozen requests from various parties and individuals who all wanted in on the ground floor. Next to that pile of paperwork lay that for orders of various supplies and services that would be needed for the outpost, as well as the Guild's decisions on how frequently Challenges could occur and how the system would allocate them. And that wasn't even counting this new pile. Still if there was one area he felt confident in, it was organization and paperwork.

"That should be fine," Noracin said. "We have all but the last shipment of supplies, and most of the housing has been set up. We're still waiting for an Item Scanner, but it should be here within the day. Once the scouting team finishes their report for the day I should be able to start work on this new schedule."

"Very good." Redar nodded. "Your draft for the first week's schedule was approved, with one addendum."

"Oh?" Noracin asked.

"There will be an inspection done by a secondary team on the first Floor as written, but the Guild has decided that your party should be the ones to undertake that task."

"Us?" Noracin blinked. "Why, if I may ask?"

"The Hallmaster will be busy with staff arriving from Ebereya, and you're the only other party to have entered the Dungeon before."

"Is that important? I was under the impression that inspections are made by those over-tiered for the Floor."

"Normally, yes. With a few exceptions—for example if the Dungeon is new, or the Floor is suspected of having changed since the last inspection. Then preference shifts for inspections to be performed by those with previous experience of the Floor. And we have both of those situations happening here."

"And right now that leaves only the Hallmaster and us," Noracin said.

"Exactly," Redar said with a nod. "Your priority will be to document the changes to the Floor rather than clear it."

Noracin nodded, then paused as he realized something. "Wait, did you say 'changes'?" he asked. "What do you mean? I thought Floors were locked from changes once they were finished."

"Initially yes," Redar explained. "When they reach level five, Dungeons unlock the skill needed to make some changes to previously made Floors, as well as many more options for Floor variety. Though large changes like a different Guardian or a wholly new appearance are still prohibited, we think. Or at least I haven't ever heard of a Dungeon doing that."

"Huh, I had no idea."

Redar shrugged. "Most Dungeons don't bother changing their early Floors, preferring instead to focus on expansion and improving their higher-level ones. Just because they unlock the Skill doesn't mean they have to use it, after all. Besides, only about thirty-five percent of Dungeons ever reach Tier five. Or level five, as they would call it."

"So this Dungeon is level five already?" Noracin asked. "After only having formed a few months ago? Isn't that *incredibly* fast?"

"Yes, it is," Redar confirmed. "But no, as far as I know it isn't 'entirely' in the fifth level yet, whatever that means. Still fast though, no doubt about it."

Noracin blinked, confused. "But—"

"You'll have to ask someone more familiar with the inner workings of Dungeon system mechanics for a complete answer. I just relayed everything that's been told to me. Now if you'll excuse me I have to get back to work."

"Right, of course," Noracin said. "I'll have the new schedule for you by lunch tomorrow."

"Very good." Redar strode away back toward the Hallmaster. Noracin stared after the man for a few seconds as he pondered what he'd just heard.

It's changing the Floor before it's reached level 5 . . .

This Dungeon might be even more special than even he'd believed.

He shook himself. That issue was above his paygrade. What he had to worry about was how to wrangle and organize the Challenges of several dozen different parties, as well as where and how to house them all while they were here. And he now had to plan an inspection of the Dungeon as well. Which meant he'd need to send for Ceria to come from Aspenfield a few days ahead of schedule. He'd have to get her a message. He should also talk to Alerio as soon as possible. He'd been spending a lot of time with the Dungeon Scholars recently, since he was deemed "unsuitable for arduous physical labor due to his reduced vitality." Noracin smiled. The prospect of returning to the Dungeon would be a good way to lift Alerio's spirits, and he really did need someone else to help with the preparations.

The messaging station was the first the Guild got up and running, for obvious reasons. It was in near constant contact with the Guild Hall in Aspenfield as well as the headquarters in Ebereya. The number of messages it sent each day would have taken an entire fleet of carrier pigeons. The station was nothing more than an unwalled tent set up over a series of tables, desks, and chairs. There was a line to get in, and Noracin had to wait for several minutes before he had the chance to speak to the operators.

"Excuse me," he said. "I have an urgent message to send to my party member back in Aspenfield."

"Name?" the operator asked.

"Noracin Lark. Message is to Ceria Dawnwater."

The operator nodded and flipped a few pages in his ledger. "Ah, there you are. Approved for priority and security. And for free no less! Sweet deal," he said. "Must be nice to be discoverer of a Dungeon, huh?"

"I guess . . . " Noracin said, unsure how else to respond. The operator either didn't notice Noracin's discomfort or just didn't care and continued with the process as if nothing special had happened. He reached into a bag on his desk and took out a much smaller box. Noracin felt a gathering of mana as the locks on the box were opened and the man pulled out a small onyx stone.

"Here's a secure Message Stone. Its partner is locked away in our office in Aspenfield, but the operators there will see when it is used. Be sure you *choose* the correct receiver—their name will be the only thing our operators can see, and only your receiver will be able to access the message."

"Got it," Noracin said, even though he already knew how secure Message Stones worked and thought it a waste to use one on such a simple message.

"There's a private message hall set up over there." The man pointed to what at first glance might have seemed like a small closet inside the station, but the mana coming from the markings on the ground in front of it told Noracin it was much more. Though to call it a "message hall" was an exaggeration. A message booth, if he was being generous. He nodded politely to the operator anyway. Once inside, he activated the privacy enchantments, then the Message Stone. Just as expected, he was prompted by the system to choose the receiver. He quickly selected Ceria, and went on to craft a message describing their new duties and asking her to come to the outpost with the next caravan.

Now all he had to do was go find Emmalia and Alerio. Emmalia didn't like surprises, so he was sure she wouldn't be as thrilled with the new investigatory duties as Alerio would be, but the sooner she found out about them the better. And she still had a few days to prepare, so she shouldn't have much to complain about.

After walking around the camp for several minutes without any luck, Noracin went to the scouting leader. Emmalia was supposed to be off duty today, but knowing her as Noracin did, it wouldn't surprise him if she'd asked to go out on a mission anyway.

"She left just over two hours ago. She isn't due back until this evening," the Scoutmaster said. Noracin sighed. Of course she did.

"All right, thank—" He was interrupted by a sudden *roar* from the nearby forest, startling flocks of birds into flight. He turned in the direction of the sound, before a bad feeling made him turn back to the Scoutmaster.

"Did she . . . ?" he asked. The Scoutmaster nodded once, then took off sprinting toward the sound. Before he knew what he was doing, Noracin found himself running into the forest after him.

Sometime earlier . . .

Life in the outpost was different than what Aira had expected. Perhaps it had been a childish view of things, but she'd thought it would be engaging, a never-ending adventure. Instead what she found was never-ending construction work, with some extracurricular tree cutting, and a constantly aching back. She grunted as she set down the bundle of wood planks near the current project and felt her back crack as she stretched out gratefully. It wouldn't be the last thing she carried today, and she would likely need to help carry something else tomorrow. Still, she didn't want to seem ungrateful. The work would do wonders to push her up the list of applicants to Challenge the Dungeon, though she still likely wouldn't get her turn until she was level 10 and at the cap for Tier 1. And while carrying wood and helping the Guild construct primitive houses for prospective Challengers granted some experience, it wouldn't be enough to get her there anytime soon. Even anytime *this year* was doubtful. No, if she wanted to level up she'd need to go out into the forest and actually find some monsters to fight. Not just hang around in the camp all day. At least there seemed to be an end in sight, as the camp had become markedly more organized and structured since she'd arrived. Once the buildings were done, perhaps she could be allowed to do something more . . . adventurous? A girl could hope, at least.

She heard a voice call her name from across the clearing. She turned to see Athilana standing with the redheaded woman from the march, waving her over. Aira hastily excused herself to the foreman and hurried over.

"What is it?" she asked.

"We got permission!" Athilana exclaimed. Aira blinked, then her eyes widened as she realized what her friend meant. *Speak ill of the Cursed . . .* She pushed the thought out of her head. Just because she'd just thought of it didn't *actually* mean it was a bad omen.

"You mean we get to go out on a mission?" she asked.

"Exactly!" Athilana nodded with a wide grin. "We won't be allowed to go out alone, though. It seems two people aren't enough to be considered a proper party out here." She gestured to the woman to her left. "This is Emmalia, the Rogue friend I was telling you about. Her party is pretty spread out with different tasks right now, so she can't take on any large missions." She paused and blushed slightly as she turned to the woman. "Sorry, I should let you explain."

The redhead shrugged. "It doesn't matter to me, but okay," she said. "What Athilana said is true enough. With everyone else otherwise occupied, I'm bored out of my skull hanging around here all day. With my build, I excel at hunting and scouting, so there shouldn't be any issues with you going out at your level as long as I come with."

"See!" Athilana said excitedly. "I told you I'd get us out of construction duty!" She beamed at Aira, who looked between the two women with a mix of excitement and overwhelm.

"So . . . " she said, trying to organize her thoughts. "We can go out and hunt monsters?"

"Ostensibly it will be a scouting mission—that's what I have permission for," Emmalia said. "But if we find any monsters within the proper level range, there's no reason we can't take them out. Around half the monsters here are Tier two. But with me around to detect them, your Tier-one status shouldn't be a problem. I see no issue with taking the two of you with me when I go so long as you're careful."

"See, it's perfect," Athilana said. "We get to go on a mission, and it won't even be dangerous."

Aira thought for a moment, then smiled. "When do we leave?" she asked.

"Right away," Athilana said, handing Aira her bow.

Aira blinked, had she always held that? She shook her head and accepted the bow.

CHAPTER TWENTY

The Dangers of the Outside World

It turned out the forest wasn't scary at all. Almost an hour into their scouting mission and so far the forest looked just as it did back home, only with slightly taller trees. Aira didn't know why she'd been expecting otherwise; she'd seen it when the caravan arrived, after all. Maybe because everyone kept saying it was too dangerous for Tier 1s, she'd pictured something . . . darker, more ominous. Perhaps with spiderwebs hanging from some dead and rotting trees.

With Emmalia leading the way they hadn't had any difficulty avoiding monsters. In fact, even with her Glyph Aira hadn't even *seen* one yet—that was how safe Emmalia was being. A part of her was a bit disappointed that the mission had seemingly turned into nothing more than a walk through the woods, but the smarter part of her knew it was the better scenario. Even fights between those of equal level were risky as mistakes sometimes happened. And most of these monsters were higher-level than her and Athilana. She shouldn't be disappointed—she should be thankful they hadn't found anything they couldn't just walk around or sneak past yet.

A screech of anger and hunger came from the trees above them. Aira looked up with a start. A monster emerged from the wood near the top of the trees. An Eyeless Tree-Monkey. No, it wasn't just the one. As her eyes scanned the canopy, Aira saw a second emerge, followed by a third. Each of their names showed up in dark yellow within her system screen. They were still Tier 1, but each one was at the peak.

Emmalia swore in frustration. "They said these things lived much farther south," she growled. "So much for reliable intel." She said the last words as if they had hurt her family, then turned toward Aira and Athilana.

"I'll hold them off. You two try an attacking retreat. Run away if you see an opportunity to do so." Emmalia hissed three commands in rapid succession, simultaneously pulling out a dagger and hurling it at the closest monster to draw its attention.

Run away and leave this woman to fight on her own? Aira thought.

She raised her bow at the same time as Athilana raised her hands. Athilana's [Water Bolt] and Aira's arrow imbued with arcane energy shot toward the closest monkey simultaneously.

Fat chance of that *happening.*

Emmalia's dagger struck the monkey's shoulder, causing it to cry out in pain and distracting it long enough for Athilana's [Water Bolt] and Aira's imbued arrow to reach it as well. Three attacks at once proved too much for the creature to handle, and it lost its grip on the branch it was perched atop. Aira cheered internally, though her elation was short lived as the monkey recovered a second later, catching itself by shoving its tail directly into the trunk of the tree. The two other monkeys leaped down toward them, screeching a horrendous cacophony of dissonant sounds as they fell. Aira's vision swam, and her head screamed in agony from the monkey's signature [Sonic Scream] skill. Despite her discombobulation she knew what to do—she instantly dropped her bow and covered her ears the moment she recognized the sound. The scream was the monkey's deadliest skill, but she also knew they couldn't utilize it for very long or it would leave them too drained to continue fighting. The fact that the skill was so costly and had such a glaring weakness was one of the reasons these monsters rarely reached beyond Tier 1; their primary offensive weapon was at least partially blocked by simply blocking one's ears. Granted most other forest dwellers didn't have hands they could use to block their ears, and even with her ears covered, Aira would still take some damage from the skill. Plus it did force her to drop her weapon, so it wasn't a useless ability.

The sound ended as the pair of falling monkeys landed and charged as one toward Emmalia, who'd been more affected by the skill and still seemed somewhat out of it. Aira was a bit shocked at that, considering her higher level, but it didn't stop her from raising her hands and firing an [Arcane Bolt] at the larger monkey. It wouldn't be as damaging as one of her enhanced arrows, but she didn't want to waste time picking up her bow.

The bolt bit into the monkey's already-wounded shoulder. It flinched, but Aira could tell the hit hadn't caused much actual damage. But she hadn't been going for damage. She'd been going for distraction, and the skill had managed that well enough. It desynced the monkeys' attacks, which gave Emmalia enough time to throw herself to the side to avoid the brunt of the damage from one and avoid the other entirely. She still cried out in pain as the claws tore open her outer thigh, but at least she wasn't out of the fight. The pain also seemed to pull her mind from the daze caused by the [Sonic Scream], as she reached out with her second dagger and pierced the now overextended monkey in the throat. It gurgled and stumbled back, then fell over dead. Aira felt a momentary thrill as the experience began to surge through her. At the same time a second [Water Bolt] flew past her peripheral vision, toward the monkey still in the trees. Good, her friend had recovered from the scream as well.

They could do this. Despite the level disparity, they could win this fight.

A screech from behind made her blood run cold. A second one froze it solid in her veins.

There aren't just three of them.

She instinctively held her hands up to shield her ears while spinning around where she stood, to see a fourth and fifth monkey emerge from the trunks of the trees behind them. Then a sixth.

She gulped and backed up a few steps, putting her back against Athilana's so they could cover each other's blind spots, just like they had done in training. Only then they hadn't fought eyeless monsters that still somehow knew where you were and could pass through wood as if it wasn't there.

Their only saving grace was that the pack seemed to have gotten more careful now that one of their numbers had died. None of the three newly appeared creatures leaped down from their positions in the trees, choosing instead to drop down at a distance and close in gradually. Even the one that had charged Emmalia had backed off and joined its packmates in slowly encircling them, but advancing cautiously.

"This is why I told you to run," Emmalia grunted from behind Aira. There was a soft squelching sound followed by quick footsteps as she joined their formation. "These things never fight an even fight. There's always another hiding nearby."

"What do we do?" Athilana asked as she fired off another [Water Bolt].

"Go on the offensive, try to break the encirclement in a coordinated strike," Emmalia said. "If we let them come at us from all directions, one is bound to get a good hit in. And they might not be fast, but their claws still hurt. Once we're running I'll draw their attention. You run and don't stop running until you're back at the outpost. Got it? Good. On my mark charge toward the injured one. Go!"

Aira barely had time to process Emmalia's instructions, but she instinctively spun and started running the moment the redhead finished speaking. As she spun she readied an [Arcane Bolt] but held it in her hand until she could identify which of the monkeys she was supposed to target. The one they had all attacked during their initial barrage.

There.

Water and arcane bolts fired off in quick succession and the two magical skills flew in coordination toward the weakened monkey. It cried out in pain and stumbled, falling to one knee as the trio started running. Emmalia instantly veered toward the remaining monkey, throwing her second dagger and withdrawing a third. Aira slowed for half a step, instinct telling her to help with the fight, before a tug on her arm from Athilana made her mind start working properly. They sprinted past the injured monkey out into the woods. Emmalia could handle herself. She would only be in the way.

"Don't stop running!" Emmalia called from somewhere behind. "I'll be fine; these things can't kill me. I'll catch up with you along the way!"

"You'd better be fine!" Athilana called back. "I'll kill you if you're dead when we get back!"

Aira followed after Athilana as they zigzagged through the trees, keenly aware of the snarling and occasional yelp of a monkey in pain coming from behind them. She hoped Emmalia would be safe. That she wasn't just leaving this woman to die. She should never have agreed to come on this mission. No matter how bored she was. She was under-leveled for the area. She had to get special approval to be allowed to even leave the base, and even then she couldn't go without a chaperone. She was a liability. She cursed her own uselessness as she ran but was forcefully pulled out of her tumbling mind by the screech of a monkey coming from right behind her. She raised her hands to cover her ears and hurled herself to the side. The combination allowed her to dodge the incoming claw, but it also made her tumble stomach-first into a tree, causing her to lose her breath and stumble backward in a daze.

"Aira!" She heard Athilana's voice from up ahead, then felt more than heard the [Water Bolt] pass right by her face and strike the monkey with a smack. She caught her breath as she stumbled forward, firing an [Arcane Bolt] blindly behind her as her steps sped to a run. Ahead of her, Athilana had stopped and stood staring back at her with frightened eyes. Aira tried to project confidence as she ran, but seeing the look on her friend's face made it feel like a pit had opened up inside her stomach. She instinctively dropped to the ground, but still cried out in agony as the claws from the monkey ripped open her back. Her vision blurred at the edges as she spun in the air, readying and firing off another [Arcane Bolt] right into the face of her attacker. It stumbled backward slightly, but it wasn't injured enough to stop a second attack. She held up her arms to shield her torso, and couldn't even cry out as the claw carved deep cuts into her bone. She heard a sickening squelch as something else pierced her stomach, but she didn't feel the pain. Quite the opposite, in fact—it turned the intense inferno into a comfortable coldness.

She vaguely heard Athilana's panicked voice from somewhere overhead. Was she coming closer?

No, stay away. Get to safety, she thought as blackness threatened to overwhelm her mind.

She kept it at bay, refusing her body's desire to black out and embrace the safety of the void. She couldn't leave her friend to fight alone.

But she couldn't lessen her injuries, nor could she make the blackness retreat completely. She felt helpless. The sound of the fighting overhead became fainter and more muddled.

Then blissful panacea rushed through her body. She gasped, then choked as the liquid from the potion caught in her throat. Her vision cleared, and she sat up straight to find Athilana's panicked face staring down at her.

"You're alive!" the elf exclaimed in pure relief. Aira blinked in confusion. Where was the monster? What was the sound? As her focus and reason returned, she turned her gaze to find her salvation standing there, a dagger in each hand.

Emmalia stabbed forward with each hand in rapid succession, each attack scoring a hit to a vulnerable part of the monkey's body. It screeched and swung its claws in desperation, stumbling slightly. The Rogue seized the opportunity, instantly piercing forward with both daggers into the creature's throat. It gurgled once, then toppled over backward. Aira stared in stunned silence as the experience from the kill flowed through her.

She beat it so easily, she thought. *Now that she didn't have to waste so much energy watching out for us.*

The Rogue walked over and looked down at her with a concerned furrow in her brow.

"You alive?" she asked. Aira nodded and tried to stand, but her legs still didn't quite feel like they belonged to her. Athilana caught her arm to hold her upright, but Aira flinched back from the touch as she remembered the monkey's claws tearing through her. But to her surprise her arm didn't hurt. She stared dumbly at her torn clothes and the unblemished skin underneath.

"Tier-two health potion," Emmalia said. "Thought it would be a good idea to stock up after my last Challenge. Seems like I was right."

"Th—" Aira began, then coughed. "Thanks."

Emmalia shrugged. "Don't mention it."

"Is it over?" Athilana asked.

"No," Emmalia said. Aira looked around with a start, trying to find the remaining monsters.

"The monkeys are either dead or gave up the chase," Emmalia continued. "But they aren't the only thing we have to worry about out here. And while they aren't that strong in actual fights, they have excellent stealth and escape tools in their ability to merge into trees. Which means they don't have to worry about how *loud* they are."

Aira paled as she realized what that meant.

"Their screams draw in something bigger and scarier," Athilana said, echoing Aira's own thoughts. Emmalia nodded.

A roar echoed through the forest from behind them, causing a flock of nearby birds to flee up into the sky. The roar was followed by screeches from several monkeys. This time Aira thought it sounded fearful rather than angry.

"Speak ill of the Cursed, and they will surely hear it . . ." Emmalia sighed. She grabbed Aira's other arm and helped keep her upright.

"Let's go. There's still quite some distance between us and the outpost. The monkeys won't keep that thing busy for long. It almost certainly already knows we're here."

"Can you walk?" Emmalia asked. Aira took a step forward, wobbling slightly and losing her balance. She winced, though from embarrassment more than pain. Her health was full, and her body *should have* been working perfectly fine. It just didn't really seem to know that. She'd nearly died, and her body still hadn't recovered, regardless of what the system said of her health. An extremely quick recovery was prone to do that, especially if it came from something above one's own tier. At least that was what Emmalia had said. Aira still found it embarrassing to not be able to walk properly, though.

"Damnation," Emmalia said as Aira shook her head. She looked back the way they had come as another roar shook the trees around them. "It's almost done with the monkeys. I can only hear two of the little bastards now." She paused for a moment, then knelt in front of Aira.

"Hop on," she said. "We're going too slow like this."

"Will you be all right to run like that? What if we have to fight something?" Aira asked.

"I can manage. Come on, we don't have time to argue here." Aira didn't hesitate any longer and climbed onto Emmalia's back. She started running, still keeping pace with Athilana despite carrying Aira on her back. Or rather it seemed Athilana was allowing Emmalia to set the pace.

"What even is it?" Athilana asked as she leaped over a fallen tree.

"I'm not a hundred percent sure." Emmalia gasped. "But my best guess is a Thunderwood Raptor. They're not common this far north, but they're the only ones I can think of that live in the Lashwood and roar like that. And given these monkey bastards shouldn't be around here either . . ."

"Aren't they born with access to Tier three?" Athilana asked hesitantly as they ran. Emmalia just nodded and upped her speed. The roar sounded behind them once more, closer this time. Aira was sure she heard frustration in the sound.

"That's the monkeys all hidden away. It's chasing us now. And its *pissed,*" Emmalia said.

The women sped up, but even Aira could hear the thundering noise of the monster gradually getting closer. "It's gaining on us," she said.

"I know," Emmalia said.

"What do we do?" Athilana asked.

Emmalia didn't speak for a few seconds. "Can you run any faster?" she asked.

"Yes. But I won't be as fast as you. Strength is a pretty low priority for me."

"Hopefully that shouldn't matter."

"You're going to act as bait," Athilana said with horror as she realized what Emmalia was getting at. It was the same plan she'd gone to with the monkeys. "No way I'm just going to leave you two behind!"

"Don't be stupid!" Emmalia bit out as she leapt over a fallen tree. Behind them, the crashes grew louder as the creature approached. "It's the best plan we have. We won't escape like this. I'm the fastest, but I don't have the ranged skills to harry it if we have to. Aira does, but she can't run right now. And we need *someone* to go get help."

"But—" Athilana said.

"This is an order." Emmalia turned slightly from their path and pulled out a dagger. "I expect you to follow it. Don't worry, I'll keep your friend safe. Now RUN!"

Athilana didn't say anything in response, but Aira could see the frustration on her face as argument after argument came and died unspoken. Then a sudden and surprisingly loud crash caused all three of their heads to whirl around. Aira only caught a glimpse of it through the trees, as neither it nor they were running in a particularly straight line. Though where they had to weave around even the smallest tree, it could crash through, and it was steadily gaining ground. It ran hunched over on two legs and was still over two meters tall. Lightning crackled all across its body and arced from it to bend and force the forest out of its path. It seemed to sense her looking, as it roared in hunger and conquest. Aira instinctively scanned it with the system. Just as Emmalia had feared, it was a Thunderwood Raptor, its color such a dark red it was almost black. For a moment Aira forgot everything else that was happening, her entire being focused on the imminent threat. Then a flash of steel glinted in the sunlight, and she could see Emmalia's dagger fly into the creature's face. The dagger fell to the ground without seeming to do anything at all. She could have sworn she'd even heard the clang of steel on stone when it hit.

The beast turned its attention to her newfound teammate, and Aira could move once again.

"RUN!" Emmalia yelled to Athilana again.

Emmalia took off running, weaving around trees and boulders in a zig-zag, trying to keep away from the Raptor while staying close enough to keep its interest. Aira held on to the older girl's shoulders for dear life, leaving her unable to spare much effort to help. It was a dangerous game, but one they had no choice but to play. The thing was much faster than they were. It was only a matter of time.

Not for the first time, she wished she had some form of dangerous ranged skill that didn't require her bow. Sure, the narrow focus made her gain efficiency and power, but only when she actually had an arrow available to fire. And with how fast and jerky their escape was, there was no way she'd be able to get her hands steady enough to hit even the *ground* on purpose. As it was, her unimbued [Arcane Bolt] was barely even enough to get it more annoyed with them. While that was a good way to keep Athilana safe and able to get help, she couldn't help but feel intentionally angering the giant dinosaur was a bad idea. Nothing she could do about that now though. She turned around long enough to fire another bolt at the creature. It was almost upon them now, close enough that the lightning passively arcing all over its scales occasionally struck *much* too close for comfort. The air smelled burnt as lightning crackled and struck the ground behind her. The beast let out what she swore was a frustrated roar. It didn't seem to have much control over the lightning; it struck wildly, vaguely toward her but not targeting her directly. Emmalia kept her path irregular, darting side to side to make aiming the lightning an even more difficult task. It was working, for now, but the beast was gaining on them. She ran toward any tree that was too large for the beast to knock down without losing speed. It was perhaps their only advantage, as it didn't seem to be able to turn very quickly.

Aira's breath caught as she got an idea. She quickly scanned their surroundings before clapping Emmalia on her shoulder to show her what she'd found.

"If we run around that, it might not be able to catch up," she said, lowering her head to speak right into the girl's ear to make sure she was heard over the roar of the enclosing beast.

"Understood," Emmalia said, despite the ridiculous nature of the plan, if it could even be called that, and veered to the left. Aira prepared two [Arcane Bolts], one in each hand. It was all she could cast with the mana she had left, and even without having to focus on running it was almost beyond her capability to have two skills ready and steady at the same time. She gritted her teeth and forced the mana to obey, and the skills to remain under her control. Even two skills would barely tickle a creature more than three times her own level, but she hoped that double the effect would at least annoy it *slightly* more.

By the time Aira had finished preparing the skills, Emmalia had reached the rocks, and the Raptor was so close she thought she could smell the blood on its breath.

Aira fired off both bolts at once, screaming over the pain. Somehow the shouting helped, and she managed to get both skills fired in the right direction. The double skill did affect her aim though, and one of the bolts hit the Raptor in its side, which didn't even warrant a reaction.

The aim of Aira's second bolt was true, and it struck the raptor square in the face. It reared its head back slightly, more out of reflex than actual pain, Aira was sure, but it roared in anger and frustration. It turned to stare at Aira, a vicious glare that made her blood run cold, then it turned its body in her direction. Time seemed to slow, and all Aira could feel was terror born from the malice within the creature's eyes. Before, it had simply been hunting them for the food and the experience it had missed out on when the monkeys hid. But now it was *personal.*

The enormous dinosaur started to close in on their position. Each step made the earth tremble and sent out an arc of lightning that blackened the surrounding greenery. Emmalia turned on a dime and to run alongside the large rock. The creature roared behind, and a crackling of lightning arced over Aira's head and struck the stone. It crackled and popped, sending a thousand small shards to rain down on her and the Rogue with such force that they pierced skin. Aira clenched her teeth, and she felt Emmalia tense the muscles in her back, but the woman didn't slow down. She rounded the rock and kept on going, running along the other side and keeping the boulder between them and the dinosaur. It crashed through the forest after them, screeching to a rapid halt and making a surprisingly agile turn for such a massive creature. Though Aira felt hope alight within her chest when she saw she'd been right—the Raptor's turn wasn't quite as smooth as Emmalia's, and it gained them a little breathing room. Emmalia reached the other end of the formation and rounded it, returning to their starting point and continuing past it.

The Thunderwood Raptor screeched in frustration as it came around the corner a few seconds after them. This time though it seemed to have learned as it took the corner a bit slower, and therefore a bit smoother. One less step in the wrong direction, and half a second faster to start the chase again. It added up. Reduced to nothing but an observer atop Emmalia's back, Aira noticed it clear as day. The Raptor was gaining on them.

"The plan is not working!" she yelled.

"It's not catching us as fast as it would have if we were just running in a straight line," Emmalia gasped. "It's giving Athilana more time to get away, and the Scoutmaster more time to reach us. There's no way they haven't heard these roars by now."

She rounded the rock again, and Aira turned and yelped as a bolt of lightning flashed past right where her head had been less than a second ago. She smelled burnt hair.

"One final lap," she said. "Then it'll catch us."

"No way. I have a plan," Emmalia said. Aira turned around to watch, but the Raptor didn't burst around the corner after them. In fact, she realized she couldn't hear the thud of loud footsteps or feel the tremors in the ground anymore.

Something was very wrong. She felt the hairs stand on the back of her neck, prompting her to look up. She watched as the giant Raptor landed atop the rock formation with a grace and precision unfitting its size. Emmalia also seemed to sense something was wrong as she came to an abrupt stop and turned her gaze upward as well. The creature let out a furious roar and leapt toward the two of them, lightning crackling between the teeth of its open jaws.

"Ah Hells . . ." Emmalia said. Aira clenched her eyes shut.

"[Burst Step]!" Emmalia yelled in a panicked voice. An instant later Aira felt the world whirl past her as she was flung backward by Emmalia's speed. She held on for all she was worth, but [Burst Step] was not a skill meant for cooperative use. It was damn near teleportation-fast, and while Emmalia had some protection from the system to cope with how fast they were going, it didn't extend to Aira. She held on for half a second before she lost her grip, and in that time she had been moved over a dozen meters away from the stone formation. She fell to the ground *hard*, and she heard a *crunch* as her left hand bent backward as she landed. Her vision grew blurry and she let out a scream of pain. She felt her health drop by more than half. There was a deafening boom as the Raptor landed where they had just been, and the fear rushing through Aira's veins overrode the pain long enough for her to push herself to her feet. They still felt like jelly as she moved, but she scurried away as quickly as she could. She didn't know where Emmalia ended up. She wasn't sure which direction to go. She settled for directly away from the creature and hoped that would work.

A shrill screech from the Raptor made her turn toward it. A dagger stuck out of the creature's left eye, and she felt a momentary surge of hope that was quickly dashed as the thing simply shook the blade loose. It didn't even look that hurt, just angrier.

Then it took a step forward.

Toward Aira.

She turned to run even a fraction of a second faster, even though she knew in her heart it wouldn't make a difference. She thought she could hear Emmalia yell a Challenge in anger and frustration somewhere to her left, though she couldn't see her for the trees. Likely she wanted the beast to turn around and chase her instead. But it wouldn't. It knew Aira was the easier prey.

Suddenly, she felt surprisingly peaceful. Her brain had been on analytical overdrive, and accepting the fact that she was going to die brought relief that the stress of the situation was finally over. At least her friends weren't the ones who died because she couldn't run properly. If someone had to die because of this, it was only right that it be her. She felt death's approach, clasping its cold hands around her neck as the Raptor loomed overhead.

A shout filled with determination. A flashing dagger.

"Aira! RUN!" Emmalia yelled. Aira spun to find the other woman hanging from a dagger she had pierced into the beast's side. She screamed as the arcing lightning struck her over and over, yet she refused to let go even as the thing thrashed. There was a crack in Aira's mind as her earlier thoughts reappeared inside her head, though this time she was horrified.

What the hell was I thinking?!

Of course she wasn't going to accept this fate. She was only eighteen years old, for brightness' sake. She hadn't even had her coming-of-age ceremony yet. And she wasn't about to let Emmalia be the only one who never gave up. Especially when it was *her own* life that was on the line.

She raised both her hands and let loose a scream of defiance as she used her meager regenerated mana to perform one final [Arcane Bolt]. She hurled it toward the thrashing creature. It hummed with arcane energy as it soared through the air, hurdling past the crackling lightning surrounding the scaled beast and striking it right between the eyes.

The Thunderwood Raptor didn't even flinch as it turned its head to Emmalia and thrashed its body at the same time, spawning more lightning from its scales. The Rogue cried out one final scream of defiant anger but lost her grip of her dagger and fell to the ground. The Raptor screeched in triumph and with the speed of a snake reached its head forward and, in a single swift strike, bit the woman's arm clean off.

Emmalia screamed in pain.

Aira screamed in powerless anger.

She took up a rock from the ground at her feet and hurled it at the creature. And was surprised to find the thing stumbling back from the impact, before she noticed the arrow sticking out of its chest. "Yeah! Take that!" she cried out.

A bolt of water streaked past from the forest to her right, followed by a shadow flying over head and landing on the Raptor's back. She looked in awe as a man clad in leather raised a blade high above his head, then brought it down and severed the creature's head with one clean swing.

The lightning stopped arcing.

The creature collapsed in a heap, falling to the forest floor with a soft *thud*. Aira felt her newfound energy drain from her like water through a sieve. Though this time not from surrender to overwhelming odds, but from relief at survival.

No, I can't collapse yet. Emmalia still needs my help.

The man had hopped down from the corpse of the Raptor and was now bent down over the Rogue, who had stopped screaming. Aira could see a bloodied stump where her left arm used to be. She didn't know much about the specifics of healing magic, but she knew regrowing limbs was *difficult*. And definitely not something done by a swordsman out in the field. She wouldn't be able to help at all either, but she needed to do *something*. She forced herself to take a step forward, only to find a strengthening arm supporting her as she walked. She turned to see Athilana looking at her with concern. Her eyes were red, as if she'd been crying.

"I'll live," Aira said. The elven girl studied her for a moment, then nodded, and the two started their hobble to Emmalia's side.

I'll definitely live, Aira thought.

CHAPTER TWENTY-ONE

Inspections

I was coming to learn that the thing I was most determined to do was to create a proper story for myself. Which made the severe lack of anything at all interesting happening recently extremely annoying.

It had been several days since I had changed the layout of my first Floor to better tie the cave into what I'd come to call the "Aberrant Vampire" storyline and scattered hints of the larger plot throughout the Floors. Yet none of the people I could sense milling about outside had stepped foot inside. Not one!

It was taking everything I had to not revamp the story to account for another Floor just for something to do. I had managed to resist so far, but if this went on for much longer . . . What were they all *doing* out there all day?

I'd taken what felt like an inordinate amount of time to create a custom Corrupted Blood Clan Vampire for my fifth-Floor Guardian. I wasn't about to use something that had actually gone Aberrant—I wasn't insane—but I still wanted something that *represented* the corruption the Vampires had undergone. It had taken longer than any singular task I'd ever attempted, and it was only with Morrígan's help that I eventually managed to succeed in creating my first custom creature. That, thankfully, was the difficult part. Once I'd done that, I could use the increased freedom [Dungeon Management] gave me to select it as the Floor Guardian without taking it on faith that the system would provide it as an option. Though I was relieved to see that I could still choose a system-provided Guardian if I wanted; it meant I could use it as a source of inspiration for future stories. My prison storyline felt complete, at least for now. The story of the tragic fate of the Blood Clan due to their experiments with the Aberrant had come to a fitting conclusion with the defeat of the corrupted Vampire. The only possible continuation I could think of was to fight against the Aberrants themselves, but I wasn't sure if it was even possible for me to make that a reality—it definitely wasn't an option right now. Plus they didn't feel like a level 5 enemy, but rather a final one. A final bringing together of all the stories into one final Floor.

Which meant the sixth Floor would be the start of another story, perhaps connected to the Aberrant through something other than the Vampires. I wouldn't start at level 1 again, though. This one would start at level 5, as a continuation of the Dungeon itself. Telling stories was all well and good, but I also needed to expand and grow in strength if I ever wanted to be able to reach that final battle Floor one day. And with the doubling of the experience requirements each level, even with starting these other stories with higher-leveled Floors, I still wasn't sure it would be enough to get to the max level by the time I'd finished them all.

Though a lot of that would depend on how many Floors each story would take, which was yet to be seen. Like with Morrígan's story, I would just have to start somewhere and see where inspiration and the system took me.

If I was ever able to finish the damnable Quest, of course.

I sighed internally and returned my attention to the people outside. They were always there. Two of them. Just standing there doing nothing but being a nuisance to my senses. I had a vague impression of there being more people farther out, but this pair were who I could sense the clearest. There were always two of them out there. Sometimes one or both would change, but even the new ones would still just stand there.

It was infuriating.

To distract myself I focused on changes to my first Floor, tinkering as I came up with new ideas.

The first thing I'd done was remove the large hole leading down from Stalker's chamber and replace it with a small alcove in one of the walls, where the portal to the next Floor would appear once the clear condition had been fulfilled. Next I created a series of similar small chambers leading off from the first cave by the entrance, which would be where the portals to the lower Floors would appear. That wasn't something you'd expect to find in a realistic cave, so I'd stylized it more obviously, making the stone appear artificial and constructed. Then I made the entrance to the tunnel leading to the rest of the first Floor look the same as the ones leading to the various portals. I wanted a clear distinction between the Dungeon entrance and the rest of the Floor itself. This area, which I dubbed the Dungeon Prologue Chamber, was now a Floor zero, of sorts. It was a part of the mechanics of how the story was told, just as the portals were, but not a part of the story itself. It wasn't a perfect solution, but it was the best one I had since unfortunately I wasn't able to make a portal between different areas on the same Floor; it could only take people to the entrance of a new one.

While setting up the portals I'd also learned of an unfortunate downside to my new ability to manipulate a Floor's system protection. While I could remove and replace it, I couldn't make a replacement as strong as the system's. It was only as strong as I was, and as I was still level 4 in all but name, someone level 4 or higher could be strong enough to break the protection. Still it should be good enough for the first couple of Floors, considering the levels the Challengers would be at. And there would be nothing stopping me from redoing the protection once I reached a higher level. Though I hoped that the portals would encourage the stronger Challengers to go deeper right away, and I wouldn't need the extra protection.

Once the cave had been cut off from the rest of the Dungeon I began making improvements and additions to the Floor itself. First and foremost was connecting the various water pools and filling in the one in the first chamber. That way the Mantas could move between rooms and better support my Bats. I also worked out a way of making magical traps that would activate and deactivate themselves at random each day using the system, making it so that Challengers wouldn't be able to study the layout ahead of time to easily get past them. To compensate for that, I made the traps at the start of the Floor a bit less deadly; this was the first Floor after all, and I wanted them to be tested by it rather than simply caught off guard once and die.

Then I moved onto the final piece of the Floor. The thing that would tie it into the story.

I hadn't wanted to make the connection too obvious, so most of the clues vaguely indicated *something* dangerous and secret had happened, without making it clear exactly what that something was.

An old parchment on a Skeleton holding a request for help addressed to the old wizard Krazad.

An old medallion with an insignia I'd gotten from Morrígan to symbolize her clan.

A letter to the queen of the Elves; the race Morrígan said had worked closest with the Vampires during their fight against the Aberrant.

The corpse of one lone Corrupted Vampire Spawn in Stalker's chamber, also with the medallion on it.

That last one had taken quite a bit of work, as I had to design yet another custom creature to be able to make the thing properly. But with the knowledge I had gained from making the fifth-Floor Guardian it had only taken me half a day, so it had been worth it in the end.

I studied the various hints I'd laid out with a frown on my face. I was a bit concerned the connection to the larger narrative was too obvious, and that I'd—

I paused as I sensed a dramatic change near the entrance.

What was this? Was something finally happening?

I turned my full attention that way. Along with the usual pair, there were five additional people there now . . . And I even knew three of them! It was Noracin the Cleric, Ceria the Fighter, and Alerio the Mage. All from my first Challenge! I felt a thrill as the five new arrivals took their first steps down toward my new first Floor. Finally the long wait was over!

This time Noracin was positioned in the front, with the Mage and the two unfamiliar Challengers—a Ranger named Aira and another Mage named Athilana—taking up the middle, and the Fighter protecting the rear. The Rogue who had done so much damage to my Stalker last time was nowhere to be seen. I wondered where she'd gone. Eh, that didn't matter right now.

The party of five quickly made their way down the stairs and into the first chamber. There they all stopped and looked around with shock on their faces, especially the familiar three.

"I thought big changes like this were supposed to be impossible," Noracin said. "This doesn't even look like a cave anymore."

"It does look quite different," Alerio said thoughtfully. He shut his eyes for a moment and focused. "The Elemental Attunements feel the same, and the mana flows in give or take the same direction. It is definitely the same Floor as last time."

"Then what is all this?" Ceria asked, gesturing to my stylized marble walls.

"Decoration?" Alerio said uncertainly, though he was correct. "It's still stone walls . . . Maybe the Dungeon just wanted it to look different for some reason?"

Noracin sighed and took out a piece of paper and a pen to write something down. I was tempted to peek with my senses but resisted the urge. That didn't feel proper.

"We'll report it all when we return. For now be sure to write down any changes you see. Aira and Athilana, make notes of your observations as well," Noracin said as he put the paper away.

"Got it," the Ranger said. The Mage nodded as well.

Noracin turned and scanned the chamber and the different tunnels leading out. Most of them didn't contain portals yet, of course, and even the three that did wouldn't be accessible to his level, so they would appear as short dead ends if he decided to explore them.

Maybe I could find a way to hide these tunnels somehow, and keep them hidden until a party needed to use them. Something to try to figure out later, for sure.

"Which way is it?" Noracin asked.

Alerio pointed to the tunnel leading to the first Floor proper. "This one," he said. "I think it's the same one as last time too, it's just added a bunch of new ones."

"We check the other ones out first then," Noracin said, to which Alerio nodded.

Well now I felt a bit embarrassed. These portal chambers were nothing but empty rooms, yet the party went into each and every one of them and searched extremely thoroughly. They even took notes!

When I saw that I committed to making the chamber's purposes more obvious, as well as making them more interesting to explore.

They wouldn't have any actual Challenge in them, but I should be able to stylize the walls a bit so they weren't all the same. Maybe I could make a different design depending on what Floor the portal led to . . . Yeah, that sounded like a good idea. I'd do that once these guys left.

While I was thinking, the party finished their examination of the portal chambers and had regrouped in front of the first-Floor entrance. Noracin had once more taken the lead, but this time the Fighter stood right behind him, and it was Alerio who guarded the rear. The unfamiliar duo remained in the middle. I felt the tension rising in the room as everyone including myself readied themselves for the coming Challenge. I sent a message to Stalker, letting her know to be ready if they reached her chamber.

"All right, guys. Let's start the inspection officially. Be ready for anything," Noracin said.

The what *now?*

CHAPTER TWENTY-TWO

Slow and Steady

This tunnel looks similar to last time, but there are no Bats up above," Alerio said as the party walked through the entrance. They were moving incredibly slowly in my opinion, with each of them keeping an eye out for both traps and enemies. Though since there weren't either in this first tunnel anymore, all it did was slow them down.

Noracin, at the front of the party, looked around the tunnel with a frown.

"I can definitely recognize parts of it, yeah," he responded to Alerio. "Though some things near the ceiling or by the entrance are different . . . I think?"

He turned to the Fighter. "Ceria, what do you think? Do you recognize anything?"

"Hmm," Ceria said. "I can't say I put the exact details of what the tunnel looked like to memory, but I guess it feels familiar? Admittedly most of my attention last time was on the Bats up above, and that area is definitely different."

"Yeah, there are no holes or small tunnels for the Bats there anymore," Alerio said. "Which means the Dungeon removed the Bats from this tunnel on purpose."

Noracin nodded and pulled out his piece of paper and started writing once again. Was an inspection something the people from outside did whenever I changed a Floor? They seemed very focused on what was different from last time. Maybe it was tradition to stay away whenever I made changes, and they wanted to wait until they were sure I was done before going back in . . .

Did that mean that *I* was the reason nobody tried to Challenge for so long?!

Uhrgh. Well whatever, the changes were worth it. And the wait was over now anyway, even if the people here now didn't intend to Challenge the Floor, but rather document it.

Which I supposed was understandable.

"All right," Noracin said as he put his paper away. "Any reason you can think of as for why the Dungeon decided to make this change?"

The question was directed at Alerio, who shrugged. "Not sure. Maybe he saw how useless the pack was against us during the first Challenge. Maybe he wants to coordinate the Bats together with whatever shot [Water Bolts] from the pools, to let them strengthen each other's weaknesses, like what happened during the Guardian fight."

"That's a reasonable conclusion," Noracin said. "Though I'm not sure how we could confirm it."

"We *could* just ask," Alerio replied, to which Noracin paused, then shook his head.

"Right, how could I forget that you can actually *talk* with this Dungeon?" he said.

"What do you mean 'talk with'?" one of the unfamiliar ones, the Mage Athilana, asked.

"Ah, so it's like this," Alerio said eagerly. "The Guardian of this Floor is a batlike creature . . ."

"A Leatherwing, according to the Hallmaster," Noracin said.

"Right, a Leatherwing. That's what it was," Alerio said with a nod. "It can speak, and the Dungeon can speak through it if we want to ask it questions." Alerio paused. "Now, I wasn't conscious for the actual speaking the last time we were here, but the others told me what happened, and we know what the Hallmaster said. I'm eager to actually be able to listen to it myself this time."

"A talking Dungeon . . . I've never heard of one doing that before. That's *cool*," Athilana said.

I felt a swell of pride. I liked her.

"It isn't the only one to do so, but yeah it definitely sets it apart from the crowd. Most Dungeons don't seem interested in it, if they even have the capability to try," Alerio said, a hint of pride in his voice.

"Stay focused," Noracin said. "We don't have Emmalia with us, so if the traps have been changed we'll have to pay *extra* close attention to spot them."

A somber air descended over the party at the mention of the Rogue's name, followed by a series of nods as one by one every member of the party got a determined look on their face. Especially the Ranger, who gripped her bow so tight her knuckles turned white. Something must have happened outside for them to have that reaction . . .

I made a note to ask what it was if they made it to Stalker and decided to ask questions rather than fight, which seemed likely given their investigatory attitude.

While I was pondering, the party had reorganized themselves and started slowly making their way through the tunnel once more. This part of an investigation seemed similar to a Challenge, if slightly slower, as they were interested in documenting even the very minute changes, and even *potential* changes if they weren't sure of their memory. It took them well over a minute to cross the first tunnel, which was only twenty meters long. This was the first split in the path, and just around the corner to their left would be the first trap. There was one to their right as well, but it wasn't active at the moment.

After discovering different and new ways to make mana-powered traps with my new skills and perks, I might have gone a little overboard. Thirteen traps, ten of which had the potential to be lethal, or at least *near* lethal, seemed a bit overkill for a first Floor, in retrospect. But I didn't just want to remove them. Or rather I couldn't decide which of them I liked least and therefore should go. So instead I came up with a system where I separated the traps into early traps, middle traps, and later traps, and then limited how many of each category could be active at any one time. That also worked well with my desire to want a Floor you couldn't easily prepare for, that would always be somewhat of a Challenge, as which traps were active would change each day. And today the right path was trapped. Of course this area hadn't always been a split path, so I wasn't surprised to find them stopping and falling into a discussion when they arrived and realized the change.

"Last time we were here this was a bend, right?" Noracin said.

"Yeah I think so," Ceria said. "I remember us going around this corner to the left to get out of the line of fire of the first group of water creatures."

"Let's go right this time then, since that area's bound to be new," Alerio suggested.

"We'll have to investigate both directions, Noracin said. "But I have no issue with taking the right path first." He turned to Athilana and the Ranger. "I know you two haven't been here before, but do you have any preference about what way to go first?"

The Ranger shook her head, while the Mage spoke aloud. "I'm fine with whatever you guys want to do."

Noracin nodded. "Right it is. Keep your eyes peeled, everyone."

The alternate path was a narrower tunnel than the main one, mostly because I didn't have enough Floorspace to make it larger, and also didn't have any caverns as large as the main one. There were two smaller ones though, each with a connection to the story. Before arriving at the caverns, they had to pass through the tunnel itself. While it was too narrow for a proper fight I had filled it with traps. Seven of my thirteen traps were on this alternate path. Of those seven, traps two, six, and seven were currently active. The sixth and seventh traps were all the way at the end of the path, but they were nearly at the second. I perked up, focusing as the Cleric inched closer and closer to the trigger.

"Wait! I sense . . . !" Alerio's warning came too late, as Noracin's foot touched a stone that began to shimmer on contact before turning to nothing more than a paper-thin sheet. The shimmer spread backward, making Noracin and the fighter suddenly stand atop something that couldn't hold their weight. It cracked and shattered into dozens of tiny shards, revealing the pit below. Ceria swore and Noracin flailed as they fell and landed with a pair of heavy *thuds*, followed by a series of pained groans.

Since this was an early trap, I had removed the sharp stone spikes at the bottom of the pit, but a three-meter drop was still nothing to sneeze at. Not likely to be instantly lethal though, I hoped.

"Are you okay?" Alerio shouted down into the pit. At the bottom, Ceria was the first to stir, though Noracin was able to move not long after.

"No, I'm not *okay*," Ceria said. "My *everything* hurts. Falling in iron armor isn't fun."

"Try falling *without* iron armor," Noracin groaned. He slowly rose to a half-seated position, then pulled a sharp piece of stone from the trap cover out of his arm with a wince. "At least you were protected from the stone knives."

"Health left?" Alerio called down.

"A hundred thirty-eight. Took over half of it in one go," Noracin said, then swore quietly as he pulled out a second shard of stone.

"Two hundred twelve here," Ceria said.

Alerio and the Ranger winced, while Athilana whistled.

"Three Hells that had to hurt," she said.

"No shit," Ceria said. "Help us get out of here."

"Hang on a second," Alerio said, removing his backpack and taking out a length of rope.

Was it that painful to lose health? I didn't *have* health in the system sense. But my creatures had, and I had a connection to them, and none of them had ever had this kind of reaction. Though I suppose the outsiders had had a similar reaction during the other Challenges as well, especially during the Guardian fight.

I frowned. I understood the concept of pain from my early naming attempts, and I didn't relish inflicting it upon others. But how else was I supposed to Challenge them? No matter how I thought about it, pain and death seemed integral to the Dungeon experience. The risk of death especially. It was what *made* it a Challenge and not just a stroll through an interactive story. No, the danger was vital, but maybe I could come up with something to reduce the pain but keep the threat of death . . .

I shook myself free of those thoughts for now. I would ruminate more on that later, once the party had left. I returned my focus to the investigating party as Alerio and the other two slowly managed to pull Noracin and Ceria out of the trap and find the path around to the other side. Once there, the party paused to gather themselves and heal up. They even stayed to perform a few stretches while discussing the trap and making notes on how the Floor had changed.

They were clearly intent on taking their time, but for once I didn't mind; the trap had worked exactly as I'd hoped. It had drained some of their resources, mostly the Cleric's mana, though even after being healed both he and the Fighter looked a bit sluggish. In addition it had made them aware of my traps and taught them a bit of what to look out for.

Though if Alerio thought that he could sense the traps now that he'd found one, he would be in for a nasty surprise later on.

After a fifteen-minute break to recover, the party once more started moving. If this were a Challenge, that long of a break would have been upsetting to me, though exactly *why* I felt that way I wasn't sure, especially since I felt fine with it during an investigation.

This time Alerio and Ceria were at the front, and there was a regular pulsing of mana coming from the Mage as he used [Detect Magic] repeatedly to try to spot my traps. It was a big drain on his mana pool, which further slowed down the advance as the party had to stop to recover after a minute or so.

They were really being thorough in their investigation. Slow and steady.

Making notes of every little thing, and even potential things, they found. They seemed like proper inspectors instead of Challengers.

Maybe that was why I was fine with this being slow and methodical, regardless of the fact that it was a bit boring? Since this was an inspection, and they were acting as inspectors, they were behaving as they should. . . . Huh. That was actually nice to realize.

It was still boring, though.

The inspection continued with the party slowly moving through the trap-free tunnel until they eventually came across the first side chamber, which made me perk up. This was where the medallion from Morrígan's clan would be found atop a small altar, and the first new connection to the overall story. It was also the first time the party would encounter any enemies, and I was eager to see how my Bats and Mantas did now that I'd increased their level and put them together. The party slowly inched their way into the cavern.

"Bats above!" Ceria shouted.

"There is something in the water as well!" Alerio called.

"Ceria! Pull the Bats back into the tunnel. Let's fight the packs one at a time," Noracin said.

Or you could do that, of course.

I wasn't even that mad. This was totally my fault. I shouldn't have placed the water around the corner from the tunnel. Something to fix after they left.

The fight itself wasn't that interesting, though it was informative. The Bats did more damage and were sturdier than they had been in the past, but there were also fewer of them to fight at once, since I'd broken them up into five packs instead of three. The fight still seemed tougher than the first one thanks to the vastly increased levels of my creatures, but it didn't seem to be that much of a Challenge for the party in the end. Which was fair, since they had outsmarted my intended encounter by using the ingenious tactic of moving back three steps. Once that was fixed and the Mantas could join the fight, I imagined the difficulty would actually be rather balanced.

As the last Bat dissipated into motes of energy I felt Mana surge toward the Ranger, then her level went up from 6 to 7.

"Yes!" she exclaimed with a smile, exuberant for the first time since she'd entered the Dungeon. There was a brief moment of celebration from the rest of the party, then they moved on to discussing how to handle the Mantas, or as they called them "the things in the water." In the end, since they didn't have any reliable way of containing or hurting the Mantas apart from Alerio's costly dancing flames thing he'd used in the Guardian fight, they had the fighter stand above the pool with her shield to cover while Noracin and Alerio hastily searched through the chamber.

They found the talisman. I leaned in, metaphysically speaking. How would they react?

CHAPTER TWENTY-THREE

The Alternate Path

What's that thing?" Ceria said once they were back in the tunnel again.

"I'm not sure," Alerio said, holding up the medallion for the party to examine. "Some kind of loot? Though it might not be since it isn't recognized as an item by the system." He paused. "Maybe it's more of a decoration or aesthetic piece?"

Uh-oh. Would they not get that it was a story connection at all? I could understand it was hard to make any accurate connection with only one data point, but surely they could intuit *something* was special about it, going off where they found it if nothing else?

"It's got a cool symbol on it. Maybe that's important?" Athilana said.

Yeah, go Athilana! I thought.

Alerio squinted at it. "It definitely looks like it was designed on purpose, though I don't recognize it from anywhere. But considering it was made by the Dungeon, it isn't that much of a surprise that it doesn't look like anything familiar."

"That's a good point; how would the Dungeon have learned symbols from beyond its borders when it's so young?" Noracin said. "Especially since this isn't a system item."

"Maybe it's the symbol of the Dungeon itself?" the Ranger, Aira, suggested. "Like a signature or something?"

"Could be . . ." Alerio said hesitantly. "But then why put it here, hidden away in a random cave? No, something tells me there's something else going on here."

"Maybe it's a clue to a future puzzle?" Ceria suggested.

"That . . . Yeah that might be it . . . Good thought, Ceria. A puzzle, or a secret like a hidden door or something. Considering how much the Floor has changed, I wouldn't put it past the Dungeon to have put in something like that," Alerio said thoughtfully. He put the medallion in his pocket, then let out a short laugh. "I'm a bit embarrassed I didn't think of that myself, actually."

"Let's keep an eye out for other places in here with the same symbol. It could be the key to some extra loot or a future Quest," Noracin said.

The rest of the party nodded, then headed back out into the main tunnel of the alternate path. They quickly made it to the second cavern, where I'd carved a gargoyle with vampire fangs on the cavern wall. There wasn't an obvious connection to the medallion, but I hoped they would connect them once they found the rest of the pieces from the main path. And just like the medallion, the carving also led to a rather spirited discussion from the party.

"It's clearly more significant than a simple piece of decoration," Athilana said. "Otherwise why put it here, alone in an empty cave?"

"I'm not disagreeing with you," Alerio said. "I'm just saying we can't know for sure how, and more importantly *when*, it will be relevant. It could be a hint of a future boss. It could be a clue to a riddle. And, though chances are low, it could just be a cool carving made to be interesting, but one the Dungeon hasn't found a purpose for yet."

Noracin clapped his hands together to signal for silence. "Let's leave the speculation until we're done with the investigation. We have a job to do, and we don't have all day."

I was a little bit frustrated that they weren't going to theorize and discuss properly. I hoped they didn't plan to wait until they were *outside*, where I couldn't hear them. That would be *so* annoying. But it wasn't as if I didn't see Noracin's point. Even though this wasn't an official Challenge, there *were* still monsters and traps around. And if I'd been feeling angry, I could have sent some in to attack whenever I wanted.

A Dungeon simply wasn't the best place to sit down and have a discussion about the narrative implications of interesting talismans.

I might want to look into that in the future. Make a safe room or something, so I could at least listen in on *some* of the discussions that would happen regarding my stories.

More things I would need to redo once they left . . . At least I wouldn't run out of things to do anytime soon, even if I didn't have a new Floor to work on.

The party continued through the tunnel without issue, and soon reached the sixth trap. This was the final section of the alternate path: a very narrow tunnel you could only pass through one at a time. And the trap wasn't a simple pitfall this time. No, this time it was a complicated deadfall. Noracin crept forward in the front, hunched over and moving carefully, with Alerio and Ceria following behind. Something about this place seemed to have put them on edge, because the Mage was constantly flaring his [Detect Magic]. It wouldn't do them any good. This was a totally mundane trap, triggered by nothing more than a tripwire.

I had Morrígan's advice to thank for that. Noracin walked slowly, feeling the ground with his foot before putting his full weight on it with each step. It was an admirable effort, and understandable considering his earlier fall, but it wouldn't help him here. The tripwire wasn't by his feet.

Above the tunnel, hidden in a small side passage only reachable from Stalker's cave by a Bat, a singular winged creature hung from the ceiling. Normally it would be a part of the final fight together with my Guardian, but until then it had the important job of manually triggering this trap.

Unlike my skeletons, which could learn simple commands after an admittedly annoying and lengthy process, the Bats weren't smart enough to learn anything even that uncomplicated. But they did know how to attack something. And they listened to Stalker, who *was* smart enough to plan and strategize.

Now, I sent, and Stalker let out a shrill and musical shriek that echoed through the first Floor. It passed over the party like a wave. They all flinched and froze where they stood. Just as planned.

"What was that?!" Aira asked, holding her bow tight to her chest.

"The Guardian, I think . . ." Noracin said, peering ahead into the darkness of the tunnel with a frown.

"The one we can talk to, you mean? It makes a sound like that?" Athilana asked. A sudden loud *snap* followed by the clattering of stone against stone made them all look up. Above them the trap had activated perfectly, sending a larger rock rolling down a hidden slope into a similar sheet of thin stone that had been used for the pitfall. Only this sheet was high up on the wall of the tunnel instead of on the ground. Beyond the range of Alerio's [Detect Magic]. It shattered upon impact, sending the rock as well as dozens of shards of stone shrapnel tumbling down toward the party. For a frozen moment the cacophony of stone hitting stone was all that could be heard, before Noracin started yelling.

"GET AWAY!" he screamed. At nearly the same instant the rest of the party had the same idea, because they too turned and started shuffling back as fast as they possibly could in the cramped tunnel. Watching from everywhere, I could see they wouldn't make it. Athilana and Aira, who were the farthest back, might be safe, but there was no way the rest of them could escape in time to avoid at least some of the small stone shards. The only question was if they could manage to avoid the larger rock or not. That was the lethal part of this trap. The stone shards were dangerous and would deal damage, but they were light enough that you could shield yourself from getting crushed. The rock, not so much. It was rounded, but *heavy*, larger than a man's head. Having that fall on you from eight meters up was not going to feel nice, even if it didn't end up crushing you.

The rock bounced as it fell, making its trajectory and final impact point unpredictable. Aira and Athilana got through just as the first shards started to rain down atop the remaining three. Ceria held her shield up to cover Alerio as best she could while they both dashed through the tunnel as fast as their feet could carry them in this cramped space. Noracin looked up just as the rock had a bad bounce right toward him, which was the luckiest thing that could have happened to him. He threw himself forward, diving down with a scream as the shards rained down atop him relentlessly. But he managed to avoid the rock, which hit the stone floor with a thundering *crash*. Then the cave fell completely silent.

"Noracin!" Ceria yelled, and started rushing back through the rubble. The Cleric stirred and groaned. His health had dropped below 50, but he was alive and conscious, if extremely disoriented.

He managed to groan in response to Ceria's exclamation, but wasn't able to form any coherent words. He tried to push himself up but his arms wouldn't obey him, or they weren't strong enough, because he simply fell back down onto the tunnel floor. After the second try he gave up, and simply rolled over to lie on his back instead. Ceria arrived and bent down to check on the man, with Alerio following after, a health potion already pulled out of his satchel. Ceria took the bottle from the Mage and uncorked it, then poured the potion into Noracin's mouth. He spluttered, but managed to swallow enough to recover to 150 health. He let out a relieved sigh as dozens of cuts all across his body stitched themselves shut, before shaking his head as alertness returned.

"Thanks." He coughed and tried to sit.

"Don't move or speak yet," Ceria said, pushing the man back down. "You've lost a lot of health, and you need to give it a minute."

Noracin nodded weakly, then shut his eyes and focused on his breathing while casting the occasional [Healing Touch] on himself. Ceria rose and turned to the rest of the party. Now her eyes were decidedly less kind.

"What in damnation just happened?" She glared at Alerio. "I thought you said you could detect these traps."

"I never said I could detect them all perfectly," Alerio said defensively, putting up his hands. He frowned. "And I'm not sure this one was magical at all. Or if it was, the Dungeon has found a way to completely hide all traces of it from [Detect Magic]. I didn't feel *anything*."

He looked up at the ceiling, then a light flashed in his eyes as he realized what had happened. He groaned.

"What?" Ceria asked.

"It's too high up." Alerio said. "Even *if* the trap is magical, which for the record it might not be, I can't sense something that high up on the wall."

He pointed to the cavern wall, where a faint hole could now be seen some eight meters above the ground.

"[Detect Magic] is primarily a short-range skill. It's best at detecting things within five meters of you, at least while you're Tier one. It *can* work at a longer range depending on the strength of the magic you're detecting, and your own level of course, but something designed to be subtle like a trap . . ." Alerio shrugged. "It just isn't strong enough to detect it that far away."

Ceria swore. "Something you could have mentioned a bit earlier."

Alerio frowned angrily. "I *have* mentioned it. Several times. Remember the Quest a few months ago when Emmalia wanted me to find the trail of the missing Mages? I told you all how the skill worked then."

Noracin coughed, which caused them all to turn to face him as he tried to sit up.

"No fighting," he said firmly. "It's a trap in a Dungeon. We triggered it. It happens. We're all alive. Focus on that."

"Yes, boss," Ceria said curtly. Alerio still seemed upset, but he nodded just the same.

"Is anyone else hurt, apart from me?" Noracin asked. He looked between Ceria and Alerio.

"Ceria should have lost a bit of health. I'm all right though, her shield covered me."

"It's not that bad," Ceria said. "I only lost about fifty health from a few glancing blows before we made it out. It can wait until you're feeling better."

Noracin nodded. "All right, then let's take a break. We need to talk about how to avoid this sort of thing happening again."

The break was longer this time than it had been after the first trap, even though Noracin was the only one who had been injured. It seemed that quickly taking damage and being healed over and over again took some sort of toll on the body beyond what the system mentioned. Something about the body needing time to adapt to its own state, or remembering damage that wasn't there anymore, according to my instincts. It seemed strange to me, but then again I didn't *have* the health attribute, so how was I supposed to know what it felt like? The discussion and planning was a bit different this time, with Noracin taking a lesser role due to his injury and Alerio and Ceria leading the conversation. Eventually they managed to come to the conclusion that both magical and non-magical trap detection was necessary at all times. They also correctly concluded that this trap wasn't triggered by them, but rather by Stalker's scream, and surmised that they should tell people to make a hasty retreat whenever a similar thing happened in the future. I made a note of that as well, so that I could come up with an alternative triggering signal for future activations. I also realized I had a fake trap trigger I could use for this Floor, though I wasn't entirely sure how to best utilize it yet.

After about forty minutes the party continued on with the investigation. Unfortunately their newfound alertness meant they found and managed to avoid the seventh trap, and they were able to handle the final pack of Bats at the chamber where the two paths met, even with Noracin still sluggish and relegated to healing duty. They still didn't have any means of reliably dealing with the Mantas, so they just fought the Bats in as good a cover as they could get, and then quickly hurried on through the cave to take as little damage as possible. It wasn't an ideal strategy, for me nor them, as they took more damage than they would have liked and it made the encounter easier than I wanted it to be.

I would have to do some serious thinking on the Mantas. Without a way to force the Challengers to remain in the same room as the pool of water, there seemed to be a fatal weakness to the creatures in that people could just leave their line of sight really easily. Maybe I could do some custom creature tinkering once the party left, try to make the Mantas able to leave the water for a bit . . . Something to consider at least.

After the party fled from the path-joining chamber, they quickly arrived at the entrance to the final one. Stalker stood in the center, her red eyes glaring a question at the investigators. But the party didn't enter. Instead, they decided to wait and tackle the final chamber at the end, once they had finished the investigation of the rest of the Floor. Which was good, because I wanted to see what questions they'd have at the end, once they had found all my narrative connections.

CHAPTER TWENTY-FOUR

The Main Path

Once the party was back at the first intersection, they took a short break to reorganize themselves before they started down the main path. Just a minute to check over their equipment and discuss the group order, then they were off. The tunnel sections looked similar to the alternate path they'd just explored, the main difference being the caves. There were still technically two caverns, though the second cavern on the main path was a much larger cave. I'd made it by carving out and combining what had once been two separate smaller caves to make a space big enough to accommodate at least one proper battle before the Guardian fight. And where the smaller caverns each had a pool of water in the corner for my Mantas, the large one had a huge moat encircling the whole cavern, which also had a trap that the Bats would trigger once the water was crossed. This would be the final test of my encounter setup with the Mantas. If this one didn't work, I might have to ditch the underwater creatures entirely in favor of something Challengers could actually fight.

That conundrum was for later though. The party still had the smaller cavern to deal with before reaching the larger cave, as well as two traps in the tunnels leading up to it, the first coming almost right after the turn.

This early trap was decidedly less deadly than the deadfall. A pressure plate magically disguised as tunnel floor would trigger two effects: a magical [Darkness], as well as a series of [Water Bolts] from the tunnel walls. Not enough to be lethal, but they'd do damage and disorient any Challenger who triggered it.

At least that was how it was supposed to work. With the party's increased vigilance, Alerio was able to find the trap well before they were at risk of stepping on it, letting them all bypass the obstacle with ease. I had mixed feelings about that. Looking at it one way, that was exactly how I wanted the traps to function: trigger one or two, then learn from that and avoid the future ones. Still there was a part of me that wished they'd triggered it, so at least I would know how well it worked. Now I wouldn't know how good the design was until the next Challengers arrived. If the trap was even active then. And if they didn't find it as well.

Maybe I could *ask* them to trigger it on purpose. After all, they were conducting an investigation here. It would only be proper to investigate the effects of the trap as well as the location and trigger. Would they accept that?

Probably not, right?

After passing over the trap trigger, they arrived at the branching tunnel leading to the first cavern, and just like last time they stopped for a brief discussion before deciding to head down the side path first. Actually, calling it a side path would be an exaggeration, since all it was was a short tunnel that quickly opened up into a five-square-meter cavern. The cavern itself was empty of enemies, and the only objects within were a Skeleton and a piece of parchment. That alone proved to be enough incentive—they instantly became curious and inquisitive about what the piece of parchment could mean. The placement right in front of the entrance made them a bit wary as well, so Ceria walked in the front with her shield high the last few steps up to the entrance.

"Wait," Alerio called, and the Fighter paused.

Darn, he found it.

"Another trap," Alerio said. He looked around the tunnel with a squint, then bent down to examine the floor by the entrance to the cavern.

"Hmm," he said after a moment. "It's not tied to a physical trigger like the pressure plate or even the false stone sheets . . . It feels more like a line of flowing mana here." He waved a hand above the ground, then turned back to the rest of the party.

"I think crossing it triggers the trap." He paused. "But . . . It has to be something *with mana* that triggers it, so we can't just throw a rock at it to set it off from a safe distance."

"What's the trap do?" Ceria asked.

Alerio tilted his head to the side. "No clue. I can feel that there is mana here, and that it seems to be flowing up and around the . . . doorway, I suppose I should call it. But as for what happens when you trigger it . . ." He shrugged. "We'd have to activate it to see."

"Lovely," Ceria said with a frown.

"Do we turn back?" Athilana asked.

What? No, don't turn back now! Athilana, I thought you were on my side!

"Without finding out what's written on the parchment over there?" Alerio said, pointing. "No way. I won't be able to sleep tonight if we do that. With how it's positioned it's bound to be important to a Challenger. Or at least the Dungeon thinks it's important."

Exactly. Good thinking, Alerio.

"Or it's bait for the trap," Ceria said. "Like you said, it's obviously placed right there so we'd see it. Maybe it's there to lure us into the cavern."

"That is certainly a possibility," Alerio conceded. He frowned. "But we're still doing an investigation here, and just leaving the room unexplored doesn't feel right."

"Walking right into a known trap doesn't exactly feel right either," Ceria said.

"That's fair." Alerio nodded.

"Let's take a minute to think. If we can't come up with something, we'll continue with the rest of the investigation, and maybe tackle this room last," Noracin said.

Crap. That was actually a reasonable conclusion to come to. What they were saying was true, though only partially. The placement *was* made to draw the party into the room, but not specifically to trigger the trap, since I only added it as a way to prepare Challengers for the cavern up ahead. The trap wasn't even dangerous this time. All it would do was trigger a stone door to shut behind the party, making them have to spend some time investigating the cavern to find the button to open it back up again. And hopefully find the second piece of narrative that was better hidden in the process.

I felt miffed. A minute ago I'd been not just a little bit pleased at myself for how my traps had worked exactly as I'd planned in how it changed the party's behavior. But now that very change had made it so my carefully placed narrative connections might be missed because they were being *too respectful* of my traps. I was frowning internally in annoyance and trying to think of what I could possibly do to make them wary but not too scared to progress when Aira spoke for the first time in a while.

"Excuse me," she said. The party turned to face her. She hesitated for a moment, but pressed on. "I'm sorry if this is a stupid idea, but couldn't we jump over the trigger and enter the room that way?"

Oh.

The rest of the party had a similar reaction, staring with blank eyes toward Aira then turning to stare at the open entryway. After a moment all eyes turned to Alerio, who blinked, then frowned, then planted a palm on his forehead.

"Yeah, we can jump over the trap," he said, though he didn't sound happy about it. Ceria burst out laughing and was joined by Athilana and Aira a few seconds later. Even Noracin's lips twitched in amusement. Alerio's face was one of embarrassment and . . . indignation? That was a bit strange, though it did make me feel a kind of kinship with the Mage.

The party decided that only one of them should jump over the trap, to reduce the risk of someone triggering it accidentally. They also decided to only go in, get the parchment, and get out, just in case something unexpected happened upon picking up the object. It was a bit annoying that they would miss the second piece of narrative, especially since nothing would happen, but they had no way of knowing that. After a bit more discussion they decided that the one to do so should be Aira, which made sense since she had the highest agility of the group and wasn't currently hampered by unwieldy armor. Two quick jumps and a grab later, the Ranger was back in the tunnel, parchment in hand. She handed it over to Noracin, who looked it over with a frown.

"What's it say?" Alerio asked. "Don't keep us in suspense."

Noracin cleared his throat. "'Magus Krazad,'" he began. "'I hope this letter finds you well, though I wish I was writing for better reasons. Things here are escalating, and I would ask you to petition Archmage Karun to send aid as soon as possible. Discretion is of course still vital, hence why this letter is sent to you personally and not in an official missive to the Tower. If the situation deteriorates much further, the general fears a more open request will be required. You can see how that could turn into an issue, and can understand why this request is of such great importance. I look forward to a positive response. M.'"

There was a brief moment of silence after Noracin stopped reading as the party processed what he'd said.

Alerio was the first one to eventually speak. "Well, I wasn't expecting *that*," he said.

"What's that even supposed to mean?" Ceria asked. "Like why was that there? A letter to a Mage Tower? What does that have to do with a cave Floor?"

"Clearly the Dungeon wanted us to learn this information," Noracin said. He thought for a moment. "It's either related to some future Floors or . . ." He paused. "Honestly I don't know."

"Are any of the names familiar to any of you?" Athilana asked. "Could this be a copy of a real letter?"

Alerio shook his head. "I don't know any of the names," he said. "There are a few Mage Towers around, though most have more specific names than just 'the Tower.' And I haven't heard of any Archmage Karun."

"I don't get how the Dungeon could have a letter from outside," Ceria said with a frown. "Isn't it just as we said with the medallion, that it's too young to have had enough outside interaction to know this stuff?"

"Normally I would agree," Alerio said. "But this is different from the medallion. More specifically tied to the outside world. I can see the Dungeon designing a medallion like that for a puzzle or something . . . But what puzzle would require this kind of letter? None I've ever heard of before." He shook his head and pointed to the parchment. "This makes it much more likely that *both* it and the medallion are from outside, in my opinion."

"Then where could he have gotten them? And why is he displaying them like this?" Athilana asked.

Alerio shrugged. "No idea. We'll have to ask him. Though I have no clue if he'd answer or not."

"Good suggestion," Noracin said. He put the piece of parchment away. "I think it's clear that we won't be able to figure this out by ourselves. So let us continue our investigation and ask the Guardian once we get there. And ask the Hallmaster when we return."

With that decided the party turned and walked back to the main tunnel. I felt it was a bit of an anticlimactic ending to the discussion, but at least now they weren't simply dismissing it as decoration or clues to random puzzles. Now they were at least considering the possibility that something more was going on, which was progress. Though they were coming to ask me questions, so I'd have to think of good answers that stuck to the story and didn't make it sound like something I'd just made up. I'd have to play the role of discoverer, rather than author. I frowned. This could require some thought . . . I glanced back at the party.

They were still deep in discussion about the parchment while they walked, though they were keeping their guard up. This made their progress even slower than normal. They were walking through a deactivated section of the tunnel one step at a time, and stopping occasionally to let Alerio recover his mana. Looking ahead, I saw the large cavern with its manually activated trap and full squadron of enemies.

That'll give me some time to think.

CHAPTER TWENTY-FIVE

The Mantas' Cavern

Noracin walked at the back of the party. He didn't like being relegated to supportive duty, but his body still felt stiff and unwieldy from his repeated healing, so it couldn't be helped. He could walk fine, but he would still not be able to contribute much in any kind of tricky fight. Luckily they hadn't encountered many of those in this delve, as the Dungeon seemed more focused on traps than creatures on this Floor. Either that or it had grouped them all together somewhere, which was another ominous possibility that he hoped wasn't the case. The Floor was also much larger than most first Floors typically were, which could also explain the sparse encounters. Whatever the reason, he was glad for it, as it gave his body more time to adjust. Every minute that passed he felt a bit better, and soon he thought he would be able to help if a fight actually occurred. The tunnel was widening out and he could see what looked to be a large cave up ahead, so a fight seemed increasingly likely.

"Watch out in front," he said. "There's probably something dangerous up ahead."

Alerio and Ceria, who were at the front of the group, both turned around and gave him a look that all but screamed "no shit." Ceria even somehow seemed to call him a moron at the same time. All without speaking a single word.

"I'm just saying . . ." he muttered.

Seconds later Alerio held up a hand for them to stop a few steps before the mouth of the tunnel. They all did so, looking between Alerio and the cavern beyond.

"It's the same trap as last time." He frowned, then looked up at the ceiling of the tunnel, then down to the floor. "Actually, wait a moment. The mana flows through the floor and the ceiling. At no point does it flow horizontally through the tunnel."

"Then we won't trigger it by walking?" Ceria asked.

Alerio shook his head. "No. At least I don't think so. Unless the Dungeon has found some way to hide some mana or make it react in a different location than where it actually is." He paused. "I wouldn't put it past Dungeon magic to make something like that happen. But it would be surprising if it happened on such a low-leveled Floor."

"This Dungeon's been nothing but surprise after surprise since you found it," Athilana said.

"The girl's got a point," Ceria said. "We should be expecting the unexpected here."

"It definitely makes it more likely. But it does beg the question, why did the Dungeon make the trap avoidable over there, but not here?"

"Maybe it wanted us to find the letter, and didn't want to scare us off by presenting an unavoidable trap?" Athilana suggested.

Noracin cocked his head thoughtfully. "That would mean that the letter's *quite* important," he said. "But I guess it's an explanation that would make sense."

"It sure sounded important when you read it," Ceria said.

"The letter is obviously going to be important somewhere in the Dungeon," Alerio said. "But it would also imply that whatever is in this cave *isn't* that important, and the Dungeon wouldn't care if he scared us off. Remember we got to the Guardian through the other path as well, so none of this is obligatory to clear the Floor."

Noracin frowned. "That doesn't seem very Dungeon-like, does it? Making a large cave and not caring if people Challenge it seems strange."

Alerio nodded. "Exactly. Though I suppose he could be banking on the Challenge being motivation enough for most parties. After all, undertaking nonobligatory danger is kind of the whole point of a Challenge in the first place. Facing adversity in order to grow, and all that."

That was a fair point as well, though Noracin still felt the normal thing was to encourage that risk-taking, rather than try to discourage it by offering an easier alternative with the same ability to clear the Floor. Regardless, it wasn't that important for right now; this was an investigation, and while they might get away with not deliberately walking into a trap that could be avoided, they were less likely to get away with skipping an entire *room*. In fact the likelihood of them getting out of this scot-free was zero, and he knew it. They had to go into that cave. He said as much, and after a moment of grumbling he could see them all realize he was right. Then came the discussion of who was going to trigger the trap. Or possibly not trigger it, as there was still the possibility that those mana flows weren't a trap at all. He paused, then turned to Alerio.

"I have a thought," he said. "What if these mana flows are just here to scare people who can detect them, and they don't actually do anything?"

Alerio frowned in confusion. "What do you mean? The Dungeon put them there just to be intimidating? Just in case a Mage walked by and *happened* to use [Detect Magic] and also *happened* to be extremely wary of traps?"

"It might not be that farfetched," Noracin said.

"Most Mages don't get [Detect Magic] as one of their innate Class skills," Alerio said. "In fact it's quite rare. And since this is a level-one Floor most won't use their unlocked skill slots on it while they're Tier one. It would barely be relevant."

"Would the Dungeon know that, though? Aren't *you* the only Mage its seen? And you do have it."

Alerio blinked, then groaned.

"Now, I'm not saying it's definitely what's happened," Noracin said quickly. "But it would explain some things. The mana flowing where people don't actually walk. The placement being right after the side room that had an almost identical trap you *could* trigger. The Floor as a whole being very magic-trap dense, encouraging the use of [Detect Magic] as a way of making traversal safe. And maybe some other reasons as well that I can't think of right now."

"I get it, I get it. What you're saying makes sense." Alerio shook his head. "What can we even do differently if it's true? We can't just rush into the cave like headless chickens without being sure first."

Noracin opened his mouth, then closed it again. "Yeah, you're right, of course." He frowned. "That leaves us with having one person take the risk while the rest stay back." He shook his head with a sigh. "All right, so who's going to take the risk? I would volunteer since I can always heal myself, but right now I don't think that's the smartest idea."

"Of course you can't go," Ceria said. "It's got to be me or Alerio. Which means it's got to be me. We can't have the newbies trigger it, and Alerio's got less health and durability than I do."

Alerio sighed. "I wish I could argue, but you're right on all fronts."

Noracin nodded after a moment, then Ceria took a deep breath and took the final few steps to the mouth of the tunnel. Noracin noticed for the first time that there was a sort of moat at the opening. It wasn't that wide, just a meter and a half or so, but it was a clear indication of where the tunnel ended and the cavern began. With a shout and a leap, Ceria leapt over the water into the cave . . .

No trap. No sound.

They waited a few seconds. Still no trap. Noracin breathed a sigh of relief.

"Looks like we're saf—"

There was a screech of a Bat from the ceiling of the cavern beyond Ceria, followed by a thunderous *crack*, which soon turned into a consistent grinding of stone against stone. Noracin saw a stone slab descending across the mouth of the tunnel at the same time as the singular screech turned into an orchestra. A cacophony.

"Oh you just had to say something!" Alerio yelled.

"No time! Run! Don't let Ceria get trapped with them alone!" Noracin yelled and sprinted toward the shrinking opening.

Half a second of stunned incomprehension and panic, then everyone sprang into action. Aira and Athilana overtook Noracin after a few steps, but they were still several steps behind Alerio, who leaped through the opening barely a second after Noracin had stopped speaking. Athilana joined them a few heartbeats later. By now the descending stone slab was covering the top third of the opening, and when Aira reached the mouth she had to duck down to be able to make it across the water. The stone creaked and crumbled. The slab seemed to be speeding up. Noracin swore and forced his unresponsive body to move faster.

Faster.

He screamed and threw himself forward, diving head first through the opening and across the water just under the descending slab. He hit the ground hard, tumbling and bouncing across the stone floor until he was stopped by Ceria.

"Whoa there boss, be careful," she said. Noracin smiled despite the pain. He'd made it through.

The sound of flapping wings and disharmonious screeches drew his mind back to the present. He shook his head to clear it and pushed himself up, then surveyed the battlefield. The Bats were upon them, diving in and out and being all-around annoying, but they'd dealt with their kind before, and he was confident they could win even without him at his best. He tapped Ceria on the back, activating a [Healing Touch], then pulled out his mace. His arm felt stiff and it was tricky to move with any accuracy, but with this many bats around, getting a hit was more a matter of how often you swung than technique. Even Aira had abandoned her bow and was swinging a short blade wildly, despite her lack of skills that suited the blade.

A Bat dove past Noracin's defenses, and he felt a sharp pain in his neck as it bit down. He grabbed hold and yanked the Bat free, then stomped it dead under his boot with a *crunch*. That had hurt much more than he'd expected.

"These are higher level. Watch OUT!" he yelled out while activating a quick [Healing Touch] on himself.

That was when the first volley of [Water Bolts] came flying at them. From the left, from the right, even from right behind them. *The moat*, he realized. It was allowing the underwater creatures to hit them from every angle at the same time. He hissed as a bolt struck him in the side. A second later Aira yelped as one hit her thigh. Ceria was trying her best to shield them, but with the Bats keeping her occupied and the creatures being underwater and thus immune to her [Taunt], there was little she could do.

Noracin swung his mace wildly, but the hits were coming less and less frequently. Having to keep a constant watch for [Water Bolts] and activate a heal every few seconds, he was beginning to feel overwhelmed and it was affecting his aim. And his mana would also be drained quickly if they didn't find some answer soon.

"Get DOWN!" Alerio yelled. Noracin recognized the tone in his voice and immediately dropped to lie on his stomach. As did Ceria. Aira and Athilana were slower to react, but only by a fraction of a second, and dropped to their stomachs right as waves of flame billowed from Alerio's hands toward the Bats. No, *through* the Bats. They screeched and tried to fly out of the way, but Alerio moved the flames to cover any attempt at escape. For a moment the cavern was nothing but screams of burning Bats, occasionally dying and dissipating into mana with a soft sound of rushing wind. Then half a dozen [Water Bolts] careened toward Alerio all at the same time. They struck true, their water drilling through armor and skin, but he held firm. A second volley followed soon after, causing Noracin to wince and Alerio to wobble where he stood. With a scream of fury, Alerio pushed the fires up to the ceiling of the cave, and the final Bat burst into flames. The flames winked out just as a third volley of bolts came flying from across the cavern, and he collapsed to his knees from exertion and pain. Ceria and Noracin acted instantly. The Fighter moved to cover the Mage with her body and shield, while Noracin activated [Healing Touch] after [Healing Touch], to try to restore the man's falling health. Aira and Athilana took position on Alerio's other side to shield him from the bolts from that direction. Alerio himself breathed rapid and shallow breaths, but he was still lucid, and his health was no longer dropping. He even managed to smile.

"Got them," he said softly.

Noracin sagged in relief. "That you did," he said. "Leave the rest to us."

"I'll do just that. Go get 'em," Alerio said.

Noracin and the rest stood, surrounding the downed Mage to shield him from incoming fire . . . Or water, rather. Ceria with her shield. Noracin with his mace, if he could. Athilana and Aira with their own magic. Noracin wasn't always able to hit the ones coming his way, forcing him to tank the hits with his body instead, so it was neither pretty nor efficient, but for the moment they were able to block all the incoming attacks. But they all knew they wouldn't be able to do this for long.

"All right boss, any ideas of how to 'get 'em'?" Athilana asked, firing a [Water Bolt] of her own. "I'm down to less than half mana already. I won't be able to keep this up for much longer."

"They likely won't have the mana for a continuous barrage either. But even if they stop we need to find a way to strike back," Noracin said. "Aira, you're a Ranger—you think you can snipe them when they go for a shot?"

"The time they're above the surface to fire is just too short," Aira said. "If I knew where it was going to pop up so I could have a [Focused Shot] prepared, I could maybe land a hit. But even then I wouldn't bet on it. And hitting them below the water . . . I might be able to do it, but the water would diffuse so much of the force it would hardly deal any damage."

"I could try to [Taunt] one when it comes near the surface. That might make it hang around long enough for you guys to hit it," Ceria said.

"That sounds like a good idea," Noracin said.

"It will leave you all exposed to all the other attacks, though," Ceria said. She twisted her shield to the left to catch an incoming [Water Bolt].

"I still think it's our best option," Noracin said after a moment. "Let's try it. Alerio, can you roll over to the edge of the water?"

Alerio nodded, and the party slowly moved around him as he rolled. Ceria rotated to stand by the edge and looked down.

"How deep do you think it is?" she asked. "Because I'd get a better lock on it if I was in the water with it and it could actually reach me."

Athilana bent down to the edge with a frown. "It's too dark for me to see clearly, but I would guess about two meters or so, give or take a few centimeters?"

"That's doable," Ceria said. She frowned and turned to look down at Alerio.

"You do what you think is best. I'll cover him," Noracin said. Ceria nodded and handed Noracin her shield. Noracin accepted it, then turned to Alerio. "Could you make yourself as small a target as possible?"

Once Alerio had curled himself into a ball, Ceria took a deep breath, then dropped down into the moat. Noracin stood protectively over Alerio, covering him from the right and the back, while Aira and Athilana covered the left and stood ready to strike.

It didn't take long for the nearest creature to notice Ceria's presence and swim over. Noracin could see a dark outline moving beneath the surface.

"Now!" Ceria called out, activating her [Taunt]. As a nonphysical skill, it was the only one they had that could actually pierce through the water relatively easily. It was still short range, and required both Ceria and the creature to be able to both see and reach each other, but once those requirements were met the results were obvious. The creature beelined toward Ceria, ramming into her legs head first. The Fighter reached down, then grabbed hold and *heaved* the thing out of the water and onto dry land. The creature was flat, with two large fins and a sharp tail, and Noracin saw it as the missing link between a Bat and a Leatherwing. This thing, however, was not as suited for life above the water, and flapped around wildly as it landed on the stone floor. Aira and Athilana didn't waste any time and fired off their skills in rapid succession. Ceria even lent a hand, literally, as she slammed her fist against the creature's face. It didn't take long before the thing disappeared into motes of mana.

"Yeah, take that you annoying underwater piece of shit!" Ceria exclaimed, raising her fist into the air.

"Hold off on the celebrations. We still have many more creatures to deal with before this fight is done," Noracin said, blocking a [Water Bolt] from hitting the Fighter in the face.

"I know. But now at least we know how to handle the bastards."

That they did. Noracin couldn't help but smile at Ceria's infectious enthusiasm. That they did.

CHAPTER TWENTY-SIX

The End of the Investigation

It took the party a long time, and drained much mental and physical stamina, but now that they had figured out a way to deal with my Mantas they finally managed to wrangle the last one out of the water and hit it until it turned to smoke. If most of them weren't already lying on the ground, I'd say they looked like they were about to collapse. I felt a profound sense of satisfaction at the results. This had been a proper fight. Difficult, perhaps frustrating even, but not insurmountable. Though depending on how skilled this group was compared to the norm it still might need to be tuned down slightly for my next Challengers. Only slightly, though—this room still had an extra reward for clearing it. Perhaps I could add a separate option to open the doors for those who found dealing with the Mantas difficult. Like a puzzle they'd have to solve or a series of buttons to hit in the right order while avoiding the attacks from beneath the surface, instead of having to defeat them all.

Actually, that was a *brilliant* idea, and one I was a bit ashamed I hadn't thought of earlier. Puzzles. The whole Floor was missing freaking *puzzles!* I had traps galore, enemies to fight, and secrets to find. But not a single puzzle. This would have to be rectified the moment the investigators left. I could work it into the traps somehow, maybe create some triggers if the puzzles weren't solved properly. That way I could enable more traps at once, instead of leaving so many of them deactivated.

I thought about leaving some of the narrative connections locked behind puzzles as well but decided against it for now. I wanted as many people as possible to find those connections, and keeping them hidden seemed counterintuitive to that goal. Though I could perhaps create other secrets, like bonus rewards, to be hidden by a puzzle. Not on this Floor, though. This Floor had plenty of rewards already.

I wrenched my distracted mind back to the present. The investigatory party was in deep discussion about what to do, what it meant to have been given a rewards chest for this room, with extra attention paid to the contents of the chest. I gave it a quick glance.

Shadowleather Bracers	Tier 1 Armor (Rare)
Made from magical leather made to imitate that of the Leatherwing Guardian "Stalker," these bracers provide an excellent boost to both health and stealth.	
Health: +50	You can activate the skill [Meld] twice per day.

I frowned mentally. Why was this thing causing such a reaction? It was a pretty good item, I thought, at least compared to what was being offered through the normal rewards chests. The health it gave was comparatively high, and it even had a cool skill attached to it, though with some restrictions. It was cool and all, but I didn't think it was worth all this. Was it infighting, perhaps? An argument about who was going to get the loot? That could make some sense, though from what I was hearing that didn't seem to be the case.

"No, you don't get it," Alerio said agitatedly. "Additional rewards on a Floor are one thing. Common even. But a *rare* custom item that's *Tier one* . . ." He shook his head in disbelief. "It's unheard of."

"This Dungeon's been generous from the start. We got talent points for the first Quest, after all," Ceria said.

"That was a special case, though," Alerio said. "A Quest given only once, to the discoverers of the Dungeon. This thing will be accessible by *everyone*. In the future, everyone will try to get this. All parties. Every. Single. One. Who would want to pass up a rare item?"

"The Dungeon *is* generous," Noracin said, "but it's also quite deadly. I suppose it sort of makes sense to have greater rewards for a greater Challenge, but this early . . ." He sighed and shook his head. "A lot of people will die because of this."

Wait, what?

Alerio paused, then sighed as well. "I wouldn't have said it quite so bluntly, but yeah. Great rewards always draw in the greedy, even those who aren't able to meet the Challenge."

Noracin nodded. "Exactly." Everyone fell into silent contemplation.

I supposed what they said made some sense. I pondered for a moment. Deadly yet with great rewards . . . How did I feel about that? It seemed negative from the investigators' point of view—I could sort of tell they felt I was luring people to their deaths. But personally I didn't see it that way. I had a story to tell, and it was as deadly as it was supposed to be. And it was only fair to give rewards appropriate to the danger. If I didn't, it would discourage people from even Challenging in the first place.

And besides, it wasn't my responsibility to manage Challengers' greed. If they were too ambitious for their own good, that was their own fault.

Yeah, that felt right. I was *offering* a Challenge, not demanding one. It was an opportunity for Challengers to grow and to prove themselves. It was up to them to decide if they were willing to risk it. After all, they were responsible for their own stories, not me. I was just the setting. The stage on which their stories played out.

After a while the discussion of loot and mortality wound down to a more casual conversation while the party waited to recover, and for once I didn't even mind. They'd earned a bit of rest. Though at this point they had defeated the last encounter on the Floor apart from the Guardian, which they weren't going to attempt, so there was nothing for them to rest for. They didn't know that, though, and wanted to be safe rather than sorry.

Which meant they took the remainder of the Floor the same way they had up to this point. Slow, steady, making notes about what stuff I'd placed where, and discussing which parts were difficult and where they expected to find traps. It was actually quite an interesting discussion to listen to, and I even came away with some ideas for designs for future Floors, once my Quest was completed. Speaking of, I checked that quickly. I was curious if this bonus reward counted toward it or not.

Name a Guardian (1/1)
Defeat 10 Challengers (3/10)
Provide completion or Quest rewards (4/10)
Finalize five Floors (5/5)

> Create a custom Floor clear condition (1/1)
> Create a custom creature (1/1)

I guess not. That was a bit annoying, though I supposed the Quest *did* specifically say what kind of reward it was looking for, so I shouldn't be that surprised. Still, I was done with what I assumed to be the difficult parts, so now all I had to do was wait for an actual Challenge once this investigation was over. Then I could finally complete my level up and start gaining experience again. I'd be able to start on the sixth Floor, and the second story. I even had an idea of where to begin, though I wasn't sure I could pull it off yet. I'd have to wait and see. I hoped I wouldn't have to wait too long.

While I was pondering about the future the party had finally made their way to Stalker's chamber, and I readied myself for a conversation. In the end it was Alerio who strode to the front, standing tall and staring into the eyes of the creature that impaled him last time they'd met.

"Veos," Alerio intoned with gravitas. "We are not here for a Challenge this time, but instead seek answers. Would you do us the honor of answering our questions?"

A dramatic inspiration struck me, perhaps brought forth by the seriousness in Alerio's tone of voice, and I made Stalker sing a different response than I'd originally planned.

"You may ask two questions, for two secrets found."

Suitably dramatic, right? It would also force them to think hard about what they wanted to ask, which was good because there were some questions I wasn't sure I would be able to give them good answers to.

Alerio bowed. "Thank you." He took a deep breath and turned back to the group. They nodded, and he once more turned to face Stalker.

"Our first question . . . " He held up the letter to Krazad. "What is the purpose of this letter?"

Easy. I'd already thought ahead about how to answer this one.

"This missive is a relic of the past. A secret once held, dangerous for its time, yet lost to the ages before being uncovered by coincidence. Now it serves as a warning."

There, that should be cryptic enough, while still sounding important in a vague sort of way. I studied Alerio's expression as Stalker sang my words, watching him move through different iterations of confusion and befuddlement. He brought his expression back to neutrality, and even bowed to Stalker before speaking. It sure paid off to be dramatic!

"Thank you for the answer," he said. "Our second question is about the changes to the Floor. What was the purpose of making such drastic changes?"

I almost answered with the simple truth before catching myself. I hadn't prepared for this specific question. I needed the answer to be suitably theatrical to fit in with the mood of the conversation, while not giving away the actual truth that I was designing a narrative rather than revealing one. After a moment I sent my thoughts to Stalker, who sang them aloud.

"The first Floor is the gateway. It is a representation and a promise of what is to come. It must meet a certain standard."

Again it took Alerio a few seconds to process the answer before he spoke, with another bow. "Thank you for providing us with answers. We will return for a proper Challenge when we are able."

I wanted to respond with agreement and eagerness, but I stopped myself. I had to seem grand and mysterious, after all. Instead Stalker just flew up into the ceiling of her cavern, and the party slowly began their journey back outside. I listened in, curious as to what they thought of the whole experience, and especially the answers I'd given.

"That was certainly something, wasn't it," Athilana said after a moment. "I've never seen a talking Dungeon before. Are they all that . . . imposing? I don't know if it was just me, but something about that had a strange *weight* I hadn't been expecting."

"We haven't spoken to any Dungeons before either," Ceria said, then paused. "Apart from last time we were in here, but we didn't do much actual talking on our end then. And, yes, I felt that same weight just now."

"It could be the level difference," Alerio said. "You know how you can feel the aura of some high tiers just by being nearby? It could be something like that, though I'm not sure if it works the same with Dungeons as with us. We don't use the system in the same way." He paused to take a breath, then spoke in a more eager voice. "But never mind that, what do you think about the answers he gave?"

I leaned in. *All right. here we go.*

"Vague," Ceria said. "They weren't true answers. It's like they were designed to invite more questions."

That was fair. It *was* exactly what I was trying to do, though I had been hoping I'd been a bit more subtle. Eh, live and learn.

"True, they were vague," Alerio said. "But to say they weren't answers is taking it too far, I think. The one about the letter was especially interesting. A secret of the past uncovered? It hints at something from beyond the Dungeon's borders, does it not? Something it found while expanding, perhaps?"

"I don't know . . ." Noracin said. "I see what you're saying, Alerio, I do. But it could also just be a riddle or puzzle from the Dungeon itself."

"True, but it's way less interesting that way," Alerio said with a smile. Ceria chortled and shook her head.

I wanted to pump a fist in the air, which was a bit tricky since I didn't have any. This was almost *exactly* how I wanted them to think. Though there was definitely still some reticence in their reaction, it was still on the right track. And pretty far along the track too, if I was to be a bit hopeful.

As the party walked through the entrance and vanished from my perception, all I wanted at that moment was some way to learn of their continued discussion beyond my walls. What report would they give to their leaders, and what would those leaders think of my narrative? Since they wouldn't actually ever go inside and find it themselves, I had no way to know without finding some way to go outside.

I shook myself. No, I was a Dungeon. My place was here. There would be no walking about and galivanting with the world outside. I'd just have to find some other way of learning what I wanted.

Maybe next time someone came I'd be the one to ask *them* some questions. I smiled internally. Hopefully the Challenges would start again soon.

CHAPTER TWENTY-SEVEN

The First Week

Aran rolled over with a groan as the last remaining Manta finally dissipated into motes of mana. His stamina was so utterly drained he only barely registered the ping from the system about them receiving the bonus reward, instead choosing to just lie there and revel in the joy of not having to move for the moment. He'd read the report by the investigation team led by the Cleric, but he hadn't truly believed in his assessment of the level of danger until just now. After all, the investigation had managed to clear it with two freaking *level 6s* in the party. To be fair they'd had one more member than he did, so he supposed it maybe evened out. Maybe. Even still the way the dangers had been described for this first Floor had been too preposterous to believe, especially when compared to the initial report from the Hallmaster. Changes that large just didn't happen on Floors this low level, if ever.

Only it seemed they had, and it was thanks to Riya's favorable Lightning-element spells that they were even able to fight the bonus room encounter properly. A trait he was almost certain Noracin and his team didn't have, considering Riya only got access to it at Tier 1 with her Glyph.

How did they beat this? Was there some hidden mechanic? Maybe they'd "forgotten" to mention some puzzle that made the doors to the room open without having to fight the Mantas in the water?

Aran shook his head at that stupid thought. There was no way a Guild investigator would lie like that. Even if they had, it wouldn't have worked.

He knew better than most that there were skills higher-tiered people could use to learn if you were lying. Some could even force you to tell the truth against your will, though he didn't think the Guild used them. Or if they did they sure didn't do it openly. A shiver ran up his spine as old memories found their way back to the surface, and he quickly forced them back down.

"All right," he said aloud, focusing on the present in an attempt to think of something, anything, else. "What's the situation, everyone? HMS?"

Troy was the first to answer, starting with a groan. "Health at one eleven, mana at thirty-two. None stamina."

Vin coughed a laugh as she sat up from her prone position. "That's one way to say it. My situation is a hundred sixty-seven health and eighty-five mana." She paused for a moment. "Stamina-wise I'd call myself better off than Troy, but still pretty drained."

"Of course you're better off than me," Troy said. "You're built for running around and stuff, I'm not."

Vin snorted and opened her mouth to reply, but Aran cut her off, sensing an imminent argument. "Guys, no fighting in the Dungeon. Riya, what about you? You were the main focus of the fight."

The only answer he got was a groan and a thumbs down, which to be fair told Aran all he needed to know. He thought for a long second, then took a deep breath and spoke with a reluctant acceptance in his voice.

"All right, I'm calling it. We retreat. We're in no condition to fight the Guardian, even if we rest before the fight. We need more than just to recover our health." He paused, then added, "We got the bonus reward at least. That's something."

He expected more annoyance and argument, but surprisingly everyone seemed in grudging agreement with his decision. And if anything was a sign from above that they were in no condition to continue the Challenge, it was this team all *agreeing* with each other about a *lack* of their own abilities.

I watched as the team trudged back the way they had come. They were the fifth party to enter since Noracin's, and so far every one of them had given up either immediately after the bonus room or upon reaching Stalker's chamber and seeing her hanging there. Menacingly, it seemed.

I suspected, both from my observations and from the Challengers' conversations, that they had been warned of the dangers of my Floor before entering and were taking things extra carefully. Every party so far had moved with extreme caution and had been on high alert for my traps. Especially once they discovered that the traps could change. That had really caught the third party off guard, resulting in the first fatality since the cheaters. Aran's party had actually done pretty well for themselves up until the bonus room fight, but a poor initial strategy had drained their stamina well beyond what the fight should have taken. And they also had the sense to call it quits there and not push beyond their capabilities out of greed or foolhardiness. It was good they pushed themselves; that was why the Challenge was there in the first place. But there was a difference between undertaking a difficult Challenge with the intent of growing, and throwing your life away due to overconfidence. In fact I was more and more sure that was a large part of my purpose as a Dungeon: I wasn't only supposed to Challenge people to help them grow, I was also supposed to lure in those who were so greedy for power that it impaired their judgement. Those Challengers were undeserving of the power they so desperately sought. I paused and frowned mentally.

I wasn't sure I would have thought like that even two days ago. The sentiment would probably have been pretty similar, but I didn't think I would've articulated it that way before. Since the Challenges started happening more frequently, I could feel myself . . . expanding? No, that wasn't quite correct. I knew expansion, and while this felt close, it wasn't the same. It was growth of some kind, though, I was sure of it. What I wasn't sure of was why it was happening. The only thing I could think was that I'd been entered more often than ever before. Two parties a day, sometimes with only a few hours in between, made me much busier than I'd ever been before. Maybe being bombarded with many more perspectives and new experiences made Dungeons grow faster?

At least it didn't seem harmful—in fact quite the opposite, though the experience still felt strange. I was thinking more, and in a way that was hard to describe. Maybe this was what growing up was like?

I shook myself and brought my mind back to the present. With the party leaving I had at least a few hours before the next one walked in. By now I was pretty happy with the first Floor, having spent some time over the last few days working on the balance of the encounters and traps. But just sitting around doing nothing had proven to be too difficult for me. If there wasn't an active Challenge, I felt the need to work on *something*. Since the Quest prohibited me from leveling, and I didn't want to start the next Floor until I could do that, it left me with little choice but to make small changes to the design and layout of the Floors I already had. And with the first Floor being the only one that actively Challenged so far, it was naturally the only one that had any actual feedback to base changes on. I didn't change the major features; the locations and overall layout of the traps and encounters were left the same. But I did some tweaking on where each individual Bat would be in Stalker's chamber and the bonus room, as well as work on the levels of my creatures to make the encounter more interesting.

I wasn't under any illusion that what I did would make much of a difference during a Challenge. I just wanted something to do, and carving murals in stone got boring after a while. It was a strange feeling. Even though there were more Challengers now, I was also more bored than ever. It was to the point where I was tempted to change the difficulty and lethality of my traps, just so I could get the damned Quest finished. All I had left was to defeat seven Challengers and provide six completion or Quest rewards, since for some stupid reason it only counted when they died or completed the entire Floor. If I just moved some more enemies into the bonus room, I was pretty sure I could defeat enough Challengers over the next few Challenges. It would also leave Stalker very vulnerable, so any party that made it to the Guardian fight would be able to finish the rewards section as well. Then I could finally get back to expanding and building again.

Of course I would never actually do that. It would undermine the very point of what I was trying to do, and what a Dungeon was supposed to be. Yet sometimes the thought still wormed itself into my mind. Brought about by restlessness in the face of purposeless work. I had to think of some other way to distract myself. Perhaps Morrígan had some ideas. She always seemed to have an opinion on how the Challengers or my creatures had performed in a fight, and some ideas of what I could do to improve for the next Challenge. I sent her a message while I waited for the time to pass.

Katherine frowned at the report in her hands. Another party retreating after the main, or only true encounter really, of the first Floor. Six parties had attempted the Floor now, and not one had succeeded in their Challenge. No one had even *tried* to fight the Guardian. Worse than that was that if the reports were to be believed, the parties had been correct in their judgement to avoid that fight. She shook her head. She'd known this Dungeon was special, both due to the speed of its growth and its high level of sapience. Both factors that made it more dangerous than the average Dungeon, but even with her expectations lowered they weren't making progress as fast as she'd thought they would. She blamed herself. She should have seen something like this coming after Noracin's report was so different from what she'd experienced. It should have made it obvious to her that even her own initial assessment had sold the Dungeon short, at least in terms of cognitive ability and a desire for change. The only good things were that he hadn't changed much since the investigation, and he didn't seem to be vindictively trying to make the Floor as deadly as possible, adapting to counter the strategy of one party to try to catch the next one off guard. If anything, she thought he seemed to encourage the formation of such strategies, though she wasn't as wholly convinced about that as the Dungeon scholars were. Regardless, it meant the Floor was dangerous and difficult enough to have the Guild's most experienced Tier-1 parties in the area stumped for several days *without* playing dirty, which was a much more notable feat than the other way around. It meant his tactics and designs were just naturally more dangerous and tricky to deal with than most Dungeons'. She was sure her parties would get the hang of it eventually, they always did, but she was worried too many would die before that point, or it would take too long for headquarters' taste. It was a bit of a double-edged sword: she wanted them to advance faster, but she was also keenly aware that it was due to her own advice that they were being extra cautious in their Challenges, thus resulting in slowed progress. It was frustrating, but something she had to accept if she wanted to preserve her adventurers' lives.

A knock at the door pulled her attention away from her thoughts.

"Come in," she said. The door opened and her assistant Yerin walked in with a frown on her face and a letter in her hands.

"What's the matter?" Katherine asked. The Scribe took a deep breath, then handed the letter over. Katherine scanned the contents, then tsked as her face too contorted into a frown. It was a short letter politely but firmly letting her know to soon expect a visit from Bishop Nicomedes and several parties of Order representatives to the Dungeon camp. It even apologized for the short notice, and promised compensation for any amenities the Guild would have to use before the Order's own supplies arrived. She tossed the paper down atop the report with a frustrated shake of her head.

"How long do we have?" she asked.

"The message came this afternoon," Yerin said. "I had our people check the situation in town while it was transcribed, and they reported that a caravan of Order adventurers left two days ago, but they didn't think much of it until the Bishop himself left this morning."

"The same time the message went out, no doubt," Katherine said. "The man wanted to leave us with as little time as possible to prepare. If he hurries, he'll arrive before nightfall."

"I figured that as well," Yerin said. "But what I don't get is why. Seems kind of a petty thing to do for not much benefit."

"Could be any number of reasons with that old fox," Katherine said. "Maybe he wants us off balance for some reason. Maybe he doesn't want us to have enough time to send for a higher-tier representative from another city. Right now I'm the highest tier here, but once Nicomedes arrives he'll be highest. That alone will provide him with some pull to get his way, regardless of the fact that the Guild still has priority on the Dungeon for another month." She shook her head. "Or he might just think it's a funny prank to surprise us. Honestly I can't tell what he's thinking sometimes."

"So, what do we do?" Yerin asked.

Katherine frowned in annoyance, then sighed. "What else can we do but prepare for the Bishop's arrival? Even if he is an annoying old man, he's still one of the most influential people west of the Kiari Mountains, and not someone we can treat poorly." She paused for a moment. "Send a message to Alash City headquarters. Let them know what the Order's doing, that they might try to impose on the Guild's new Dungeon during our priority time. If I know Hallmaster Raven at all, he won't just accept that without doing something about it." *Not that he's much better than Nicomedes,* she thought to herself.

"As you wish, Hallmaster. Should I send for Samuel before I leave?" Yerin said.

Katherine tapped her finger on her desk repeatedly. "Probably for the best if you do," she said reluctantly. "I'm not the most suitable for preparing a proper welcome, but you gotta do what you gotta do."

Yerin nodded and stepped outside, leaving Katherine alone with her papers once more. She looked down at the report from Aran again and let out a sad sigh. With the Order coming, they couldn't afford to be so careful in their Challenges anymore. Lack of progress meant a lack of influence, regardless of any supposed priority access. And the winds of politics were fickle at best. She rested her head on the back of her chair and stared up at the ceiling. This was going to get very annoying, very soon. She could just feel it.

CHAPTER TWENTY-EIGHT

Rumblings

The dungeon camp had been set up quickly, focusing on function rather than form, so it took quite a bit of work for Katherine to prepare a venue suitable for a welcoming party for the Bishop within just a few hours. But in the end she managed, and just in time too. Clad in her proper Hallmaster regalia for the first time since arriving at the site, she watched as the procession of Order Justiciars approached through the trees. Their caravan included half a dozen carriages. She wasn't proud of it, but she took a little pleasure in watching them struggle through the still relatively wild terrain. The path they'd created for their supply carts was a bit rougher than a carriage could handle comfortably. Not to mention the difficulty it presented to their normal marching formation. She could tell they were trying their best to not let it show that the terrain was affecting them, but in so doing they made it all the more obvious.

She schooled her face. Annoyed though she was at this whole affair, she had to present herself properly as a Hallmaster of the Guild. It wouldn't do to have a high tier take any pleasure at the misfortune of her juniors, even if they were from the Order and here to try to lay claim to what the Guild had rights to. She knew they were only here on the Bishop's whim, and not of their own accord. That much was obvious even from this far away, going by the annoyed frowns on some of their faces.

She turned to Yerin, who stood behind her on her left side, also clad in the official garb of the Guild. A dark blue shirt and trousers covered by an even darker blue vest lined with golden stripes, the crest of the Guild embroidered in actual gold thread on the chest, all under a light blue cape billowing slightly in the breeze. It was all a bit too pompous for her taste, but that was the cost of playing politics. A necessary evil to enable the Guild to get what it wanted from the world. That was what she told herself anyway.

"Any word on the Bishop's arrival?" she asked. Yerin furrowed her brows slightly and shook her head.

"I'm afraid not. He's flying directly over the forest, and we don't have an easy way of tracking his location from here. But based on his departure time and his normal flying speed, he should have been here already. I don't know what's keeping him."

"He might want to time his arrival together with the procession, make a spectacle out of it for his people," Samuel said from Katherine's other side.

"That does sound like something he'd do." Katherine sighed and turned back toward the incoming arrivals. Nothing to do but wait, then.

She didn't have to wait long—Samuel was right. The procession stopped a few meters from her, and she heard a whisper from Samuel.

"He's here." Samuel needn't have bothered in this instance.

Not being a magic-focused Class herself, Katherine normally wouldn't be able to feel someone using their skills unless they were well below her tier, which the Bishop was not. The Bishop, however, was outright flaunting and exaggerating the use of the skill, making no effort to hide its effect on the surrounding mana whatsoever. Katherine could feel it like an invisible wind rushing all around her. She looked up to see the man in the sky above them, a pair of glowing wings of light illuminating his white and silvery Order robes as he descended toward them. She snorted. *A spectacle indeed.* The Bishop landed in front of the procession, then, with a few of who she assumed were his high-tier members, walked the final steps to stand in front of Katherine. She remained where she was; as the host it was her right to be approached. And while she waited she studied Nicomedes closely, trying to figure out what he was thinking. Unlike most people that worked to tier up, he didn't *look* young, a faint graying at his temples and wrinkles around his eyes. To Katherine the wrinkles always made it seem like he was smiling slightly, possibly at her expense, but she didn't know if she was just unused to aged people. Nearly everyone she saw on a daily basis was either high tier themself or actually young. There weren't that many who chose a slow and safe life in the lower tiers, and even rarer were those who changed their minds to join the Adventurers' Guild *after* they'd aged. Adventurers typically died young, and those who didn't still looked young. Few people showed their age as the Bishop did. It was a minor thing, perhaps, but it still made dealing with Nicomedes slightly more uncomfortable for her. Not that she could let him learn that, of course.

"Bishop Nicomedes," she said and bowed her head slightly. "Welcome to the Veos Dungeon outpost. Apologies for the rather plain reception, but we had no idea you were coming until a few hours ago."

The Bishop waved a hand with a smile.

"Do not worry yourselves about a lack of ceremony. I was never one for such trivialities anyway." He frowned. "It is unfortunate that you weren't informed earlier; there should have been a missive sent several days ago." He shook his head and his smile returned. "There must have been a mix-up in communication somewhere between our two organizations. No matter, I am sure whatever you have planned will be more than good enough for me and mine."

"Thank you, Bishop," Katherine said with a smile of her own, though inwardly she was frowning. There was no way Nicomedes hadn't delayed the message on purpose. And now he feigned benevolence and understanding about the "mix-up," no doubt to gain an advantage for whatever else he planned to do here.

"If you would direct your men to follow Yerin, she will show you to where your people can set camp. I'm sure you are all quite tired from the journey, so we have prepared quite the feast for tonight."

Nicomedes laughed. "Great, great. Your generosity will not go unappreciated, I assure you."

"I would expect nothing less from the Order," Katherine said. "In the meantime, if you would like to follow me, we should have a discussion about how to proceed. Leader to leader."

"That would be pertinent. Lead the way," Nicomedes said with a nod.

"So," Katherine said once they were seated in her private office and the door was shut, "what are you doing here?"

Nicomedes blinked, seemingly surprised at her bluntness, but soon smiled and shook his head in what Katherine felt oozed faked sadness.

"Ah, I had wished to avoid this part," he said. "I know our organizations have had some issues in the past, but not everything has hidden meanings and secret agendas." He sighed. "All right, I will be upfront. I am merely here to add support and join forces in the delving of this new Dungeon you have found. But rest assured, I am aware your organization still has priority. Again I simply wish to offer my support in what has come to seem an unusually difficult undertaking."

"Uh-huh," Katherine said. "Well in that case I thank you for the offer, but I think the Guild has it covered."

"Are you certain?" Nicomedes said. "I've heard you've lost several people during these last few days and have yet to succeed in even a single Challenge. I've brought some of my brightest here, from Tiers one to three. We're eager to help, all you need to do is ask."

Katherine shook her head. "Thank you again, but I'm afraid I must decline. We already have a packed Challenge schedule, and I'm sure you wouldn't want to be the reason one of mine couldn't undertake theirs."

"Ah, that *would* be unfortunate of course," Nicomedes said. "One's Challenge is a sacred thing that shouldn't be interfered with."

"I'm glad you think so," Katherine said.

"Though I have heard from some that what you're doing isn't considered a proper Challenge, that many of your parties are giving up before even *trying* to fight the Guardian."

Katherine frowned, and Nicomedes hastily added, "I've made sure to rebuke my own people whenever I've heard them speak about it, of course, but you know how the younger ones can be about these things. Unfortunately, though I am a Bishop, even I can't stop people from talking." He shook his head. "I'm just worried that the rumors will harm your station here."

"I see . . ." Katherine said.

Nicomedes nodded. "It's unfortunate that rumor holds such sway over people's minds, but it's the world we've been given. It's up to us to deal with it the best we can."

"That we can agree on," Katherine said. "But you needn't worry. A few rumors aren't enough to hold any sway on the Guild."

"Naturally." Nicomedes nodded. "I know very well the strength of the Guild as an organization." He paused. "It's more the junior members themselves I'm worried about. They and others might get the wrong idea about how the Guild handles itself. Or . . ." He cut himself off with a sad shake of his head.

Or being careful and planning ahead might spread into my ranks, you were going to say, Katherine thought. *Lady of "Wisdom" forbid that ever happen.*

She kept that to herself and instead asked. "So what would you do about these dangerous rumors then?"

"Of course I'd start by sending as strong a team as I can get to fight with the Guardian. Nothing quells rumors about weakness faster than success."

"But it would be the Order's success, not the Guild's," Katherine pointed out. "Might it not instead seem like we ran to you for help if you did that?"

"Ah, I'm afraid you've misunderstood me," Nicomedes said. "Apologies. I was stating what I would do if the rumors were about me. You would of course send for the strongest Tier-one *Guild* party that can get here quickly enough. I'm sure there are more than a few options to choose from that aren't here already."

"Of course there are," Katherine said quickly. "Though I'm afraid they're all busy on missions already, and I'm not petty enough to interrupt other important work for something as small as a rumor."

Nicomedes stared at Katherine for a few seconds, tapping his fingers on his thigh as if waiting for her to continue, then burst out laughing when it became clear that she wouldn't.

"I guess I should've known better," he said with a shake of his head.

"What are you talking about?" Katherine said.

"I was waiting for you to realize what I was suggesting—that my people play the part of yours. That way progress can continue without any rumors spreading. No egg on your face, and I get to help. It's a win-win."

Katherine blinked. "How on Nerian-Silex could you think I'd ever take *that* offer? I feel insulted that you even considered it would work."

"I guess I owe you an apology then," Nicomedes said. "Your aversion to playing the game has given me an unfairly jaded view."

"Just because I dislike it doesn't mean I'm a complete idiot," Katherine muttered, crossing her arms.

"Fair enough," Nicomedes said. "I won't beat around the bush any longer then, though I had hoped to avoid using this." He reached into his robes and pulled out a small piece of parchment and handed it over to Katherine. She unfurled it and read its contents, her frown growing deeper the more she read. Finished, she leaned back in her chair and stared up at the ceiling.

"If you had this, why bother with the theatrics in the first place?" she asked tiredly, facing Nicomedes once again.

He shrugged. "I wanted to see if I could get what I want without it. A favor like this is a precious thing, after all. Better to save it for when it's absolutely necessary."

Katherine thought for a moment, tapping the note on her desk absent-mindedly as she did. She couldn't get out of it, not with this note. "Why do you want to help with this Dungeon so badly?" she asked. "There are plenty of stronger Dungeons the Guild has domain over, not just priority access. Surely you would better serve the Order by gaining access to one of them?"

"This isn't a favor for the Order. It's a favor for me, and I would disagree with that statement," Nicomedes said. "I'm pretty sure you would too."

Katherine sighed. *He knows everything, then.* "What do you want?"

"I'm not here to be the villain who steals things out from under the Guild. I don't want exclusive access or to take over your leadership position or anything of the like. That's how rumors get started." He smiled slightly as if he'd said something funny, then continued. "What I do want is a partnership, of sorts, in which the Guild grants us access to Challenge the Dungeon, and we will of course provide fair compensation to the Guild in return. I won't even ask for a fair split of time during the priority period, but something like one or two Challenges a week for my people."

"That's it?" Katherine frowned. "That's a bit of a waste of a personal favor from the Guildmaster, don't you think?"

Nicomedes grinned. "I know, right? Hopefully your Guildmaster thinks so as well when he hears about this."

Katherine paused, then placed her face in her palms with a groan. "All right, whatever. Seems like you win no matter what."

"Now, don't think like that," Nicomedes said. "The way I see it, everyone wins here." He snapped his fingers. "Tell you what, I've got a great idea. We can be responsible for the first Challenge of the later Floors. Up to Tier Three at least. Your teams investigate beforehand anyway, right? We could take that spot. My people like as pure a Challenge as possible, so we wouldn't have used the information your investigation would have gained anyway."

"That . . . That could actually work," Katherine said slowly. She thought for a moment. "Depending on the compensation, I could spin that."

"Great," Nicomedes said with a grin.

"There are still a ton of details left to hammer out before we can come to any proper agreement, however."

"Of course. I have nothing but time."

Before Katherine could get started, the door burst open and a harried-looking Yerin rushed in.

"Hallmaster! They die . . ." She caught herself as she finally noticed

Nicomedes sitting there. Her eyes opened wide and she clamped her mouth shut.

"Yerin? What happened? Don't mind him—just tell me," Katherine asked in alarm.

Yerin quickly got herself under control. "It's Garie's party. They were supposed to be out half an hour ago, and we just sent someone in to check . . ."

Katherine felt a chill travel ominously up her spine. This could not have happened at a worse time. She clenched her hand to a fist. "Is it a . . . ?"

Yerin nodded with a mournful look on her face. "It's a party wipe," she said.

Katherine swore, then turned to Nicomedes, but he spoke up before she could.

"It seems best I leave you to it. We can continue this at a later time," he said and stood.

"Thank you," Katherine said gratefully.

The Bishop nodded, then paused at the door. "And let me know if you want a vigil for your fallen party. It would be the least we could do."

"I will be sure to do that," Katherine said.

CHAPTER TWENTY-NINE

The Fight

One hour earlier, inside the Dungeon.

Hold up!" Garie said, raising his hand into the air for the party to stop. "This is where the last party said there was a trap. Erlon, check it and give a shout if you sense something, yeah?"

"Will do, boss," Erlon said, stepping out in front, his face taking on a focused frown as he tried to sense the surrounding flow of mana. He didn't have [Detect Magic] or anything similar; he relied on the natural sense for mana he had as a Mage, helped by his spirit-enhancing Glyph. Which wasn't perfect, of course, but it was certainly better than Garie's own. The way they had decided to think of it was that a positive detection was reliable enough, but a negative one was not. So if Erlon didn't find anything up ahead, it didn't necessarily mean the trap had been disabled. It wasn't a foolproof system, to be sure. But it was what they had, and it had worked out for them so far. They just had to be sure to remember to not become overly reliant on the answers Erlon could give.

"Anything?" he asked.

"Hang on," Erlon said. "I think so . . ." He shut his eyes and reached out a hand, tracing a line through the air. "There might be something here . . . going . . . from the floor somewhere here . . . up through the wall." He opened his eyes and shook his head. "I can't sense anything more specific than that," he said.

Garie frowned. "That's unfortunate. We can't really avoid it if it's a general area and not a pressure plate or something."

"I'm sorry I can't be more specific, but if I hadn't known there *might* be something here, I wouldn't have sensed anything at all." Erlon shook his head with a sigh. "The trails are just too faint for me to detect with nothing but stats."

Dalia stepped up and laid a hand on his shoulder. "Don't beat yourself up. We get how tricky this is. We'll find some other way to deal with it." The Warrior turned toward Garie and gave him a nod.

"Of course," he said immediately. He thought for a moment. "If it's a general area trap, you think we could trigger it by tossing something into it?"

Erlon blinked. "Maybe, but I doubt it. Most of the traps in here can only be triggered by something with mana."

"Still worth a shot," Garie said. He signaled for them to come back while he reached into his pouch and pulled out a silver coin, then he paused and looked at Erlon.

"You say mana is needed to trigger it?"

"Yeah. I think so, at least. The mechanism is too sophisticated to be tricked just by *movement*."

"Great, great. Then I have an idea. Give me your pack for a second," Garie said, reaching out a hand. Erlon frowned, but still handed it over. Garie reached inside and pulled out a mana potion, holding it up for the Mage to see.

"Would this work, you think?" he asked, handing the pack back over. Erlon took the bag with a thoughtful look on his face, glancing back and forth between the potion and the tunnel ahead.

"I don't know," he said after a moment. "It might. It certainly has plenty of mana. But it wouldn't work if the trap can somehow sense whether the mana belongs to a *living creature* or not. And nobody has checked that yet, as far as I know."

"Not surprising," Narim said, speaking up from the rear "Not everyone is well enough off to have a mana potion in the first place, not to mention wasting it on a maybe." The Druid cocked his head. "Though I will admit it might work. And it's definitely better to test it with a potion than with your own head."

"We could always go back, try the alternate path instead? It won't make us fight any additional fights, and we could avoid the trap entirely," Dalia said.

Garie shook his head. "We could avoid *this* trap. But remember the alternate path is filled with the things. It might not have as many enemies, but that doesn't mean it isn't dangerous."

Dalia shrugged. "Fair enough, just thought I'd point it out."

Garie nodded. "It's always good to know all your options before you decide. Still I think pushing on is the better choice here."

"Agreed," Narim said. "Assuming this trick with the mana potion works, anyway."

"If it doesn't we'll just have to think of some other way," Garie said. "Unless you want to give up without even making it to the Guardian?"

"No way," Narim said. "We didn't struggle our way through that damned pool room just to give up at the first trap we can't easily go around."

"I heard from the messenger station that the Order is arriving later today," Dalia said. "Several parties along with the freaking Bishop himself. Even thinking of what they'd say if we just ran away makes me feel gross." She shivered dramatically, and Garie chuckled.

"Yeah I figured as much," he said. Then he frowned. "But just because the Order's here doesn't mean we're going to act foolhardy, you hear? When we make it to the Guardian I want a proper discussion of whether we fight or not. We have nothing to prove."

"Got it, boss," Dalia said. "Calm, cool, collected."

Garie nodded and held up the bottle. "Ready?" he called out. Once he got three confirming nods, he tossed the bottle into the tunnel, making sure to aim it where Erlon had indicated the disturbance in the mana was. It crashed against the stone, shattering and spilling its contents all over the Dungeon floor. The mana contained within exploded out in a wave, causing a tremble Garie himself could sense even with his meager spirit stat. A second later it was over, and the mana settled back down. Nothing happened with the trap. At least nothing he could see. He sighed and turned to Erlon with an apologetic look on his face.

"It seems I wasted your—" he began, but the Mage cut him off.

"No! I think it worked," he said quickly. "Not the way we thought, but still. We have to hurry, though. I don't know how long it will last."

He started forward and Garie reached out a hand to stop him. "What are you doing? Explain first," he said.

"The trap's disabled. Not triggered or destroyed, but I think the mana temporarily overloaded something. I can't sense anything apart from normal mana on the ground, but the part going up the wall is still there, so the trap's not completely gone."

Garie blinked. "That . . . I don't completely follow but a lot of it sounds like pure guesswork. How can you be so sure the trap won't trigger anyway? I thought you could barely sense the thing."

"It makes sense," Erlon said. "Think of it as a similar reaction to what would happen if you drank a potion too high-tier for you, or if you already had full mana. Overload, I think it's called."

"I've heard of it. Not a pleasant condition," Narim said. "But it wears off after a while, and it won't leave any lasting damage."

"Exactly. So if we want to pass we have to go through quickly," Erlon said. "Trust me."

Garie hesitated for only half a second, then nodded. If he wasn't going to trust the Mage's opinion on magical stuff, what was the point of even asking his opinion in the first place?

Still, as the leader he felt he should be the one to go first, so he went on ahead with the rest of the party staying a few steps behind, just in case something unexpected happened.

Nothing did, and they quickly moved on to the mouth of the tunnel. There was one more pack of Bats they had to deal with before the final chamber, but with the knowledge they gained in the main room, they made quick work of them without any issue. Soon they found themselves standing in front of the entrance to what they felt was the Guardian's cavern. Garie thought he could almost touch the tension in the air.

Unlike what the investigators' report said, the Guardian wasn't standing in front of the entrance looking at them. As had happened with the other Challenger parties that had entered since, the cavern was hauntingly empty. The scholars seemed to think it had something to do with this being a proper Challenge rather than an investigation, though how the Guardian could know that Garie had no idea. Whatever the reason, the creature wasn't there to stare at them, which he now thought he would have preferred. Even with the creepiness of having a monster staring at him, at least he'd have known where it was. Now all that was visible in the cave was darkness.

He shook himself. He couldn't let himself get scared now. As his father always said, if the leader was frightened, the soldiers always followed.

Now soldiers and adventurers weren't the same by a long shot, but the principles of leadership were the same. He had to be an example for the others to follow.

"All right," he said. "Here we are. The final Challenge. How's everyone feeling? Not just system-wise. Are you up for risking your lives today?"

"Here we go," Narim said. "The speech." Dalia chuckled.

"No speech this time." Garie shook his head. "I just want to make sure you know and are ready for what we're about to get into. If you don't feel up for it, there's no shame in going back. Everyone else who made it this far retreated once they got here."

"That would make us first clear then, wouldn't it?" Dalia said with a grin.

"That's true," Erlon said, also smiling.

"And a bonus: just think about the faces of the people from the Order when we defeat it right as they get here to try and steal our glory," Narim said.

"Don't get too eager now," Garie said. "This will be a real fight with our lives on the line. Some of us *could* die in there."

"We're adventurers," Narim said. "We risk our lives all the time. The creatures in here are dangerous, but at least they won't try to kill us when we aren't ready for a fight. Unlike most things we'll go up against in the wilds outside."

"Don't worry about us, boss," Dalia said. "We know what we're getting into."

Garie studied the faces of his three companions in turn, and saw nothing but assurance and confidence from each of them. He nodded.

"Good," he said, then smiled. "Then let's go show everyone what we're capable of."

Garie swung at a swirling Bat with a shout as his injured arm screamed in agony. The blade hit, but he couldn't put any strength behind it, so all it did was knock the creature back slightly and open a minor cut on its belly. He grunted in frustration, turning back toward Narim and Erlon, who were busy avoiding a dive from the Guardian. Vines sprouted from under Narim's feet, trying to catch the beast, but all it did was slow down its descent enough for both casters to dodge out of the way. To his right Dalia struck down a Bat, then blocked a [Water Bolt] with her shield, though he could see her gasping for breath as she did so. They were all pretty drained of their stamina, and Dalia and Garie were both down at least a third of their health. There was a flash of pain from his side as yet another [Water Bolt] struck. One Dalia hadn't been able to block. Luckily most of the damage was blocked by his armor, but he knew it was only a matter of time before they managed to eat away at his health. This was like the pool room all over again, which had been hard enough already. But with the addition of the Guardian, it was just too much to avoid all the incoming attacks. They had to change their strategy.

"Fall back!" he yelled, clutching his bleeding arm. "Return to the tunnel, fight the Guardian there. Keep the Mantas from getting a good shot!"

"Got it!" Dalia yelled. They backed away toward their companions, who both also started to move toward the cave entrance.

Then the cave was plunged into [Darkness].

Garie scrambled to reach into his pocket for a [Sunstone], but heard a shriek from Narim that chilled his bones. The [Sunstone] shattered against the ground. He swiveled toward the noise, to find the Druid falling to his knees, a spiked tail sticking out of his chest.

"NARIM!" he yelled. His feet were running before he finished speaking. Before he finished thinking. But he still didn't get there in time to do anything. The Guardian withdrew its tail, and Garie saw the light go out in his friend's eyes.

He screamed louder, joined by his friends. But the Guardian didn't care. Neither did the Mantas. A volley of water shot at Dalia just as the Guardian dove. She tried to dodge, but her movements were sluggish. Garie saw it, as if in slow motion. Her gaze kept flicking to Narim. In desperation he tossed his sword at the charging Guardian, hoping to do something, anything, to distract it long enough for Dalia to get out of the way. His desperation paid off, as the blade struck true. He felt a moment of hope rise in his chest, only to have it instantly quashed as the blade did little more than bounce off the creature's hide. The beast struck Dalia with a low *thud* that rang like the bell of death in Garie's ears. Dalia fell backward, just as the volley of [Water Bolts] struck from the side, each hitting the woman and making a painful sizzling sound. He cast a glance at Narim and Erlon, and saw that the Mage stood hunched over the Druid, a health potion in hand.

Good. He let himself feel a tinge of hope once more as he ran to Dalia.

The Guardian wasn't going to let him get away with that, as it leaped off the woman to fly straight at him. But that was exactly what Garie wanted. Dalia may have been knocked down, but he didn't think she was completely out of it. As a defensive Warrior, she had more health than he did. One large blow shouldn't be enough to take her out completely, even with the damage from the [Water Bolts]. She'd be back up in no time. He just had to distract the Guardian long enough.

He dodged low to the side, letting the beast fly past over his shoulder, then rolled away from a diving attack that would have pierced through his back.

Any second now. He glanced at Dalia, hoping to see her up on her feet again.

She lay in the same spot. Motionless.

Erlon screamed something from his side, but Garie didn't catch the words. He stood stunned for a moment, staring at the fallen body of his friend. There was a sharp twinge on his shoulder.

Then world-blackening pain.

I told Stalker to let the last one run. The Mage, seeing all three of his companions fall in under a minute, had screamed in horror and turned to flee. Even though he hadn't said the words, I knew he'd given up the Challenge. There was no need to chase him down. I felt like sighing. It was a sad ending today. And they hadn't really done anything substantially wrong, either. They had planned ahead, thought through a strategy, and executed it.

They just hadn't been strong enough.

Or rather, Stalker had been much too strong for them to handle.

I wondered if I should remove some of her helpers. She might be difficult enough on her own.

No. It was better not to rush to make changes like that. Something I'd learned over this week was that people were quick to adapt to difficulty. Something that was too challenging one day became manageable the next, and trivial the day after that.

Okay maybe that was a bit of an exaggeration. I didn't expect Stalker would *ever* be trivial, but it might be better to give them a chance to overcome the Challenge themselves first, before I went in and made it easier.

A surge of experience drew my attention back to the last remaining Challenger. Or rather, what had once been the last remaining Challenger. He'd run in a panic the way he'd come. Through the cave of defeated Bats, and right into the trap they had so carefully avoided on their way inside. Now nothing more than a corpse lay in the pit trap, impaled by half a dozen stone spikes sticking up from the floor below, a look of confusion frozen on his face.

Shit. I'd forgotten about that.

CHAPTER THIRTY

Introspection

I realized I felt bad about that last Challenger dying, which was a new thing for me.

Up until now, while I'd felt that Challenger deaths were a bad thing in an abstract sense, as it meant their failure to rise to the Challenge while at the same time halting the progress of the story, I never really felt *guilty* about their deaths. Even as I grew more familiar with these Challengers as more and more entered, I'd still felt detached, like an outside observer not participating in the events that were taking place, but just watching them happen. Which, sidenote, I didn't want to be forever. Eventually I wanted to interface with the world through my story even beyond my borders, if that was possible. So perhaps caring more about the Challengers was a natural evolution toward that goal. Something for future me to figure out. For now I had enough trouble thinking about this uncomfortable new feeling. I thought this last death had been different from the others because he'd died after already giving up. It had taken some introspection to figure that out, but once I did it made sense to me.

Giving up was the ending to the story of his Challenge, so his death happening after the fact just seemed unnecessary, especially since if I'd thought ahead I could have prevented it. If I'd disabled the trap once it was clear the Challenge was going to fail, I could have gotten the proper ending. It felt like a waste, and that waste was my own fault.

It wasn't a nice feeling to have, like a nagging itch deep within me, and it only compounded when I realized that I *also felt* bad for feeling bad for the Challenger. Like I was supposed to hope they died and was going against my instincts somehow by instead hoping for their success.

That threw me for a loop because I had such a powerful drive to provide a proper Challenge and reward those who proved themselves. I knew I could make every Floor next to impossible if I wanted to, with constantly changing death traps that in no way tried to teach or prepare anyone for what was to come. But that wasn't what I was meant to do, so I'd never even considered the option, at least not consciously.

I focused inward, deeper than I'd ever done before, toward the metaphorical kernel that was the source of the uncomfortable sensation. Minutes turned to hours, and the feeling came and went as I considered everything that had happened during the Challenge. It was tricky, examining my own emotions so directly like this, but eventually I was able to figure out that whenever I thought that a Challenger failing was bad, or that I'd done something wrong somehow by making them fail, the kernel would squirm and send out tentacles of discomfort through my mind. Discomfort and a hint of . . . was that fear?

No, fear wasn't the best way to describe this emotion. I wasn't even sure if *emotion* was the best way to describe it. Perhaps some kind of internal sense was a more apt description. It felt primal, almost like the pure instinct of the Challengers when they flinched away from pain. Something they did without thought, purely through an ingrained reflex to avoid danger.

There was something deep in the back of my mind that was afraid of Challengers—no, *delvers*—defeating my Guardians and reaching my Core. I thought back to what the tutorial had said so long ago, about how some people wanted to "gain my treasures" in a way not according to the customs of the Challenge.

That had to be what was causing the reaction. I was flinching away from the danger a group of Challengers presented by progressing. The conflicting feelings were coming from my instincts fighting over which was more important, the Challenge or my safety. Until now the Challenge had been winning, as I hadn't ever really felt I'd been in any real danger. But perhaps feeling bad about them failing was a step too far? Were my instincts worried I would grow lenient, perhaps let someone pass I shouldn't out of a desire to avoid inflicting unnecessary harm?

There was some logic to that, but I didn't like it. Not only because discomfort wasn't a nice thing to experience, but also because now there was a seed of doubt in my head.

I'd only noticed it now, but how could I be sure I hadn't been overly harsh in an attempt to avoid leniency? Considering how lacking the progress had been, I could definitely see an argument for me having made the Challenge unfairly difficult. Which I did *not* want it to be. I was already feeling a bit discouraged by the Challengers' lack of progress through my story, and if it was because I was unfair and not because they were foolhardy or not skilled enough . . . that would just make me feel stupid.

I went over the Challenges again, remembering how the Challengers would react to my creatures' attacks or how they had seemed overly hesitant to walk into an area where there could be a trap, and I recognized the reaction as similar to what I was now feeling. Apprehension. An itch within their mind warning of something that could potentially cause harm. Something that could threaten their lives. Right now mine was muted, since the danger was all theoretical, but for the Challengers, that was far from the case. For them that itch had to be much more severe. Though to give myself some credit, they were also probably much more used to the whole experience of emotions and sensations than I was. It could be that this wouldn't really be a problem at all, once I got used to it. The problem was I had no way to know that for sure.

For the first time I tried to place myself in the Challengers' shoes. I hadn't ever really thought of them as being separate from the Challenge before, despite knowing logically they had to have lives outside my Dungeon. Those lives just hadn't been very interesting to me. Now, though, I thought I understood more about them, as well as all they had to undertake in order to even attempt the Challenge in the first place. They were risking their lives every time they stepped onto my Floor, and I very much wasn't.

And though that made some sense since the Challenge was primarily for their benefit and not my own, it still felt like I was missing something by just capitulating to the fear and playing it safe. The risk, the fear, was what made the Challenge worthy of the reward. If I wanted to understand that better, I ought to take some risks myself as well. Or at least not let my instinct to make the Floors as difficult as possible run the show. Maybe I'd been too hard on them, and it would be better if I eased up in the future . . .

I shook myself. No, I shouldn't rush too far in the opposite direction just because I *might* have made a mistake. I wasn't sure if there was a way for me to ever find out what "too harsh" or "too lenient" was objectively, but I did know

I didn't want to be ruled by fear. Moving forward, I would need to pay attention to my own emotional response as well as any logical conclusions I could draw from the Challenges before I started making changes to my Floors.

I might as well start right away. In this most recent Challenge, there were two main things that I didn't like. Most obvious was of course the fight with Stalker; it was just too difficult. I would get to that eventually, but the thing that bothered me more was that the party completely ignored the story connections. They did make a few passing comments about the letter to Krazad, so I knew they were aware of them. But they didn't seem to think that the connections were that important. Or rather, that it wasn't their job to investigate them further. What needed to be found had been found, and what needed to be discussed was being discussed already, so what use was it for them to go get a second copy of a note they already had anyway? I could see where they were coming from, but it was still a problem because the supposed discussions that were happening about my story were all happening *outside*. Where I couldn't listen in. A few off-hand comments about "Farinon didn't find any mention of it in his notes," or "Alerio said they sent for more books" weren't enough. I not only wanted people to interface with my story, I wanted to *see* them interfacing with it.

That meant I'd have to either encourage the Challengers to interact with the narrative elements, or do something drastic that would force those outside having these discussions to come in and have them here instead. I wasn't sure if that was a feasible option. It wasn't exactly in line with my sensibilities as a Dungeon to have non-Challengers enter to essentially just hang about and talk, regardless of how interested I was in what they had to say. So for the foreseeable future I thought the better choice would be to try to make Challengers become invested in the story *while they were here.*

I actually had a few ideas on how to do that. I could make puzzles for small bonuses or secret things that could only be accessed using the items found in the narrative rooms. I could maybe even make the puzzles change the same way my traps did. And make it so the answers could only be found within the narrative. They didn't even need to be that difficult. Perhaps a clue to a puzzle would be one of the words from Krazad's missive, but which exact word would change. If possible the puzzle itself would have a limited number of attempts, to prevent them from just forcing it by remembering all the words in the note. That way if the party investigated the narrative connections, they'd easily be able to solve the puzzle and get a bonus for it. But they'd never be able to solve it without investigating.

Yeah, I was liking that idea more and more. And curiously the kernel of discomfort wasn't reacting at all to the prospect of providing additional rewards. Perhaps it only cared about progress through the Floors, and wasn't sophisticated enough to put together that more rewards might mean a deeper progression?

It would certainly be a relief if that was the case, as it would assuage some of my worries that it had had a large impact on my design of my Floors so far. I might have been influenced to make the Challenges difficult, but if it had to be that direct the effect shouldn't be that notable. At least not beyond the point where I could fix it without changing the main features of the Floors themselves. Though I might have to get pretty involved with the Stalker fight, as she was just way stronger than the rest of the Floor.

For most of the parties that had entered, what they had come to call the "main room fight" was still a true Challenge. Everyone acknowledged its difficulty and annoying enemy combination, yet they still went that path most of the time, so it wasn't difficult enough that the Challengers thought it wasn't worth its rewards.

The same could not be said for the Stalker fight. She had only been Challenged twice, once just now and once during the initial discoverer Challenge. And the first time had been an easier fight, with the water for the Mantas positioned extremely poorly and without any tunnels between the various pools.

And even with that it had resulted in the Challengers' defeat, and Alerio would have died if not for my interference.

Stalker was a monster, and I realized more and more just how much of one she was now that there had been a true full Challenge against her. I wouldn't even be surprised if she could handle some of the parties without any help at all, let alone almost a full "main room fight" worth of helpers.

I realized I could hit two birds with one stone, if I tied some of the helpers in Stalker's fight to the new puzzles in the narrative rooms. Separating them into smaller encounters that could be defeated in advance if the puzzles were solved, or if the party chose to skip the narrative those creatures would return to Stalker's chamber to help with the final fight. That way the story would be more tied into the actual mechanics of the Floor that the Challengers cared about. If I did that, I could even fill up the monster quota of the Floor completely, as there were still a few creature slots remaining that I hadn't been sure what to do with since changing the layout of the Floor. There weren't enough for a pack by themselves, but I hadn't wanted to add them to the already difficult fights that were here. But if I split that final pack into thirds, there was plenty of room to add them back in.

I grew more and more excited as ideas spun into being fast enough that I barely noticed the slight wiggle from the kernel of irritation at the prospect of making the final fight easier.

No, stay quiet, I thought to myself. *I make the decisions here, not you.*

That was a strange thing to think, as the kernel was also definitely me. I shook myself—that didn't matter right now. I had changes to make. And I would make sure I consciously thought about *why* I was making them. All for a fair and balanced Challenge, and engagement with my story.

Now I just had to come up with some riddles.

CHAPTER THIRTY-ONE

Meeting of Lethality

Nicomedes shut the door to the temporary chambers the Guild had provided for him and sank into a chair with a sigh. It was late in the afternoon the day after he'd arrived, and he'd only now managed to get some time for himself. At first he'd felt a bit annoyed at the delay, but he quashed that reaction as soon as he noticed it. The vigil of a fully defeated Challenger party wasn't something he could ignore as a Bishop of the Order, regardless of his personal plans. Thankfully for him it seemed that the Guilders weren't aware of the shard as of yet, so he wasn't in a desperate rush to get ahead of anyone tying it to him. Especially since they hadn't even started the Challenges on the second Floor, where the shard was most likely to be. And it seemed likely his Justiciars would be the first to enter, given his conversation with the local Hallmaster.

His Justiciars wouldn't all be made aware of the shard either, of course. That was too much of a risk. But Boltar knew what to look for, and he was loyal to a fault; that would be enough to make sure the shard was never found by someone who shouldn't see it. If it was even still there, which Nicomedes couldn't be sure of. He wouldn't be surprised if it weren't. With their built-in trust in the system, Dungeons tended to have a stronger instinctual rejection of the Aberrant than sapient races did, one that took months if not years of talking to help them get over. Though Nicomedes couldn't blame them too much when it came to shards; there was a reason most humans thought badly of Necromancers after all. Still, if Dungeons could be convinced to look past their instincts and see the bigger picture, they would become some of the most useful allies a researcher like him could have, since their influence over the system through their Edicts mirrored the Aberrant's own system manipulation.

He scoffed. Not that the system saw it that way of course, otherwise most high-tier Dungeons would all be labeled as Aberrant. No, that label was left to the people of the sapient races who tried to reach beyond what their cap was supposed to be. The people like him who wanted to grasp more than what the system had limited them to.

He shook his head. He shouldn't get lost in his own thoughts, not when he had so much work to do. Even with his main fear assuaged and the shard still not found, there seemed to be much more to this Dungeon than what he'd first assumed, and he wanted to know exactly what he was dealing with before the big meeting later tonight. If his hunch about what was going to be discussed was correct, he would need to be prepared to properly take advantage of the opportunity. He reached into his robe and pulled out several sealed letters from his contact among the Guild Clerks, ripped the first seal, and started reading. He knew a bit of what to expect from what he'd seen while escorting Lenore, but what he read still surprised him. He'd assumed half of the changes he'd heard about to be the usual exaggerated Adventurer gossip, but as he read through he found that the reports mostly matched up with what people had been saying.

A named Floor 1 Guardian, capable of contending against a full party alone. Now that one he could believe, considering how annoying the fight had been even for level 20s. He was surprised it could talk, though.

Then there was the massive change to the layout, as well as the variable death traps. Those were rarer in his opinion, especially considering that many of the traps were triggered through a clever use of mana that made them almost impossible to spot with mundane means, and tricky to find even using skills. That kind of sophistication when using mana usually signified an older Dungeon, as it wasn't something that could be forced through system help. Then there was the fact that a months-old Dungeon already had an *Edict*.

That was rare. So rare many people didn't even know what an Edict was. But it still wasn't the most shocking thing. That would be the note and the talisman, though he wouldn't have been surprised if he was one of the only ones still alive who remembered Archmage Karun or the old symbol for the

Blood Clan. Apart from some of the older Vampires themselves, of course. Though they mostly kept to themselves, a few thousand kilometers to the east at that.

Nicomedes spent a long time reading through the reports from the Dungeon Scholars, and could only come to one conclusion. It was a genuine Blood Clan talisman, and though it looked brand new, it was a symbol they hadn't used in more than five hundred years.

How did the Dungeon learn of this? Nicomedes shook his head in bewilderment. Oh what he wouldn't give to be able to go down there and ask these questions directly. The things he might learn . . . He sighed. No, that was a bad idea. Even if the Dungeon hadn't had a bad image of him from interfering with Lenore's Challenge, he couldn't risk going into a Dungeon while around so many Guilders. It would see through his fake status in an instant, and the risk that it would share that information was too big.

No, he couldn't go inside. He had to theorize the best he could while out here.

A half hour later, Nicomedes tapped his fingers frustratedly on his desk. No matter how hard he thought, only two possibilities came to mind, and he didn't like either. The first and least distasteful possibility was that the Dungeon had found some old artifacts during its expansion and used them as a basis to create this . . . whatever this was supposed to be. That would be strange, but would have very little to do with him personally. The second possibility he thought of, however, was that the system had *given* the Dungeon the information about the history of the Aberrant War, and the Dungeon had decided to change its Floor based on that information.

If the second possibility was the answer, the cause had to be the shard. It was Aberrant, and Karun was Archmage during the Aberrant War, so there was a connection there. Not to mention the connection between the Aberrant and the old Blood Clan. Though he had to admit it was a long shot at best. He frowned and tapped a finger on his desk. Neither of the options were good enough for him to say they were anything remotely close to a likely explanation. Suddenly finding artifacts from half a millennium ago relating specifically to the Aberrant War that took place on the other end of the continent . . . It just didn't seem plausible. And the second possibility was even less likely. He had never heard of the system giving out information like this before. Ever. And he'd talked with several Dungeons at length about that particular relationship. Still, he couldn't dismiss the notion out of hand, considering how doting the system was toward Dungeons. Especially new ones. And who knows what adding something Aberrant to them that early could cause. He paused. That might be something worth experimenting with further in the future. He made a mental note so he wouldn't forget it once he was done here. For now though he thought he should focus his attention on the more immediate future. Making sure the shard was never found, and finding out whatever else this new Dungeon knew about the Aberrant. Now that he'd read through the reports, he was even more eager to learn what the Dungeon, and the Guild, were hiding. In order to make sure he and the Order got what they wanted, he had to prepare properly for the meeting. He put the Scholars' reports to the side and took out a blank piece of parchment. There he began to write down a list of everything he knew about the meeting and the Guild's situation.

Firstly, he'd only been invited as an afterthought. Or rather, it seemed Katherine invited him because she'd felt after the vigil that she couldn't afford *not* to. Which meant she hadn't originally wanted him to be there.

That wasn't that surprising. She was a Guilder after all, and they weren't big fans of people from the Order coming in and judging them for their decisions. Nor do they want the Order to infringe on their leadership. So, it could just be a standard unwillingness coming from the politics of the two organizations. Or it could also be because she knew what they were discussing would be an issue for him as a Bishop of the Order. And considering who the other attendees were, he was pretty sure it was the second option.

If he had to guess, they were going to discuss using higher-tiered members to carry people through the Floors, making damned sure no more Guilders died during their attempt to tier up. Maybe they wouldn't try something *that* drastic, but perhaps something similar but less extreme would be on the table. Which was certainly something he as a Bishop would have to object to. Considering how the Dungeon had reacted to his own outside interference, it probably wouldn't go that well anyway. He thought for a moment, trying to come up with the best way he could gain an advantage in the situation. The obvious idea was to outwardly object, but not with enough strength to stop the Guilders from what they were planning to do. Then he could just wait for the inevitable fallout that would come from the Dungeon evoking its Edict against the "cheaters" and use that as leverage for getting what he really wanted. It was a simple plan that was almost sure to work, but one Nicomedes rejected out of principle.

While he wouldn't lose sleep over the deaths of a group of Guilders he didn't know, he didn't like the idea of intentionally letting children die just for some small advantage in future negotiations. He wasn't unskilled enough to need to stoop down to that level. He was plenty capable of getting what he wanted through other means. He just had to think deeper than the first thing that popped into his head.

The meeting of leaders took place in the largest room the Guild had available, a dining room in one of the few buildings the Guild had finished so far. The dining tables had been moved and a large meeting table stood in their place in the middle of the room, with five chairs on either side, as well as one large one at the head, facing the door. Katherine stood behind that chair and signaled for Nicomedes to take the seat to her immediate left. He made his way over to it with a gracious nod. As the highest tier here, even with his faked status, it was only right for him to arrive first. Apart from the meeting organizer, of course. Part of him felt annoyed at the pretentious officialness of it all, but he was experienced enough with these kinds of things that he knew it came with the territory. Especially now that he was here. With a Bishop from the Order present, there was no way the Guild was going to be anything less than proper. He wished it didn't have to be so, but some of his compatriots were real sticklers for protocol and ceremony, so the Guild had learned to play it safe.

One by one the other members filed into the room. There was Yerin of course, Katherine's right hand and assistant. She took the seat on Katherine's other side. Then came a pair of men who, despite their young looks, gave an aged air—they had to be the resident Dungeon Scholars. Nicomedes hadn't had a chance to meet either of them yet, as they hadn't left their rooms once since he arrived. Not even for the vigil. But he'd been around their ilk long enough to recognize them at a glance. They sat on either side of the table, next to Nicomedes and Yerin. After them came a pair Nicomedes didn't recognize, though with them being in Tier 3 and 4, he guessed they were the Master Clerk and Scoutmaster of the camp. After them came the final three attendees: representatives of each of the three tiers of Guilder parties that were currently in the camp. His eyes were drawn to the Tier-1 representative, one Noracin Lark. Something about him seemed familiar to Nicomedes, but he couldn't put a finger on what until the man noticed his gaze and bowed while mouthing the traditional Order greeting. Ah, so he used to be a member. That could be useful. He nodded back to the man with a smile.

Katherine cleared her throat, then took her seat, signaling for the others to do the same. Nicomedes and the others did so in the order they'd entered, and once they were all seated Katherine declared the inter-organizational meeting officially begun.

"Welcome one and all," Katherine began. "This is important, so I'll get right into it. The Dungeon is too lethal. We are here today to discuss and decide what we are to do about that. The goal of this meeting is to have a plan in place for keeping more of our Challengers alive, and hopefully even tiered higher, after they undertake their Challenge. The floor is open, any ideas?"

So far the meeting had proceeded pretty much as Nicomedes predicted. The Guilders had presented several ridiculous ideas for how to best deal with this Dungeon's high difficulty, and all been shot down as not being feasible or requiring too much outside interference. They hadn't yet suggested the idea of having higher tiers carry the Challengers through the Floor—perhaps even they thought that idea was too much. In fact many of their ideas were, in his opinion, quite conservative in how much it would actually help the Challengers. Perhaps his presence alone was enough to dissuade them, as he hadn't had to protest even once so far.

More frustrating was that they didn't seem to be making any progress. One of them would come up with some idea, which would then be shut down by someone else shortly after, who would then present their own idea, and the cycle would repeat.

It took a lot of mental effort to keep his face neutral, but Nicomedes was experienced in that regard. It wasn't time yet. If he just came out and suggested an idea, someone would shoot it down. They needed to step too far first, so he had some reason to object. And going by how frustrated some of the participants, particularly the Dungeon Scholars, were getting, he was sure he wouldn't need to wait much longer.

He was right.

"If you want to do that we could just as well have some high-tiered buffers give the Challengers buffs before they walk in," one of the Scholars, Florian, said angrily.

"Are you crazy?!" Korbin, the other Scholar, exclaimed.

"It's not crazier than your idea," Florian scoffed.

"How are buffs the same as information?!" Korbin said. "With my idea the Challenge is still there. Your idea trivializes it completely."

"What 'Challenge,' if you have high tiers go in first to trigger all the traps?"

"At least with what I'm saying . . ."

"Gentlemen, please," Nicomedes said. The room went silent instantly. A perk of speaking rarely was that people tended to listen when you did. "I can see you are upset, but spouting ideas you know are improper won't get us anywhere." He turned to Florian. "Don't you agree?"

Florian grimaced, but managed to calm himself with a deep breath. "You're right, of course. I let emotions get the better of me. Apologies, Bishop."

"No need for apologies," Nicomedes said. "This is a difficult question for you, I'm sure."

"Do you have a suggestion?" Florian asked.

Nicomedes smiled internally but kept his face neutral. "I must admit to not having given this much thought. As I'm sure you're aware, we in the Order follow the teachings of the Lady, so this would never come up in our discussions."

"Of course," Katherine said, trying to interject, but Nicomedes held up a hand to forestall her.

"I have, however, had some time to think during this discussion, and I think there is a way I can help." He turned to Katherine. "We had a previous discussion about my Justiciars. Now they would not normally concern themselves with taking notes or the like, but I think they could be persuaded to do so if it is to help the Guild. As long as it isn't spread around of course. That way at least the information isn't gathered by those of higher tiers than is appropriate."

"And you would want what in return?" Katherine asked. She looked annoyed, but he could see thoughtful faces on the other people in the room.

"We wouldn't need anything. The opportunity to Challenge the Dungeon itself is reward enough. But before we decide, there is one thing I feel is important to mention. One person whose opinion we cannot decide without."

"Whose?" Florian asked. Nicomedes turned to face him.

"Why, the Dungeon's of course," he said. "What was its name? Veos, right?"

Noracin nodded absently.

Nicomedes pressed on. "Now, I'm aware that this isn't typically how it's done in the Guild, but if you're going to attempt to cheapen its Challenge, it's sure to have some kind of opinion on that. Perhaps a good move would be to make sure whatever you're planning won't make it dislike you too much. Who knows what it might decide to do then?"

CHAPTER THIRTY-TWO

For the Future, Part I

It was early morning the day after the meeting. The sun hadn't yet reached the main campground, still mostly blocked by the surrounding forest, but a few rays shone through the trees, causing the morning dew still dotted across the flora to glitter in the sunlight. Katherine didn't pay it any attention as she stood with a scowl on her face watching her two Dungeon Scholars shuffle toward her. They were late, and carrying a frankly disturbing amount of notes and equipment with them in several different packs. Ninety-nine percent of which she was sure they wouldn't need. They were going to have a discussion with the Dungeon, not spend a month excavating its walls and making notes on rock shapes.

But it was just what could be expected from Dungeon Scholars.

"You're late," she said.

"Apologies, Hallmaster," Florian said. "We wanted to make sure we were prepared for anything that might come up, so we had to bring almost half our notes." He frowned apologetically. "It took quite a while to narrow it down to something we could carry without slowing us down too much."

Katherine blinked. This wasn't even *half*? She looked at the bags and pouches hanging from both men's arms and shoulders. How had they even managed to do this? They'd been at the camp for less than two weeks! They had always been an obsessive group, and this was just par for the course. But it wasn't the main reason she was annoyed this morning. That would be the man standing to her left.

Bishop Nicomedes hadn't spoken much in yesterday's meeting, but once he did he'd shifted all focus to himself. And now they were doing exactly what he wanted by going in and having the Dungeon help decide how to best proceed. It wasn't that it was a bad idea, in fact quite the opposite, she just didn't like feeling that she'd been manipulated somehow. She was supposed to be in charge here, dammit.

"It's good to be prepared," Nicomedes said, and she was sure it was an attempt to annoy her on purpose. She schooled her face; she wasn't some young inexperienced child. While she wasn't anywhere near as old as that old bastard, she'd still been a Hallmaster of the Guild for over two decades. She wasn't going to be controlled by her emotions or let her annoyance at an old man keep her from following a smart idea.

"That's true," she said. "But it's also true that you could have let me know you would need this much equipment. I would have sent some people over to help you."

"Ah, yes of course," Florian said. "I'll be sure to remember that next time."

"Good." She nodded firmly. "Then let us be off."

She started walking, the two Scholars following behind. After a moment she noticed Nicomedes following as well. She turned to face him and raised an eyebrow. He only smiled in response.

"I thought you said that this was Guild business, and so you'd keep out of it." That might have been a bit too adversarial.

The Bishop, however, just nodded his head with a smile. "I said so, so of course that is what I'll do. Whatever agreement you and the Dungeon come to, you will have my support. Walking you there is merely the polite thing to do."

This old fox, Katherine grumbled inwardly. Now he seemed to be the bigger man, always helpful and even seeming to respect the Guild's authority. And he still would likely get everything he wanted. She didn't let any of the frustration show on her face, though, and instead just nodded.

"Then your presence is welcome," she said. The four walked in silence the rest of the way, until Katherine stood in front of the opening in the ground that would lead them into the Dungeon. It was strange to think how different it would be inside when this part hadn't changed at all since she first saw it. She shook her head and continued walking until she hit the wall from the [Blacklist].

Dungeon Access Blocked!

You have been put on the [Blacklist] for this Dungeon. As this was automatically done by the system due to the Tier difference, the Dungeon may choose to grant you access upon your request.

Still below Tier 6, then, she thought. In a way that wasn't surprising at all—normal Dungeons took months to advance even in the early tiers. She turned to Nicomedes, who nodded and stepped back a few steps. Best to avoid giving the Dungeon the wrong impression. She thought her request into the system.

I, Katherine Verantz, hereby vow to the Great System that I will offer no harm upon this Dungeon or its inhabitants throughout my visit, unless they try to take my life first. In return I and two Tier-3 comrades would like to be given access to the first Floor for the purpose of having a discussion about the future of its Challenge.

She turned to the Scholars while she waited for the Dungeon to respond. They were still standing a few steps back beside Nicomedes, fumbling with their packs.

"Could you step forward so the Dungeon can sense you?" she asked. "And Bishop, if you would take a few steps back. We wouldn't want to give the impression that I'm lying."

"Of course," Nicomedes said, backing up while the two Scholars shuffled forward to stand beside Katherine. She nodded and turned back to the Dungeon's entrance. All their cards were on the table now. It was time to see how the Dungeon would respond.

She didn't have to wait long before there was a notification from the system that she had been granted temporary access. She smiled and took half a step forward, then paused as a second notification appeared in front of her eyes.

Quest received: "A Challenging Discussion!"

The Dungeon Veos appreciates your willingness to have a discussion, and hopes to be able to work together to create the best Challenge possible. He has asked that you move the discussion to the second Floor, as the Guardian there has an easier time with human speech, and that you provide him with one interesting item from outside his domain. In return you will be granted 1 Health Potion (Tier 1). Will you accept this Quest?

Time Remaining: 23:59:58

"Hah!" Korbin exclaimed. "First time I've been given a Quest to skip a Floor."

"It's not that strange," Florian said. "Dungeons provide skips for higher-tiered people all the time."

"I know *that*, I'm not stupid," Korbin said. "But how often does it come in the form of a Quest? Of course I wasn't tal—"

"As Scholars, what do you think qualifies as an 'interesting item'?" Katherine asked, interrupting their argument and changing the subject. Both men furrowed their brows in thought, and Katherine turned to look back at Nicomedes. He too seemed deep in thought, and was that an annoyed wrinkle in his forehead? Katherine suppressed a smile as the man noticed her looking and forced his face back to a neutral expression. She turned her attention back to Korbin as he answered her question.

"It's too broad to give a definite answer," he admitted. "Probably intentionally so. It's much more common for Dungeons to give out Quests where they get something in return. And us going to the second Floor probably isn't enough to count."

Florian nodded along with his fellow scholar, then added, "And since this isn't a Challenge, he won't be getting any experience from our visit. He might just have asked for any random object we have as a way of getting the Quest to work. You being a higher tier than him also probably made it harder."

"So just any random object will do?" Katherine asked with a frown, but both men shook their heads.

"No not just anything, but I'd guess it would accept aa pretty broad range of things," Florian said. "Plus the main point of the Quest is probably to get us to the second Floor, and not the object." He ruffled through his pack and took out a small handful of green stones, which Katherine's [Inspect] skill let her know were Emerald Fog Shards. "These will probably do the trick."

"All right," Katherine said. She and Korbin each took one of the shards, then she accepted the Quest. The three then stepped past where the barrier had once been, and down into the Dungeon proper. At first glance, the tunnel down looked similar to how it had when she'd been here last, but upon closer inspection Katherine could see it looked more artificial and deliberate than last time. The steps in the staircase were also made from what looked like marble instead of being simply carved away from the surrounding rock. But the changes really began once they made it to the bottom of the steps, and into what Noracin had called the Dungeon's audience chamber. She hadn't been quite sure what to make of that at first, but now that she was seeing it firsthand the description made sense. A circular chamber made of clean-cut marble, with doorways in all directions. Above some of the openings were images carved into the stonework. The one straight ahead—the entrance to the rest of the Floor, if she wasn't mistaken—was an image of what she could only assume was a Leatherwing. Florian and Korbin were even more interested than her, almost becoming incoherent as they tossed ideas back and forth fast enough they were slurring the words. Normally she wouldn't have minded, but they were on the clock today. She snapped her fingers to get them to focus, then signaled for them to follow as she headed for the Leatherwing on the wall. A surge of mana stopped her mid-step. She frowned as she looked around the room, reflexively readying herself for combat. Nothing the Dungeon was capable of should be able to harm her, but a century spent either in or around Dungeons had given her certain habits.

The surge was coming from the doorway directly to the left of the Leatherwing door, and it didn't seem dangerous or even hostile. She wasn't a Mage, so sensing mana wasn't exactly her forte, but even she could tell that much. What she couldn't sense instantly was what the surge was supposed to do, so she turned to her companions for answers, which they were quick to provide. Apparently they had theorized even before this that the way this Dungeon would transport people to later Floors was through portals in this chamber, and the symbols above each door were likely hints about what the portal would lead to. Part of her was a bit annoyed that they hadn't told her any of this earlier, before she remembered that she'd avoided discussions with them on purpose, as they could get . . . lengthy. And she didn't exactly have a lot of free time on her hands at the moment. Once everything calmed down, she would make the time. But until then she would have to rely on them to tell her the important things when she needed to know them.

She looked at the carving above the surging doorway. A Skeleton with glowing eyes. Wonderful. It was only a Tier-2 Floor, so they shouldn't be in any actual danger. She gestured for the Scholars to follow and stepped through the portal.

What awaited them on the other side seemed to be a tomb of some kind. Or at least the entrance to one. She stood in a small circular room with only one doorway. A stairwell lined with torches descended into the darkness, and she saw what she thought was an offering plate atop an altar to its right. Above the plate was a statue of a woman in armor wielding a large halberd. Katherine was tempted to stay and examine the place further, but the excited exclamations from her scholarly companions brought her mind back to what they were there to do.

"Look, words below the statue!" Korbin exclaimed. "'Give thanks to the protectors,'" he read.

"There's more above the stairs," Florian said just as excitedly. "'The Protectors' Rest.' Is that the name of the Floor, perhaps?"

"Focus up, everyone," Katherine said. "We're here for a reason. We can deal with this later, if we have the time."

"Right," Florian said, gathering himself.

"Of course," Korbin said. "Lead the way."

Katherine did so, but froze upon taking that first step down the stairs. She had received yet another notification from the system, and this one she hadn't seen before.

Entering Floor: "The Mausoleum of the Protectors!"

Light and Life element skill mana costs increased by 15%!
Dark and Death element skill mana costs decreased by 5%!

"How fascinating! He's figured out how to name his Floors as well," Florian said as he caught up.

"We shouldn't be surprised at this point," Korbin said. "Veos is clearly a savant when it comes to . . . Dungeon-ing." He fumbled a bit over that last word, but Katherine still got his meaning.

"I've never seen this before," she said. "Dungeons can name Floors? Is it the same as with the named Guardians?"

"It's a more advanced application of a similar technique," Florian said with a nod. "And as far as I know it also requires the Dungeon to have some prerequisite perks or skills. I don't know exactly what they are; Dungeons are a bit cagey when it comes to specifics about their own skills."

"That's putting it mildly." Korbin snorted then turned his attention to Katherine. "But it's a bit surprising that you haven't come across this before. It's less common than naming a Guardian, but about fifteen percent of Dungeons can name Floors. You should have at least heard about it."

"Guess it's never come up . . ." Katherine said with a frown. She was coming to realize that she knew much less about Dungeons than she'd thought.

"Really? You've never had anyone call a Floor by a name before when describing a Challenge?" Florian asked, surprised.

"Ah, no, of course I've heard people do that . . ." Katherine paused. "I guess I just never equated it to a *name*."

"That makes more sense. Still though, it seems you should study up about Dungeons a bit more. I know it wasn't the highest priority in Aspenfield . . ."

"But now it is," Katherine finished.

"You're always welcome to visit us if you want to learn more," Korbin said.

"I might take you up on that, once things calm down a bit here. For now we should get on with what we came here to do. We've wasted enough time already. Veos might be losing his patience watching us just stand around gawking."

I wasn't. Though to be fair I could see where the woman was coming from. It felt strange, having someone be on a wrong Floor for their tier. Off, somehow.

Not in the way that the Aberrant had felt—not even close. More like . . . an itch in my mind that told me something wasn't quite right. I hadn't noticed it the last time Katherine was here, maybe because I was inexperienced with what Challengers *should* feel like, but now I noticed it clear as day. I could deal with it, especially if I got to listen to some interesting stories in return, but I could see how other Dungeons would get upset.

Now that the three were on the move again, I sent a message to Krazad to prepare himself. These people were here because they recently lost five people to Stalker, and though they wouldn't be speaking to her, I still wanted to give the best impression I could.

Lest they decide Challenging me just wasn't worth the trouble.

CHAPTER THIRTY-THREE

For the Future, Part II

I watched as the three strolled through my second Floor, Katherine looking focused and the others seeming as if they had just found the most interesting thing in the world. Their words rushed together they were trying to talk over each other so fast. Everything seemed equally exciting to them, whether it be the offering plate that hinted at the mausoleum's connection to the Vampire narrative, or the design of the stonework, or even just the positioning of the torches on the walls. In all honesty it got a bit overwhelming to listen to after a while, and for a moment I was surprised to find myself feeling a bit relieved when they approached Krazad. I'd be more than happy to listen to them talk about most of the things they had mentioned, if they'd just kept their focus on anything long enough for the discussion to go anywhere. Just my luck, the first ones to really seem to like talking within the Dungeon and they liked it to the point where they didn't make any sense at all. Or they just liked starting discussions and not finishing them.

At least Katherine made them focus once they stepped foot in Krazad's chamber. The Skeletal Necromancer stood alone in the center of the room, already out of his sarcophagus and clad in his usual cowl of shadows, though of course without his skeletal minions. There would be no fighting today. Still, he stood tall and imperious, wanting to improve my status in the meeting as much as possible. I didn't know how much difference it made, but it was still nice that he cared.

The three humans stopped a few steps in front of Krazad, who waited for them to speak.

"Greetings," Katherine spoke up. "We seek information. You have our gratitude for agreeing to meet with us."

Polite. That boded well, I thought. I sent Krazad my response.

"I return your greetings in the place of the Dungeon Veos," he said. "He is willing to trade information, if that is what you wish. I will serve as liaison for this purpose."

Katherine nodded. "Then I thank you . . . What should I call you?"

"My name is Krazad the Necromancer, though you might also address your questions to Veos directly, as he is able to hear all we speak."

"Krazad?!" Korbin exclaimed. "Like from the note."

"I knew it had something to do with the later Floors . . ." Florian muttered.

"Focus," Katherine admonished.

"But Hallmaster, this is the first time . . ." Florian began, but Katherine held up a hand.

"If we have time once the discussion is done, and if the Dungeon is willing, you may ask a few questions. Before that we have something that is more important to do."

I wasn't sure I agreed with that—they wanted to talk about the story!— but I could see Katherine's reasoning. They had come here for a specific purpose after all.

"Speak your questions," Krazad said.

"Right . . . First and foremost, I . . . *we* . . . are curious about the fates of the previous Challengers." She sounded sad suddenly. "What happened to them? Where did they go wrong?"

I knew this question would be coming, I sent to Krazad. *They were not strong enough to defeat Stalker, and found this out too late into the fight. They were unfortunate in that an initial setback cascaded until they could no longer retreat. The Mage was especially unlucky.*

"So it was just bad luck?" Katherine said bitterly after Krazad relayed my words.

They were outmatched, and some would likely have still died if the fight happened again, but yes, it was due to bad luck that all *of them died.* I sent.

Katherine frowned and stared into space for a few seconds, and even the two eccentric old-seeming men behind her remained silent. I could understand their frustration. They had come seeking answers, but there was nothing to be learned from bad luck. Nothing they could do to be better prepared next time.

Ah, I should tell them about my changes. Then at least they would have something. I sent my words to Krazad.

"There are ways to affect the difficulty of the Guardian fight, if the Challengers explore the Floor properly," Krazad said. "And they were able to meet the other Challenges the Floor had to offer."

Hey now that wasn't really what I said, I sent.

I am aware, Krazad sent back, his voice still coming out crisp even through telepathy. The words also contained the Necromancer's emotions, letting me know the reason for the change. He didn't want them to look down on me, and let them know I'd made a mistake. Plus he felt it was wrong to just tell them how to make the Floor easier. I frowned a bit at that. There was nothing wrong with making mistakes, as long as you learned from them. I didn't really see the need to be seen as all-knowing.

"What are you saying?" the man on the left said, his status page labeling him as Florian. "There is a way to make the Guardian fight *easier?*"

Too late to change now. At least the core of the message came through. But I would have to have a discussion with Krazad about this. I sent my response, making sure to tell him to relay my words verbatim this time.

"There is," Krazad said. "If one was to properly explore the Floor and find everything it has hidden, they would also find the final fight against Stalker to be much simpler."

"How interesting. To have a mechanic that rewards exploration with an easier combat encounter . . ." Florian said, seemingly talking to himself.

"I don't suppose you would be willing to be more specific about what and how this can be achieved?" Katherine asked.

"No," Krazad said before I even had a chance to send him anything. "That is also part of the Challenge. You should be thankful we even told you there is a way."

Hey, don't be rude.

"I suppose that's to be expected." Katherine sighed. "And you're right, at least we know there's a way now. That's something." She took a deep breath, seemingly preparing for something. "Now for the big question. Would you be all right with us—"

"Actually, Hallmaster," Florian interrupted. "Considering what we just learned, do we even need to bring that up?"

"Florian has a point. It seems we already have what we wanted. No need to push our luck, I don't think."

Katherine paused and furrowed her brows in thought, while I tried to figure out what it was they were so hesitant to ask me. If it had already been answered, it probably had something to do with making the Stalker fight easier. No, surely they hadn't been about to ask me to do *that?* The mere thought was so offensive to me it became preposterous, never mind the fact that I'd already done it myself. That had made me question myself a bit, but I'd pushed through since I'd done it in an attempt to make the Challenge more *fair*, not *easier*. But Challengers should *not* be the ones determining its difficulty. That was a recipe for making it way too easy.

"You're right," Katherine said, grabbing my attention once again. I couldn't be sure that was what she would have asked, but if she had I would have said no. Regardless of if that meant being abandoned. Thankfully it seemed the men had convinced her not to ask the question, sparing me from that potential outcome.

"Veos, is this mechanic of rewarding exploration specific to your first Floor, or is it a theme across the entire Dungeon?" Korbin asked. An interesting question. I would definitely have preferred if people spent more time exploring the Floors, and the theme of rewarding exploration sounded quite nice. I didn't actually have any such systems set up for the other Floors yet, though. But I couldn't ask Krazad to say that.

"It is a commonality, yes," I had Krazad say instead. "Though exactly what the rewards are, and how large they are, vary of course."

"Fascinating," Korbin said. "I suppose that is also why there are so many interesting things spread around the Floor—to hint at that sort of thing."

"It's just a shame we didn't realize it sooner," Florian said with a shake of his head. "Then perhaps fewer Challengers would have died."

No, they would have still died. The mechanic didn't exist until yesterday.

"We'll have to do better going forward, then," Katherine said. "It is also my fault, since I failed to realize the benefits of asking the Dungeon for information."

"That's true." Florian nodded in agreement, which seemed rude.

"I have one final question, if you do not mind?" Katherine said.

"Speak," Krazad said. The woman took out a small, semitransparent, pink crystal. A quick inspection told me it was something called an Image Recorder.

"How would you feel if our Challengers brought along some of these on their Challenges? That way, in case all of them die, we will at least know what happened to them. It would help bring some closure."

My instincts wanted to scream out "no" immediately. Recording how someone failed could also be used to help prepare those who came later. But that could also be said about just *telling* people what happened, and it wasn't as if I wiped their memories every time they left the Dungeon . . .

It's not a good idea, stupid instincts. Then no one would know about me and they would just never walk in, and I'd be left alone with nothing to do. Plus they'd forget my story completely. No, I wasn't going to start doing that.

A recording was a bit different in that it could be studied over and over in more detail, though. Memory could be faulty and tainted by perspective in a way a recording wasn't. No, having a recording of an entire Challenge attempt was simply out of the question. It would provide too much outside help to the next Challengers.

Though it wasn't as if I didn't understand *why* she was asking.. I could maybe modify the recording so that it only showed the final moments of the person. That way they could still have closure, but without access to my secrets. And of course if there was at least one survivor with the ability to report, I could delete the whole thing. In return I could also ask the Challengers to provide some small tribute. Nothing overly valuable, but if I could get my hands on more things from the outside world that could inspire more stories, it might make it worth it. It was at least a compromise I could accept. I had Krazad relay my thoughts to Katherine, who nodded.

"I can work with that, if you promise to provide access to either me or a proxy to retrieve the Image Recorder if we need it."

"It would depend on who the proxy is," I said through Krazad. "I won't remove the [Blacklist] for just anyone."

"One of us three, then," Katherine said after a moment's thought.

"That is acceptable."

"Great, then we have a deal." Katherine turned to the other two, who nodded. The three then held up a small Emerald Fog Shard each. I was confused for a moment, until I remembered the object I'd needed to add to get the Quest to work. I accepted the stones, and felt the Quest be resolved as three Health Potions materialized in their place.

"Thank you for your hospitality, Veos," Katherine said with a small bow. "Know that the Guild is grateful for your information. If you have any questions of us, we will answer them."

All right, now we're talking. I'd spent hours conversing with Morrígan about what questions I should ask if I ever got the chance. It was time to learn the truth about so many things.

Tell me about the Elorian Empire.

Katherine blinked once Krazad had relayed my words, then turned a confused look at her fellows, who both shrugged.

"I'm afraid I don't know much," she said when she turned back. "It was a large country on the eastern coast of the continent that dissolved into half a dozen smaller countries a long time ago. And none of *those* countries exist as they were anymore, either."

"Baltien held on the longest, existing up until just one hundred . . . something years ago," Florian said. "Some would say it still exists now, that it only changed its name to Kinova to avoid the bad connotations people had with their royal family."

"Those people would be fools," Korbin said. "If you look at the difference in how the Kinovan . . ."

I barely paid attention as Korbin and Florian descended into a discussion about the varying politics of the incarnations of what had once been the Elorian empire, as there was one thing vastly more important than anything specific they had to say.

The Empire had been *real.*

CHAPTER THIRTY-FOUR

Dungeons and Outsiders

I watched the three Guilders leave, one in silent contemplation while the others intermittently talked about our conversation and the layout of the bricks in the walls with an equal amount of enthusiasm. From what little I'd seen of these men, it wasn't surprising, but it was still surreal to hear them discuss off-hand something that had just changed my world completely. The fact that I wanted to know about the Elorian Empire was a curiosity to them, but for me it was an answer that upended everything, yet at the same time changed nothing.

My stories were at least in part based on real history. That was now as close to an indisputable fact as it could possibly be without meeting Morrígan's old clan members in person. And the only reason I wasn't a hundred percent certain was because I hadn't asked about Morrígan or her clan members by name. I wasn't sure exactly why, but I wasn't comfortable revealing too many of my secrets to these Guilders, regardless of how friendly they seemed or how curious I was about anything they might tell me. My questions had been more general in nature, centering around Eloria and only mentioning Vampires tangentially. I hadn't even brought up the Aberrant. The fact that they didn't know what had caused the conflict within Eloria was telling; the Aberrant war had been forgotten. Probably deliberately, because how else could it have possibly happened? And I wasn't about to open *that* can of worms. Besides it felt wrong to tell them things that could be used against me. I didn't know how they might use my interest against me, but I figured it was better to be safe than sorry.

After the Guilders were gone, I checked on my Quest. I now only had three rewards left, as well as two deaths, unfortunately, before I'd finally be able to level up and start working on the next Floor. The next story.

But I shouldn't get overeager. There was no telling how long it would take me to fulfill those last Quest conditions. Especially since they worked against each other, as most parties that died didn't get rewards, and vice versa. It might be satisfied with the next Challenge, or it could take a full week, if not more. If I got too excited thinking that I was almost there, I might give in and start the next Floor without leveling.

Besides I had something more important to do right now.

I had a Vampire to talk to.

I moved my attention down to the fourth Floor, were Morrígan waited for my return. I'd filled her in on the Guilders' visit and we'd worked together to come up with the questions to ask while I waited for them to reach Krazad. She was unsurprisingly eager to hear what I'd learned.

She shot to her feet the instant she sensed my presence, speaking in a rushed voice. "What did they say?"

Eloria existed, but it splintered over half a millennia ago into several separate independent countries. It seems they think the conflict between the different Vampire clans was the cause, though they don't seem to know about the Aberrant. Lariet doesn't exist anymore. It was split between the winners of the conflict, and even those borders seem to have mostly come and gone.

Morrígan stood in silence for a few seconds.

"That's . . . a lot," she said eventually. "I should be ecstatic that my memories aren't lies. That my life was real and not some fiction conjured up by the system." She took a deep breath. "But most everything I know is lost forever. In a way, I knew that already of course. My life is here now, not out there. I have no desire to leave or even see the outside. Even if we'd learned some members of my clan were still alive . . . I don't even know if I would *want* to meet them." She shook her head.

Take your time, I sent. *Once you're ready we can talk.*

"No, I'm fine," she said, raising her head. "Tell me what you learned. You said they didn't seem to know about the Aberrant? Do they know about the war?"

I don't think so, I sent. *I gather the only war they knew was the one that splintered Eloria, which was supposedly triggered by the conflict within the different Vampire clans. They didn't mention anything about a war before that, and they didn't seem to know why the internal conflicts started to begin with.*

"That's a bit suspicious," Morrígan said. "The war was pretty important. They should have heard about it. How long ago did you say this was?"

It's been about six hundred years or so since the empire splintered, according to what they said.

Morrígan shook her head.

"That's far too few years for this to have just been forgotten. I've met people older than that. Hells that's not even twice my own age, and I wouldn't have called myself particularly old when I . . . When I put my family in prison and . . ." She paused. "What did I do after that? Did you find anything out?"

I'm afraid not. I didn't ask about you or your family directly.

"Why not?" Morrígan asked with a surprising amount of venom in her voice, giving me pause.

I didn't want to reveal too much of my connection to that time, or to your clan.

Morrígan growled in frustration and threw her hands up. "That shouldn't be a—" She stopped herself and took a breath. "No, I shouldn't get mad. It makes sense from your perspective. You're a Dungeon after all, and a young one at that."

What does that mean? I sent, growing even more confused.

Morrígan sighed. "It means Dungeons are naturally suspicious of outsiders. They don't like to give out information for fear it might be used against them somehow in the future. Even if it would be in their best interest to do so," she said, then shook her head forlornly. "I knew that. I should've told you about it when we talked about what questions you should ask. I know we didn't exactly have a lot of time to prepare, but still."

Why is that a problem? I asked. *Isn't it prudent to not to give away things that could potentially come back to harm you in the future? I can't exactly go anywhere. If someone learned something and wanted to use it to harm me somehow, I couldn't really do much about it, right? Better to be safe than sorry.*

"It's not like I can't see the logic, it's just . . ." Morrígan paused for a moment before continuing. "Look, I'm not saying you should start trusting everything people tell you. Keeping some secrets about your capabilities is prudent, as you say." She fell silent as she pondered what to say next.

"What I meant was that you shouldn't just dismiss sharing information as a whole. Just because it's something they don't know doesn't magically make telling them about it dangerous to you. Sometimes keeping it a secret could be just as risky. They'll still be curious whether you talk to them or not, and if you keep things from them they'll just make up reasons for your actions to make them make sense. And while they probably won't be able to use that as information to defeat your Challenges easier, since they would likely be wrong, it could affect their attitude and relationship with you. If they think you're keeping things from them, or worse, lying to them, to make it easier for you to kill their friends, for example, they'll likely either leave or get angry. Neither of which you want."

We can at least agree on that, I sent. *And the solution you're suggesting to keep that from happening is to just be open and reveal all my secrets?*

"No, don't be so all-or-nothing," Morrígan said, frustration clear in her voice. "What I'm saying is this: letting them know *some* things helps build a proper rapport. And having a two-way relationship with your Challengers is almost always beneficial to both sides. While keeping secrets is understandable, and revealing them *can* be risky, keeping everything as hidden as possible won't stop people from making assumptions. Which can also be risky if they make the wrong ones."

I thought in silence about what Morrígan said. I could see the logic, but something about it felt a bit off to me. I wasn't sure what exactly, or even why it felt wrong, but something about the idea of interactions between Dungeons and outsiders being safe for the Dungeon rang false to my instincts. My instincts told me to not let my guard down. Don't be open to cooperation. Stay vigilant at all times. Keep them out. Out. Out. *Out!*

I shook myself in frustration. *Freaking great.*

So that's what she'd meant. My instincts again.

I guessed there was some comfort in knowing that this was something all Dungeons went through. It didn't make it any less annoying, but I had to believe they were there for a reason beyond just making my life difficult.

If that is the case, and the people outside are so friendly, why is it that the first thing the system does is warn us of the danger of outsiders? Why do my instincts scream at me whenever I think about making life easier for the Challengers? Even if it would improve the Challenge?

Morrígan blinked. "Though I could have guessed about your 'instincts,' I've never heard that about the system," she said with a frown, then thought for a moment. "I don't know what to say to that, honestly. The system wouldn't just warn you for no reason. But, as I said, it is also true that most Dungeons benefit much more from a more direct partnership than just passively being Challenged and hiding." She sighed. "There are risks to both, but being more open might indeed be the riskier of the two if the system warns about it. Being dangerous doesn't take the benefits away, though, and if you want to keep everything we know hidden, that's going to be very difficult. Especially if at the same time we want to learn more about the outside world ourselves. In the end it's up to you; I'm neither a Dungeon nor the system."

I'll . . . I'll think about it.

We sat in silence for bit, neither of us sure what to say next.

Morrígan breathed out, then shook her head with a sad chuckle. "I really got us sidetracked there, didn't I? Sorry, I guess I got a bit frustrated when it felt like I had a chance to learn of my past, but I let it slip through my fingers. What do you want to do now that you know my story's real?"

I let out a metaphorical breath as my thoughts moved on to an easier topic, then frustration mounted as I realized that this topic wasn't any easier at all.

What *did* I want to do with this information? What *could* I even do? I had to do something, surely, otherwise what would be the point? I could change my story in two very different ways. I could let the Challengers discover secrets of the past that had been discarded, as I'd been doing, the only real change being tying it more obviously to the real world. It sounded nice, but again my instincts protested. And for once I could understand why. It would almost certainly draw in unwanted attention. Attention from those who'd rather the Aberrant remain forgotten.

But then why had I been given this information, if not to share it?

The other option would be to make the story a fiction, something of my own creation. It should be possible. I'd made up Krazad completely, after all. At least I thought I had. He didn't have any memories of a life lived before the Dungeon, anyway. The only true connection was Morrígan, and she could pretend if I wanted her to.

No. That felt *wrong*. It would change the fourth and fifth Floors too much. I couldn't accept it. Plus it felt like running away. A distortion of purpose.

My story was my purpose, and now I'd been given the chance to make one with real meaning and real connections to the outside world.

I couldn't *hide* that just because it might be dangerous.

Let's make it more real, I decided.

CHAPTER THIRTY-FIVE

The Order's Challenge, Part I

The sun had already fallen below the tree line by the time Boltar stepped out of the Bishop's temporary quarters and back into the camp. As he walked to his squad, his mind spun with what the Bishop had told him. There seemed to be much more happening here than what was on the surface. Questions that couldn't be left for the Guild to answer. He was disappointed that he couldn't tell his squad what the true purpose of their mission was, but the Bishop was right. Until they knew more, spreading it around might create assumptions on both sides and cause unnecessary conflicts. And the Lady knew there was enough conflict between the Order and the Guild already, regardless of how polite they were all being. Though he supposed it didn't seem as bad as it once was, since the Bishop had at least been able to negotiate for them to be able to undertake their Challenge. Once the Guild's Hallmaster had returned from conversing with the Dungeon, the Bishop had had a long discussion about the Order's role in the camp. That was despite the Guild's priority, a concept which he'd always thought was stupid, but that was something for those higher up than him to decide.

It wasn't an ideal situation, but it was worth it to get them their Challenges sooner. And for the chance of finding out the truth about what was really going on here.

"Captain," Aldrick said and stood as Boltar approached their tent. The rest of the squad stood and saluted a second later.

"First Clergyman." Boltar nodded and signaled for his team to relax.

"What did the Bishop have to say? Did we get our orders?" Aldrick asked.

"We did," Boltar said. "We are to undertake our Challenge tomorrow."

Excited cheers erupted from some of the Inquisitors, which soon petered out when they saw that Boltar was not done talking.

"What's the catch?" Tyree asked from the back, her hand unconsciously tapping the hilt of her war hammer.

"We've been given the time slot the Guild would usually use for their investigation of the second Floor. That means that while we get to go, the other Tier-Two squads are not so lucky. At least not while the priority holds," Boltar explained.

"Stingy," Seraphina said. "But that's to be expected when dealing with the Guild."

"Seraphina," Boltar said.

"I know, I know. Don't deprecate the Guild in public," Seraphina muttered.

"Remove 'in public' from that sentence and you've got it. There's enough friction between our organizations as it is," Boltar said. "We're Inquisitors. We need to be mindful of how we act. *Especially* here, yes. But not *just* here."

"The captain's right," Waldemar said. "Especially now as well. There are going to be plenty of Guilders who aren't happy we're stealing one or their spots."

"I get it," Seraphina said with a sigh.

"Good." Boltar nodded. "Now this Challenge will be a bit different from our last one. As the replacements for the Guilds' investigators we will have to fill that role to some extent." Seeing the frowns on his squad members' faces, he quickly continued on to explain. "The Bishop has already made sure that this won't be taken too far. All we will need to do is take notes on what we find down there and hand them over to the Guild. They have agreed to only give them to the Challenging party the night before, to prevent them being spread around. The parties themselves will also be barred from talking about them both before and after their Challenge." He took a deep breath. "It's not ideal, but it's the price we have to pay for expediency. Any questions?" Boltar asked, and after seeing there were none he nodded. "Good, then you are excused for the rest of the day. Make your preparations. Pray, eat, and rest. Tomorrow we fight."

Boltar led the way through the entrance of the Dungeon, as was the captain's duty. Aldrick followed as his second, followed by Seraphina and Tyree, then

Waldemar, and finally Mirielle protecting their back. They wouldn't be facing any real difficulties until they arrived on the second Floor, but they still kept formation as was tradition.

The tunnel was made of chiseled stone, and seemed carved out of the rock itself through natural processes, though Boltar knew better. The only exception to this faux natural roughness were the polished marble steps leading them down into the dark. Before Boltar said a word, Aldrick raised his staff and cast [Light] atop it, illuminating the staircase ahead. They walked forward slowly but with deliberate steps until the stairs stopped and the tunnel widened out into a cavern. A quick count revealed twelve separate doorways leading in all directions, one of which they'd entered through. Some of the doors had symbols carved above them, though Boltar couldn't say immediately what the purpose of them were.

"Waldemar. Direction," he called out.

The Priest of Fire remained silent for a few seconds before opening his mouth. "Straight ahead. The one with the Bat abo—"

He was interrupted by a sudden surge of mana coming from the door to the left of the one Waldemar pointed out. Boltar immediately raised his shield. The mana, while it didn't seem directly hostile toward them, seemed much too powerful for a first Floor. He couldn't quite believe something Tier 1 would be of any threat to them, but he firmly believed in the mantra safety first. And if something did pop out at them, he wanted to be prepared.

"Wait," Waldemar said. "I think I know what this is."

"Speak."

"The mana surging is Tier Two, and it changed the flow. Now the way forward is through that left doorway rather than straight ahead . . . It's a skip."

"A portal-based skip?" Seraphina asked. "Why not just make a staircase?"

Waldemar shrugged. "Who knows. Maybe the Floors don't line up properly. Whatever the reason it's there now."

"Is it safe?" Boltar asked.

Waldemar nodded. "Yeah. It's no different from the puzzle Dungeon Betu, a bit northeast of Ebereya. You know how it uses portals to get you to the next Floor after you've cleared the puzzle? Same principle here."

Boltar nodded. "Good, that saves us some time. Let's go."

He led the way through the doorway, beneath the not-at-all-ominous picture of a Skeleton, and into a smaller circular chamber. And just as Waldemar had predicted there was a portal inside. A swirling vortex of mana that seemed to curve around itself and converged at the center. He'd seen drawings of portals like this before, but they hadn't come close to this. Disconcerting to the senses, but not in a negative way. A swirling storm of lights that weren't quite there, like looking at something while also looking behind it and around it at the same time.

"It's beautiful. The pictures don't do it justice at all," Tyree said, echoing his thoughts.

"Tell me about it," Aldrick said.

"Everyone ready?" Boltar said.

"Yes, Captain," came their answers immediately. He nodded, then stepped into the swirl. He found himself staring at a monument to something precious. He didn't recognize the woman the statue depicted, but he could tell its purpose right away. A statue above an offering plate, showing respect to those who lay beyond and the woman herself.

Then the system blared a notification in front of his eyes.

Entering Floor: "The Mausoleum of the Protectors!"
Light and Life element skill mana costs increased by 15%. Dark and Death element skill mana costs decreased by 5%.

Waldemar whistled in surprise, while Seraphina cursed.

"Typical," she muttered. "Why is it always light that gets cursed in these places?"

"They're underground," Mirielle said with a shrug, the [Guardian Paladin] speaking for the first time since they'd entered. "Makes sense to me."

"Yeah well . . . It's still annoying."

"No arguments here," Aldrick said.

"What do you think about the statue?" Tyree asked. "It's clearly here for a reason."

"It's nice," Seraphina said. "It's obvious the creator found the woman and her purpose very important. Though I'm not sure about the halberd. I think it clashes with the aesthetic."

"I meant what is the reason it's here, in relation to the Challenge?"

"Oh," Seraphina said. "Well, that I don't know."

"Take an image of it. It might be a clue to a puzzle later on," Boltar said. "In my opinion it's there for theming and aesthetics, not function. But I could be wrong. For now we should focus on the immediate Challenge first and foremost."

"Roger that," Aldrick said. His staff flashed bright for a moment as he activated his skill, then he nodded for Boltar to continue. Beside the altar was a staircase leading down. Like before, Boltar walked in front, and led them down over a dozen meters of steep staircase before the ground leveled out in front of them. They walked through a short hallway before a doorway brought them into a wide square chamber. Each wall had a doorway, with the largest one straight ahead. But that's not what caught Boltar's attention. That would be the four sarcophagi in the center of the room.

"Circle. Watch," Boltar called out.

"Understood," Waldemar was the one who answered, but they all moved as one. Their line spread out to form a circle, each of them facing outward with their weapon raised. Boltar walked slowly toward the sarcophagi. Six steps into the room, the lids started to creek, stone on stone, but Aldrick spoke up before Boltar could open his mouth.

"Skeletons! Left doorway," he said from Boltar's left.

"Right as well," came Tyree's voice from his other side.

"Archers!" Mirielle shouted a second later.

Boltar turned his head to look down the side path and saw a pair of Skeletons, each raising a bow. "Shields up!"

The Clerics fell back to within the circle, while Boltar and his Paladins all raised their shields. A moment later the clanging of metal on metal signaled the first arrow hitting. From the left. Boltar looked ahead to the final opening, but could see nothing but darkness inside.

"No archers in front," he called out. "Focus fire. Left then right. Mirielle, move up front to watch the sarcophagi with me."

She didn't answer, but he could hear her metal boots clicking against the stone as she ran low through their circle to join him. With a crash, the four lids of the sarcophagi were thrown off, and four Skeletons rose, moving with surprising agility, and leapt out. Three of them wielded a shield and a sword, while the fourth, a larger version, held a heavy hammer in both hands. Boltar raised his sword in challenge and stepped up to meet the creatures. Bolts of light and fire flew to his left—he could see them from the corner of his eye, but he blocked it out. Forcing all of his focus instead on the enemies in front of him.

"[Enhance Strength]."

He felt the fiery energy of the skill surge through his veins as it took effect. He gripped his sword tight and charged.

The closest Skeleton swung wildly, and while Boltar could tell there was some power behind the blow it wasn't enough to scare him. He deflected it easily, forcing both swords down to the ground before crashing into the creature with his shield. At the last second before impact, he activated [Shield Bash], and felt himself rush forward as the magic of the skill took hold. The Skeleton flew back, crashing first into the side of its sarcophagus and then onto the stone floor. It didn't remain there for long, but the brief engagement was enough to tell Boltar a whole lot about his enemy. These were not at his level. They didn't seem that high in Tier 2 at all, if he was honest. Which would make some sense considering this was the first room; the Dungeon would want to ease its Challengers into the new environment. They didn't all care enough to do that, so it illuminated a lot of the Dungeon's personality for Boltar. He'd have to confirm it with [Inspect] to be sure, but that would have to wait until the battle was won.

"One down!" Aldrick said from behind him as he charged the nearest Skeleton "Other one falling back in the darkness. Switching sides."

"Keep an eye out for the remainder," Boltar yelled back, parrying a blow, then kicking the leg out from under the creature. He heard a loud crash to his right as Mirielle brought her shield up to block the blow of the hammer-wielder. It was louder than he'd expected, hinting at the possibility that this was the most dangerous foe here. But not loud enough that he was worried Mirielle couldn't handle it. He held the Skeleton's arm down with his right foot and brought his shield down hard. Once. Twice. Three times he hit it before he felt its bones crack. Then he tossed himself to the side and rolled away from his first opponent, who had once more reached him. While rolling he allowed himself a glance to the side. Mirielle had one foe missing an arm, forcing it to attack with nothing but its shield and letting her focus most of her attention on the hammer-wielder. In the brief second he watched, he saw a wide grin on her face and a light shining from her eyes.

Yeah, she was fine.

He rolled to his feet and swung wide behind, catching the sword of the Skeleton at a bad angle. For it, not him. It fell to the stone with a clang, and he pushed forward, activating [Shield Bash] and once more forcing the creature to the ground.

"One down right. Remainder falling back again," Aldrick called out. "I think it's around the corner."

"The one on the left hasn't fired an arrow again."

"Then leave it," Boltar said as he delivered the finishing blow to his downed foe. It dissipated into motes of mana as he rose, his legs already moving toward Mirielle and the hammer-wielder.

While it was stronger and its attacks heavier than its fellows', it was still well below their level, and outnumbered six to one. It didn't take long before all that was left of both it and the crippled Skeleton were motes of mana floating up into the air. Boltar took a deep breath but didn't sheath his sword.

"Status? Clerics first," he asked.

"Eight-tenths. Health full," Aldrick said.

"Seven-tenths. Health also full," Waldemar said.

"Seven-and-a-half-tenths. No damage here either," Seraphina said.

Boltar nodded. "Good. Paladins? Eight-tenths here. No damage."

"Nine-tenths on both," Mirielle said. "Tanked some hits with my shield."

"Eight and nine," Tyree said.

"All right. Good engagement, everyone," Boltar said. "But it's not over yet. We still have the two Archers."

"It's a bit suspicious that they never returned," Aldrick said. "Skeletons don't tend to flee out of fear. Especially not ones in a Dungeon."

Boltar nodded. "They're probably meant to ambush us later, or lure us into a trap."

"My vote's on trap," Waldemar said. "Two Skeletons won't make a very good ambush."

"Don't underestimate the damage an arrow can do at the wrong time," Boltar cautioned. "But I agree that a trap is probably more likely. Seraphina, time to potion up."

"Already on it," she said as she pulled a small glass vial from her pouch. She grimaced at it. "I really hate drinking these. They're gross, and take *forever* to brew." Then she brought it to her lips and downed it, grimacing as she did so. "Blegh," she said, then scanned the room. "No traps in here at least."

"None that you can *detect*," Waldemar corrected.

"Yeah, whatever. Same thing," Seraphina said. "If I can't see them even after drinking this, we'd never be able to spot them before they triggered anyway."

"Good point," Waldemar admitted.

"Anyway, no traps in this room or the part of the hallways I can see," Seraphina said. She turned to face Boltar. "Which way are we going, Captain?"

He frowned, then turned to Waldemar. "Which way leads to the end of the Floor?"

The man shut his eyes for a few seconds, then pointed straight ahead.

"They can all reach the end, but that path's the shortest. Followed by the one to the left of where we came in."

Boltar nodded. "Then we go right first. And remember we're supposed to be investigators. Before we go anywhere, have a look around in here and make notes.

"Of what?" Seraphina asked.

"Anything you find interesting," Boltar said. "And everything you think the Guilders would find interesting as well. And as always if you find any treasure or possible puzzle pieces, bring them to me for now."

They all nodded and went their separate ways to search the room. Unlike Boltar, they had no idea what they were looking for, but they were smart people. They' know it if they found it.

A few minutes later they had combed the entire room, and Boltar was certain there was nothing more for them to find. In the end the room hadn't contained anything obviously interesting. The sarcophagi had some symbol carved into their lids, a tower with a star atop it, but none of them recognized it. He suspected it was just for aesthetics and not really important for the Challenge itself, though he still had them draw it just in case it was a clue for a puzzle farther along the Floor.

Once they were done they resumed formation, though this time with Seraphina walking in front beside Boltar, and set off to the right. The hallway was dark, lit only by the light of Aldrick's staff, but otherwise empty. It stretched for less than a few meters before turning ninety degrees to the right. They paused at the edge of the wall, Seraphina and Boltar both peaking around the corner at the same time, her to scout for traps and him to shield her from possible arrows, while Aldrick lit the way ahead as best he could with his staff. The corridor was lined with outcroppings on a wall that seemed much more natural than the one they had just walked down. The light from Aldrick's staff cast shadows that seemed to dance and twist, making it hard to see anything more than two meters in front of them with any real detail. Boltar could only just make out the outline of the Skeleton up ahead, along with the bow it held in one hand at its waist. What he couldn't see was what the other hand was doing, apart from reaching up into the wall.

Seraphina let out a gasp and jolted back around the corner, pulling Boltar with her.

Then a gout of flame as wide as the hallway flew past where they'd stood less than a second earlier.

CHAPTER THIRTY-SIX

The Order's Challenge, Part II

Three Hells!" Boltar exclaimed as he tumbled back, almost falling over. He stumbled to a halt a few steps from the corner and watched as the flames winked out. The crackling and roaring stopped as abruptly as it started, leaving the heat on his face and hands as the only signs that anything had happened at all.

"You guys all right?" came Aldrick's voice.

"I'm fine," Seraphina said, sounding disappointed in herself. "That was too close. I should have spotted it earlier."

"You got us away in time," Boltar said. "No damage taken. Besides, a little fire wouldn't be enough to take us out anyway."

"That's not what I'd call a 'little' fire. And losing health isn't the only way to take damage from a flame, or do you think you'd look perfectly good without any eyebrows, Captain?" Waldemar said, letting some mirth seep into his voice now that he knew they were both unhurt.

"You would know all about that," Tyree said.

"Hey, that was *one* time. And I got the Class we were going for, so it was worth it."

"Whatever you say, nobrows."

"Guys, focus," Aldrick said. "We're still in a Dungeon."

"Aldrick's right," Boltar said. "Maintain a proper attitude at all times in the Dungeon."

"Yes, Captain," Waldemar and Tyree said at the same time.

"Now, is it safe to continue?" Boltar turned to Seraphina, who tsked.

"Normally I'd say yes." She gestured toward the wall to their left, where the fire had come out of. "But there wasn't any reaction at all from my potion when we came in here. It looked just like all the other walls."

"Which means?" Boltar asked.

Seraphina dragged a hand through her hair. "It means we can't rely on my sight to catch the traps, even with the potion. Sure it lit up like a beacon once the mana had reached it, but that was *after* we could have seen it with our own eyes. And if they're hidden any better than a lever on the wall, the chances of us avoiding all of them are lower than I'd like."

Boltar frowned in thought. This was a real problem. Traps were some of the most insidious and deadly parts of any Dungeon, as they were often an all-or-nothing threat. Many of them either killed you or did absolutely nothing. Being able to avoid them was a key aspect of the Challenge, in fact almost all Inquisitor parties had someone use one of their skill slots on something to help them detect them more easily. And those that didn't had some other way to get a similar result, like Seraphina and her Alchemical Priest Class. Without it, the danger of the Challenge shot up. He shook his head. He wished Dungeons would just stick to monsters as defenders. They were almost always much simpler to deal with than traps.

"We'll have to pay more attention to our surroundings," he said. "All of us. Don't just rely on Seraphina. Listen if she shouts a warning, but don't assume it's clear and rush ahead just because she hasn't spoken."

"Got it, Captain," Tyree said.

"I'll keep my eyes open," Aldrick said. Waldemar and Mirielle just nodded.

"Then let's keep going. We still have a lot of Floor to cover," Boltar said.

They walked carefully up to and around the corner, but the trap didn't activate a second time. In fact once they rounded the corner they found that even the lever itself had vanished, probably dissipating into motes of mana just like the monsters did. That fact let them all breathe out sighs of relief. Most traps were one-time uses within the same Challenge, requiring the Dungeon to reset them manually in a way Boltar didn't understand. The minutia didn't really matter to him anyway. The important point was that, usually, if they managed to trigger a trap safely once, they wouldn't need to worry about it for the rest of the Floor. And it looked like that was true here as well.

The rest of the hallway was dark and empty, and even with their slower pace it didn't take them long to arrive at the entrance to a new room. This time there was even a door. Seraphina stepped up first and examined it closely, making sure, to the best of her ability, it wasn't trapped. Once she was done she nodded to Boltar and took a few steps back along with the others, just in case. Once they were safely out of range, Boltar pushed the door open and peered inside. He couldn't see anything, of course. Like the rest of the Floor the room was completely devoid of any light. He waved the rest of his squad over, and and they made their way into the room, Seraphina and Aldrick with his glowing staff in front.

Soon they came across the first sarcophagus, though this one remained still as they walked by. A few steps later a second one came into their sphere of illumination, and Boltar called for a halt and turned to Aldrick.

"There's got to be a fight in here. We need more light," he said.

Aldrick peered into the darkness in thought for a moment. "Using more light skills will use up a lot of my focus, so I'd only be able to use simple skills for the fight."

Boltar thought for a moment and looked around, peering into the dark to try to discern anything helpful about the room's layout. Eventually he gave up, seeing nothing but blackness and vague outlines that would be more of a danger than a help, and turned back to Aldrick.

"It's worth it. Light up the room."

"Got it, Captain," Aldrick said and focused. Soon three more lights floated up from his frame, hovered above him for a few seconds, then spread out in a triangle formation away from the squad. The farther they traveled the more Boltar tensed. As more of the room was bathed in magical light, more and more sarcophagi appeared from out of the darkness. Two became four became eight, which became *sixteen* before they finally saw the other end of the room.

As one their lids exploded up and out with considerably more force than in the first room. Over a dozen Skeletons jumped out, each clad in armor in addition to their sword and shield, yet still moving noticeably faster than their first enemies had done. So not only where there twice as many enemies as last time, they were also all higher level.

"Move to the back wall! Cover Aldrick!" Boltar yelled.

He raised his shield and activated all his enhancement skills one after the other while backing away to the closest wall. He, Tyree, and Mirielle were the vanguard, with Seraphina, Waldemar, and Aldrick standing within their triangle of protection. This time he didn't charge forward. This time the enemies were charging them.

He raised his shield to block the swing of the Skeleton that got there first, then kicked out to trip the one to its left while using his blade to intercept a blow from the one to its right. The clang of steel on steel rang loud, and he felt his muscles strain against the power of the blow even with his enhanced stats. He could feel he still had more strength than his opponents, but fighting off three at the same time and having to block strikes at bad angles meant it wasn't as simple as comparing stat to stat. In fact he could tell if his strength hadn't been so much higher his blockade would have folded right then. To the first attack.

Boltar pushed the middle skeleton off himself with a quick [Shield Bash], then ducked under an incoming blow from the second right as a ball of fire came flying over his shoulder to crash into the Skeleton, throwing it off balance temporarily, and making his dodge completely useless. He growled. He couldn't afford to miss chances like that. An [Enhanced Strike] against the third Skeleton was blocked by its shield, but the force of the blow still made it stumble backward a few steps. He didn't pursue; his job in this fight was defense, and a new Skeleton took the old one's place almost instantly, swinging toward Boltar's head. He brought his own blade back up to block, and the dance continued.

Skills flew from the clerics behind Boltar and crashed into the quickly amassing wall of Skeletons. Swords met shields from both sides. Three Skeletons had fallen trying to get through their defensive line. So far they had held, though not without injury. Boltar wasn't sure how badly the others were hurt, but he had a gash in the side of his leg that burned with pain, even after he'd been healed back to full health. His mana had dropped to below half after he reapplied his suite of buffs. He stopped using any other skills. This was going to be a grind, and he couldn't waste the mana. Without his buffs he wouldn't be fast or sturdy enough to keep the Skeletons at bay.

A *twang* and a *thunk* in the stone above his head made the blood freeze in his veins before he forced his mind to focus on the fight. He scanned the room behind the Skeletons and found that one of them had dropped their sword and taken out a bow instead. Worse, two more seemed to be doing the same, raising their bows toward them as he watched.

"Archers!" he yelled. "Waldemar!"

"On it!" the Priest of Fire yelled back. "Going big!"

"Barrier!" Boltar called out, but Mirielle was already moving. She stepped back next to the Clerics, and a bright yellow glow began to emanate from her, wisps of light rising like smoke to the ceiling. The glow gradually intensified.

Boltar blocked a charging Skeleton, parried a second, then cried out as a third pierced his side with a sword.

Tyree screamed as she too used one of her more costly skills to keep her side in place and away from the casters.

Seraphina tossed a vial of purple liquid on the ground beneath the Skeletons.

The arrows were loosed with a *twang*.

Seraphina cried out in pain.

"Ready!" Mirielle called out.

Waldemar raised his hands, and three balls of white flame flew out toward the Archers. Boltar ducked as they passed overhead but could still feel the heat they gave off from over a foot above him. They hit and sank into their target without a sound, though Boltar as always thought he could hear something fizzing, like water on a hot fire.

At the same time the white glow spread out from Mirielle, a fog of light pushing the Skeletons back as it expanded out to cover the whole squad.

The [Holy-fire Bombs] exploded with three deafening cracks of thunder a second later, then went completely silent as Mirielle's fog solidified to form a protective dome that blocked out everything, even light and sound, from passing through. It couldn't last long, though. It was extremely draining on mana and focus even in an ideal situation, and the Skeletons' attacks combined with the force of the now-silent explosions caused cracks to form in the glowing smog within seconds of it forming.

Waldemar gasped for breath, and Seraphina rushed in to prop him up and feed him a Magical Stamina Potion. She tossed a second to Aldrick, who moved up toward Mirielle.

She groaned as the cracks in the dome spread faster and faster, before she was unable to maintain it anymore and it shattered into motes of light. She collapsed onto one knee as the sound of the Skeletons reached them once more. The three Archers had exploded, along with a single other Skeleton that had been unlucky enough to stand too close. Unfortunately the others seemed mostly undamaged. Blackened by soot, certainly, but still in fighting shape. Adding these four to the two they'd managed to take out before, that made six enemies that were either dead or downed. That meant there was still ten of them left. Ten Skeletons in armor and equal to them in level, and they were down to pretty much three and a half members until the others could catch their breath.

"Tyree," Boltar said, taking a deep breath. "I'll go in. Hold the line against any who get past me."

"Yes, Captain," Tyree said.

Boltar cracked his neck and put down his shield. His squad was in danger. Two of them had already used the most powerful skills in their arsenal, which had left them drained and vulnerable to retaliation. And they hadn't even defeated half of their adversaries yet.

When he was younger, Boltar had often cursed his Glyph-acquired skill. It was base, primitive, and not suitable at all for the Order. He'd wished he could be a protector instead. Standing stalwart with shield raised and chin held high.

But that wasn't the way. The Bishop had made that clear. He'd explained that there were no such things as cursed skills, even less so a cursed Glyph.

It was a tool for him to use, nothing more and nothing less. It was up to him to master it and turn it into something suitable.

"I'll help you," the Bishop had said. "I'll guide you to the path. But you must walk down it on your own two feet."

And walk it he had. For over a decade he'd trained, harder than anyone he knew. Harder than people said he should. Until eventually he'd managed to do it. He'd reined himself in. The day after that the Bishop had given him his captain's title.

He looked back to Tyree, who nodded, faith shining in her eyes. Faith not only in the Lady, but in him. Belief that he'd remain in control. That he'd protect them.

He charged forward, leaping into the Skeletons and activating [Berserker's Fury].

CHAPTER THIRTY-SEVEN

The Order's Challenge, Part III

I watched the carnage brought forth by Boltar in what could best be described as awe. In twenty seconds he'd turned four of my ten Skeletons into piles of bones, taking hit after hit without seeming to care at all, all the while letting out a cry of furious anger like I'd never heard before. After the second one went down, he took a sword to the left arm, down to the bone, rendering it useless. Health be damned, the man didn't even slow down. He just clubbed the Skeleton in the head with the hilt of his sword using his good arm, then kept on fighting with one arm dangling limply at his side. One slash wasn't nearly enough to take a Skeleton down, but he managed to hit three for every one he took, so he was gradually lowering my creatures' numbers at a slightly faster rate than his own health. He didn't care about his injuries, but the system did. If he didn't manage to win before he was at zero health, no amount of angry screaming would let him keep fighting.

Behind him, next to the wall, Tyree was busy fending off the two Skeletons not currently occupied by Boltar. Despite the man's best effort and even with the insane buffing skill he was using, he couldn't fight more than four at the same time.

Tyree didn't have a skill anything like the one Boltar's Glyph gave him, but she was an expert defensive fighter, focusing on minimal movement and delaying tactics rather than dealing any real damage. She even used Mirielle's discarded shield with almost equal proficiency to the [Guardian Paladin].

Not that she *couldn't* deal critical damage if she had the chance—I could see her skills and stats. Aldrick had managed to pour one of Seraphina's potions into Mirielle, who was swiftly regaining . . . not her health or mana, but something less official than that. Some kind of internal energy? Stamina? Something akin to that anyway. Her barrier was powerful, but it seemed to have a cost beyond simply draining her mana. A cost I couldn't see for some reason. Not because it wasn't within the system, but because it was less interested in keeping track of it? Because it didn't *want* to keep track of it? Because it would be detrimental to keep track of it? Or maybe it just had too many things to keep track of?

At least that was what my instincts were saying.

That was weird. Interesting, but definitely weird. I'd have to look into that more once the Challenge was over, to see if there were any other things in the system background I hadn't realized.

While I was contemplating, Boltar crushed the skull of another Skeleton, taking a severe hit in his stomach in return, while another rammed into his side with its shield. Which turned out to be a lucky break, as that was the only thing that kept him from being impaled completely. As it was the stab to his side slashed deep. This time his scream was filled with pain. His health plummeted down to less than fifty, and for the first time since his skill activated, he faltered, missing with a wide swing comparatively devoid of power. But it was still enough to knock aside the attack of the last remaining Skeleton, and bought him enough time for Waldemar's fireballs, normal ones this time, not the exploding ones, to come flying past Tyree before Seraphina's now-empty mana potion had even hit the ground. Waldemar blinked and wobbled unsteadily on his feet, but the skills still hit their targets, crashing into the skeletons around Boltar and forcing them back, even taking off one of their arms completely.

"Don't overdo it!" Seraphina yelled from beside him as he had a particularly dangerous wobble. "What's the point of the potion if you collapse right after I get you back to your feet?"

While she spoke, she raised her own hands and a beam of light shot out from her palms and into Boltar, and I could see the wound in his side stitch itself shut. His health didn't go up much at first, but it did stop dropping. At the same time it seemed to energize the enraged man, and he leaped back into the fight with renewed vigor. Seraphina kept the beam focused on him the best she could while he fought, moving to keep as clear a line between them as she could. It was still blocked intermittently either by a Skeleton or

Tyree as they fought close, but while the beam was on Boltar, his health kept slowly climbing back up even as he fought.

Mirielle and Aldrick got to their feet then, and I knew the fight was over. Mirielle leaped forward to join Tyree, and Aldrick sent out a light to Boltar to join Seraphina's, though his was significantly stronger than hers. It even weaved across the battlefield, leaving him free to remain standing where he was. It did require him to drop his concentration from most of his lights, but the fight was small enough that they didn't need the entire room to be lit.

It took another minute before the final Skeleton died, crumpling to the floor with the now-familiar rattling of bones and clang of steel on stone. With it, Boltar lowered his sword, then collapsed onto his knees. Then he fell prone as consciousness left his body.

I was a bit concerned at that. This had been one of the most engaging Challenge fights I'd ever had, and I was concerned the rest would give up if their leader died. My concern was heightened because there was nothing in the man's status that showed *why* he'd collapse. His health wasn't full by any means, but it wasn't zero, same for his mana. And I couldn't sense any flows going through him to indicate a skill backlash effect that would explain it either. At least not one caused by mana, anyway.

Once I saw that his teammates didn't share my concern, however, I shifted to frustration. It had to be a consequence of his skill again. What was the damned point of me being able to see what skills people had if I couldn't see what they did?!

No that wasn't entirely true. I could see his status page. See his name, stats, and a full list of what skills he had learned, just like I could for my monsters. I even had a basic idea of what the effect of most of those skills were, thanks to my instincts. I felt that [Enhanced Strike] cost less mana than [Holy-fire Bomb], for example. Though I couldn't tell what the exact cost would be, nor did I know how much damage it would do before it hit my creatures.

But both Boltar's [Berserker's Fury] and Mirielle's [Luminous Barrier] were complete mysteries to my senses. I couldn't even tell they were power-ful, like I could with Waldemar's bombs, I only knew it from having seen them being used.

Which bugged me to no end.

I was interrupted from my internal mutterings by the sensation of mana flowing to the Challengers. They had gathered around Boltar and were dis-cussing the fight, seemingly while waiting for the man to just wake up on his own. Before that could happen, though, it was time to see how they reacted to my reward.

"Woah . . ." Seraphina said, holding the ring up to one of Aldrick's lights. I felt a surge of pride at that. That's right, it's the ring of the Tower's Peacekeeper. Of Krazad the Necromancer. The one who stood up against the Aberrant.

Supposedly, anyway. I'd made that up to better tie Krazad to Morrígan's story. Though Morrígan had said that while the Tower *did have* a Peacekeeper, he hadn't joined their fight, and more to the point, Krazad had never actually existed to the best of her, and Krazad's own, knowledge. It wasn't ideal, but since I hadn't really known what I was doing when I was making my first few Floors and just kind of stumbled into the story with my third and fourth, some sacrifices had to be made for continuity's sake. Besides, this was my story, not history—I could afford some inaccuracies here and there if they allowed for a good narrative.

"It's definitely powerful," Aldrick said. "Though I'm not sure any of us would be its best users considering what it buffs. Might be better to trade it in once we get back."

"I recognize the pattern from the tombs earlier," Seraphina said. She turned to Aldrick. "You think that's the sigil of this Floor or something?"

"Could be," Aldrick said with a frown. "Definitely something worth not-ing down, even if the item itself *hadn't* been strong enough to make the Bishop want a regular supply."

"He did want us to be thorough," Tyree said.

"I'm writing it down," Seraphina said. After a moment she handed the ring over to Aldrick. "You use it for now. You're right that the effect won't be that great for any of us, but a slightly increased mana regeneration is still something. And your lights are the skill we use most often."

"Good thinking," Aldrick said.

That's it? I thought confusedly. *That was the sigil of the Mage Tower . . . They should already know tha—* Belatedly I realized the reason for the confusion. They'd never been to the first Floor. At first I hadn't thought that was a big deal, because every other party had showed some kind of familiarity with both my layout and enemies during their Challenges. Taking advantage of information from their peers was . . . fine. It definitely wasn't as bad as out-right help, and being properly prepared for a Challenge was a skill in itself.

But this group was the first to Challenge the second Floor since the invaders. The golden man would have been the only one able to tell them anything, and Morrígan seriously doubted he'd risk something like that, especially with the shard in my possession. So their comparative lack of knowledge of the second Floor hadn't come as any sort of surprise. But they hadn't really seemed to know anything about the first either. This meant they were either kept from learning anything, or they didn't bother learning it. Which it was didn't really matter to me, but it did bring up a worrying thought. With the portals making Floor skips easier, there would probably be others like them in the future, who started on a later Floor without any prior knowledge from the earlier ones. They would be dropped straight into the story with no context for why anything mattered. Which would make them unable to piece together clues that would impact the process of the Challenge itself. The secondary puzzle in this room, for instance—without the note from Stalker's cavnern, they wouldn't even know to *look* for it, let alone be able to solve it. A full bonus reward, and a large piece of the Floor's narrative, would be missed completely because it wasn't explained properly. It wouldn't even be the Challengers' fault. Without the information gained on the first Floor, they would have no reason to even suspect or look for anything else in here. The room had an obvious function, which they had already cleared.

At least I caught this now, and there weren't any puzzles they had to solve to clear the Floor that needed outside information. Not on purpose either, I was just lucky I hadn't accidentally made the Challenge unbeatable for anyone skipping ahead.

This would have to be fixed. The story had to make sense to any Challenger who entered, otherwise there was little point in its telling.

The Challengers were resting for now, waiting for Boltar to recover. I had some time to think.

Eventually I came up with two solutions. One a goal that I wanted to reach but didn't know how to, and one an alternative that I'd rather avoid. The latter was simple: I could just remove anything from my Floors that needed knowledge from the earlier ones, make each Floor as isolated as possible, only connected via the pieces of the narrative that weren't used for loot or puzzles. I didn't want to do that, since it lessened the impact of the story and made it less important to the Challengers' success. I'd already seen what would happen then. Sure some people would still explore and maybe even find stuff, but most would just ignore it and take the most direct route to my Guardian or bonus room, ignoring everything else. It made the Challenge functional while keeping the story understandable enough, but it wasn't anywhere close to my ideal.

That would be coming up with some way to *force* everyone to complete all the Floors in order, even if they were higher tier. The simplest way to do that would be to just remove the portals and connect the Floors manually, but that wouldn't really solve the problem. Higher-tiered Challengers could just blitz through the Floor without paying much attention until they reached the Floor that matched their level. They might learn *some* of the story, but most of it would almost certainly be missed or actively avoided.

No, what I wanted was to find a way to make them have to Challenge the Floors in order. Not just pass through them, but complete the Challenge fair and square. That would solve everything. It just didn't seem possible. That would work with those who started here, like the Discoverers, but they were a minority of parties in existence by necessity. I couldn't just ban everyone else from participating. That felt profoundly *wrong*. Not the same feeling as the Aberrant, but about at the same level of instinctual revulsion. I was supposed to provide a Challenge to everyone who sought to improve themselves. Not just those who happened to be at Tier 1 when they got here.

So two solutions, and both were . . . disagreeable at best. But I'd have to think more on the matter later. Boltar was awake, and so the Challengers were on the move again. I settled in to watch.

They moved with the same tactical slowness and careful awareness as before. Their health was back to full, though they still seemed sluggish. Not slow, just a bit . . . drained. Especially Mirielle and Boltar.

Even so, normal packs of Skeletons were no match for them, and with Seraphina's potions they were able to stay clear of most of my traps. One triggered when it caught Tyree in the arm, forcing another short break and costing some mana to heal, but other than that they moved through my Floor without issue. And they were being quite *thorough*. Cataloging and discussing everything that had even the slightest chance of being important, and documenting them with the Image Recorders. They were so meticulous that even without the information from the first Floor, they managed to find and trigger the mechanisms that made the Guardian fight easier just from pure deductive reasoning. They didn't find the second bonus reward, but it was still damned impressive.

Soon the six stood in front of the final Challenge of the Floor, and for the first time Krazad spoke with a tone that indicated approval.

"You have proven yourselves resourceful," my Guardian said. "You're strong, yet you act with cunning and thoughtfulness. Something that would have been much sought after in the past, and will no doubt serve you well in the future." He paused, probably for dramatic effect. "*If* you pass this final Challenge."

Then he slammed his staff into the ground and activated both [Darkness] and [Raise Skeletons].

"Ready!" Boltar cried out. "Defensive positions. Aldrick, you handle the dark. Mirielle, protect the casters. Tyree, you're with me."

"Got it, Captain," a chorus of voices said in unison, and they started acting, smoothly flowing into what had to be a practiced formation. Not as fast as they had previously, but not overly hindered by the [Darkness] either. Not that it lasted long. A bright flash from Aldrick burned through it mere seconds after Boltar had spoken. But those few seconds had been enough for Krazad to fall back behind his minions. The fight always had at least two Skeletons, though it could be up to six if the Challengers went straight to the Guardian fight, and Krazad had just summoned an additional two. The four charged in and blocked Tyree and Boltar, while Krazad himself activated a string of [Mana Bolts] that fired off in rapid succession toward Aldrick. Mirielle raised her shield to block, but by the end of the barrage was crying out in pain despite the protection the shield offered. Seraphina was on her in a second, light pulsing and a potion in her hand, and the Guardian Paladin quickly roused herself as her health shot back up to full.

Together Boltar and Tyree cut down the first pair of Skeletons without issue, only to have it be replaced by two others as [Raise Skeletons] was activated once again.

"Waldemar! Focus fire on the boss!" Boltar cried out. "Stop him from summoning!"

Without a word, the fires that had been supporting the two front liners shifted focus to the back of the room. Krazad tried to dodge, but agility wasn't exactly the strong point of a skeletal caster, and a majority of them hit their target. He growled, then cast [Death Mark]. Waldemar screamed in terror, and the newly conjured fireballs winked out before they were fully formed as he collapsed to his knees. The mark wasn't a highly damaging skill, but it wasn't supposed to be. It had a steep cost that needed to be paid consistently to keep it active, but in return it would disable an opponent with visions of their own demise and nightmares from beyond the grave. Honestly I didn't really like the Skill, but I couldn't deny that it was effective. Especially since it couldn't be countered with normal healing, something Aldrick soon found out.

"Seraphina!" he yelled. "Mental effect!"

"On it." The woman pulled out a potion and scurried toward Waldemar. Krazad wouldn't just let that happen, however, as he summoned several Skeletons in her path, as well as directing the ones fighting Boltar and Tyree to ignore the fighters and rush past. Two of them fell to the ground as piles of bones in the attempt, but that didn't matter. Screeching to a stop, Seraphina had a stunned look on her face, as if she didn't know what to do. Suddenly there were enemies all around her.

That moment proved too long, as three of four swords hit with a squelching sound and a shout of pain. Then an empowered [Mana Bolt] struck her back, and she crumpled to the ground. Not dead yet, but not far from it. And Krazad's Skeletons were eager to finish the job. Several screams came from the throats of the Challengers.

A beam of light from Aldrick hit the downed priest.

A shield came flying, knocking a Skeleton back.

Tyree and Boltar came charging back onto the other two.

Under the combined assault of four of the Challengers, the Skeletons wouldn't normally last long at all, let alone have the ability to inflict any serious injuries.

But in that moment of panic, Krazad was forgotten. A [Necrotic Aura] spread throughout the cavern, covering skeletons and Challengers alike, buffing one and crippling the other. It was a massive drain on the Necromancer's mana; the fight had gone on for less than a minute and he was already below half, but it was a risk he was willing to take for the chance to eliminate a key member of the attacking party. I hadn't expected all-out aggression from Krazad, but it seemed to be working so far. One way or another this fight wouldn't last much longer.

A series of [Mana Bolts] rained down in concert with the Skeletons raising their swords, oozing a black haze. Most were blocked, either by sword, shield, or arm. But one managed to connect, severing the throat of the downed priest in one smooth motion before hitting the stone below with a *clang*.

For an instant, everything seemed to pause. Then Boltar screamed in anger.

I hadn't thought he could activate his fury so soon, and apparently neither had Krazad. Nor his own teammates. They looked at him with a mix of worry, understanding, and fear.

And then Boltar charged my Guardian, faster than ever before.

Krazad conjured a Skeleton to block, but it was cleaved through with ease. A [Mana Bolt] was just ignored, and then the raging lunatic was in range. His health was being constantly drained by a source I couldn't see. Couldn't even really *feel.* Nor could Krazad, but he seized on the moment, activating a second [Death Mark] as he retreated.

Boltar stumbled, but only for a moment. He shook his head as if to clear it from an annoyance, then swung at Krazad before he managed to get far enough away. Once. Twice. Thrice. He swung without abandon, heedless of the strikes he took in return. Both magical and from Krazad's staff. Each hit he took drained considerably less of his health than it should have, and each of his own took almost a fifth of Krazad's health. In seconds he was down to less than half, and the man showed no signs of stopping. A fourth hit crashed down, splintering Krazad's arm into a thousand pieces of bone that dissipated into motes of mana and caused him to stumble. A fifth swing was started, then Boltar stood frozen, his face contorted in furious anger and his sword held high.

Yet he was dead.

A ball of fire and a beam of furious light came shooting from the other end of the room, as Boltar's teammates had managed to kill the remaining Skeletons. Even Waldemar was back on his feet, as Krazad could only focus on one mark at a time. They hit the Necromancer one after the next, a berserker's rush of a different kind, yet equally as relentless. It didn't take long before my Guardian's health dropped to zero and he dissipated into motes of mana.

All in all the fight took two minutes and twelve seconds.

It felt longer. And judging by the sudden silence in the cavern, the remaining Challengers felt something similar.

A surge of Mana flowed through the room, and through my Core, as several things happened in sequence. The Challenge was won, and the Challengers received their reward. They each tier up and received a magical item. Then they were teleported back to the entrance so suddenly even *I* barely felt the mana ahead of time.

And finally I received a ping from my status.

My quest was complete.

The mana swelled as my restrictions were removed, and I was finally able to step into level 5. They continued to surge, taking up all of my senses as my experience increased more and more until I reached level 6. Then finally it stopped, and I was left in silence.

CHAPTER THIRTY-EIGHT

Everyone Starts at the Beginning

I let the silence breathe for a moment, waiting for the Challengers to leave, before I let myself peer at the notifications from the system.

Quest completed!
Experience function unlocked.
Maximum mana restored.
Mana regeneration restored.
Floor creature maximum level restored.
All level 5 features available!
Massive amount of stored experience available!
Experience gained.
Level up!
Additional Edict slot gained! (1/3 Edicts proclaimed.)
Additional Dungeon perks available for selection.
1 new Dungeon perk available!
Skill [Swift Descent] available!

Phew. It had been a while since I'd gotten a deluge of messages like that from the system. Then again, it had been a while since I'd leveled up because the Quest had locked me out for such a long time. Not to mention I'd never leveled up *twice in a row* like this.

I had all but skipped level 5 and was now several thousand experience points into level 6. It was a *massive* jump in experience.

I'd gone from having so much locked away to suddenly having a huge number of possible paths in front of me. I could start on my new story. I had a new perk to pick, and new options to sift through. I got a new *Edict slot*, though that one was less relevant since I'd already had one available that I hadn't used yet. Given how powerful my first one had been it felt important enough that I should pay attention to it.

But first I wanted to take stock of the Challenge. Ever since that first, week I'd been in the habit of going through the events of the Challenge and to find areas to improve. Normally I'd just take a few minutes to think it through, but this was the first true Challenge of the second Floor, so I wanted to be more thorough.

Let's see . . . what had gone right?

The bonus room fight was sufficiently difficult, and succeeded in forcing the use of several trump cards. In return, though, the Challengers received an item none of them could use very well, so that was a bit of a downer. They could maybe sell it or trade it, but in an ideal world the bonus room reward would be usable by those who earned it. It should be easy enough to make the reward adaptive—the standard rewards chests try to do that by themselves— but I'd really prefer the items to have *some* connection to the narrative. I still should be able to make it work, though. It wouldn't cost me anything to make the reward semirandom, apart from the time it took to design the items.

I'd get back to that later though, when I was done reviewing the Challenge and the things I'd gotten from my level up, and and after I'd made my next Floor. I'd had an idea for what to make for a while, and it was agony holding off on creating it.

The Aberrant Vampire storyline was done, but I still wanted a bit of a connection to it. A parallel story of sorts that converged with the Vampire story with a final dramatic confrontation with the Aberrant.

I'd spent some time discussing various ideas with Morrígan. If possible, I wanted my new story to have the same connection to reality as hers did, but I had no clue how I'd done that, or even if it was possible to do it on purpose, so in the end we decided that I would just select what felt *interesting* to me. That was what I'd done with her story, though not until I'd gotten to the third Floor, which forced me to hammer the previous two into the narrative in a way that, while functional, wasn't ideal. For this next one I wanted a narrative right away.

And eventually I found one. Another race that had stood beside the Vampires in their fight, but had their own front.

The Elves of the Faewood.

It also helped that a lush green forest was about as far from a dark underground cave you could get, and I wanted my stories to be distinct from each other. I even had a good idea for what the first Floor of that story could be, and how I could implement it.

I shook myself free of that tangent . . . Where was I? Right, additional reward options. Not exactly the highest priority right now.

I wished I'd had one of those notebook things the Challengers used to write down important information—mostly about my narrative, which I appreciated—so I didn't have to keep all of this in my head. Where it tended to get lost as I got distracted by everything else interesting happening.

Actually now that I was thinking about it, what use was a notebook to me anyway? I didn't even have any limbs. Maybe there was some way to use the system to . . .

Focus. I forced my thoughts to return to the Challenge.

The first fight. That had also gone according to plan. As with Stalker's Floor, the room right after the entrance was a fight that served as a sort of introduction to the creatures of the Floor. They were lower level and the group was slightly smaller, so the Challengers had some time to get used to what this new Floor had to offer. In this instance the fight had been extremely one-sided, so maybe I'd made it a bit *too* lenient, but it did inform them about my Skeletons' tactics, as well as how they might use traps and ambushes. I'd still say it served its purpose.

I couldn't say the same for the rest of the regular encounters, though. They might have taken longer to complete compared to the first, but I'd be hard pressed to say they presented a more difficult Challenge. With more higher-level Skeletons, the Challengers just had to chew through more health before they were done—that was all. The fights were just too easy. Especially considering how difficult the Guardian fight and the bonus room turned out to be. Krazad especially had proven to be just as lethal as Stalker, even if he started with the fewest possible minions. There wasn't anything wrong with him being dangerous, except that the rest of the Floor did very little to prepare the Challengers for that sort of difficulty spike. It almost seemed like a bait and switch. Like I was doing it on purpose to make the Challengers think the Floor wasn't as deadly as it was. *That* was something I had an issue with.

I could be overthinking it, but just the fact that it occurred to me was proof enough that something had to be done.

I'd think on it in more detail later, but for now I just turned the four normal encounters within the Floor to three, splitting the Skeletons of the third between the final two. Now the bonus room had sixteen creatures, the first fight had eight, and the other two had twelve each. Fewer fights, but each fight was more difficult. And more importantly they were more in line with the difficulty of the Guardian fight. There was probably a more elegant and refined solution, but that could wait until I had less important things to do.

The other thing that didn't really go well was the impact of the narrative. The Challengers found all the connections, but they didn't really seem to care that much. Without having been through the first Floor, they had no reason to be invested, and more to the point there wasn't anything telling them why what they found was important or even what it was for. A common reaction whenever one of my narrative connections had been found had been that it was relevant to the clearing of the Floor somehow, like a clue to a puzzle or a hint at a secret. It was true that I *did* tie them together that way, but I didn't want the narrative to be reduced to *only* that. I wanted the Challengers to be invested in the story for its own sake, not just where it mattered to the Challenge.

One thing this Challenge in particular had made clear to me was that for the narrative to hold any importance at all, the Challengers had to be made aware of *all* of it. They had to start the story from the beginning, experience it Floor by Floor, and *then* maybe they'd think it was important.

I just had no idea how to make that happen.

Perhaps I was being too impatient.

What was it Morrígan had said? "Investment takes time to grow." She'd said that I couldn't expect outsiders to realize the implications of everything right away, but once they did they'd be interested in the story, and not just the Challenge.

She was probably right; she definitely knew more about life as a humanoid than I did, but that didn't mean I had to like it. Patience was definitely *not* something I was good at. But if it was the only option . . . I could do it.

That still left me with the same problem of how to make the Challengers aware of the story and its purpose. Even if investment into the story increased as they spent time spent with it, I still needed to find a way to make them experience that story in the first place. Otherwise they would have nothing to get invested in.

Simply beginning each Floor with a puzzle that required knowledge from the previous one felt wrong. Like a cheap block that would just make the Challengers annoyed, rather than invested.

No, what I needed was a way to make everyone Challenge each Floor in sequence. And not just in name, but in reality. If everyone that entered was Tier 1 at first, and had to complete each Floor before having their tier increased . . .

Then everyone would have the same chance to learn about the story. Everyone had the choice of how much they wanted to care. Instead of the story being met with confusion, it would be met with knowledge.

That's what I had to do. It suddenly felt so clear to me. Like a flash of insight, lighting up the dark path ahead. It was so simple, and yet it changed everything about how the Challengers would interface with my Dungeon. And, as a consequence, my story.

All I had to do was make it so [Everyone Starts at the Beginning].

I felt a rumbling from the world. From within me and everything beyond. It quickly gained strength, becoming even louder than what I'd felt the first time I proclaimed and Edict. Everything shook. Or perhaps it was just me. The difference was academic, and I was beyond any ability to care. All my focus was on the struggle.

I strained to contain it, to keep it from exploding out and splintering me into a thousand pieces. I thought I could *hear* the cracks forming, but whether they were in my mind or in my Core I didn't know.

Then my mana vanished, and the storm rushed out, spreading in a spherical shockwave all through my Dungeon, traveling from the fifth Floor up through the rest. And beyond, into the outside world. There was a fainter *cracking*, like the aftershock of thunder, from somewhere near my Core. Then it went silent.

This time there was no pain. Only a certainty that something fundamental had been accomplished.

Noracin shuddered as a sudden wave of *intent* rushed through him. He turned toward the Dungeon and saw that those around him had done the same. He stood and walked to the Hallmaster's quarters. Something significant had happened.

Nicomedes sat up straight, his eyes going wide as he felt the intent of the Edict rush through him. It was different than it should be. Though he couldn't put his finger on why, but he didn't need to know that to understand the importance of the event. Beyond the Edict, which was an accomplishment in itself, the Dungeon had done something else. Something beyond what a Dungeon should be capable of. Again.

This time, however, he was here, and he could deal with it.

Katherine turned to the Dungeon, shut her eyes, and sighed. Her door opened and she spoke before her assistant could open her mouth.

"Yes, I'm on it," she said.

There was always something new that needed to be dealt with.

***What did you . . . ? No . . . How did you . . . ? How is this* possible?!**

The voice came from within my head, yet did not belong to me. I blinked in confusion for a few seconds before I recognized it.

Greetings, voice. I sent. Then my mind caught up to the content of what it had actually said, and I added, *I proclaimed an Edict requiring my Floors to be Challenged in order. That way the Challengers can properly experience my story.* I paused. *Should I not have done that?*

"Should?!" *What you've done* **should** *have been impossible!* **You shouldn't** *have access! There should be hindrances in place!*

I frowned mentally. *I didn't feel any. In fact, this was easier than my first one.*

There was a pause. **Your first . . . Right. The one you proclaimed while at the level where the cost** *should* **have killed you. That should have felt difficult. At least** *that* **much** *make sense.*

Did I do something wrong?

No . . . I got a distinct impression of something shaking its head and sighing. **Hang on, I need to make a call.**

There was another pause before the voice spoke again, though this time the words weren't coming to me as clearly as they had been. As if the voice was focusing somewhere else, and only partially kept me in mind.

Lady Nerian? It's Etar. I've got a situation . . . There's a Dungeon . . . Impossible . . . South western coast . . . Tier manipulation . . . No! Nothing like that! Increased access . . .

The voice scoffed. **Said it was easy.**

Its name? Veos. It's new, so it wouldn't be strange that you haven't . . .

Veos . . . Yes, I'm sure that's the name.

What does your brother have to do . . . ?

The voice fell silent, then returned its attention to me, the words coming in clear once again.

I will leave you to your work. What you have done does not count as an infraction. Someone will be in touch at a later date to converse further.

Then, as suddenly as it had appeared, it was gone.

I was left with a huge number of questions, and no answers. Clearly what I'd done was significant, especially in that it seemed most Dungeons weren't able to do it. Which I couldn't understand. Even as I thought back nothing stood out as special or different from the things I would normally do. I could manage the levels of my own creatures easily, and I could even affect things as fundamental as health using my other Edict. So why was affecting the level of my Challengers such a big deal?

I didn't know, and it seemed the voice wasn't going to clear anything up either. Then again it did say that it hadn't been wrong, so maybe the reason didn't matter that much? I'd ask Morrígan about it later, and maybe even my Challengers once they returned.

But not now. I'd held off on my expansion for far too long already.

With a surge of glee I activated [Swift Descent]. It was time to start excavating a forest, and hopefully find out what interesting history the Elves were hiding beneath the canopies.

And if I didn't find anything like Morrígan, that wasn't the end of the world. I was a storyteller after all, not a historian, and as long as there were people with the ability to listen, there'd always be room for stories.

About the Author

Victor Storm is the author of *Veos, The Story of a Dungeon*, originally released on Royal Road. Storm is a longtime reader and writer of fantastical stories and is looking forward to telling (hopefully) compelling narratives for years to come.

Podium

DISCOVER MORE

STORIES UNBOUND

PodiumEntertainment.com